BELOVED--

IN

ANOTHER TIME, ANOTHER PLACE

Book One: The Prophecy

By

Annabelle Blythe

Read all about it!

What Southern Battle almost turned around the results

of the whole Civil War?

Beloved: In Another Time, Another Place
by
Annabelle Blythe

Publisher:
Annabelle Blythe Books

Cover Design: Delia Latham (Heaven's Touch Designs)
Editor: Lisa Maine

Print ISBN: 978-0-9969161-0-3
Digital ISBN: 978-0-9969161-1-0

Previous Publication:
ITOH PRESS
Bowling Green, KY 42103
www.itohpress.com
Print ISBN: 978-1-939383-80-8
Digital ISBN: 978-1-939383-78-5

All rights have reverted to author

Dedication:

This book is dedicated to
Jesus Christ
&
Mom,
who after trial by fire,
came through to pure gold.

"But all things are naked and opened
into the eyes of Him with whom
we have to do." Heb. 4:13

Acknowledgements:

No man or woman is an island. We all owe others for helping us arrive at our destinations. My list is lengthy. Many of these won't be re-listed in the other books. So, bear with me and/or find your attributes! If any are left out-- forgive my memory loss and pray for me! May God richly bless all of you for blessing me, especially any personalities I may have copied from!

Thank You Jesus- for this opportunity, adventure, and experience of a lifetime!

Alyce P.- Knowledgeable, willing, giver. You shared the most practical advice of all. "Entertain them, don't pull 'em down and leave 'em down!" You lived that. Thank you. (Deceased 2008).

Goldie A.- What a dear friend. You were my most joyful critique! A servant to all. You didn't have much will to go on after you lost your best friend, Ms. Alyce, but you did it. Thanks for being there for me. (Deceased 2011).

Harvey H.- A great man. Guess what? They finally came back around to loving westerns! Thanks for giving me the title of my book. (Deceased 2011).

Bayou Writers Group- I had no idea what I was getting into when Alyce brought me and Goldie to your group! I was pleasantly surprised. Randy and Pam, your goals and courage to follow through has helped many others-- exponentially. Then, finding most of you were Christian writers-- such an added bonus. I certainly hadn't planned to dig out my old manuscript and polish and finish it. Pam-- Nona-- Linda-- most experienced critiques. I have been "educated, encouraged, and inspired"!

Pam T.- What a well-balanced, knowledgeable, encouraging Author/Editor/Proofer/Prez/Critique/Christian! Keep it up!

May G.- Thanks for the "push" I needed to take the course I needed to get me organized. What a good friend to the end. Thanks for backing me still.

Shonell B.- Ingenious-- wow! I thank my God and May for introducing us. Writers Boot Camp and the Creole Heritage classes at the library were two turning points in my life. Thanks!

Mary W.- What a sweet, Christian friend! My "blythe spirit", Beth. I like hanging out with you and "Anne of Green Gables". You make me feel like I'm really somebody!

Dee B.- Your last name should be "Encourager"! And, strong shoulder. Plus, giving heart. Thanks.

Barbara B.- Sweet, generous, encouraging friend. What's amazing is that you still back me after all these years. "Thank you" seems inadequate.

Susan F.- You know who you are-- dear encouraging friend. You and your husband hired me and kept me-- against all odds and hurricanes. You even let me write and study in-between my work. Tell your "other" boss-- Nah nah nah nah nah! You and your crew were my consolation in my transition of life. God's angels.

Lessie O.- Who would have ever thought you would be my best critique? Or that I'd ask you and you would accept? You stayed with me from the inception of the story to the end. I will be eternally grateful. And, you'll probably have to wait that long for compensation! Thanks.

Mitzie D.- What a gorgeous, generous person you are. As I said before, "You have backed me through all the stages of my life". What were you thinking?! God bless the godly-- you, Dan, and your children. Thanks.

Rachel D.- Gratitude for your encouragement and critique! We've each traveled down a long road-- never knowing they would end up together. Thank God, they did. Now, it's your turn. Write about it! But change my name!

Robert D.- You and Deb never doubted my ability to do this. You even liked the story. That amazed me. Now, go, discover your own abilities that give you joy!

Billie D.- The excitement you and Jessica and your family generated about this book was a miracle. The encouragement-- a gift. May God bless you with all your dreams coming true!

Attoyac Writers Guild- After Hurricane Rita chased me from Louisiana to Texas-- I found you. I had no idea God would bring me to another such knowledgeable, Christian group again. It's like falling in love twice in one lifetime—unbelievable! Ed and Treasa, thank you so much for allowing our meetings at the Attoyac Art Gallery and Coffee Shop. None of us will ever forget the comraderie. Andi, you stuck it out amidst all the odds practically alone as leader, a position you never intended to have. Thanks for finding us another great place to meet again when Ed and Treasa moved. Thanks for sharing, and persisting with your knowledge, guidance and encouragement. Terri, sharing your experience with us through all the tragedies of your life has been an inspiration. You and Andi have provided great programs and speakers and seminars to help educate us, plus giving your compassion. Q & M, we miss you. Ms. Ellen, thanks for a tremendous friendship and sharing your art. I pray you and James publish those awesome, miraculous, anointed, entertaining poems in a book! Betty, what a fun friend you are, even after your trials. Who says you can't mix politics and religion? You're a writer-- go for it! Deb, sweet Deb, thanks for the Youth Writers help. Shelby County longs to read your adventurous book about them! Now just do it! Hilda, thanks for the friendship. We may not like the same slap-stick, but our goals are the same-- writing and God. Thanks.

Quincy B.- Constant encouragement, strictest critique-- with a dash of compassion mixed in the recipe! You and Mur are friends till the end. God bless.

G.W. & Bettie- There's no bookkeeping ledger that has enough room to list all the good deeds you did for me. God's the best Bookkeeper. Thanks.

Dois G.- Friend through all those years. We faced the devil head on in this county-- and with Jesus' help, we won. May God bless you and your husband and family richly for blessing me.

Marcie M.- Even after trial by fire, you are still a bundle of encouragement. We were least likely to become friends. But, you shared your feelings and we became deep friends. All the info and research you have shared with me-- has been invaluable. You even let me write in your newspaper. Most of all, thank you for leading me to my publisher!

Carol Itoh- I thank my God always for you. Thank you for being a readily available, kind, knowledgeable, no-nonsense publisher. And, for taking a chance on me. May God reward thee!

Mark K.- Constant computer friend. I owe you throughout eternity. You may have to get in that same line Lessie's in to collect! Mega blessings to you.

Tim V.- Impeccable, computer friend. Most interesting conversationalist and Christian. God bless you-- for getting me out of many troubles!

Sandy P.- My old friend. I've known you about the longest. What a joy to have re-united after all those years! What a blessing-- that you-- who were published before me—backed me! Forever thanks.

Annette D.- O.K. I've known you longer than Sandy. My brilliant tax consultant and friend since birth! Many memories. And, many thanks, for helping me.

Hazel S.- Thank you for encouraging and hiring me. Also for letting me visit you so often in that beautiful Victorian home! May God bless us both with the ministry in it.

Fannie W.- Relative, dear person, knowledgeable, teacher and trainer. Thanks. And, thanks for employing me to help with your husband.

Ruth S.- You are a generous spirit, relative and joy to be around. Thank you for your encouragement and employment. Most of all, thanks for being a living example of Gratitude personified.

Susan W.- "Cuz". You know you own the beautiful lake I wrote about. Through many troubles we have already come. And, we have always loved and prayed for one another and each others parents. I will never forget it. Thanks.

Steve C.- God bless you for letting me write about your gorgeous land. Get ready for the film crew! You and Joyce are tremendous backers and Christian cousins.

Pat S. & Sylvia C.- My other great, backing, encouraging cousins. God shall bless you!

Plus, Nurse Donna- You're backing has been a blessing.

Thanks to all my Pastors over the years and everyone who did anything to every further this book or encourage me.

Introduction

This book dares to compare the oppression of one white woman, a Southern state and a Negro nation. Enslavement of their spirits was not an option. Sophya Blackwell almost lets her destructive marriage cripple her emotionally. Her wish comes true when she and her sister, Anya, are sent back in time to witness life during the Civil War. What they happen upon-- the dark side of slavery-- amazes them.

Anya meets love, face to face.

Sophya gets a view of the bravery of Gen. Richard Taylor, her hero.

Taylor led the state of Louisiana, against all odds, to one of the few Southern victories against the North, in the Battle of Mansfield, almost turning around the outcome of the war.

In this process Sophya gets more than she bargained for, too: *The courage to allow real love to heal her own heart, from an unlikely Source.*

This courage thrusts them forwards in time. It teaches Sophya to suppress her impatient nature, forget the mistakes of her past, and to wait on God to take care of her future.

Foreword

There are three chapters in this book that are fact not fiction. They are: Hero Hall of Fame, The Civil War in Louisiana and The Battles of Mansfield and Pleasant Hill.

Some may choose to skip these chapters. They have nothing to do with the fictional characters of this book. That would be sad.

Granted, not everyone cares for history. Not all are even interested in fiction. Even less, probably, love romance novels. Then, there's even a smaller percentage that would bother to read a Christian novel. This book contains all of these genres.

I did not plan for this story to start formulating in my mind, some twenty-something years ago-- it just did. And it wouldn't go away until I wrote it down! Nor did I place the interest in my mind for history—it just came. Fiction, though, has always carried me through the rough spots of divorce in my youth and adulthood: that wasn't planned either. My mother placed the first book in my hand and allowed me to escape reality and dream. Lastly, I didn't seek Jesus, He sought me. I just thank Him for finding me. These things formulated my interests. Our lives form our loves, I believe. The publishing industry might be said to be molded along the same lines. The writer has an original thought. Then, they go through a heck of a lot of research, rewrites, and critiques. And then there's God-- directing them, hopefully-- to try and tie in life's lessons with actual historical facts. One needs to obey God above man.

So, I could write about what someone else wants me to write about, or I could obey God, and write about what I know and love and feel led to write about, which I did-- after spending years learning how!

Some may wonder if this book will be worth reading, I assure you, you will miss out on an adventurous treasure if you don't.

My belief is that fifty percent of the readers of this book will be male, due to the chapters on the Civil War. Next, in process (if they read the other chapters, too) they will learn how women want to be loved. The women reading the Civil War Chapters will end up being very able to hold an interesting conversation with the men in their lives. A valuable swap! Plus, my wish to get the truth out will come true. This would be the truth of the history of the characters and the Civil War in Louisiana and the forgotten or unmentioned importance of the Battles of Mansfield and Pleasant Hill.

Also, the truth will get out about God's love.

Thanks,
    Annabelle Blythe

Table of Contents

Chapter One
Like Mother, Like Daughter

("Is it lawful for a man to put away his wife?" Mark 10:2)

"Sophya! Mikalina! Get in here, right now!" I heard my daddy yell. My older sister and I were outside playing. I had been swinging. She had been digging in the sandbox. We glanced at each other and ran nervously inside only to hear words that changed our lives forever.

"Sophya, *who* do you want to live with-- Mommy or Daddy?" my daddy asked me.

Shocked, I just stood there in my baby blue pinafore. I loved this dress because people said it made my eyes look bluer with my light brown hair. At that point, though, my eyes began to cry. The kitchen seemed to start spinning. I leaned against the bar-type counter we were standing near. It separated the kitchen from the dining room in our large, two-story house in southwest Louisiana.

I looked at my tall, handsome daddy. He looked like my granddaddy, I'd been told, with his purely Ukrainian features. Granddad once came to stay with us in the smaller house while he and Dad built the bigger one, but I don't remember that. Dad had light brown hair like me. He looked mad standing there in his khaki work pants and shirt, with his arms folded.

I looked at my mom to see if she would help me to decide. Her dark hair and pretty face showed the beautiful Indian part of her. I heard people say that, too. I couldn't tell by her face what I should do. I couldn't tell anything at all. She seemed distant, almost numb, empty of emotion. She held my baby brother, Urich, in her arms. She still had her nurse's uniform on. People called her Mrs. Edvard Stolsky, but her real name was Christian.

My older sister, Mikalina, was called "a daddy's girl." She had dark hair like my mom. My sister had on her jean overalls from playing outside. She liked to dress like a tomboy. She always acted tough like that little girl, Scout, in that movie, "To Kill a Mockingbird." But, Mikki was crying really hard then.

***

Hearing her name being called startled Sophya awake. When she opened her eyes she realized, *I must've been dreaming.* The dream, a flashback actually, shook her like it had just happened, but it hadn't. Some people say you can't remember that far back, but she did and she was only three years old. *How could someone that young make that kind of decision, though?*

Mikalina chose to live with their dad. Their younger brother, Urich, an infant, had his choice already made for him. Sophya chose her mom. Somehow, they all ended up with their mom, not remembering how. They moved to the projects next, to what was called, "Black Town" in Houston, Texas. Mrs. Stolsky worked as a nurse at night and slept in the daytime. A Negro woman, Sara, from the next neighborhood, became their sitter. They played in both neighborhoods, never thinking there was any difference between the two. Later they moved to Alabama, about fifteen miles from Mobile, and missed their sitter a lot and her good country cooking.

This is a story about Sophya Blackwell. Some people called her Sophie. She's trapped in a marriage she hates--to William Blackwell-- because his actions show he regrets marrying period.

She rolled over and ached as she sat up from sleeping on the sofa. She remembered the argument with Will last night. He had already left for work this morning, leaving his cold chill behind him. Hands propped on her knees, she rubbed her eyes and slid her feet into her slippers. Then she remembered something from the argument: nobody won.

"Sophie, come in here a minute!" she remembered William

barking at her.

Sophya went into the living-dining room. "What? What's the matter now?"

"Look at all these bills!" Will flung the stack down onto the dining table.

"What about them?" she asked, puzzled.

"How can you dare say you are still going to that stupid re-enactment when we have all these bills?"

Sophya sighed. "That's the same stack of bills we always have. What's different?"

"You're squandering my money is what's different!" he advanced to hollering.

She sighed again, "Your money? I saved back some from my paycheck for gas and for the fee to see the battle. That's just a total of *ten* dollars, Will. Will that break the bank? How much does it cost you to go out every night—yeh, I know, you *say* you're working out at the gym. I happen to know, now that I have my own little car, too, that you were nowhere near where you said you'd be when I needed you to go to the ER with me and Billy the other night. Let's square away what the *real* problem is: *I'm* finally going to get to do something I love. *I'm* finally going to be the one that gets to get away for awhile and you can't stand not having control of me or the money!"

"You b--"

He walked out the door, slamming it, got in his car and drove off.

***

Oh, how I wish I could just disappear. Maybe that would make him happy. That might please my church, too, since they don't believe in divorce.

She walked down the hall to the bathroom in their middle-class home. *I am grateful these walls can't talk like one song says.* She

3

looked into the mirror and saw nothing looking back at her. There were teeth to brush, a face to wash, and hair to fix, but she searched for a reason why she should do it. Then, she thought about her trip: she planned to go see the re-enactment of the Battle of Mansfield. Her soul began to fill with hope again.

"At least that battle was won!"

Sophya thought about getting to be with her mother, brother, and younger sister. As she went to the kitchen to flip the coffee pot button on, she wondered if that big fight for this little bit of freedom had been worth it.

The phone rang and startled her out of her thoughts.

"Hello?"

"Hey, Sophie, are you about to shove off?" her older sister asked.

"Yes, Mikki, I'm about to shove something *somewhere*!"

Silence.

"Uh, I was going to call you before I left, though."

"I know, I know. How was it last night, or should I say how was *he*? William?"

"Oh, you know. I couldn't leave without a good sendoff. So much for a night alone together to talk. His temper still raged because I planned this trip. But it only costs five dollars in gas to go to Mom's. So that must not be the reason. I've planned this so long, too. I invited him, but it is his turn to work a weekend holiday, you know. I even invited him to go another weekend, though."

"Mercy, after you've longed to go for so long. What did he say?"

"He said, 'That doesn't sound like fun.' I don't know if he meant going with *me* or the trip or the re-enactment. He used to love to go to Mom's."

"Sophya, I'm so sorry."

"Thanks, but I guess I made my bed, uh, sofa, and I'm lying in it, as Dad says."

Mikki tried to suppress a laugh.

"It's humorous, all right, humorous but sad," Sophya sighed.

"What *did* happen last night?" Mikki persisted.

"Oh, Mikki, it's just life. It's just choices. I made the wrong choice pushing Will to marry so young. He's never going to forgive me for taking his freedom away, even though, as you know, we were engaged at the time. He dislikes being financially strapped with a family while he's so young, I guess."

"So, he doesn't want *you* to have any freedom?"

"I suppose that's my punishment," Sophya replied with acceptance.

"What did he do? What did he say? What's got him so upset, this time?"

"It doesn't matter what he said. But lately, after fourteen years of misery, I've gotten to where I rebel and try to get revenge. I hate that. He won't give money, so I take it. He won't give freedom, so I take that, too. I'm not even letting his German temper scare me anymore. That aggravates him even more."

Mikki sighed.

"Church teaches me I have to be blameless as a wife. I get up early and prepare his breakfast and his lunch to take with him to work. He just looks at it and walks out. I cook supper every night, try to keep the house clean, and tend to the kids all night when they are sick, even after *I've* been at work all day, too. Nothing pleases him enough to help me, or have any compassion or gratitude."

"Sophie…"

"Last night I point-blank asked him if he's being unfaithful again. He put on his shoes, walked out, and slammed the door. Guess he just wanted an excuse to go out again."

"Sophya, all these fights aren't normal, especially when y'all are having them around the kids."

"Oh," Sophya interrupted, "just *try* to get him to *wait*!"

Mikki sighed harder, "Please, ask him to go for counseling with you again."

"I have."

"He refused?"

"Yes."

"Sophie, I'm worried about you…"

Sophya laughed weakly and changed the subject, hoping to calm her sister's fears. *And her own.* "But, Scarlett's OK and I'm going to take a quote out of her book and 'think about that tomorrow.'"

"I love you," Mikki said, her tone comforting.

"I love you too, Sis. And thanks for giving in to the kids pestering you to let them stay at your house for Easter, even though it hurt my feelings!"

Mikki laughed.

"I know they think of you as a second mom and their cousins as siblings. Thank the Lord-- I guess!"

"Yep," she said. "Especially since our voices are just alike and people say we favor more than you and Anya."

"Huh! She's too short and I'm too tall. You are just right and you look and act like that actress, Sally Field. You're the strong, motherly-type with the logic. I've been *told (cough, cough)* I look like *Stephanie Powers.* She has beautiful high cheek bones, though. If I could just harness my impulsive nature! Oh well, I'm just glad I'm going on this trip."

Mikalina chuckled. "Oh, Sophya, you and that fascination with movie stars! You are strong, too, though, you just don't realize it yet."

"If I don't have my dream world, what do I have to hold on to? Besides, I just feel like a *single star*, out there in the universe, alone."

"You are not alone. You have us and your children, and *God*!"

"You are right. Well, better get this show on the road!'

Mikki laughed again. "Be safe, honey."

"Oh, thank God you didn't say, *'Behave and have fun.'* That's such a dichotomy!"

"Let me go look that up in the dictionary," she said, laughing again.

"I got that word from Dad!"

"Figures!"

"Well, I'm packed, so I'll be leaving in about fifteen minutes. I'll call you when I get to Mom's. Are the kids handy for me to tell them good-bye?"

"Girl, they stayed up so late watching movies last night. Today, we are all going to swim in the pool and just relax. Don't you worry, they'll be fine."

"OK, I'll take them to church Sunday night after I get back so you can go to your church that night."

"Thanks, honey. Well, good-bye. Chill out and enjoy."

"Yes, *ma'am*!" Sophie answered with a Texas drawl and hung up the phone to the sound of her sister's laughter.

She thought about her children, her real reason for living, other than God.

She kissed and hugged them when she dropped them off at Mikalina's yesterday afternoon. Diedra was thirteen, Bobby was ten. Billy was five, and wanted to be anywhere his older brother was. Their sister preferred to be anywhere they're *weren't*, but she adjusted fine to them when she got to play with her cousins. Sophya considered herself blessed that they were all beautiful, healthy, and intelligent to boot.

"I could *squeeze* them right now-- but I'm not! I'm going on this *trip*!"

She carried her suitcase outside and put it in the trunk of the car. She locked the front door of the house, and got into her car. Sighing, she shut the door and locked it, too. She felt safe, and she felt free.

***

Once on the interstate, Sophya thought about the dream she had the night before. *Probably that fight with William brought it on.*

George Jones and Tammy Wynette's song, *Two Story House,*

came to her mind. Each said they have 'their own story' and then together sing, *"How sad it is, we now live-- in a-- two-story house."*

When Sophie's mom and dad divorced they lived in that two-story house they had built. Mrs. Stolsky and her children never lived in a house that decent again, until she re-married her husband when Sophya was a teen. The only other good thing that came of that union was their youngest sister, Anya.

Then they split for good.

Sophya thought about her two-faced marriage and her husband's double-standard. He reminded her of the parable in the Bible about the cup that looked clean on the outside, but in reality, was dirty on the inside. *No wonder my children don't want to believe in anything or go to church with me. Not even on Easter Sunday.*

She used to think Will was so good-looking. When she first met and fell in love with him, she just noticed his appearance. He was tall with sandy-blonde hair. He reminded her of that actor, Robert Redford, from the movie, *Butch Cassidy and the Sundance Kid.* Mikalina had a crush on his co-star, Paul Newman. Wow.

Her mom left when her children were young. The kids did without a father and a lot of other things. Sophie decided to wait until hers were all out of school if she divorced.

Stephanie Powers had won William Holden's heart, and he had stolen Sophie's when she was just a child. She saw him in movies. He seemed so-- *handsome and passionate and exciting and protective!* "No, Stephanie, I am not married to William Holden. I, unfortunately, am married to William Blackwell."

The Civil War re-enactment came to her mind. "Oh, how I wish I could go back in time and do it all over again! This time I would do it right. I would win."

Chapter Two
Arriving on an Adventure

("For now we see through a glass, darkly..." I Cor. 13:12)

The sun finally shone after the shower and felt like a warm friend on this Good Friday morning. Sunbeams streamed into Sophya's car window. They seemed to be saying 'goodbye' to all the clouds left behind in Louisiana.

She prayed her regular traveling prayer: for good weather, light traffic, and no car trouble. This feeling of gliding down the highway, free from all worries, came as an added blessing from the Lord.

Texas always seemed so big and full of promise and adventure. Sophie laughed. Many of the people leaving Texas probably think the same of Louisiana!

Trips are like that; momentarily, at least, problems and pain can be put on hold.

Spring flowers popping out along the side of the road embraced her senses and made her smile more. It's amazing how they gave comfort deep into her soul.

Her three favorite things were beautiful, fragrant flowers, gorgeous sunsets, and the laughter of small children. Two out of three would be great this trip!

***

Mixed emotions filled her heart as she turned off the highway onto the long, shell drive-way that led up to her mom's house. It didn't look much different from most of the other modest homes in this small northeast Texas town. But it was.

Her Great-Aunt Sadie's house was on the right side of the drive near the highway: so pretty and white. Sophya would call it middle-class. An inviting screen porch extended between the house and the garage on the left. The porch continued across the back of the house.

Many peaches were peeled, and pecans cracked, right there on that screen porch. They would listen to all the latest news Great-Aunt Sadie had. Oh, alright, not news but gossip. Sophie smiled again. Why, Sadie knew everything about everybody! She even knew all the current football players on all the teams. That must've helped, because she married and was widowed three times. She always managed to find a man interested in what she had to say-- and cook!

The old relic barn nestled in the corner of the pasture adjoining Sadies's back fence brought peace to Sophie's mind somehow. She loved the pines and red dirt along the fence line beside the barn.

The next fence squared off her mother's property and small brick house. The glider on the concrete patio shared many early morning cups of coffee, prayers, and conversations between Sophie, Mikki, and Anya. The backside of the house was bordered by a barbed wire fence, and the north side by that same fence and the railroad track.

If one turned left at the fork of her mom's drive, they'd be at Great-Aunt Sheila's house. It was surrounded by beautiful landscaping, and faced a gorgeous eight-acre lake. She was more refined than her two sisters, Sadie, and Priscilla, Sophie's grandmother. Sheila's daughter, Susie, lived with her, too. She tended to her mother very loyally.

This place--the small town of Morristown--was what Sophya really called home. She loved being in the country. And, most of her mother's kin had lived right there in that county since before the Civil War.

That was what Sophie called roots.

When her grandparents, the Braden's, died, they left the place to Christian Stolsky. She had taken care of them after she and Sophie's dad divorced that second time.

Mammaw Braden was Sophya's idea of the Bible's "Virtuous Woman". She adored her. She always kept her hands from being idle

10

and loved the Word of God.

Their home had been built for Pappaw Braden like an old-fashioned barn-raising ceremony. He was a circuit minister and his parishioners had lovingly built it for them.

Bro. Richard Braden's retirement ended ten years after he settled his wife back home near her sisters, when he died of a stroke. Grandmother Braden lived ten more years after her husband died, much to her unwelcome surprise. It was no surprise to Sophie, however, for she had been the one that prayed for that.

Now, five years later, she still felt her grandmother's presence in her home. Such a shame, to have to drive this far to feel that loved and accepted.

She put her car in Park. *How much should I tell Mom and Anya and Urich about my battles? I don't want to spoil our time together, but I need their support.* It unsettled her.

"How'd the trip go?" Anya asked as she came out from the side carport door.

Sophya pulled her long, tired legs out of her small economy car and stretched, then affectionately tapped Anya's nose. "Oh, cloudy with a few sprinkles. But it got better the closer I got to home."

Anya wrinkled her nose back at Sophya, then smiled. They started walking toward the house arm in arm. Sophie still hated how tall she was. Some say the way she wore her hair long and layered emphasized her height. *Oh well.* Anya hugged her. People thought they looked like Mutt and Jeff together, Sophya, being a full foot taller than Anya. Their dad's father was where Anya got her short stature. Edvard Stolsky's mom was tall. Sophie never researched the rest of that family like her little sister had. Not too many of their dad's Russian relatives were still alive. Anya and Mr. Stolsky longed to go to Russia to search for descendants.

Sophya concentrated her research on her mother's side of the family. Christian's dad, Bro. Braden, the minister, had been tall, dark, and handsome. There was a mysterious reserve about him. It had been said that his grandmother, a Cherokee Indian Princess, had married a

Spanish general that fought in the Spanish-American War. *That* intrigued Sophya!

"Have any trouble getting *permission* to come?" Anya asked. Her facetious tone pulled Sophya's wandering thoughts back to the present.

"Ha! You know it! He said we couldn't afford it. At least that's the excuse he tried to use to clip my wings. I swear that man is so tight he squeaks. My car doesn't take much gas to get here and I felt like I would *explode* if I didn't get away for a while."

"Uh oh, I thought you sounded desperate on the phone."

"I know he worries about money all the time. I wonder how he can go out every night, though. If he wanted a family, he sure didn't think they would cost him anything. But I needed a break from being hated."

"Do you think Will can be trusted while you're gone?"

The sarcasm in her voice wasn't lost on Sophie. She stopped and looked at her sister. "I don't think he can be trusted *period*! That's why I am glad to get away and *think* for a while. Thank goodness this trip was already planned."

Anya looked up at her. Sophya sadly began to tell her what had been nagging her. "I found an earring on the floor when I cleaned the other day, and it's not mine. I found it in our *bedroom* no less!"

Anya looked down, probably to keep from letting Sophya see how she hurt for her. No one escaped pain with an unfaithful husband.

Her gaze sought Sophie once again. "What did you do?"

"I asked him about it. He said it must belong to Buddy's wife. So I asked what they were doing in *our* bedroom. William said they came over after I went to work the other night at my second job at the grocery store. You know it's now open twenty-four hours a day. He said they were just horsing around. I started to tell him I know it's not Buddy's wife Buddy wants to horse around with! But I didn't."

"Should have!" her sister showed her anger.

"Well, I knew then, this graveyard shift he insisted I take, wasn't working. I'll just have to figure something else out to catch up this lull in my beauty shop business."

"Hmmm," Anya commiserated.

"I can't believe this is happening again! He *promised* last time if I took him back one more time, we would live together in a *Utopian* life-- perfect! I'm doing all I know how to do. I work full-time and over-time! I hand over the money to him, and he still says I don't help. He's so controlling and demeaning. I can't handle my suspicions anymore."

Anya shook her head, but let Sophya vent; also didn't remind her that they warned her not to take him back the last time.

"When I look in the mirror I see *nothing* looking back at me. He makes me feel like I'm *nothing*. Surely that can't be what God meant when He said, 'Husbands love your wives like Christ loved the Church.' Surely submission and helpmeet, as a wife, do not mean being a doormat to wipe your feet!"

"Ohhh, you need this trip more than I imagined!" Anya hugged her sister again.

"Well," Sophie added, "he stays gone six nights a week, until time for me to go to work. He's either working out, or going out to the bars to show himself off. It's so sad. He's just got to see that look in one more woman's eyes, other than mine, that he's still got what it takes. Whatever 'it' is, I guess he doesn't get it from me anymore. But, I don't respond to abuse very well either."

Anya raised her eyebrows and sighed.

"I'm getting older, Anya. It hurts when he puts me down instead of seeing I have a good heart and brain. I've been such a fool to think he ever loved me," Sophya's eyes began to tear.

"Ah, what's thirty-five? Wait until you've turned *fifty-five* then complain, Sis!"

"Ugh!" she made Sophie smile instead of cry. Sophie hugged her back. "Well, here I am."

"As Dad always says….'Atta, girl!' "

"Shhh, let's change the subject." Sophya opened the door to her

13

mom's house.

Her mom, Christian Stolsky, had been teased a great deal by her seven siblings because of her name. To rebel, she made a point of being as wild as the wind (according to the girls' father), who admitted that he mistakenly thought he could tame her. He also accused Sophya of being just like her mother. Even though he meant for that to offend, it had the opposite affect. Well, Sophya *used* to be free as the wind, also. Until marriage.

Mom just rebelled at being a preacher's daughter. Some said the acorn didn't fall far from the oak tree. Sophie thought they were referring to Granddad Braden before the Lord changed him-- well, the Lord, and Grandmother Braden!

But, life, itself, had changed Christian Braden Stolsky.

Her presence now made everyone feel loved and accepted. This is probably over-compensation for when she felt she didn't measure up to her father's expectations.

Hmmm, there are dreamers and realists. Too bad they attract to each other. Sophya smiled. Her mom wasn't the apron-type, but standing there by the window at the kitchen sink, she made a welcomed sight.

"Hey, Mom!" Sophie hugged her and ran her fingers through her mom's short, dark hair. She had had that style as long as Sophie could remember. The beautiful dark part had grey streaks in it now. Thank God, she kept her Katherine Hepburn airs about herself!

"I'm going to call Mikki, Mom."

"OK, Sophie," she replied and kissed her cheek.

Sophya called and left a message.

"I'll get the rest of the things out of the fridge for lunch," Anya stated.

"How was your trip?" her mom asked.

Excitement returning, she exclaimed, "Ohhh, Mom! I told Anya, it began cloudy and rainy, but ended up gorgeous and sunny!" She smiled when Anya snickered.

"Good, honey," her mom lifted the chicken pieces out of the frying pan.

"The flowers," Sophya continued, "that are coming out now just take my breath away! The fuchsia pink azaleas and white bridal wreath and the lavender wisteria, lock like crocheted drapes around the trees. Plus, those little yellow wild flowers look like carpet for the cows in the pastures. And Anya's favorite, the red clover mixed with the purple, the redbud trees, the lime green buds on the other trees, and blue bonnets-- are picture perfect, like a painting!"

Mom and Anya laughed at her analogies.

"OK, OK, we get the picture," Anya said.

"She'll make a good writer," her mom added.

Sophie ignored her sister's remark. "I wanted to stop and sneak some flowers out of the yards for you, like when I was a little girl."

Her mom smiled and patted her cheek. "I'd just have to set them outside on the patio because now my *sinuses* take *my* breath away!"

"Amen!" Anya quipped. "I second that *e*-motion…mine too!"

Sophya shook her head at those two.

Anya was precious. She wiped her almond-shaped eyes with her hand. Her little pointed chin with that dark hair reminded Sophya of Elizabeth Taylor when she played in a movie, *National Velvet*, as a child. Anya's hair was cut in a wedge-cut like her favorite ice skater, Dorothy Hamill. *Sophya* was the one who cut her hair like that the first time!

Their brother, Urich, came into the kitchen from being out back, burning the trash. Sophya bounced up and hugged him. He stood tall and rigid. He looked so much their dad, with light brown hair. They reminded Sophie of the actor, Jon Voight, but an accident at birth had damaged a spot on Urich's brain. This left him marked as a slow learner, but Sophya knew Urich was better at things like math than her.

Urich, non-demonstrative like Grandfather Braden, didn't back away from her hug. He'd lived independently in Shreveport for years, doing yard work for a living and pushing his lawnmower for miles across town. He refused to give up that part of his independence in spite of adversity. He would come to visit to their mom's place on a bus from Shreveport.

He looked in all the pots on the stove to inspect them for onions or cheese, both things he disliked very much. He put his tall glass of tea at the spot where he wanted to sit to make sure no one else would sit in his place.

"Well, how the heck are you?" Sophya tapped him on the shoulder.

"Alright," he muttered. He sat in his chair acting like she'd never been away, though it had been since Thanksgiving.

They sat around the table waiting for the blessing. Their mom asked Sophie to pray.

"Lord, thank You for my safe journey. Thank You for blessing this food to our bodies. And, thank You for helping us to be a blessing to You and each other. Amen."

"Well done!" Anya said, and began eating.

Their brother's revere wasn't greater or lesser, that anyone could tell.

Commotion began to stir again.

Her mother had placed her delicious country-fried chicken, steamed green beans from Anya's garden, mashed potatoes, gravy and squash in front of her family.

"Ummm," Sophya savored the taste of potatoes and noticed her mom managed to sneak butter in. "And banana pudding, too. If Urich leaves me any!"

He kept on eating. The meal seemed to please him. He had entered into his solitude and slowly, methodically, *perfectly* picked his chicken off the bone.

Sophie rolled her eyes at Anya, who, in turn, blinked hard to keep from laughing.

Their mom looked at Anya and asked, "What's the matter, did you swallow a bone?"

That did it. The girls burst out laughing.

Urich raised his eyebrows and went on about his business of eating. Guess he realized he was probably the butt of the joke, but didn't care.

Sophya missed Mammaw Braden's chicken and dumplings. And, *three* desserts—a "must." Her excellent country cobbler couldn't be beat. She always encouraged the girls to go berry picking. Priscilla Braden knew the stomach went straight to the heart.

Mom's pudding will suffice for now!

"Pass me the pudding, please, Mom." Sophie smiled at her mother.

***

After they put the food away and did the dishes, their mom asked, "Will you girls go up into the attic and find my embroidered tablecloth in Mammaw's chest? I want to wash and iron it for Easter Sunday."

Although she rarely stood on ceremony, she could set a pretty table for holidays.

"Yes," they answered in unison.

Once in the spare bedroom, Sophya pulled the foldaway ladder down from the ceiling. "I'll hold it for you, Anya, since I'm *bigger* than you. I won't need you to hold it for me."

"O.K., but don't *push* me!"

"I'm not *pushy*!" Sophya answered haughtily.

"Boy, *that's* an opinion shared only by *you*!" Anya retorted.

Sophie swatted her sister's rear end and laughed.

"Hey!" she gruffed, then began coughing. "Ugh, it's musty up here."

"Ohhh," Sophya said, upon arriving. "Let me open this little window. Yuk, it's tight!"

She finally got it opened, then pulled the string to the overhead light bulb.

Anya turned on the floor fan near-by. She coughed again. "Ugh, dust!" Then she walked over to the dark, walnut brown, hand-carved wooden chest and opened it.

"Boy, that would bring a pretty penny at the auction or antique market," Sophya pondered out loud.

"Not in this life!" Anya barked, possessively stroking the chest.

"That gold liner is pretty old. Look it's torn and needs sewing."

"Yeah, yeah, one day, one day," her sister responded. She lifted some things out of the chest and looked for the linen tablecloth.

Sophya reached in and almost knocked her sister over.

"Hey!" she yelled.

"Anya, look at this old Bible!" Sophya grabbed it and sat on a stool near the chest.

Anya glanced over then looked through the folded things again.

"It's Grandmother Braden's! 'Priscilla O'Reilly married Richard Braden. They bore: Roberta, Reuben, Daniel, Christian, Elijah, Ezra (infant son that died), Paul, Jedediah and Rose.'"

"My goodness," Sophya continued, "*look* at Mammaw's grandmother!"

Anya leaned over the Bible and looked at the old picture. "Isn't she the one that fed the Confederate soldiers on her dog-trot porch when they came by?"

"Yes," Sophya answered dreamily. "Oh, how I've longed to live back then."

"Why?"

"Ohhh, the balls, the gowns, the *romance*!" She stood and twirled around in what little space they had and sat down.

"What romance?" snapped Anya. "You mean devastation and *poverty*!"

"Well, that came later."

"Not everything happened like in *Gone with the Wind*, Sis, get real! You need to come out of that dream world and face reality."

"Look who's talking. Besides, what's so great about reality?

What if..." a dreamy feeling came over her. *She gazed above Anya's head, her mind in another place and time.*

"What if we got the chance to go back in time? What if we got the chance to do it all over again, and this time get it right?" Sophya sighed.

"I haven't even had the chance to get anything *wrong* yet. Do you mind? This is too deep a subject for just a linen trip. Can I have time to think this over first?"

Sophya exhaled the rest of the way and relinquished her thoughts.

Anya patted the folded tablecloth. "Here it is. Let's go."

"Huh!" Sophie gasped. "Who's in *this* photo?"

Her sister peered over her shoulder and caught her breath. "That's *her*. When she was *young*!" she slowly mumbled.

"Who?"

"Great-great grandmother *Morris*! The one this town is named for, the one who fed the Confederate troops!"

"Wow," Sophya gawked, "so young and beautiful. And that *gown*! It's *gorgeous* and *slinky* and black *velvet*. Woo, woo, Lou!"

Anya laughed, "And that *scoop neck*! How *scandalous*," she whispered, like they had discovered some deep, dark secret, as dark as the dress.

"How did she get away with that back then?" Sophya wondered out loud. "Didn't they wear hoop skirts and high necklines?"

"I dunno," Anya still murmured-- practically--and gritted her teeth and talked even lower to keep the secret.

"Maybe she was beginning a *trend*, treading in *deep* waters!" Sophya laughed and pointed to her own chest to where the neckline would dip.

They both laughed.

"Hey!" Anya picked up another old photo that fell from the Bible. Brown and faded, it portrayed a young man standing beside a horse. She turned it over and strained to read the hand-writing, "Earl Beddoe with Trusty Rusty."

"Hmmm, isn't that Susie's dad, Uncle Tim's great-great-cousin or something? You know the one who rode his horse across the Sabine River that night? He had ridden through the county, changing horses in different people's barns. He infiltrated enemy lines to get the message to Gen. Richard Taylor's troops near Mansfield about Gen. Banks' location."

"Yeah!" Anya exclaimed.

"Are you girls setting the table up there?" their mom shouted jokingly. "That hot air is coming down here. Come out, come out or you're forever locked in!"

***

"Mom, Anya-- I'm going walking down through the pasture to the creek!"

"Spray with bug spray!" Anya shouted back.

"Okay!"

Sophya walked out into the sunshine and enjoyed the freedom. There was a breeze so it didn't seem so hot. She climbed through the barbed wire fence, walked down the woodsy hill to the railroad track, and placed pennies on it. Then she did her balancing act! She had actually gotten pretty good at it, walking on tracks and pipelines.

A quarter mile down the track she cut over to a gate and slipped the barbed wire off the post. There stretched a great pasture and peaceful cows in front of her. Her cousin, Cleve, never seemed to mind her meanderings all these years. He and his wife, Ann, lived nearby and his mom lived next door.

"Oh, Lord, thank you for freedom, and fresh air, and peace!" Sophya ran across the field for exercise, careful not to be too close to the cows and disturb too much. One more fence to climb through, a wooded area to pass, then down the little hill, across another field where blackberries grew, and the comfort of the stream awaited her!

"Oops!" Sophya stopped a moment and glanced at a spot where

Will and she…stopped once and…. "Oh well," she said and walked on.

She sat by the rippling stream and saw an occasional minnow swim over the sandbar, longing to join them. She loved to come here every time she visited her mom, who'd said her brothers used to skinny dip here! Recon how she knew? Sophie smiled and took time to pray.

***

Later, standing by the kitchen sink, she observed the evening sun as it gave a most beautiful sunset, like a sweet promise of better tomorrows. It looked like a huge orange ball of fire, leaving behind streaks of pinks and lavenders. The clouds appeared like cotton candy against the clear blue sky.

"Two out of three ain't bad," she said out loud thinking of sunsets, flowers and children.

Standing there brought so many memories of her grandmother. The knotty pine cabinets and dark brown appliances had been here since the house was built.

According to the weatherman, the forecast for tomorrow was good weather. Easter Sunday was questionable though, with a cool front moving in. Rains would be more welcome in Texas than in south Louisiana. Her mom said it had been a drier spring here. "Oh, Lord, help the rain to hold off until Monday so families can go to church, then have their outdoor activities." *I hope my children are content. I'll call them after while.*

Her prayer life. Now there was a subject she hadn't practiced much lately-- prayer. Her prayers had been shorter and shorter and less intense. Probably because she had become disillusioned with her marriage. She hadn't meant to blame God for the failures in her marriage, but she guessed she had. Seemed like all she could pray lately was, "Hold on to me."

Apparently, He had.

21

She became very active in her church, until they had a church split. That could happen in any church, of course. Hateful things were said and done-- things that wouldn't be forgotten-- but must be forgiven.

Her mind came back to the present when she heard a lonesome dove sing its sad song. She looked out the window at the bird perched on the telephone wire. "Mates for life. Amazing. Why is it so hard to win the prize of love in real life, Lord?" she whispered.

"Earth to Sophie. Earth to Sophie," Anya came up behind her and grabbed a dish towel and began twisting it to pop her on her rear.

Sophya turned quickly and grabbed the towel and pulled her sister close. "That will be your *last, biggest,* mistake, *little* sister! Then I'll turn you over my knee and give you the whoopin' you have been *needing* all of your life!"

Urich sat at the table, sipping another big glass of tea. He laughed his deep belly laugh. They got tickled and couldn't stop laughing. An indignant Anya looked at Sophie and her brother harshly.

Their mom came in. "Private party?"

They all laughed again.

Sophya thought of the scripture that said laughter was good medicine for the soul.

"I get the shower first!" Anya shouted.

"PLEASE!" Sophya remarked.

Urich laughed deeply again.

Sophya smiled.

"Well, I'm tucking in to read. We have such a busy day tomorrow," her mom said.

"Give a kiss, Christian!" Sophie begged her mom.

She smiled and kissed her girls' cheeks and hugged Urich tight and went to bed.

***

Nighttime settled quietly in the home that still seemed to echo Bro. Braden's schedule. The family all went to their private spots to read and pray, each in their own way. Sophya wished it would be that way with her family in Louisiana, even though she was tempted to read her romance novel instead.

***

She awoke to a slow-moving train whistle blowing near her mom's house. Six a.m. That used to be her morning time with God. She wondered if He was trying to tell her something? She traipsed into the kitchen and turned on the coffee pot that Urich had prepared for the girls the night before. That was one thing he liked to do even though he didn't like to drink coffee. Then, going into the bathroom, Sophya closed the door behind her.

The mirror by the sink stared back at her. "Why can't I be a blonde or raven-black-haired beauty with vivid green or blue eyes? Why do I have to be just a mousy-- brown-haired-- grey-eyed-- *mediocre*?"

She brushed her teeth and hair, then she left, with no answer given back.

Sneaking quietly out of the sliding door, Sophya sat on the glider swing with her coffee and Bible. She looked at her Bible, her best friend. Her church had started a program of giving a certificate to everyone that read their Bible through in one year. She got hooked. That was ten years ago. She had done it every year since. That was one addiction she didn't mind having.

About an hour later, Anya pushed the glass door opened and closed it to come sit with her sister on the glider. "Hey, watcha doin', talkin' to the birds?"

"Well, sometimes they talk back to me quicker than God does," she smiled at Anya.

"Sophie," she started.

"Yesss, Anya."

"*What* are you going to do?" she finished.

"Breathe, walk, and talk," Sophya answered.

"*No!*" she persisted. "You know, are you going to leave Will for good?"

Sophya looked up to the clear, blue sky. "I'm hoping this trip clears my head and gives me some answers. Actually, I'm probably counting on this trip more than I should. We have separated many times, you know."

"I never really believed in divorce. Didn't want to end up like Mom and Dad. When they split we were young, we did without a father and sometimes didn't have much food or clothes. So, I figured, if I ever did take the leap, I'd wait until my kids were out of school. But, there's no good age for divorce, I've noticed.

"I've spent a lot of time wondering: What if I never met him? What if I never married him? When should I have left? After child number one, two, three? I wonder, but no solution comes."

"Well, you know what happens when you spend too much time looking back…"

They touched foreheads and simultaneously said, "Pillar of salt!" Then they laughed.

"Come, let's change the subject and go get ready for a good time!" Anya slapped her knee and they got up to go into the house.

***

Saturday afternoon, after the re-enactment of the Battle of Mansfield, Sophya stood staring out of the sliding glass door. The lake looked so beautiful and calm this time of day. *Wish I could be that calm inside.*

Anya came into the living-dining area. "Aren't you going to take a nap?"

Sophie dreaded going home to face William tomorrow. She

smiled at her sister. "My time here is so short. I want to take all this country living in while I can. Think I'll take a walk."

Her mom came into the kitchen from the wash room, and through the spare bedroom, in time to hear her answer to Anya. "Will you check the mail in the box, then?"

"Yes," she smiled at her mom. "Come with me, Anya!" She went and kissed her mom's cheek and bent over to get her tennis shoes. All the girls in the family hated to wear shoes, from their mom down to the grandkids.

"All right," Anya mumbled. "I'll get my tennis shoes."

"Here, Sophie, take an ink pen in case you have to mark through some mail that doesn't belong to us and send it back. We have a new mailman," her mom said, then thanked her when she took the pen from her.

Walking out of the door into the cool of the afternoon brought a peace to their minds. The pink azaleas and blue hydrangeas were such a colorful contrast. The honey-suckle vine growing on the tall pine beside the house smelled so fragrant. The lake's stillness still shone like glass. What a moment to behold.

Anya's calico cat brushed past her leg, begging for attention. She picked Callie up and made her paw wave at her sister, so Sophya petted the cat's head.

Anya put the cat down and returned to her conversation. "Sophya..."

"Yes, Anya."

"Are you coming up with any answers yet?" They turned to walk down the shell road to the mailbox. Many times Sophie had walked on it for exercise or just to think. Now, it seemed-- longer.

"No," she replied then changed the subject. "Hey, how'd you like that *Battle* today?"

Anya just looked at her sister and shook her head, then said, "It was *hot*--ugh! I don't see how they could stand to wear those *wool* outfits. But, it was good."

"Amen. I didn't realize there would be such a crowd. And, they

25

put the concession stand so far from the parking lot! Guess we are spoiled these days."

Anya looked deep in thought. "There's a movie I want you to watch with me tonight!" she said excitedly.

"*Gone With the Wind*!?" Sophie guessed.

"No, but it's cool! You will *love* it! Please?" she batted her eyelashes, begging. "It's about this guy that falls in love with this girl, by going back in time to the Civil War!"

"Ummm. Anya, do you remember that research we did from the library when I wanted to write that love story that took place during the Civil War?"

"Yes. You mean your *divorce* therapy? What's your point?"

"Just think, what if the Feds' boat didn't get stuck in low tide on the Red River? What if General Banks hadn't chosen that long path away from the river, losing so many of his men to General Richard Taylor's expertise? What if Taylor and General Kirby Smith could have put their differences aside and won the whole war for the South?"

She thought of her own battles.

"They could have won more victories than just Mansfield and Pleasant Hill! General A. J. Smith and General Banks set *their* differences aside for the good of the North."

Anya looked at Sophya's enthusiastic face like she might have fallen off the planet.

"I guess," she mumbled through gritted teeth.

"Hey!" Anya exclaimed, "Have you ever been inside that old barn of Great-Aunt Sadie's?"

That got Sophie's attention. Anya always had more *bravado* with her sister around. She said, "Why bother going on an adventure alone?"

They looked at each other mischievously. Sophya walked over to the fence to hold one line of the barbed wire up for Anya to crawl through. Then, she held it for Sophie, who then scraped her shoulder and tore her shirt. "Hey, squirt!"

"Well, you're too tall!"

Sophie climbed through. "No, I'm *not*! You're too *short*!"

"But," she declared, "I happen to be the only one here to help you through!"

"That's a scary thought," Sophya smirked.

They looked at each other a moment and laughed. Anya held out her hand, directing her big sister to go first.

"Oh, it's *your* idea, but *I'm* supposed lead the way?"

"Of course," she smiled demurely.

Sophie trudged on but then Anya knocked her out of the way, going around the corner to be first to open the barn door.

It squeaked when they opened it. An eerie feeling came over them.

Sophya slowly followed Anya in. They began sneezing and coughing.

"Ugh! What's that smell?" Anya asked.

"I can't tell and I can't see-- a thing. Ouch!"

Something hit her head and made her feel as though she was falling. Then it felt like a vacuum sucking her down, down-- "Ahhh!" together they yelled.

Sophya heard a voice say, "Gold, frankincense, and myrrh, to refine you to pure gold."

When she began coming to her senses, she realized she sat on a straw floor in the barn. When her eyes cleared, everything felt different.

Chapter Three
Tour of the Mansion

("In my Father's house are many mansions." John 14)

Anya began to get up, dusting herself off.

Sophya sat still, mesmerized, trying to regain all her senses *and* make some sense of the words she had heard. *What* in the world-- or in the world *to come*-- had happened just then? What was that aroma? What hit her on the head? And that sensation of falling—and those *words*-- they sounded straight from the Bible.

The barn had so many of the smells she loved, horses, hay, and leather. For some reason, that other sweet smell from when she fell no longer existed.

Sophya began to look around. Ahead of her, Anya still appeared to be in a daze. She faced the north corner of the barn and saw what looked like a blacksmith's corner. A large stone bowl-type fire pit apparatus was half-way buried into the ground with metal stokes and clamps propped in it. Horseshoes and tools to shape them hung on the wall near-by.

On the wall to Sophie's left were leather work items, then an opening to some horse stalls. The supplies were nailed so neatly: brushes, grooming equipment, stirrups, and bridles. There were some brackets with halters and lead ropes and cinches, hoof picks. A small table had shampoos and scissors and a bucket. Two saddles were draped over some wood stumps and blankets that were laid over wooden limbs made in a saw-horse shape. Someone had stacked hay above in the loft.

Then she saw *him*! There stood her husband! She turned to see if Anya saw him too. Anya had been turning around looking at the barn also. She froze when she saw Will.

"What are *you* doing here?" Sophya asked indignantly. He

looked as tall and good-looking as ever. *Looks are so deceiving,* she mused. His sandy hair had grown longer than usual and he had a mustache! She glanced back at Anya and raised her brows. Anya seemed too stunned to react. *Maybe this is my imagination from the hit on the head.*

Sophya turned back to see if William would still be there. He was. She surmised, *He's still a cross between Robert Redford and Chuck Norris. Too bad he isn't really like them: Romantic, kind and brave. He is a little bit witty, though, or at least he fooled me in the beginning to believe that.*

He had on an old western-type suit. He stood near a desk and window by the other side of the barn. He just stood there staring at them like they came from outer space. They felt like they came from there, too. So Sophya decided to encourage a conversation. "How did you grow your mustache and hair so fast and why are you *here* and wearing that old suit?"

"*Who* are you, what are *you* doing here, and why such an entrance?" he demanded.

Sophya looked at Anya--who sat amazingly quiet for a change-- then she glanced back to William. She couldn't figure out why he acted and looked so strange. "You *know* who I am. And we were just out for a walk and decided to look in this old barn."

She looked around again, realizing it wasn't old inside at all. "What are *you* doing here?"

"You mean *fell* in! My name is *Reverend* William Hawkins. I do not know you, nor how you know me. And, as you can see, this barn is not old! Furthermore, how dare you question my mode of dress when you are barely covered and dressed so indecently?"

Anya laughed. Will glanced at her disdainfully. Sophya began to get up, brushing herself off. She stopped and looked up shocked. She began to feel self-conscious about her Bermuda shorts, even though Anya wore shorts too. She felt the torn spot on her shoulder from her shirt jump right out at her, but decided to ignore it and retaliate for a change.

"*Reverend? Hawkins?* Ha! And that's a switch; and you never wanted me to dress decently before!" she laughed sarcastically.

"Before? Why do you keep acting like you *know* me?" Will asked haughtily.

Then she mumbled to where only Anya could hear, "Be careful what you wish for."

"Hmmm," Anya mumbled back.

Sophya walked up close and looked William squarely in the eyes. Ordinarily, she would never have been this brave to mock him, but this weekend she wasn't in the mood to coddle him either.

He broke out in a sweat with her being so close to him!

"You are William *Blackwell. I* am *Sophya* Blackwell, your *wife,* remember?"

He let out a sigh and shook his head then laughed surreptitiously. "I would never marry someone as immodest as you, nor would I encourage such dress. I am a minister of the gospel. The Bible says to cover yourself *and* your *legs*, for heaven's sakes!"

Anya whimpered a shy laugh at this remark, got up and sat on a stump nearby. She continued watching the discourse, wondering how Will pulled this off, probably.

Sophya's mouth fell open. She had never been able to snap back quickly with words when caught off guard.

"I repeat, *who* are you and *what* are you doing here?" he waved his hand over toward Anya. "And, who is this-- our *child* I suppose?"

She jerked her head as if she had been slapped.

"You know that's Anya, my sister!" Sophya began to get angry.

"Where do you live?" he began to show more agitation.

"Up the road," Anya finally spoke and pointed north. "Remember?"

"That's a lie," he hissed. "There's no road that goes north. Maybe you are spies."

Anya and Sophya looked at each other questioningly.

Sophya spoke up, in her low tone to gain control of the

situation. Will hated that tone. "Now wait just a minute, if *anybody's* a spy it is *you* spying on *me* this weekend. And if anybody's *lying*-- it's because *you taught them how!*"

She began to fume. Something seemed different about him other than the clothes and hair. Sophya couldn't quite put her finger on it.

"Spies?" she mocked the word.

"Look, I don't know *you* or *her!*" he said pointing to Anya. "But, I am busy practicing my sermon for Sunday, so you need to leave before I have you arrested."

He sounded almost bored with their presence. He usually would have been in a rage by then.

"I am entertaining Andrew Hamilton, General Xavier DeBray and Major Thomas Green tomorrow night at a ball in their honor," he boasted.

Sophya felt like she couldn't breathe, she was so filled with indignation. "Sermon!" she exclaimed. "Ball!"

She looked at Anya and tried not to laugh. "If this is your ploy…" Her eyes widened and her mouth contorted.

"Do you usually act like this?" He took another out-of-character calmness.

That did it. Anya burst out laughing.

Sophya looked back at her--twice--to shut her up. She breathed deeply in and out. "Like…what?" she asked while simmering inside.

"Domineering, presumptuous, and disrespectful," he sighed disgustedly at her.

"Woe!" Anya mumbled.

Sophya swirled around to look at Anya and back to Will. She stepped closer and got nose to nose with him. He would never have let her be so insolent before. Now, she didn't care anymore.

In her calm, low-toned voice, she spat out, "You never *let* me be *before*! All I have been allowed to do is shut-up and go to work, remember?"

This took him by surprise. There seemed to be even a hint of a gleam in his eyes.

All of the sudden, something began to dawn on Sophya. "Wait just a minute. Did you just say you are entertaining Hamilton, DeBray and Green tomorrow night?"

"Yesss," *Reverend* William Hawkins began to look at her as though she really *might* be a spy.

She began shaking her head. She felt like she might faint. "Oh no, oh no…"

Anya gasped with the realization settling in on her, too.

"What-- is-- the-- date-- today?" she stammered.

William stared at her as though he couldn't believe how stupid she was acting.

"Friday, March 18, 1864."

"Oh, Sophya, let's get *out* of here…before we find out…" Anya stood up quickly.

"Yes, *please* leave!" William said adamantly.

"Come on, Anya." Sophya looked at him like this was all his fault. That seemed to be the easiest way to handle it. She put her arm in Anya's to go with her to the barn door. She pushed it open. When they stepped outside, hoping their *adventure* to be over, everything looked different. Sophya's mouth fell open and felt very dry.

"Oh, Sophie."

"Oh, Aunnie."

"Sophie, pray this spell *off*!" Anya sobbed.

"Aunnie, I didn't pray this *on*, how can I pray it *off*?"

The small pasture was a large one now. There were horses and cattle and no barb wire fences. A homemade wooden fence petitioned in the livestock.

"Where's Mom's house?" Anya asked sadly.

Sophya stood amazed. "And the railroad track and Aunt Sheila's house?"

They looked to the left where they had started their journey. There was no longer a shell driveway. Walking away from the barn, they, fearfully, turned left. The wooden fence separated the pasture from a huge white plantation home further down the hill, near a dirt road that ran east and west where Great-Aunt Sadie's house used to sit.

Sophie looked back at Anya. "Oh, my, God. I didn't...I didn't..."

"Wish for this?" Anya said bitterly. "Oh *didn't* you?"

"No!" Sophie insisted.

William walked out of the barn door. "What's the matter with you two, now?"

"Look," Sophya said exasperatedly, "someone is playing a cruel trick on us. We live in 1980. It was *Saturday, April 8, 1980,* when we left to go walking down Mom's *shell driveway* over there!" She pointed in the direction where the road should have been.

"We decided to look inside this old barn at least it was old *then.* When we walked through the door, I was hit with something on my head and felt like I was falling. Anya?"

She shook her head. "Yes," agreeing.

Sophya kept the rest to herself. "And there you were!" She threw her hand in his direction. "Dressed in that old suit, with that mustache you never had before, needing a haircut and with that haughty attitude-- something *new.* Now, everything is different outside. Huh." She sucked in her breath then sighed sadly.

"Haughty? Old?" William shook his head and sighed also.

She continued in Anya's silence. "This pasture is supposed to be *small*. It has a *barbed wire* fence around it."

Tears started welling up in her eyes. Her conscience seared, digesting the fact that she could dream this up and hope it to be true. Then, it would happen *and* involve her younger sister. *How can I get back? What will happen to my children and Mom and Urich?*

She panicked. Then her shoulders slumped. As she looked back at Will, she believed she actually saw compassion in his eyes, for one brief moment. Then he turned his head away. His eyes followed Anya. She walked to the corner of the barn from where they had fallen "out of time."

"Oh, God," she whimpered. "There's no lake, either."

Sophya came up behind her. There stood in its place, a beautiful valley where the lake would be years later. The woods were still behind it, but much thicker.

Anya cried with a loud sob, "*Who* will look after Mom and Uri?"

Sophya hugged her. Surprisingly, under the circumstances, she let her.

William broke the silence that followed, "What you two are saying is impossible."

"I'll prove it's true," Sophya proclaimed. "Those men you are entertaining tonight? Well, Andrew Hamilton is *not* here for the good of Texas *or* the South!"

"How could you know that?" spat *Reverend* William Hawkins reverting back to his snobby voice.

"I've, we've, *studied.* This is the time of the Civil War, am I right?"

"Yes…" he spoke like he still doubted her.

"Well, Andrew Hamilton, though he's a governor, is here to get Texas to join the cause of the *North, against* slavery. The *real* cause of this war ends up being *cotton and greed.* Lincoln wants Texas instead of allowing Mexico to have it!"

William's shoulders now seemed to exhale in a slump. He regained his composure. "Look, you two need to leave. Get off my property, *now*!"

Anya's temper flared. "We have no place to *go*! Our home…" she struggled, "is *gone*! We were walking along that shell road, or drive-way, that used to lead to Mom's house! We were just day-dreaming and wishing we could go back in time…to *this* time period. Sophya wished to change something in her life. We had *no* idea…" she couldn't even finish her sentence.

"We?" Sophya looked at her questioningly.

William caught it.

"Well, we'll see," he said, sighing, apparently still not convinced. "I *will* find the truth!"

He thought for a moment. "For now, I guess it's my *Christian* duty, I suppose, to put you two up for a while until we can find this out."

He glanced over at them exasperatedly. "After you've refreshed and rested..." he hesitated, "we'll examine the matter."

Anya and Sophya looked at each other like he was weird for sure--not them. They sighed, resigned and nodded.

William sighed again at that and waved his hand in the direction of the plantation home to the south of them, instructing them to go first, they guessed. They stared--amazed--at the big plantation home. Sophya put her arm around Anya, and she put hers around Sophya's waist and they trudged onward.

William began to make conversation, as if to take the edge off the circumstance. "Do you always mess up your *real* husband's life like this?" he asked Sophya.

Whether he meant it as a joke or to lighten things, she didn't know. She raised her eyes to his, and then looked down at the parched ground as they walked southward. Then, she glanced over at Anya on the other side of her. Sophya raised her eyebrows matter-of-factly and replied, "He seems to think so."

As she watched, Anya raised her brows back to Sophya as if in agreement. From then on they walked in silence. No attempts at words came until they arrived at his house.

The dry ground beneath their feet brought to Sophya's mind how irrigation would be introduced years later for grass and livestock. Right now it seemed as dry as their souls. She looked at Anya again. Even though her eyes faced the ground, Sophya could see tears streaking down her sister's cheeks.

William turned to them, sighing again. He probably wondered how to explain bringing them to his household.

The walk to the mansion took a few minutes. Sophya became

grateful it was downhill.

She couldn't believe the changes in the scenery; especially for what had appeared to be a small town that never changed.

Well, I got what I wished for, apparently. Is this man a Godly man? Or, will he be full of hate also? she wondered, but she found herself not caring either way.

***

"Land's sakes, Mastah William, you didn' tell me you'd be bringin' compny!"

Anya and Sophya looked up as they approached the cook's house, connected to the back of the plantation. A rotund black lady in an apron and long cotton dress stood at the door.

"I didn't *know* I'd be bringing any company, Mama Sara."

Sara. Anya and Sophie glanced at each other upon hearing the name of Sophie's former sitter. William looked back at them impatiently. "This is Sophya and Anya."

He didn't point to which was which. "Feed them well. Then we'll decide later if we are going to roast them for supper or not."

His humor had a chill to it, as he hopped up the steps, skipping some with his long legs.

Mama Sara let out a long sigh, and then turned around from watching William Hawkins leave without an explanation.

They both looked from where he had left back to Sara, their confidence deflating, if any had been there at all.

"Commone," she said, motioning for the girls to come in.

Sophya looked at Anya and raised her brows again. She shook her head and started up the stairs.

"You mays well sit heah on dez stoolz. Dez commendashuns not fo' compny, but dey do fo' now."

Mama Sara stirred the ingredients in a container on the pot-bellied stove and began humming.

They obeyed and sat on the "stoolz."

Sophya looked around and noticed that the small dark kitchen, though far from modern, could be very serviceable. The counters were more like wooden table tops. Bins provided storage underneath. Some cabinets were covered with homemade curtains to match the two windows, one by Sara and one on the opposite wall by the girls. *At least they are colorful.* One of the counters, on the wall by Sara, had a makeshift sink with a large porcelain bowl that had a hole in it. It probably drained to the outside. A pump handle had been rigged to let water flow into the sink. Maybe a water well had been dug close to the house. *Now that is modern!*

Anya and Sophya sat on two of the three stools in the small kitchen, across from where Sara cooked. Pots hung on the wall in a handy manner. Dishes and bowls might be kept in the bins below, behind the curtains. There were no knives in accessible sight. *We may need them later,* Sophya contemplated.

Anya had, momentarily, forgotten her sadness, Sophya noticed. She looked hypnotized watching Mama Sara cook.

Sara checked a pan of cornbread cooking in the skillet on the stove and turned back to them. She caught Sophya glancing around intensely. She also noticed Anya watching her. She nodded politely to Anya, then looked at Sophya and spoke. "You lookin' fo' sumpin,' missy?"

Sophya jerked from her thoughts. "No! No, ma'am. I was just thinking about how different kitchens are today." Sophya quirked her mouth in a fake smile.

Anya looked at her sister with a warning expression. Sophya raised her eyebrows questioningly. Mama Sara saw the silent communication between the two of them. Then she turned around to cut two pieces of cornbread. She reached under the cabinet to her left and brought out two plates from behind the curtain. That got their attention. Then she moaned from bending and said, "Gots ta git sum top cabnits bilt sumday."

The girls watched as she put a slice of cornbread on each plate.

Then she dipped some greens from one of the pots on the top of the cook stove and some beans with ham in it from another pot onto the plates. Then she slowly turned to bring them the plates. Anya, being the closest, got hers first. Sara nodded to her again when she said, 'Thank you.'. Sophya hopped down to get hers and save Sara some steps. She smiled and looked her in the eyes to see if she trusted her yet, but only saw distrust looking back at her.

"Thank you," Sophya said, noticing Anya didn't mention she didn't like greens!

"Hmmm," was all Sara mumbled and turned around to begin washing a chicken.

Anya spoke up with interest. "What are you making now?"

Sara proudly answered, "Chick'n frik ah say. Mastah William's fav-rite."

"Master?" Sophya and Anya spoke in unison, mockingly, and looked at each other.

"You guls gots sumpin' agin' Mastah William?" she looked back from the sink without turning her body. She probably wondered what had transpired between them all.

"No!" Sophya hurriedly answered, and looked at Anya smiling. Anya just ignored her.

When she spoke, it was to Sara, "How do you make that?"

"What do *you* care? We're supposed to be going home soon!" Sophya lashed out.

"You're just jealous because *I'm* a better cook than you!" she slammed back at Sophya.

This is good, Sophie thought, *at least I'm getting a response.* "Jealous? *Please,* chile!" She didn't realize how she had said it and sucked in her breath. "Huh!"

Sara glanced back at her, raising her brows.

Gees, I not only have to win Anya back, but the whole crew! At least the food is good.

She heard Mama Sara chuckle.

"Ummm," she said, as she tasted the food, not caring who she won over at the moment.

Silence ensued for a while. Sara hummed and they ate. Then she spoke to Anya.

"You cum back latah," she looked back at Sophya. "By you self aftah you gits settled. Ah tells you then."

Anya smiled at her and returned to eating, slowly, in deep thought.

Sophya ate hurriedly, wishing she could break that habit. It always agitated her dad. He said food was made to be enjoyed, especially in Europe, where he came from. Fast *was* not good for the digestive tract. That was his regular lecture when he took Sophya out to eat once a week. She knew he did it for them to spend time together. He also did it to aggravate her husband, who never took her to restaurants. Will said it was due to his shyness. Sophya knew it to be anti-socialness. She also knew he took other women out to restaurants when they had separated in the past.

She looked at Anya and just shook her head, watching her play with her fork in sadness.

Mama Sara spoke up, probably to change the mood. "You guls hav' ta wait till suppa fo' dis peach cobbla."

"Supper?" Anya twirled around on her stool and looked at Sara, then back to look at Sophya, worriedly.

Before they could speak, a young black woman came into the kitchen. She entered hurriedly across the walkway made of wooden planks. It looked to be about ten feet long. It separated the kitchen from the main house. What appeared to be strong, round tree logs cut to size, supported it.

"Mama Sara, ah needs to bring dees laydees to Mastah William," she sounded excited and out of breath with her mission.

"Go 'head on, chile." Sara raised her brows like she would be glad to be rid of them as her projects. She turned from the younger woman back to the sink, to cutting vegetables, like they were already gone.

39

The younger maid looked at them and said, "I'm Lihlee. You all can cum wid me."

She nodded her head and smiled at them both.

"Thank God for a friendly face. *Finally*," Sophie mumbled and forced a smile at her little sister then to Lillie. They followed her across the plank. "I'm Sophya, this is my sister, Anya."

Anya raised her brows nonchalantly at Sophya. That looked to become a regular form of communication between the two while in their present predicament.

Lillie smiled and half-curtsied once across the plank.

Stepping into the plantation home, they entered a large dining room. Sophya loved the medium blue walls, but not the heavy, navy blue, velvet drapes. They were beautiful, but *dark* and *heavy*! The two French windows were tall and the drapes were opened, letting in a lot of the noon sunlight. The gorgeous chandelier reflected the light with many star-shaped, crystal prisms hanging from it. Now *that,* Sophie approved of! By today's standard it would probably seem a little bit dressy for the dining area. Apparently, it wasn't too ornate for *then,* or for *Reverend William Hawkins.*

At that moment, Sophya wondered if she had been bitter because she married for love instead of money. Her mom's older sister, Aunt Ruth, helped raise her when she lived outside of Mobile, Alabama. Ruth let it be known she thought Sophya was crazy marrying for love instead of money. She remembered Sophya as the little girl that used to dress up in Ruth's fancy ballroom dresses. She'd dance and sing and declare she'd be rich and famous one day.

Sophya snapped back to reality. *Was that me*? No, she still believed that love was more important than money. *Too bad it's unrequited love,* she sighed.

"The real William would be very uncomfortable in these surroundings," she whispered. That's one thing she had fallen in love with. What she had failed to notice was his "shyness" was an anti-social attitude. His aloofness must've been bitterness toward rich people because he had been jealous of them. She also failed to realize she was just a wife, not a psychologist. *God forgive me if I brought this on myself.*

"Sophya, look at the carvings on this table."

In her awe of the room and her retrospective thoughts, she hadn't noticed her sister's mood had lightened. She ran her hand along the carvings of what looked like a walnut, Mediterranean table. It surprised her even more that the maid, Lillie, had slowed her pace to let them view the gorgeous dining room. *Maybe she doesn't have to move as fast when she's not under Mama Sara's watchful eye.* Sophya smiled.

"Yes, Anya, it looks like it's from Spain, and *ten* chairs!" she showed excitement.

"Yes'm," Lillie piped in. "Mastah William had it come from deh. Dis ma fav'rite room. Das ma 'sponsibility. Ah cleans dis one and da utta ah shows you downstaihz." She began leading the way again, walking proudly.

Thank goodness she's still making eye contact with me. Maybe I can make at least one friend while I'm here!

"Oh this *vase!*" Sophya stopped to touch the gorgeous tall, Mosaic vase on the hutch nearby. Lillie smiled.

Anya and she walked past the beautiful hutch that matched the dining table. It stood the same height as the table, about to Sophie's waist. The candelabras matched the bronze sconces on the wall behind it. The wall was opposite the windowed wall. Between the sconces hung a gorgeous picture of The Lord's Last Supper.

"W. Hawkins. *William* painted this picture?" Sophya bellowed out.

Anya looked up after touching the candelabras.

"Yes'm," Lillie said, almost reluctantly, not losing eye contact while nodding her head.

The painting had intricately detailed the emotions of Jesus' face as He served each one of the apostles. Sophya couldn't take her eyes off of it. The dim lighting was awesome and probably difficult to achieve. *But, what do I know? I only had three lessons.*

She started to walk off, but Anya lingered a little longer.

"You coming?" Sophie asked.

"This is too weird," she stated, then shook her head and began walking away.

From the 'blue room' as they decided to call it, Lillie led them through a narrow hall. It ran the width of the dining room. Bronze walls greeted them.

"Oh how *dark*!" Sophya stated nonchalantly.

"I like it," Anya countered.

"Of *course*!" Sophya stated coolly.

Lillie laughed.

"I like you," Sophya told her.

She smiled.

"Of *course*!" Anya remarked.

"Hmmm," Sophya murmured.

Lillie smiled shyly.

That passage brought them to a fabulously large hall painted light yellow. To the left stood an elaborate staircase. Turning right, they would be facing south and could have walked out the large French double doors onto a huge front porch. Instead, they walked straight across the hall, entering French doors that opened into the ball room. There were more paintings, apparently family portraits, all along the east and west wall.

"W. Hawkins, W. Hawkins, W. Hawkins. I can't *believe* this!" Sophie exclaimed. Anya followed her, gazing at the portraits. Lillie watched them trying to figure out their opinions.

"Who are these people?" Sophya asked.

Lillie came and touched the one nearest to Sophya. "Das Mastah William's mom. She die 'bout ten yeah ago when Missy Beth be eight."

The woman had strawberry blonde hair. Anya and Sophie glanced at each other, knowing the lady in the portrait resembled her mother-in-law, but not totally.

Lillie continued to the next portrait. "Das Missy Beth, Mastah's little sistah. She be out heah fo' da pahty tomah. She real quiet, d'on cum outta huh room much. But, he *encuhged* huh fo' da ball. She *sings* like a buhd. Bee-u-tee-ful! But not when fokes aroun'."

Then, she pointed to the next one. "Das Senyah Mastah Hawkins. He die when Missy Beth be two. I nevah knowed him," she smiled sadly.

The gentleman had raven black hair, like Sophya's father-in-law, but he was *not* Mr. Blackwell, Sr. Same stern look, though.

Anya raised her brows to Sophya.

Lillie looked from one sister to the other with the questioning look again.

Sophya came to the last portrait. It was of a raven-haired, beautiful woman. Her eyes, a gorgeous green, were stern, like Mr. Hawkins, Sr. Her smile certainly didn't reach her eyes, as some would say.

"Wow!" Anya stated. "Is that another sister?"

Lillie actually blushed. "No, das Mastah's fee-an-say."

"Fiancee'?" Anya and Sophya exclaimed together.

"Yezzz," Lillie stretched her words while looking from one of them to the other. She seemed to really wonder what they knew about her *mastah*.

Sophya took a step closer to the woman's portrait. Eyeing her flawless skin and hair, she said, "Good. I hope she's as tough as she looks."

Lillie snickered.

That brought a suppressed laugh from Anya.

They were near the double French door that opened to another room. Sophie peeked in. It looked like a large ballroom with even brighter yellow walls. "Is this what I *think* it is?"

"Yezzz," Lillie drew out the word again and tilted her head so cute it made the girls laugh.

The room looked beautiful. It probably stretched to the size of two large rooms. More white French windows were encased on the east wall. Sophya said, "I love the drapes! They are softer, more romantic. The print has yellow and blue and green in it. My favorite color combination. The figures on the drapes are English aristocratic ladies and gentlemen, aren't they?"

Lillie shrugged her shoulders.

"No, there's *French* furniture in here and *French* doors. It must be *French* ladies and gentlemen! Wow," was all she could say.

Anya giggled.

"Ah tendz ta dis room also," Lillie beamed.

Anya pushed past Sophya at the doorway to take a look. "Gosh," came her reply. The paintings in the room were mainly outdoor scenes and more portraits. One may have been a picture of Sam Houston, also, one of the Confederate governors of Texas. Sophya wasn't sure about the other one, maybe Jefferson Davis, the president of the Confederacy. She didn't venture near; fearing the name of the artist might be the same.

From across the room she spoke though, "Looks like the artist has actually *been* to all these places, and really *knows* these people personally."

Anya and Sophya looked at each other and stated simultaneously, "Nahhh."

Lillie whimpered a laugh, but didn't answer.

Sophya figured William would never be alone with his thoughts long enough to go fishing by himself, as one scene showed. *Maybe afraid of being alone with the devil within himself!* She mused. He did like the outdoors though.

Two romantic, traditional Victorian fireplaces were on opposite ends, north and south, in this bright room. Elegant chairs were lined along the wall. *Must be for guests at the forth-coming ball.* Two long French tables which matched the chairs, graced the west wall where they stood--maybe for the food. There were tables to accommodate people, and chairs to sit and eat near the north and south fireplaces.

The orchestra instrument stands, and a piano, were in the middle of the east wall. French windows on each side overlooked a courtyard outside. They must've camouflaged the servants quarters out in back area the girls had seen. The oak floors of the ballroom were so shiny and inviting.

"Look, Anya, perhaps I could be like Julie Andrews!" Sophya stepped onto the ballroom floor. She twirled around and bowed like Julie did in her movie, *The Sound of Music.*

Anya frowned at her for daring to enjoying this so much.

Of course, then, *Reverend* William Hawkins opened the door across the hall, and stepped out to see what kept them so long. He leaned against the opening and watched Sophya's charade, and shook his head.

She stood straight up and began walking towards him, brushing her sister aside, like she had done her.

"*Gol-lee!*" Anya mumbled as she backed up.

Sophya looked at William and spoke with a chilled voice, "You always *did* know how to ruin my fun."

Lillie became very uneasy as he walked near to them. She excused herself, knowing her duty to bring them to him was over.

Sophya walked back across the hallway to Anya, but spoke to Lillie on her way to leave. "Thank you, Lillie."

She turned back and glanced at Sophya.

Then Sophya whispered, "*If he ever gives you any trouble, you tell me. We'll fix him so he won't bother you again!*"

Lillie's eyes got so big. She blinked and then turned and walked away.

Sophya jerked her head in the direction of William, motioning for Anya to follow. Anya leaned against the doorway, hitting it hard with her body then pushed herself off from it, defiantly.

Sophya stopped in front of William to stare at him.

"We must've wasted a lot of time," he retorted, "ruining each other's fun."

She walked past him indifferently, then realized there was

45

another man in the room--or study or library.

The man had a suit on, similar to William's. He smiled a *wicked* smile that stayed on his lips as he nodded to Sophya, then to Anya. He had black hair and a mustache that accentuated his skinny, lanky self.

"This is Sledge DeVille," William told them as he walked into the room. "This is Sophya Blackwell and Anya…"

He turned, eyebrow arching waiting for Anya to supply her last name.

"*Stolsky,*" she murmured, poutingly.

Will stared at Anya a moment then stated, "Mr. DeVille wants to ask you some questions." He nodded to DeVille to proceed.

The visitor motioned for the girls to sit down. He looked from Anya to Sophya with lingering eye contact, then looking at their bodies.

"We are fine, standing, thank you." Sophya looked at Anya. She apparently decided to go along with the decision, choosing not to answer. Sophya presumed Anya allocated her as spokesperson at that point.

"Fine," he said hastily.

William leaned against the large desk, almost sitting on it, facing them.

Mr. DeVille strolled around them like the cock of the barnyard.

"Where are you ladies from?" he asked snidely.

"Why should we tell you?" Sophya asked insubordinately, knowing William had probably told him already.

"Because he is the constable here and has the power to *arrest* you for trespassing, if I ask him to," William responded with smug authority.

Sophya sighed and glanced at Anya. Anya closed her eyes for a moment, and then turned her head away. Sophya took that as confirmation of her refusal to get involved.

"I am from southwest Louisiana," Sophya replied. "My sister is from here…*wherever* we are. Northeast Texas, I guess."

46

"You *guess*?" the stranger questioned. "You don't *know*?"

"I know where *she's* from. It's *you* I'm not too sure of." Sophya tried not to laugh but couldn't suppress it. Anya even laughed a little.

William couldn't keep a smile off his face, either.

DeVille fumed. He got so close to Sophya's face she felt his breath on her. She moved her head back, insinuating he had bad breath.

"Do you two girls know there's a *war* going on?"

Now they were demoted from "ladies" to "girls."

Anya and Sophya looked at each other, then back to him, and Sophya sighed.

"Well, there wasn't one when we left home, but apparently, there is one now." She chose insolent humor again.

Anya didn't stop her laugh.

William straightened up in his indignant manner. "Your cooperation with Mr. DeVille is *mandatory*!" he reminded them.

DeVille looked Sophya up and down brazenly. "You have told Rev. Hawkins an astonishing tale of some time zone, or something."

"Yesss," she stretched it out.

"Why should we not believe you and you sister to be Yankee spies?"

He seemed so evil and Sophya still did not trust *this* William. *Should I proceed with caution?* Sophya wondered, but decide not to.

"You would be a traitor to the Confederacy before I would," her voice held no humor that time.

"*Sophya*!" Anya whispered.

DeVille caught it and glanced at her.

To take the heat off her direction, Sophya continued, deciding to end this farce. "The South does not win this war, anyway, gentlemen," she said softly and sadly and looked from one to the other.

William stood up.

"There's no way you have of knowing that!" DeVille spat.

Sophya thought of William's invited guest, Andrew Hamilton

47

and looked at DeVille coolly. "Just as there's no possible way you two guys could be involved in using this war to put money in your pockets, trading with the enemy, eh?"

He cursed and William corrected him. Apparently he wouldn't treat them as anything but ladies until proven guilty.

DeVille started to walk out in anger.

"Sledge," William stopped him. "Please, come back for the party tomorrow night."

Sledge looked from Sophya to Anya. "I hope the *rest* of your guests will be more agreeable!"

William looked at Sophya. "I assure you, they will be." He calmed him down, but Sledge left in a huff, like an injured dog, without the yelp.

Then William sighed. He looked from Sophya to Anya again. "What am I going to do with you two?"

We didn't have a clue.

He walked over to the back side of the desk, took out a bell, and rang it.

Lillie soon came in.

"Lillie," he sighed again. "Show these-- ladies-- to the spare bedrooms upstairs." He then sat down at his desk as though they were already dismissed from his presence.

Lillie curtsied stiffly, nodded to them, and began to direct them to walk out. She looked back to see if they were coming. Sophya noticed Lillie still acted different around the "Mastah." She led them to the "great hall" as she called it, and up the stairs.

Sophya waited and let Anya go ahead of her. She looked back at William, wondering how he could be the one that painted that deeply intense picture of The Lord's Supper, but he never looked up.

Lillie gracefully ascended the stairs, Sophya noticed and smiled.

Anya, on the other hand, stomped up them, emphasizing her misery.

Sophya took the steps slowly, gliding her hand along the

beautiful, varnished and waxed wooden banister. The spindles under it were carved and painted ivory-colored.

Lillie rounded the column when Anya and Sophie stopped. There, at the top of the stairs hung a large painting of a river with shady, green trees along each side. They were drawn to it. That would be Sophya's idea of heaven…a beautiful stream running right by her own mansion.

In the scene, a man stood in the middle of the water, baptizing many people of all nationalities. Little children played alongside the bank. Picnics and blankets were spread all around the grounds. That one did not have William's name on it! *Come and Dine* were the words written below it. Sophya remembered the Lord had said that.

Anya glanced for a moment more, then continued to walk around the banister and up the last step, that turned right, to the second floor.

Sophya looked at that peaceful painting again. Then she looked back down to the door of the study of the man who called himself a minister. Anya walked into the bedroom door where Lillie stopped and pointed. Sophya smiled and Lille smiled back at her.

Another maid came out of the door in a rush. She stopped to look at Sophie. She appeared to be about twenty-eight years of age, probably three years older than Lillie. This maid was Caucasian, though. She also lacked the beauty and kind face of the first one.

"Dis Katy," Lillie said. "Katy, dis Miss So-fe-ya, and dat young lahdee in dere, Miss Ahn-(she struggled)-yuh."

Sophya smiled. Katy nodded and walked across the hall to go into another room.

"She d'on need *no*-body!" stated Lillie.

Sophya raised her eyebrows and smiled again as she walked into the bedroom where Anya stood waiting for them. The walls in this first room were sky blue and a velvet comforter on the bed had patchwork squares of blue, red, green and purple. Sophya sat on the bed and bounced. "I want this one!"

Lillie pushed the door open to the room to the north of the one they were in. Sophya could see the walls were lavender. Anya walked in and slammed the door behind her.

Lillie raised her brows.

"She'll love it," Sophya said smiling. "It's her favorite color."

Lillie shook her head, smiling and said, "If you needs sumpin, missy, you call me."

"OK," Sophya said and stretched out on the bed.

Lillie walked back through the door that went to the great hall. Looking back at Sophie, she closed the door.

Chapter Four
The Revelation

("In the day when God shall judge the secrets of men ..." Rom. 2:16)

Sophya awoke and found a lantern beside her bed the next morning. The flickering flame looked like figures dancing around the room. She tried to remember where she was. Then it hit her, "Oh, God, it's not a dream. This is real!"

She moaned and sat up. The door to Anya's bedroom was shut.

Supper last night had been a snack with just her and Anya in a quiet mood. They had peach cobbler for dessert, though.

She opened the curtain to let the morning sun greet her. Then she heard loud voices coming from downstairs. Sophya got up quietly and pried open a small slit in the door so she could see out. The voices were coming from the hall near the study, where they last spoke with William. She recognized William's voice but couldn't make out the other man's. It certainly didn't sound like that snake, DeVille, they met yesterday. She got on her knees to peek.

"When Hamilton arrives tonight, it would do you and some of your people good to be waiting outside in the courtyard to meet him. He holds great authority with the ranchers and farmers in Texas. He can also get your people weapons from the fallen Union soldiers."

A calm voice answered, "My people do not need your type of weapons. The God *we* serve protects us. Is He not *your* God, also, *Reverend* Hawkins?"

William shuffled his feet at this rebuff.

Gotcha, Rev. Sophie smiled.

This new visitor, about the same height as William, exuded humble confidence. His frame appeared to be about six foot, or so. His buckskin breeches and western shirt were filled out very well with muscle. He looked like he had Indian blood in him, probably Cherokee. Maybe he didn't leave on what had been called the *Trail of*

51

Tears, when the Indians were led out of Texas and put on a reservation in Oklahoma. Sophya had read that that had been a painful departing. Their grandfather's grandmother had been a Cherokee Indian.

Maybe we're related!

The man downstairs had medium brown hair pulled back in a short pony tail on his neck. She didn't like long hair on men. But on him…

"Suit yourself, Brooks." William eyed the man up and down like he was a fool, and shook his head.

Lillie came out of the dining room about that time and started up the stairs.

"Lillie!" William called to her.

She jumped so much that Sophya wondered again what made her so afraid of him.

"Lillie, will you show our visitor out?" William spoke lighter then, and turned to walk into the library, dismissing the man abruptly.

He acts like everyone around here is low-life except himself! Humph! "That jack…" Sophya muttered to herself.

Lillie turned to look at the one called Brooks in his eyes for a moment. Even from where Sophya kneeled on the floor, She could detect a hint of admiration in Lillie's eyes and a slight smile on her lips.

Then, she looked up and saw Sophya's face peeking through the slightly opened door.

Brooks' eyes followed her eyes and turned to look in Sophya's direction.

"Oops!" Sophya pushed the door shut quickly and fell back on the floor on her rear end.

She heard Lillie say, "Dis way, Mistah Brooks." Then the big French doors to the front porch squeaked open and closed.

At that same time, Anya came in from her bedroom rubbing her eyes.

"What..?" She acted surprised to see her sister sitting on the floor.

"Shhh!" Sophya put a finger on her lips, even though Anya had never known how to be quiet in her life. Sophie rolled over onto her knees, got up, and whispered, "I just overheard *Reverend* William Hawkins trying to work out some kind of weapons deal with some Indian!"

Her little sister looked doubtful. She still had not awakened enough to interact.

"Look, Anya, I know how mad you are at me over this situation. I'm just as mad at myself. But, I've been thinking. You know how the Bible says, 'One day is as a thousand years, and a thousand years is as one day with the Lord' or whatever?"

Anya nodded slowly, distrustfully.

"We don't know why this is happening. God is not so cruel as to play some kind of trick on us as this! He might be holding Mom and Urich's lives just as if they are passing normally, while we are here doing *whatever*, for whatever reason, for however *long*!"

They heard Lillie clearing her throat to warn them she was at the door. She knocked. Sophya lowered her voice, "We've got to make up and forgive one another and *trust* each other. We have no one else here, but each other. We got in this together and that's the only way we're getting *out* of it. We just have to figure out *why* we're here, so we can!"

Anya sighed and nodded, submitting.

"Come in," Sophya said.

Lillie opened the door and looked at Sophya. She tilted her head sideways and asked, "Missy, wus dat you peekin' out dis doh?"

Sophya rolled her eyes, acting surprised. "I'm so sure." Then she slowly shook her head. "Yes."

Lillie smiled at her.

Sophya spoke real low, "What's going *on* around here, Lillie? Is your master a man of God and honestly for the Confederacy, or is he not to be trusted?"

She slowly shook *her* head and said, "Dis is Mastah's proppity an' you da in-trudah. Das what he say. Annn…" she hesitantly added, "Das none you biznis. Plus, he say you two cain't reelly cum and go, less you aks."

Sophya acted offended and looked at Anya. She just raised her brows, non-committally. Then Sophya turned back to Lillie. "I don't believe you really want to be part of such!"

"Missy, ah jus da maid, as you see."

Sophya closed her eyes and swallowed hard.

"But," she continued, "we hav' sumpin' bettah ta talk about."

Anya spoke up, "Good, when do we get to go home?"

"Ah d'one know, Missy." She looked at Anya sadly. "But, ah fetch you sum warm watah from da basin ta wash off wid. Den, ah brings you laydees sumpin' ta weah ta da pahty tonight. It'll make you feel reel good!" She smiled, trying to encourage them.

"Now, you stay rite heah, doh." She pointed to the floor of the room while watching Sophya's face.

Sophya nodded as Lillie began to leave, looking back at them as she closed the door.

Anya looked deep in thought.

"What?" Sophya asked.

"Nothing," came her reply.

Sophya glanced behind her sister and saw a crack opening from the third door in her room. So she began, "Oh, Aunnie, I hear that Master William is sooo *mean,* he even keeps his sister locked up, too!"

Anya blinked her eyes twice, trying to follow where Sophya was going with that.

"Matter of *fact,* I'm *glad* it's not just *us* he locks up!" She looked mischievously at her sister.

A small voice entered the room and said, "He doesn't keep me locked up."

The shy creature, apparently William's sister, Beth, came

through the other door. She stepped softly into the room and stood before them. At least, Sophya figured this to be her. She looked like an angel, with her auburn hair aglow near the lamp by the bedside.

They were silent a moment, in awe of this picture before them. Then Sophya replied, "I see."

She slowly walked to the meek creature. Not losing eye contact, she continued, "And, who might *you* be?" even though she thought she knew.

Anya followed slowly also, to win the wisp of a girl and not scare her off. They were, however, almost the same height. Beth had maybe a few inches more on her.

"I'm Beth, don't you know?"

Anya brushed ahead of Sophya. "We have seen your picture on the wall." She seemed to be searching for a way to befriend Beth. "You are more beautiful in person."

Beth blushed and looked embarrassed at this comment.

"You are!" Sophya reached for her hand.

Beth smiled and looked down.

Anya came closer and bent her face forwards to catch Beth's view. "Do you want to help us plan what to wear for the party tonight?"

Ahhh, Anya will be alright now. Now she has a pet project. Sophya breathed a sigh of relief.

***

After they washed up and put on the day clothes Lillie and Beth brought them, they had breakfast in the big dining room. William tried unsuccessfully to engage them in small talk. They pretty much ignored him. The girls had lunch, later, in the kitchen and found the *Master* had left on an errand.

Once back up in Sophya's room, the meeting place, Lillie knocked and came gracefully in through the hall door. She smiled when she saw they had won Beth's friendship. She had a large kettle of very warm water in her possession. She poured some in the bowl on the dresser, and then went into Anya's room to do the same.

"Are you coming to the ball, tonight?" Anya asked Beth. She looked to be about eighteen years of age, closer to Anya's, at twenty-one.

"Yes," Beth stated. "But I'd rather not go."

Lillie walked into Sophya's room from Beth's with the water pitcher in her hand. "Mastah en-cug you to go, Missy." She looked at Beth, motherly, though only about ten years her senior.

Beth smiled, accepting.

Lillie handed Sophya two bars of soap and a cloth and towel for her and her sister. Sophie turned and handed hers to Anya. She smelled the soap. "Ugh, what *is* this, *lye*?"

Lillie looked at her rather scornfully. She reached in her pocket and pulled out a little metal box with her free right hand.

"What's this?" Sophya asked, almost laughing after she didn't answer her question.

"Das for dis." She pointed to her teeth, handing her some homemade toothbrushes.

Sophya opened the box. It looked like baking soda but smelled like it had some mint mixed in. She smirked and curtsied to her. All three women laughed at her.

Lillie had something made of black velvet draped across her left arm. She held it up to Sophya, testing the length.

Sophya gasped. "Oh, my, God!" Tears welled up in her eyes.

Anya walked around to the front of her sister. When she saw the dress she let out a loud sob, and cried, "Oh, Sophie, Sophie. What's happening to us?"

They hugged each other with the dress between them and cried together.

Lillie must've thought she didn't like the dress. She calmly laid the long black gloves that matched, on the bed. She and Beth remained silent.

Sophya swallowed hard as Anya pulled away and ran her fingers over the dress gently.

"Where did you get this dress?" Sophya asked.

Finally Lillie spoke, "Was da mattah, Missy, you d'one like dis dress?"

She held it out to look at it better. "Oh no, I *love* it!"

She looked to Anya to give her words for a change.

Anya's tears did not stop. She looked at Sophya, pleadingly, not to expect anything more from her at that moment.

"I…it looks like one we saw in a picture, that used to belong to our grandmother. We…" Sophya nodded toward her sister, "we just saw it recently."

"Ohhh." Lillie dragged the word out pensively. She looked from Sophya to Anya to Beth

"Where did you get it?' Sophya asked.

"Mastah William got it from a laydee from church." Lillie glanced from one sister to the next. "She too ole fo' dat now, she say. She be glad ta loan it ta his compny. But he d'one hav' one fo' you, Missy," she nodded to Anya.

"Oh," Beth said, coming out of deep thought, "I do!" Then she got excited.

Anya smiled through teary eyes at Beth.

"What is the lady's name?" Sophya asked almost fearfully.

"Dat laydee's name…" Lillie seemed reluctant to answer. "Is Miz Louanna Morris."

Anya and Sophya sobbed out loud and grabbed each other hugging and crying.

Lillie and Beth got silent again.

After a while, they pulled apart.

"Lillie," Sophya spoke, wiping her eyes. "That *is* our relative. She's actually our great-great-grandmother, on our mother's side."

Lillie's mouth drew in a smirk trying to figure that out. She sat on the bed. "How'z dat? She not even be fifty."

"Can we see her?" Anya's voice practically croaked. She had

actually found something to be glad about in their circumstance.

Dazed, Lillie looked at Anya.

"Lillie," Sophya decided to try to explain. "Something has happened to us. We were merely walking down the road to my mom's mailbox and stopped to look in this old barn. We went through the barn door and got hit on the head with an object, and entered some sort of different time zone or something. We really do not expect you to believe us, but it is true."

She looked at Beth. "Anya and I don't live in *this* time period, really."

She looked from one to the other, and bit her lip, awaiting their reaction. "We live in 1980."

Lillie looked from Sophya to Anya to Beth again. Tears still flowed down Anya's cheeks.

Beth raised her eyebrows and smiled a quick, compassionate smile.

They could tell Beth and Lillie tried not to show doubt or mockery. To hold their judgment must have been very hard.

Sophya continued. "We live in the *twentieth* century. We don't know how we got here, or why. I…" She took a deep, shaky sigh and looked at Anya and began to exonerate all blame. "I have always longed to live during this time period."

She looked from her to Beth and smiled.

"In *my* time period, I have been very unhappy in my marriage. I have longed…" She now hesitated to try to and explain…"To go back in time, but to *another* time, and have the chance to do my life over, or for sure, my marriage. And, *this* time, I hoped to get it right. I wanted to correct all the pain, I have obviously, but not deliberately, caused my husband and my children, for making wrong choices or to make him stay faithful to me. But I think I know what to do differently now."

Compassion showed on all their faces.

She looked at Beth intently.

"In *my* time," Sophya spoke as though she'd rather not be revealing the next thing, "I am married to your brother. But our last name is Blackwell."

Lillie and Beth gasped.

"I came here to visit my mother and sister." Sophya nodded to Anya. "And we have a brother, Urich, whom I'm visiting also. Our older sister, Mikalina, lives in south Louisiana, where I do. I came contemplating divorce from my unfaithful husband."

Beth blinked and looked frightened. Then, she sat on the bed beside Lillie, as if in a daze.

The quietness seemed so heavy.

Anya slipped over to Beth and put her arm around her.

Lillie sighed and shook her head.

"Please, just be our friends, while we work through this. And, can we keep this conversation between us, even though William already knows?"

Beth and Lillie looked at each other slowly.

Beth looked at Anya and smiled. Then she turned to Sophya. "We'll be glad to. Surely, God has something good for you in His plan."

Sophya couldn't stop the tears from falling. She put her hands to her face.

Beth stood and hugged her.

Anya hopped in and put her arms around both of them.

"Lor-dee!" Lillie exclaimed. She stayed seated, probably not knowing if they wanted to hug her, too.

None of them had dry eyes. Sophya reached over to hug Lillie and include her in their circle as she wiped a tear away.

They all laughed as the tension relaxed.

Beth looked up to Sophya. "Did I, was I...In your time-- did you like me, in your other life?" she asked, showing her lack of confidence, but belief. "Were we related then, too?"

Sophya smiled at her. "Yes, to both questions, and you were just as beautiful!" She glanced at Lillie. "But I must not have met you, yet."

She shook her head, still taking it all in, Sophya guessed, and smiled.

"Sophie likes *everybody*!" Anya blurted. "She's just too dumb to know when they don't like *her*!"

Sophya took a pillow and threw it at her sister.

Beth giggled.

"Lawsey, Lawsey," Lillie piped in, then stood up to leave, but looked at Anya. "You havtah ask Mastah William if you go sees Miz Louanna, doh."

Anya's eyes got big in disbelief.

Beth wanted to cheer her. "I need to go get the dress that I think you might like!" She left hurriedly then came back in with a beautiful purple, satin dress.

"Purple!" Anya gasped. "No hoops! I'll take it!"

"Thank God, "Sophya said.

They laughed.

Chapter Five
Claws of Competition

("We have piped to you and you have not danced;" Matt. 11:17)

Lillie came back for the girls at about 5:30 pm. She knocked on Sophya's door and she asked her to come in. She smiled pleasantly when she saw her in the black velvet gown. The neck had a draped-scooped yoke. The sleeves were capped. The long black gloves added elegance. "You da mos fine woman heah. You hairh up like dat, *it finish it off*!"

They giggled.

Sophya twirled around slowly, pretending she felt as splendid as Lillie said, hoping to hide her blush. Then she stopped and said, "I've been hearing people arrive already."

"Dats way sum are. Anyway, Mastah William wants you laydees enta little late."

"Why?" Sophya asked.

"Be mo….mo…pro--foun," she said with emphasis.

"Why?" she asked more emphatically.

"He a proud man. Probably want ta take credit, like he in-vent you." She shook her head.

"But if he has a fiancee', *why* would he do that?" She couldn't imagine, with his attitude against them.

"You know men. Dey be fas-nated wid beauty," she sighed.

"Oh," Sophya coyly curtsied. "I'm a beauty?" Then she saw Lillie blush, even beneath her light brown skin!

"Yeh," she said dryly and approvingly. "Giv' huh a run fo' huh money'!"

They laughed.

"That's carrying it a little bit far." Anya walked in from her bedroom. "However, you might actually pass, tonight, Sis." She looked at Sophya, then her eyes trailed the dress down to the floor.

"Thanks, Sis," Sophya bluntly stated. "You may *actually* pass, also!" She stroked the satin of Anya's dress with her finger. Anya watched her finger until Sophya tapped her underneath her chin, to make her look up at her. Anya had shampooed her hair and brushed it until it dried and shone fluffy. She was stunning tonight, but Sophya wouldn't tell her that! Her neckline wasn't as low as Sophya's, lucky duck, and her sleeves were three-quarter. Sophya mustered up a compliment, "That is very slimming on you, though."

Lillie nodded in agreement.

Sophya added, "Well, for someone who seldom cares *how* she appears, or *what* people think about her, you might just turn a head or two!"

Anya's face brightened, in spite of herself.

Lillie tilted her head and looked at Sophya disdainfully, like she ought to be more polite.

"Thanks, Sis. And, *you* just might steal *Reverend* William Hawkins from his *Flo*! What would you say *then*?"

"I'd say I'd have double trouble!"

They all laughed.

Beth came into the room. "I think I might *like* that!"

They burst out laughing again, and then gasped over how beautiful she looked. She turned red.

"Oh no," Sophya said and twirled again and bowed. "*I* want to be the *Belle* of the *ball* and dance with *everyone!* But, go home *alone! You* might out do me!"

Hearty laugh, again.

She touched Beth's hair. She had hers arranged on top of her head with tendrils hanging down to frame her face. She was wearing a long, turquoise taffeta gown. It looked so pretty with her auburn hair. "You are exquisite!"

She smiled "Thank you."

Beth touched her hair. "Lillie fixed it."

"Wow," Sophya said surprised.

Anya walked up to Beth, took her hand and patted it, admiring her. "And whose heart will *you* steal?"

"Probably no one's," she responded shyly.

"Now, now," Lillie spoke up like she knew another secret. That made Beth blush again.

Anya and Sophya looked mischievously curious.

"She got sum one on huh mind. Weth-a he cum ta his senses, ah d'on know," Lillie gave her account.

"Lillie!" Beth whispered with embarrassment.

"Well, I have ta lead you beauties in ta da pahty, now."

"Oh, I wish you could go, too, Lillie!" Sophya exclaimed.

Lillie smiled "Ah may not shine like you tonight, but, *one* day, mah *shinin' star* intercep wid da one God has fo' me!"

"Ohhh," Sophya was over-whelmed that Lillie had a romantic spirit, also. "Wonderful!"

"Mistah Brooks tole me dat," she stated with a confident air about her.

They laughed at her charade and Sophya commented, "Mr. Brooks?" picking on her.

"Yesss." Her face showed that was a closed subject for now.

"We needs ta go," she prompted and led them out of the room and down the stairs.

"Sophya, just *do* what you need to do to get us through and out of here tonight," Anya stated, as they descended the stairs. "Don't do what you usually do."

"Oh," Sophya acted offended. "What's that?"

"*Flirt* with everybody!" she added adamantly.

Beth whimpered a laugh.

Lillie only murmured, "Hmmm," but kept walking, like she was as proud and graceful as the rest of them, which she was.

When they came to the ballroom door, the hum of voices ceased in the room until all eyes turned towards them. *Do we meet with their approval or just stir their curiosity because we're strangers?* Sophya wondered.

Lillie spotted *Reverend* William Hawkins across the room. Sophya noticed definite approval in his eyes. She smiled, acknowledging it. *No point in irritating the enemy.* She purposely showed no other emotion. William walked across the ballroom to greet them. Lillie dismissed herself as *Reverend* Hawkins led them back across the floor to his guests.

"Colonel DeBray, these ladies are guests in my home," he nodded to them and looked back at the gentleman. He introduced Sophya, Anya and his sister Beth by name.

Sophya wasn't sure if she was allowed to say anything, being a woman, but *nothing* could have kept her from it at this momentous occasion. She reached to shake his hand. "I am so honored, Colonel DeBray!"

He would be made Brigadier General *after* the Red River Campaign, she'd read. "I've heard so much about your triumphs here in Texas and Galveston Island."

She curtsied and smiled. He was jovial and stocky and had prematurely balding, grey hair and beard.

"Overrated words, I'm sure!" He assumed humility. "But tell me, *how* does Reverend Hawkins have such lovely guests?"

He looked from her to Anya to Beth.

Sophya wanted to say a million things. She heard William suck in his breath. "We are imposing on him while we have a lay over in plans."

She wouldn't even *look* at Anya while she said it, hoping not to anger her. But, she was usually shy around famous people, a rare but true trait. Beth, of course, would always be shy around strangers.

"Well, I doubt *he* feels it's imposing," DeBray stated and the other men laughed.

William ushered them to the next gentleman. "General Thomas Green," he introduced. His voice had an air of pride in it.

They curtsied again. Sophya took hold of his hand and held it, relishing the moment. She would have bent and kissed his feet if she could have without humiliating everyone else. Instead she looked him in the eye and said, "Bravery is so well represented here tonight!"

The clean-shaven, sandy-haired, hero sometimes known as *wild* on horseback replied, "Whoa! We might get too big-headed to ride through the trees!" but he didn't release her hand. "Thank you for your kind comments. When the womenfolk at home back our cause so heartily, it keeps us soldiers fightin'!" He smiled.

Sophya relinquished his hand with a solemn smile, knowing his life would soon be taken from this world in battle.

William seemed almost reluctant to introduce her to the third man. She was pretty sure why. "Ladies, Mister Andrew Hamilton, acting governor of Texas."

The other two girls always curtsied and scooted past each man without speaking. This they did once again, leaving Sophya to face and speak to each dignitary. She stood right, square in front of the proud Hamilton, who extended his hand expecting a handshake also. She looked at his hand and wished to ignore it. Then she felt William squeeze her elbow. Anya, out of character, tapped the back of her other arm as if to remind her he would betray the South. She made it even harder for Sophya to keep her composure, but she took Gov. Hamilton's hand.

"Charmed, I'm sure," she said and let it go.

Once again, many things came to mind to say, but William quickly interfered. "Excuse me, gentlemen, while I escort these ladies to their table."

Hamilton looked surprised, but they were glad to accompany William and find their table.

The others commented, "Certainly."

The women nodded, smiled and left their presence.

As they departed, William took Sophya's gloved hand and brought it to his lips and kissed it. He looked into her eyes in a way she could not understand. There seemed to be a great debate going on within him. She couldn't decide if that was because he wasn't sure whether to believe her (or not just yet). Or, he may have just been showing off in front of his friends. But if unnerving her was his purpose, she pulled off some of her greatest acting at that point, and remained calm. That, she had learned from years of practice.

She knew if she looked at Anya right then she'd burst out laughing. She also decided for that moment, a cloak of humble fear would be wiser. The feminine side of her, however, wanted to use any admiration at all to her advantage.

William glanced at his sister lovingly, as they walked. "I hope you've found some friends. I'm so glad you decided to join us."

He nodded to Anya and Sophya and began to seat the three of them at the table.

"Hello, William, this must be our company you told me about."

Sophya turned around to find the source of the icy voice. Next to William stood the dark-haired woman they had seen in the portrait. Her eyes still showed the chill of her personality. She was wearing a red velvet dress. Her neckline appeared to be as low as Sophya's. Her sleeves were long and graceful. Sophya smiled, admiring her beauty.

"Florence," William said. He turned to look at her then back at Sophya. "This is Sophya and her sister Anya, and you know Beth. Ladies, she is Major Tom Walker's daughter."

Sophya couldn't detect either fear of the woman's disdain nor affection for her in his voice. Maybe, just a touch of pride.

Beth curtsied and smiled. Anya nodded and so did Sophya.

"Just call me Flo," she extended her hand to shake Sophya's, and made sure William let go of it.

She smiled pragmatically. "It's nice to meet you. I've seen that gorgeous picture of you in the hall. It was intricately done by a, W. Hawkins, I believe."

She looked at William and laughed a flirty laugh.

He chuckled, assuming humility: Sophya didn't really know if it existed.

Then she looked at Flo. "You are every bit as beautiful in person as your portrait," she said sincerely.

66

Flo smiled and accepted her compliment with uneasiness.

William looked at her in surprise.

To end the chilled, still, moment, Sophya added, "We were just sitting down."

But she didn't invite Flo to join them.

Beth and Anya were watching Sophya, as if awaiting her cue. She nodded her head towards them and they sat down.

William put his hand on Sophya's bare shoulder and with a lowered voice said, "There will probably be many suitors that ask for your hand tonight to dance. But, may I, as head of this house, ask for the first one?"

He looked at Flo and back to Sophya. "You are my guest, you know."

Sophya looked back across her shoulder, caught off guard. Then she saw the green-eyed monster overtake inside Flo's eyes. She glanced down at his hand. He removed it as if stung. She looked from Beth to Anya. Then she stared down into the pretty, reflective, mirror-mirror, china plate in front of her. She looked like a different person in the gorgeous, black velvet dress.

Tonight, for once, I'm going to act like I feel beautiful.

"Sure!" She looked up at William, ignoring Flo.

Florence walked off in a huff.

"Thank you," he said. This time there even seemed to be a ring of sincerity in *his* voice. Then he left.

Sophya smiled at Anya, who sat to her left and Beth was stationed to Anya's left. The china got Sophya's attention again. She picked up the pretty cup. A teapot had been placed by every third plate. Thin, curly-cue type cookies, some dipped with chocolate tips, some with cream filling, were on saucers, probably for hors d'oeuvres to curb one's appetite.

"Can we have this now?" she asked Beth.

She excitedly shook her head 'yes'.

They began tasting the dainties and pouring their tea.

"Ummm, sweetened cream cheese!" Anya exclaimed.

Sophya glanced at the older woman next to her and said hello. She turned to face Sophya. She had died red hair that showed her grey roots and she had a real buxom chest. "Oh, ma'am, you ought to let me do your roots. They have so many other type dyes other than that henna!"

She sucked in her breath, shocked and looked away. About that time Anya kicked Sophya under the table.

"Ow!" She hollered and looked at her in surprise. Anya tried to whisper a warning to her.

About that time, music from a waltz, began to be played by the small orchestra nearby. The music floated through the air so gaily.

"Oh, Sophie, it's the Byerly Waltz!"

"You know this dance?" Beth asked Anya.

"Yes, our father made sure we knew the waltzes. If no one asks us to dance, though, let's dance together!"

"Anya, they probably didn't *do* things like that back then!" Sophya now corrected her.

The two younger women giggled.

"Miss Blackwell,"

Sophya felt a cold, forceful hand on her shoulder. She looked up to see Mr. DeVille.

"May we dance?"

William came and tapped him on the shoulder and gave DeVille a placating smile. "My house, my guest, my first dance."

Sophya looked down at her dish a moment for comfort. Beth and Anya were silent. *Uh oh.*

"Why, yes, how inconsiderate of me, *Reverend*," he reminded William of his title.

William watched him walk away, and then touched her shoulder lightly. "May we?"

Sophya took a deep breath, and eased from the chair as Reverend Hawkins pulled it out.

He gallantly took her hand and guided her to the dance floor.

With the corner of her eye, She caught Flo watching. *I'll give her a show, a show for all the women my husband danced with instead of me.*

She let William begin the conversation.

"You look very lovely tonight, my dear. That dress looks like it was made perfectly for you."

"Thank you," Sophya answered. "Lillie said a lady from your church loaned it to me."

"Yes," his tone turned benevolent.

"Lillie also said the lady's name is Mrs. Louanna Morris," Sophya pressed on.

"Yes." He seemed to want to end this topic of conversation. He obviously thought she was carrying it on just to pass the time.

"She is my great-great-grandmother," Sophya said lowly, watching his reaction. "She is married to Isaiah Morris."

William almost stopped mid-step, then began to dance again. *At least he can dance well!*—she concluded.

Regaining composure, William responded, "What you are saying is not possible. Why do you persist with this?"

"Are you afraid of things that you don't understand?" she asked, testing him. *Is he as fearful as the bully I know of as William Blackwell?* she wondered.

He looked down at her condescendingly. "Afraid? Ha! If anyone is in a position that should cause fear, it should be you."

He smiled as if to lighten that blow. He tilted his head as if to try and figure her out. Then he questioned her. "How about you, *are* you afraid?"

Something made her feel ill at ease when he asked. She couldn't quite put her finger on it. "No."

She looked at him with defiance. "But they say there's a fine line between being brave and being a fool." She smiled coyly.

At that he laughed and whirled her around.

She didn't dare meet Flo's glare at that moment. She just let William lead and hoped she could find the grace to follow.

"Tell me, how does a *preacher* learn to dance so well?"

"Practice," he said with a gleam in his eye. "And the right partner."

She actually smiled at that deduction. Then the dance ended.

William ushered her back to her chair, pulled it out, and excused himself.

Anya was alone, watching people dancing.

"Where's Beth?"

"Oh, Sophie, I went to look at the food table and maybe get another appetizer or something. This guy made small talk about the food and the music. He was really nice, and *cute,* too! He was just the right height. But when I got back to our table, Beth looked real sad. I asked her what the matter was. She said, 'Well, at least *one* of us got his attention tonight!' Then she left. What can I do?"

Sophya sighed deeply as she sat down. "Wow, what a night."

She thought of Flo's hateful eyes. She decided, at that point, to stop hating the women her husband had been with. From then on, she'd place the blame squarely on the liar it belonged to, William Blackwell.

"Beth seems to have a level head," Sophya said. "I'm sure, when she rethinks this, she will realize that you weren't guilty of *flirting* with that young man." She drove the word in.

Anya sighed, realizing her point. "I can see it is not fun being accused of that. I'm sorry," she added.

"Well with you it's unintentional, I know. With me, not always. I hate to admit what I've become just to build my own self-esteem."

Anya tightened her lip with an understanding look, and then changed the subject. "Wasn't it neat to meet the generals? They are so cool! And did you get a glance at that food? That fricasse' looks great! There's little thin ham rolls all decorated up, and that peach cobbler, and chocolate cake...ummm!"

Sophya laughed. "*When* I'm *allowed* to, I will! It looks and smells wonderful! That's *one* good thing to come of all this. Did you notice Sara's name is the same as the woman who kept us back *before* your time? And her cooking's every bit as good!"

"Yes. Did she look like her?"

"No." Sophya laughed. "The first one was *thin* from smoking those *Camel cigarettes*!"

Anya smiled. Then Sophya felt another touch on her shoulder. she hadn't noticed but a waltz began to play again.

Sledge had re-appeared. "Shall we?"

She sighed again, and glanced back at Anya with a dreadful look.

"And what if I say, *no*? Don't you have a wife to harass or something?"

"That wouldn't be friendly, row would it?" came Sledge DeVille's snide remark. "Besides, my wife couldn't come tonight." He pulled out her chair with her still in it.

I bet, she thought.

Anya held her hand ever so lightly, though, to encourage her as she stood up.

Maybe he'll try to make up for being so rude.

He began dancing kind of stiffly, she mused. She decided to try to follow him anyway.

She noticed William had left the ballroom with the most unhappy Miss Florence.

"What's the matter? Afraid William is not here to protect you?" DeVille questioned flatly.

"Do I *need* protecting?" she bluntly asked, while looking around at the other dancers instead of him.

"It's the Confederacy that needs protecting from *you,* probably," he said harshly.

Sophya stopped looking around and focused her attention on him. "How dare you speak to me in that tone! *You* are probably in on the cotton deals with that Yankee General, Banks, and he, probably, with Confederate General Kirby Smith!"

DeVille took her by the arm and pulled her over near one of the windows, away from the orchestra. Her back faced the window.

"You insolent hussy. How *dare* you speak to *me* like that!" He lowered his voice. Then he squeezed her wrist until he saw pain on her face.

Before Sophya could smart back with some snide remark-- something-- or someone-- outside got his attention. He let go of her quickly and practically hissed in disgust. He left before she could speak, not finishing the waltz.

She slowly turned around to look out of the window, but saw no one.

Anya had been watching this exchange.

"What was *that* all about?" she asked as Sophya came back to the table. "Thought I might have to grab a fireplace poker or something!"

She smiled at her defense. "I don't know, but I aim to find out," Sophya said and picked up her plate. "Right after I taste some excellent food from *this* century!"

Her sister smiled back, but looked saddened by the reminder.

She stopped and touched her cheek. "I'm sorry, honey, so sorry." Her eyes moistened, so did Sophya's.

"I'm taking my plate outside and sitting on the front porch to see if I hear or see anything. I think ole devil DeVille just saw something out there that scared him. I'd like to find out who or what that is. Maybe someone can help us. Wanna come?"

She brought her beautiful, fortune-telling, china plate to the elegantly decorated food table and exchanged it for a dinner plate. Anya followed.

She shook her head slowly. "You go on. I think I'll go see if I can mend a friendship. Don't eat too much, though. You might look too fat in that dress." She had a twinkle back in her eyes.

"Thanks, for your concern, Sis, but I may never get to eat in this century again! Besides, this empire waist hides a *multitude* of sins!"

"Yeah, right. Well, we may never get to *leave,* either, if you get to liking it too much."

She stopped right in the middle of dipping her chicken fricasse and the juice. "Anya, I know I do things impetuously sometimes, but I'm taking this *seriously!*"

Her mouth fell open. She twisted her tongue between her teeth to keep from speaking. She looked at her sister with disdain though, who was making sure to have some of the chicken, ham, cucumbers, green beans, peach cobbler, a pinch of buttermilk pie, and some teacakes. She motioned for Anya to follow her out into the hall.

"Anya," Sophya said firmly, exercising her big sister authority. "*Where* is your *faith*? Do you think *I'm* not getting scared? That devil DeVille has threatened me, *twice,* and *now* so has *William*! Do you think I like that, and missing Mom, and Urich, and my *children*? What if *I* never get to see them again, either? This has happened to *both* of us for a reason. I don't know what it is, maybe just to teach me a lesson, and have you watch. But, I believe it's more than that. All the wishing in the *world* couldn't make this happen, or *un-*happen! This is *God.*"

Anya's head jerked back like she had been slapped.

"I can't keep fighting your attitude and this too! What if..." she looked around to see if they were still alone.

"What if we are given the chance to *change* something in history for the better or something?"

Anya's demeanor began to relax a bit. She looked at Sophya's ambitious eyes with sympathy. She could read her thoughts like the ones that Mom and Dad had insinuated..."*Poor Sophie, always trying to change the world.*"

"I'm going to find out the, whats, whys, and wheres, like a real reporter. Then, I'm going to *write* about it someday!" she said excitedly.

"All-right," Anya muttered through her gritted teeth, which she sometimes resorted to, when giving in, even if only temporarily.

Sophya smiled with love for the kid sister she helped to raise. She smiled back.

"I've had enough of a *ball* though. I'm going upstairs to wash my real clothes out, since it looks like we'll still be here, tomorrow!"

She turned to go up the stairs before Sophya could see sadness come back in her eyes, who watched her until she turned the corner and went towards the bedroom. Anya looked down and smiled one more time to comfort Sophya.

"Can I relieve you of that plate, and have this next dance with you, ma'am?"

She turned around to a young man's smiling face. He had sandy-colored hair. He reminded her of the actor, Nick Adams. The orchestra played a very inviting tune, the Cally Polka Waltz.

"You are very kind, indeed." Sophya smiled. "But, I promised to meet someone else right now." She stretched the truth.

"Shoulda known you'd be taken," he bashfully looked down.

I'd love to tell him I'm just going on a mission. If he weren't too young to understand. "Otherwise, it would be an honor to dance with such a kind, handsome, gentleman as you. I'll be back in a moment, OK?"

He smiled, blushed, bowed, and turned back to go into the ballroom.

Her thoughts turned to her plot. She looked around and no one else was nearby. Sophya glanced down at her delicious, now cooling plate of food. Then she went out the front door, determined to sit on that gorgeous porch and eat.

She eased through the beautiful, glassed, French doors that squeaked. *Looks like no one's here to enforce house arrest!*

The plantation's porch had handsome, tall, Greek, Corinthian columns. They stretched the whole two stories upward. *Probably imported, like his furniture.*

She sat in one of the wooden rockers. It felt wonderful. It had been painted green to match the shutters. She sat near the window, so she could hear the music and have some light. The air felt cool but not too crisp. Pretty, fuchsia azaleas surrounded the porch. She drew in a breath of honeysuckle and wisteria. She tasted the delicious food. *God, what a dream to wake up from.*

"Ummm, this fricassee is almost worth the worry," she whispered to no one. The fried green tomatoes made her taste buds stand up. "Oh, and these tomatoes!"

She downed it with the peach cobbler *and* the cucumbers.

Then, from the side of the house she heard, "Brooks, this is Andrew Hamilton. He is the one that can help your people get weapons."

She jumped up, set her plate on the rocker, and peeked around the corner. Brooks had five of his men with him. He looked at Hamilton with distrust, like he sensed something wicked about him.

"This is Major General Thomas Green, and Colonel Xavier DeBray. They are here to solicit your people's help with the fighting in Louisiana.

Brooks nodded to them with apparent admiration. The ball lights shined on his face. He glanced back to his men and then to William. "Our tribe will discuss this decision and let you know in twenty-four hours, whether we will fight or not."

William nodded slowly, as if trying to read the expression on the Indian's face. But, he was unreadable at that point. Brooks and his people left quickly. The grass didn't even shuffle.

William spoke, "He would be wise to help us."

"It won't hurt your pocket, either," Hamilton added.

The other men chuckled. Sophya heard the movement of their feet in the grass.

She hurried back into the ballroom. The gaiety lightened her spirits from the somber mood she'd just felt. She saw the young man that approached her before, dancing with a young woman with beautiful, light blonde hair. Then he caught her watching him. *Why not?* Sophya thought, and gave him a flirty smile before she picked up a few more teacakes from off the table.

She joined some others at her table. She placed her half-empty, non-prophesying dinner plate on the table in front of her. Just as she pulled her chair out to join the others, the music ended and the bashful blonde, young man was standing near her.

"The Blue Danube Waltz" began to play. She closed her eyes and took a deep breath. *Oh, to be with someone I really loved right now. Someone that loved me back.*

"My name is Johnny, Johnny Sims. What's yours?" He flashed a shy smile.

"Sophya, Sophya Blackwell." she smiled back. He looked like everything good and pure represented in one person.

"May I have this dance, now, Miss Sophya?" came his hopeful request.

Why couldn't someone twenty years older and this good, look at me this way?

"Yes." She took his hand and he led her onto the dance floor. Sophya decided to let the music soothe her soul.

"Your name suits you," he said, in a pensive, analytical way.

Her head went back as she laughed light-heartedly.

He looked surprised. He had no way of knowing he was her best dance partner yet.

"My name suits me?"

"Yes," her young companion answered.

He must be about eighteen or nineteen, she speculated.

"It's aristocratic," he replied.

Now she showed surprise. "Oh, my mother would thank you."

Johnny seemed pleased with this grown-up compliment.

"You are a *great dancer*! How'd you learn so well?"

He blushed.

She cringed. She did not mean to embarrass him!

He quickly spoke to hide his shyness. "*My* mother would thank *you* for *that*! She made me learn to dance with her and my twin sister, Jenny. My dad's away fighting, so I don't mind filling in for him."

"She's done very well! *You've* done well! Bet Jenny's glad, too!"

He smirked at that and added, "Maybe. That's Jenny." He nodded to the pretty blonde girl he'd just danced with. She had another partner, at that point.

"What's your mom and dad's names?"

"Mona and David Sims," he answered.

"Oh, I don't believe I know them." She relaxed in his sweet arms, enjoying the music.

"I'm going off to fight, myself, next week!" he added.

A warm feeling came over Sophya for his pride for his country. Johnny noticed it and whirled her around to keep her from looking at his face, she imagined. She smiled and looked away to keep him from feeling awkward.

"Where do you live?" she changed the subject.

"Down south of here, about five miles south of the sawmill lumber place, near the river."

William Hawkins came back into the room with his guests.

In a few minutes, the waltz ended. Johnny led Sophya to her chair. "Thank you, ma'am. It was a pleasure I hope to come across again."

"Me too, Johnny," she said sincerely.

He pulled her chair out for her.

"Ladies and gentlemen, I'd like to have your attention, please," William said.

Sophya nodded that Johnny could leave but she wouldn't be sitting down.

William continued, "This is Major General Thomas Green and Colonel Xavier DeBray and you all know, acting governor of the state of Texas, Mr. Andrew Hamilton. General Green and Colonel DeBray will be going to help the Confederacy fight the Union Army in a few days. Let's give them applause for their bravery. Then, I'll lead a prayer for their safety."

A glorious round of applause ensued, then a hush fell over the crowd as William began to pray.

"Lord, we thank you for these brave men. We pray your Hand

of protection upon them as they prepare, and go, into battle for this Great Cause. Guide them. Keep them. Bless them and their families for this great sacrifice. Then, bring them back *victorious!* In Jesus's name."

A loud applause followed. The two men were obviously touched by the prayer. Hamilton shuffled his feet.

A tear appeared in Sophya's eye. She felt for them and for the South. "Amen," she said.

She felt sad for her and her sister's situation, also. Sadness remained in her eyes as she stared at William, wondering, how he could be such a hypocrite?

She had wished for her own husband to be the spiritual leader of their family, as much as she longed for a love to love like God. Would she, also, lose too, like the naïve South?

The music began again. She turned to pull her chair out.

"My, my, aren't you the popular one tonight? May I have this dance before another one beats me to it?"

Her sadness sank further. *William.*

She glanced at him and turned back toward the table. "I was just going to sit for a while."

"Please?" he asked.

She stopped. She looked at her mirror, mirror plate, not even hanging on the wall to tell her fate. *Half-eaten delicacies that no longer meant anything.* She turned back to William. He held out his hand to her. It looked so familiar, yet so strange. Her eye caught the beautiful, black velvet dress in the background of his hand. "Why?"

She looked back at him.

"Because," was his only reply.

She took his hand and began to dance to a tune almost as somber as her mood. She did not want to speak to him, but decided to concentrate on the lovely Spanish Waltz.

Although he seemed not to want to talk either, he proceeded, "Will you accompany me tomorrow on a horseback ride?"

Good grief, how many years did I long for him to love horses, or me, or anything connected to me?

She must have looked as shocked as she felt, because then he asked, "What's the matter, don't you like horses?"

"I *love* horses! You, in your other life, *hated* them!"

He laughed out loud.

The somber mood had passed.

"Why do you want me to go riding with you? Why do you want me to dance with you? What are you up to? You don't even *trust* me! What about Flo, your *fiancée*?"

"So many questions!" He whirled her around even though the music had stopped.

I should be dizzy tonight!

Then, he began to usher her to her chair. "I have decided to trust you. Louanna, Mrs. Louanna Morris *is* married to Isaiah Morris, but everyone here knows him as 'Seth.' Only she and I know his full name, because I wrote it on his baptismal certificate. Someone would have had to trace their ancestry to have known that."

Sophya couldn't detect anything in him at that moment, not trust, not compassion, not attraction. Not even deception or honesty. *What a cold, cold, poker-faced person,* she deducted.

"And," he continued. "Florence and I are *not* married yet. Our marriage will be profitable, however, for both sides. My marrying into her family name is an asset for me. *My* assets to use as collateral for some of her father's business investments will be, favorable; for them now, and me, in the future. But, she will have to accept the fact, that a man of my position, both business-wise and clerically, will have many dealings with many people, some women. She's been told she will have to adjust."

Sophya tilted her head watching his face in wonder. *So different, so different. But not even for the better. Is that what you are trying to tell me, God?*

"Now, surely we can put our two heads together and come up with a solution to get you back!"

Back to where? She wondered. It must have shown.

'Wouldn't you like to go riding? I thought you might like it."

"Oh, I do, I do," she stated blandly. *What reason would he have to do this?*

"I will answer any questions you have tomorrow. Maybe you will answer some for me?"

That got her interest. Maybe he *was* starting to believe her. She gave in. "Alright."

***

Humming, she ascended the stairs. Most of the guests had begun leaving the party. Sophya heard laughter coming from Beth's room when she entered her own room. She peeked into Beth's door that had been left ajar. The room appeared larger than the others and had been painted a lovely, pale pink. Anya and Beth were playing cards in the middle of Beth's bed. When they become aware of someone else's presence, they shrieked and covered up the cards!

"My Lord!" Sophya said as she walked in. "Are you two gambling?"

Beth's faint laugh seemed so childlike. Anya's that followed was shrill, like always, when she got caught doing something wrong or got tickled.

Then her sister gathered her protective tone, and spoke up for Beth. "She's not allowed to play *cards* in the house because of her *brother!*"

"Oh, please," Sophya said, practically spitting out her words.

Beth looked shocked. Anya smiled knowingly.

She realized her bluntness. "Then *who* taught you for heaven's sake?"

Beth blushed. "A handsome traveling man-- when my brother had gone on a trip once."

They all laughed with glee at the wickedness of it.

Sophya took Beth's hand. "I'm sorry. I don't mean to sound so critical of your brother. Sometimes I get him mixed up in my mind with my real husband. Forgive me."

"That's OK," Beth smiled. "I imagine that would be easy to do."

Anya dug to where the cards were hidden in the quilt. She straightened the deck to put it away. "It's late, and you *promised* to go down with me tomorrow to Mama Sara's kitchen and bake cookies!" she reminded Beth.

Beth nodded and smiled.

Sophya rolled her eyes at the mention of Sara's name. The younger girls caught her expression. "Oops," she said and slapped her cheek at the second *faux pas* of her mouth. The girls doubled over laughing.

"Good *night!*" she said, resolutely excusing herself before she made another mistake after such a weird night! She waved them off and walked out.

Anya hugged Beth then followed Sophya, closing the door behind her. She continued on past Sophya as though she were going to bed without saying good-night again. Sophie tapped her shoulder lightly, then harder when she kept walking.

"Hey!" she exclaimed.

Sophya tilted her head and nodded in the direction of Anya's room, for them to go talk. She stretched one side of her mouth down and blinked her eyes grudgingly. She had not been in the habit of staying up late. She didn't like getting up early either!

Sophya went behind her and closed the door. "Anya, I overheard the *Reverend* talking to that Indian, Brooks, or whatever his name is, again, outside tonight. He's still offering him *weapons* if his people will help fight!"

"So," her unconcerned sister stated.

"That's why William had all those *dignitaries* here tonight!" she expounded.

Anya stretched *both* sides of her mouth down, trying to act

81

interested. "I don't remember any Indians fighting with Colonel DeBray or General Green in Louisiana."

"I don't either." She looked around the lavendar room with approval, finally seeing it for the first time. "Tomorrow William wants to tell me something. He's asked me to go horseback- riding with him. I'm glad you have something to occupy yourself. But keep your eyes and ears *open*!"

"Yes *ma'am*!" She saluted and sat on her bed. Now she fell back on it to let Sophie know she was tired.

Sophya shook her head, walked over and kissed Anya's forehead and then left the room. When she got into her own room she checked the drawer to see if Lillie had brought some paper she had asked for to journal their experiences. She had not.

She looked down at the beautiful black velvet gloves and dress. She pulled the gloves off and laid them on the night table. Then she pulled the dress off gently and draped it across the chair. She realized again the impossibility of it all. She unlaced the corset loaned to her, and the shoes. She fell onto the velvet down comforter without even taking the hair pins out of her hair or having water to wash with or brush her teeth. Her tears moistened the pillow as she fell asleep.

Chapter Six
What I Thought I Wanted

("Yea, mine own familiar friend, in whom I trusted, which did eat of
my table, hath lifted up his heel against me." Ps. 41:9)

The sun crept into the window by the headboard of Sophya's
bed. She blinked her eyes open, trying to get her bearings. Then it
dawned on her where she was. There lingered not so much fear as
before, only sadness.

A fresh bowl of water to wash with sat on the bedside table. She
noticed the small container of mint powder and her toothbrush. A
fresh towel and face cloth lay with a bar of lye soap on top of it.
Across the chair Lillie had laid some clean clothes. The beautiful,
black velvet dress and gloves were gone.

Sophya got up and splashed the warm water on her face. An
oval mirror had been placed nearby. She blotted her face and picked
up the mirror. "Ugh, those puffy eyes. Wish I had my make-up. Oh
dear, my *hair!*"

She brushed out her hair and fluffed it with her damp finger
tips. "Thank God I had a new perm before all this happened!"

She sighed a deep sigh. "I am almost too tired to face my new
adventure today."

Someone knocked on the door.

"Who is it?"

Lillie opened the door. "Me," she said lightly, then smiled and
looked at Sophya a while. She too, must be wondering what Sophya
would be going through that day. She handed her a dish of cream-
looking lotion.

"What's this?"

"Dat," she rubbed some on her own face and hands. "Makes
you smell nice."

"I could've used some of that last night!"

"You do pretty good fo' yo'self, I huhd," she stated, as she began draping the clothes Sophya would wear on the bed. She lifted her eyes to Sophya jokingly, without lifting her face.

"Why whatevah do you mean, Missy?" Sophya joked with a southern drawl.

One item she brought looked like a riding skirt. "This is a *skirt*. Not even a *split*-skirt! How do you expect me to ride with this?"

Lillie placed some riding boots by the chair, also, then crumbled and laughed. "You *tuck* it *under* you and ride wit bote legs on one side de hoss!" She acted exasperated and showed her.

Sophya shook her head in disbelief.

Then they stared quietly at each other for a moment.

"Lillie," Sophya spoke softly and peered into her eyes so deeply it made Lillie look away and then down at the riding skirt again. "Is William trustworthy?"

Lillie blinked hard, took a deep breath and stared blankly into space. Then she looked Sophya in her eyes searchingly. "Are deys many mens trustworthy, Miss So-fe-ya?"

She had a pretty face with soft rounded cheeks and full feminine lips. Her medium brown skin looked perfectly flawless.

Sophya smiled a smile that showed compassionate woman-to-woman understanding. "What about *Mr. Brooks?*" Sophya emphasized his name and shoved a friendly shoulder into her new friend's shoulder.

Lillie snickered, "Now das a hoss of a differnt *breed*!" She blushed!

Sophya laughed so hard, her head reared back!

Katy knocked hard and entered the room. She looked at them with a disdainful look, for wasting time. "Reverend Hawkins said you two need to hurry up!"

Sophya blinked her eyes tight and raised her eyebrows, glancing over at Lillie after being reprimanded.

Lillie brushed Katy on the shoulder with her hand and bore

down to direct her out of the room. "Some people 'fraid the wurl might smile."

Katy huffed and left, realizing *she* had been rebuffed.

Lillie looked back at Sophya and smiled. Then she said, "It pays to be on you guard when you is a woman, Miss So-fe-ya, spesh'ly a pretty woman."

Sophya smiled, grateful for the compliment *and* the advice. "You ought to know."

Lillie smiled and sighed, withholding any further words of wisdom. Then she left.

***

"Well, seeing you so refreshed is worth the wait!" William said politely. Then he reached out for both her hands. He had come out of his study while she descended the stairs.

She looked at those strong, slim hands that she had loved. Reluctantly, she took one.

"There, you see? We are going to have a fine time today!"

She smiled, resolutely, and followed his escort as he guided her by the arm.

"Sorry you missed breakfast, but I had Mama Sara pack us a picnic lunch." He glanced down at her. She acted grateful. A pleased look crossed his face. He looked away to hide it, while he led her by the hand. They walked away from the study and passed through the two halls and the beautiful dining room, across the walkway, and across to the cozy cookhouse.

Mama Sara closed the picnic basket.

Uh oh, Sophya thought, as she smelled the fried chicken Sara packed. Sophya loved it but didn't usually eat that or spaghetti very gracefully in front of people!

Anya and Beth were cutting out cookies on the other counter. It amazed her they were up before her. Beth looked intent on her project. Anya looked up when they walked in. She glanced at

William's hand holding Sophya's and turned back to the counter.

Sophya cringed and dropped his hand. "Oh, that smells so good, Mama Sara!" she said, still trying to win her over.

Whether for *Reverend* William's presence, Sophya knew not, but Sara raised her eyebrows in appreciation of the comment.

Sophya let out a deep sigh.

William noticed it and laughed lightly, grabbed the basket with one hand and her hand with the other again. "Beth, keep Anya happy," he ordered.

Beth looked up and smiled at her brother.

Anya looked at him with no expression.

"We're off! Thanks, Sara," he said, continuing on through the back door with all his charges.

When they stepped outside, Sophya saw two gorgeous quarter horses, one tan and one reddish-color. They wore the pretty saddles she had seen in the barn at the beginning of their journey. She stared in appreciation.

William tugged at her hand when she stopped. "Come on, woman!"

This surprised her, even though he said it jokingly. Her face must have shown it.

He laughed again, stopped and bowed and pointed his free hand to the red horse.

"I take it *this* is the horse I get to ride?"

"Yes," he said. "Any objection? You said you liked horses."

"Oh, yes!" she said truthfully. "But when is church?"

"Church is at two."

William smiled a smile she couldn't figure out.

Is he bribing or buttering me up? Horses...surprises...hand-holding...so out of character from what I'm used to!

She faced the horse, but when William put his hands on her waist to help her, she froze.

He dropped back. "What's the matter, now?"

She turned to face him. "I know we danced together last night, but you know, in real life, I'm married *to someone else*! Besides, I can get on by myself, thank you."

William stepped back more, in disbelief.

She studied his face a moment. A hundred thoughts went through her mind. But, at this rare moment, she only said, "OK?"

"Yes, m'lady." He took a pair of riding gloves out of his pocket and handed them to her. He assumed a cautious, mannerly, behavior and bowed.

"Thanks."

She turned to face the horse again. She petted its jaw and spoke softly to him. Then, she put her foot in the stirrup and made sure she *gracefully* pulled herself onto the saddle, tucking her skirt under her.

William visibly showed his admiration. "You don't ride side-saddle?"

"No, and you could've gotten me a split-skirt that was more *modest!*" She smiled.

"Ready?"

William just shook his head at her.

"What's the matter, aren't you used to women going horse-back riding with you?"

"No!" He walked around her to mount his horse easily.

"Why ever did you order one for me then? And, whose fine boots are these?"

William settled into his saddle and sighed. "Maybe to impress you?" He looked at her questioningly. "And, those boots were for Florence, and most of the other clothes and shoes, but she refused to go riding."

Sophya laughed with surprise. "Where are we headed?"

"We're headed..." he hesitated, smiled then said, "I'm not telling you where we're headed."

Uneasiness came over her.

He caught it and added, "If I tell you, you may *beat* me there, if you know how to ride and you really know this area."

She sighed and tilted her head. "Like the back of my *hand*!"

She stretched her left hand in front of herself and examined the back of her riding glove like it was a map. With her right hand she held the reins of the horse.

William laughed. "Come on, Rusty," he tugged at her horse's bridle to follow him.

"Rusty?" she questioned. "You're kidding."

Rusty leaped forwards as she quickly grabbed the reins tighter after startling him.

"Nope!" William commented with a tone that ended the conversation. He looked ahead and clicked his tongue for the horses to gallop off.

It amazed Sophya how he made sure it was him that controlled the conversation. It also amazed her he could ride so well, seeing how the other William was so afraid of horses. *I must be crazy for going with him. But for now, I'll just relax and enjoy the ride.*

William looked over, observing her calm mood, and smiled.

She wondered about that smile, but she always picked everything apart, every mood, every action, *everyone*. She hated that, but couldn't seem to stop *analyzing* everything!

She gazed at their surroundings-- the yellow patches of field flowers, the dried cow patties in the midst of grass that needed rain. The trees were green with Spring, though, and the smell of eucalyptus lingered in the air. She loved that pasture smell. She loved Spring. She loved that area of Texas that usually meant time with her mother and younger siblings. *But Mom isn't here right now to make me laugh my problems away.*

Her eyes misted over. She wouldn't let *Reverend* William see her cry anymore than she'd let William *Blackwell*! She let the fresh air hit her face and dry her tears.

She figured they were headed to the valley by the stream that circled around to the old ferry and the Sabine River.

Her mom told her of times when her brothers got caught skinny-dipping at the bend in the creek by the sandbar. Mom and her female cousins had gotten away with it. Her brothers didn't fare as well and suffered Bro. Braden's rod of correction!

Her heart sank as they traveled over the spot where her mom's house really was. She swallowed hard.

William looked over at her. She wondered if he remembered her sister had pointed in this direction for its location. The *real* William would have never remembered anything she had said or done, unless it was something bad to throw up to her later. *Probably the same for this one.* She glanced over at him but looked ahead quickly. She intended to be as unreadable as he was.

They crossed over the place where the railroad would be one day. Her children put many pennies on that track. And to think, it wasn't even here yet!

Pasture lay ahead before the woods, then the valley, then the creek.

William looked in her direction once again. "Ready?" he asked. Then, he kicked his horse in the flanks and took off in a race.

Totally out of character from the other. I'm the adventurous one!

Although she usually used caution with horses she did not know, this time, she patted her horse's neck and gently kicked his flanks. "Come on, Rusty, let's go!" she said and clicked her tongue.

William didn't bounce in his saddle at all. Being out of practice, she tried hard to tighten her thighs and hold a good form. *Tomorrow, omigosh, tomorrow, my thighs!*

William beat her to the wooded area and reined his horse in.

She galloped towards him and began to wonder if Rusty would slow up. She remembered a tree limb and clothes line she went under too close when she was a teen. Oh, and the barn door one horse headed for when she said, "Whoa!" and he thought she said, *Oats!*

She pulled tighter, kicking up dust on arrival. "Whoa, boy!"

"Great gods!" William exclaimed, waving away the dust.

"On a little bit longer haul, and with a little bit more *warning,* 'trusty' Rusty and I would have beat you!" she stated, laughing.

He looked shocked for a moment that she call the horse by that name. Then he smiled at her laughter.

"You're probably right. But, as you see, you weren't given the chance!"

She acted indignant.

He laughed out loud.

"What *is* it about *men* and *winning*?"

William feigned a smug look on his face, showing he wouldn't divulge the secret. Then he said, "We were created *first*, to *be* first, in *all* things!"

She shook her head and faced forwards. *He probably really believes that,* she speculated, and then gave him a quip smile.

"Recognize anything?" he asked and looked around.

She held out her left hand again and pointed to the back of it with her other glove.

He steered the way for their horses again. "You mean, I can't get you lost out here, even if I wanted to?" He looked a bit mischievous.

"No," she said solemnly, not knowing if that might be his intent.

"Aw," he clicked his tongue again and cut a trail through the trees, ducking his head once or twice.

"Watch out for those limbs," he muttered.

"Yes, *sir*!" she answered, aggravated about the path. "Can't we walk from here?"

He stopped, looked back like he had been offended, and then said, "Texans don't walk, they ride."

She thought, *Yeah, and that got y'all into trouble going into battle a couple of times when you needed to march instead of being such a good target on horseback.* She sighed.

"Oh, alright," he said and, to her surprise, stopped and dismounted, after he ducked a limb again.

At least, the real Will, Mr. Safety, *would have already suggested that by now. He was real kind to animals also. Too bad he loved animals better than he did people.*

Sophya dismounted, too.

The path became narrow. William kept glancing back.

In all her figuring, she couldn't decide if he wanted to see if she were OK, or gone. She guessed the latter.

She had the strangest feeling they were being watched at this point.

They were approaching the brook. She came to it so many times before. She would pray, or cry, or just spend time there pretending. Fantasy would always be better than reality to Sophya. She had pretended to be in her ancestors' time. Now, fantasy had become reality, and she had become fiction.

"Do you hear from that Brooks fellow very often?" she asked for a thought change.

"Who knows," he said nonchalantly. "He comes and goes. Most of the time, his own people don't even know where he disappears to. He has an uncanny knack, though, for being present when most needed or most not wanted."

"The stream is down here a bit," he said, after a while, breaking her thoughts about Brooks.

"I know," she said, patronizing him.

He looked back at her, taking that in. He shook his head and turned to look forward, leading his horse again.

About that time, a rabbit ran across her horse's path. Rusty whinnied and reared up. She grabbed the reins tighter and watched the cotton-tail scurry off. She used to think that meant good luck, even though she didn't believe in superstition. *Wonder what it means now?*

William stopped to hold onto his horse tighter at that time, also. It would have been hard to squeeze past his horse and the brush to help her. "Are you alright?"

"Yes," she answered, calming her own spirit.

"Close call, eh?" He started down the trail again.

"Yeah, close," she repeated. *Not much chivalry here, either.*

She relaxed again and looked around. So familiar, yet so different. Her cousin's cows kept a path through here in her time. Occasional rains must keep it now.

There's a little clay ridge right about here…yes…where Will and I had lain once…

"Recognize anything?"

She jumped and startled the horse again.

"No! I mean, yes!" she struggled to regain her composure.

William stopped and turned his whole body around to study her face a moment.

She felt her face flush. She could never keep a poker face, especially when guilty. She smiled innocently.

He smiled, shook his head, and turned back around to lead his horse again.

She wondered what William Blackwell would think of her now? He had been over-protective. She had to practically give up friends and family and hobbies so as not to cause any trouble. Then verbal abuse followed. *Had I caused all that, like he accused me of?* He wasn't very brave, either. She had to kill all the bugs and mice and chase off burglars. *He must've just been a coward that didn't want me to go anywhere and discover his activities.*

She looked at Reverend William Hawkins, while he walked ahead of her. *He's not very protective. What else is he not? Not always talkative-- now that's a switch! Wonder what he's in deep thought about!*

"There's a pretty, sandy-bottom bend in the creek up ahead. The embankment makes a good picnic sight." William said.

"Yes," she answered.

He laughed but didn't look back.

The trees had thinned out. There were still more shrubs than she remembered. Maybe her cousin cleared some grazing area for his cattle near the water.

William stopped. He took his blanket from his saddle to unroll it and spread it on the ground. "Someone else has been here," he noticed, looking at the ground.

"Who do you think?" Sophya asked.

"No telling. Indians live near here. Or, could've been a hunter. Hope there's no *ants* though!" He changed the subject and took the picnic basket from the saddle and put it on the blanket.

"In my time, we have bug spray." She tied the horse.

He studied her face again. "Oh, we have things, too. Some of it we've gotten from the Indians and it doesn't *smell* so great."

Did she detect a note of prejudice?

He stretched out his hand and waved for her to sit down on the blanket.

She walked slowly over, deciding whether to obey.

William opened the basket and poured some lemonade out of a jar into a cup and handed it to her. "Mama Sara's best!" He smiled and poured his.

Sophya tasted hers and nodded agreement.

Her husband never had a take charge attitude, except when bullying. And, he certainly wouldn't have waited on her, it would be vice versa. Maid for life.

She decided not to speak until spoken to, totally not her usual personality. She still wanted to know why he brought her here.

William took a big drink of his lemonade and spoke, "The Union soldiers reached Alexandria last week."

She turned her cup in a circle on her bent knee. She knew men back then didn't like to engage women into their political conversations. "Is that why you brought me here, to ask me questions about the war?"

He laughed. "Do I have to have a reason? Do you analyze everything?"

"I believe everyone has a reason for doing everything. And, yes, I'm sorry, but I do analyze everything, I can't help it." She tilted her head.

Silence. Then...

"May I paint your portrait?" William totally surprised her.

"No!" She surprised herself with her harsh response.

"Why not?" he asked flippantly.

"*Why*, for heaven's sake? Why would you want to paint *my* portrait when you are engaged to someone else?"

"Does that bother you?" he goaded her.

She couldn't hide her shock. "*Bother* me?"

"Yes, that I am engaged to someone else."

She stared at him. She didn't want to *antagonize* the enemy--until proven *not* to be the enemy. "Why *did* you bring me here, when you are engaged? Why didn't you bring Flo? Why do you want to paint *my* picture?"

He sighed. "Whether I'm engaged or not, doesn't detract from the fact that you are a beautiful woman."

She jerked her head at that announcement.

"And, I simply want some intelligent conversation. Engaged or not, I am my own man, and free to do whatever I want. Within reason."

"Within *reason*? Intelligent *conversation?*" she said both rather sarcastically.

"Florence limits her interests, and her topics. I am a preacher. That carries with it certain boundaries, certain responsibilities."

He appeared as though he were trying to think up reasons to qualify why he became a preacher before she even asked.

She bit the bait. "Why *are* you a preacher?"

"My father was a minister."

"That's why *you* became a minister?" she sounded more shocked.

"In *my* time," he glared at her, almost mockingly, "A man usually does, or is *expected* to follow in his father's occupation. He had been a planter and a minister. I expanded that into cattle also."

"In *my* time, men are called by *God* to be ministers."

"Well, all the Levites were priests in the same lineage," he replied, as though testing her knowledge.

"They were *still* called by God," she answered.

He could tell he struck a chord. He then changed the subject, almost as if he didn't want to get too spiritual.

"Where are the Union soldiers headed next?" William persisted on going back to that.

"Are you going to keep trying a different subject until you get one with the right response?" she questioned.

"Maybe."

He has a good poker face, but a cold, cold soul backs it, she perceived.

"Why did you have Andrew Hamilton at your party?" *I must find his true colors.*

"Why not?" He chose nonchalance.

"Look, William, we can keep dancing around each other, or you can really reveal some motives here and maybe get some real info out of me." She showed her agitation.

"Info?" He acted as though that were a new word, taunting her still.

"Information," she added flatly, realizing that slang word might not have been used yet.

"Alright. What's wrong with Hamilton?" His question seemed genuine.

"He is a *traitor*! That is what's *wrong* with him!" She showed surprise at his assuming ignorance. "He's *Union* underground!"

She watched his response.

William looked at the stream water rippling over some rocks.

Still unreadable, she surmised.

"If this is true, and I will search it out, I will distance myself and my associates from him. To sever totally, though, might not be beneficial to keeping an eye on him."

"You have, also, made reference to those who have aligned themselves with the Yanks for profit," he continued. "I am not one of them. I may even be perceived by you, upon closer scrutiny, to be more sold out to the Confederacy than to the ministry."

Her head snapped up in surprise at his perceptiveness and gall.

"The Confederate Cause is a more urgent need right now. Besides, one day, I plan to run for office here in Texas. That would be if Texas stays independent from the North, which you infer, it doesn't."

The sadness in her eyes showed, that he would choose something temporal over something eternal. *No difference in the two men there.*

"I'm sorry if that disappoints you."

Her eyes blinked wide that he even made that statement.

"And about Hamilton, I am more friends with Edward Plumb, of Mexican Affairs than I am with Andrew Hamilton. Andrew was introduced to me through another person. And for your *info,* I'd rather see Texas go to Mexico than to the Union!"

She contemplated that for a moment. She looked at the cluster of wild violets that grew near the bank of the stream. This territory had always been about a month late compared to Spring in south Louisiana with regard to flowers blooming. She couldn't believe he was watching and waiting for a reply.

"I guess things aren't that easy in your time."

He looked surprised.

"I still have *one* more item to settle, what *do* you suppose your *fiancée* thinks of you bringing me here?" She tilted her head again and peered hard into his eyes for the answer.

"*Florence,*" he emphasized her full name. "Has gone to Missouri to visit her cousin for a while."

"You sent her away, or she left mad?" She hated that inquisitive female side of her personality and bit her lip as soon as she said it.

"Neither," he remarked with a glint in his eyes. He watched her sit back as if rebuffed. Then his amusement went to his lips.

"Her father, Major Tom Walker, sent her," he continued. "In

case the battle crosses over into Texas."

Sophya sighed.

He laughed out loud.

Sophya smiled coyly, and decided to tell him about some of the conflicts to come.

"You are probably aware that General Banks already placed the Union flag at Brazos Santiagos?"

William nodded in agreement. "That doesn't mean anything, though."

"He won't cross the Sabine. He will be held back by a fine group from Louisiana. The Union soldiers will attempt to travel the Red River with Porter's fleet by water. They want to accompany Banks and General A. J. Smith, who is traveling by land."

It amazed her that he listened intently.

"Shreveport is their goal, then Texas. You probably already knew that, though."

"Yesss," he said.

Sophya didn't know why he did that, whether failure to commit or refusing to divulge. *Oh well.*

Then he spoke. "The Yanks blew up Ft. DeRussy after General Taylor and General Kirby Smith ordered it rushed to be 'completed'."

"Yes, that jackass, A. J. Smith! But that wasn't Richard Taylor's idea to complete a stationary target...so easy to shoot at!"

William looked shocked.

"That's a Bible word." She felt her face flush.

"Yes, but from a *lady?*" he pressed.

She cringed. She forgot what century she was in and that she was alone with someone she did not know *or* trust! Her mouth fell open. She realized it and shut it.

"Aren't you a *lady?*"

Something in his voice.... "I *am!*" she insisted.

His smile looked wicked.

"I mean, I'm just not usually very *ladylike* or *graceful!*" Her face felt hot.

97

He smiled smugly. "You are graceful when grace is needed."

She blinked hard. *He must need more information.*

"Getting back to the other subject at hand," he cleared his throat and smiled.

She gulped.

"Why do you despise A. J. Smith so much?"

Sophya let out a sigh of relief for the change of subject.

"He's callous and destructive like General Sherman his teacher! He burns or destroys or *steals* everything in his path! There's hardly even any antebellum *furniture* left in the South!"

She caught herself revealing too much emotion to someone whose motives she still was not sure of. She took a deep breath and rearranged herself on the blanket.

William took the hint and stayed silent, speculating, she presumed. She almost thought she saw compassion cross his face.

This William likes nice things, also. Maybe that's why the compassion…who knows?

"Ft. DeRussy is a big, expensive, dangerous waste," he agreed.

She caught his agreement with amazement.

"What about Shreveport? Will they take it?"

She hadn't seen him this apprehensive before.

"I hear Steele is dragging his feet about coming down from Arkansas to help Banks." His face did look anxious. This was a new side of him.

She couldn't imagine this William being fearful. *He must have some investments he needs to protect or something.*

"Steele will start to come, Grant makes sure of that." She pondered how to continue. "But Shreveport will *not* be taken," she answered and waited.

William relaxed immensely.

"The navy will get bogged down because of the low tide on the Red River. General Banks will have to go on alone by land."

William looked pleasantly surprised.

"Then, there's a decisive..." she chose her words carefully..."victory at Mansfield."

He showed real excitement. "How can that be? General Kirby Smith..."

"General Richard Taylor will grow weary of waiting for that wishy-washy General Kirby Smith to give orders to take troops from Shreveport. He *knows* the timing and opportunity will be right and the situation strategically set with his troops at Keatchie, so, he heads for Mansfield and *takes* it!" she said with pride.

Reverend William Hawkins appeared amazed at her knowledge and her interest in the battle.

"My, my," he murmured.

That time, she almost felt she could read his mind, which seemed to be racing.

William sighed. He rearranged his legs and sat, engrossed in thought.

"You seem to admire General Taylor immensely."

"He's *brilliant* and *brave!*" she countered, probably too quickly.

He absorbed her comment, and then responded. "And yet, you say we lose?'

She blinked away a painful look. She'd never believed in slavery. She had come to love their sitter, Sara, and her cooking, and playing in her neighborhood. And, Sara was good to them. And, the *Southern pride* that the North felt needed to be *broken* had wearied her.

"Taylor and Kirby Smith never could mend their differences for the South to have more victories. A. J. Smith and Banks had the same ego problem, but decided to let it go, for the good of the North."

"Well now, let's eat!" She ended the conversation which astounded the Reverend.

"All right," he said reluctantly.

She smiled that the issue had been settled.

William put the plate of chicken on the blanket, then the biscuits, unwrapping the cloths around them.

99

"Ohhh," she gasped.

He laughed. "I can see the way to *your* heart!"

She blinked hard at that remark. But, chose to answer. She would only compromise by revealing *some* parts of herself. "That's a *known* secret from where *ah* come from."

A chuckle came out of him.

He might not be so bad if he were real all the time. She felt proud that he looked so perplexed, hopeful he couldn't read her thoughts.

A jar of warm green beans and peach cobbler! *Delight must be on my face.*

"It seems Mama Sara has won you over, Sophya," William proclaimed.

"I don't think I really matter, so it must be you."

He burst out laughing.

She laughed too.

He stopped to stare at her a moment.

This dude better not get mushy with me.

"Win some, lose some," she said matter-of-factly.

"Oh, it's a good idea to win *her* over," he advised. He held a piece of chicken, showing he'd taken the first grateful bite. "Ummm, she never lets me down, though."

Sophya grinned and picked up a piece of chicken from the plate.

"How did you win her over?" she asked.

"Does it surprise you, that I did?" he feigned hurt feelings.

"Sometimes." She averted her eyes down to her piece of chicken. "Ummm, you're right about this, though!"

He smiled. "She's known me since my birth," he answered then tasted the other delights. She could tell *he* now closed the subject.

She stopped chewing and sighed.

He waited.

"And what about you? Are you hard to win over?" he asked.

"Win over to what?"

He looked mischievous.

So different from the William I know, she mused.

"Win over…approval of," he stated.

"Approval of what?" Sophya asked bluntly.

"When will I win your approval of me?" Reverend William Hawkins raised his eyebrows. A smile didn't quite reach his lips, but a spoon of cobbler did.

She contemplated her response long and hard. Her eyes pierced his. She had fallen in love with those green eyes, and listening to his soul being poured out about all the woes of his childhood. But now, even though the features were the same, she felt nothing. He looked totally different…like a ghost, or reincarnation…even though she didn't believe in such.

"I don't really know you," she replied.

"You said I looked like your husband."

"Oh, you do, you do," Sophya assured him.

"Then what's the problem?" William questioned.

"I know *him,* his life, his likes, his dislikes, but not yours."

He still did not venture into that territory.

"How did you meet your husband?" William inquired.

It was a beautiful Sunday, and still having time before church, Sophya decided to play his game a little longer.

"I met him at a beach, through a mutual friend," she said without emotion.

"What attracted you to him?" His curiosity seemed genuine.

"His looks," she laughed and looked down at the patterns in the quilt. She knew that meant she liked William *Hawkins'* looks also.

When she looked up, he had a contented smirk on his face.

"I thought he was gallant."

"You *thought?"* He picked up on that one quickly.

"Well, yes. In the beginning. My friends and I had car trouble when we started to leave, and he insisted he and his friends help."

"Car trouble?" He looked confused.

"It's something in *my* time," she bit her lip because she forgot the situation.

His brow raised.

"Anyway, my friend had her dog with us and William was kind to it, worried it needed more water in the heat that day and all. I love animals too."

"I can tell," he quickly interjected.

Surprised, she stopped, then continued.

"I judged his character that day by those incidents."

"So soon?" William Hawkins questioned.

"Too soon, probably," she said, retrospectively.

William sat back to think a moment, then asked, "Did you fall in love with him?"

"Yes, I did."

"Are you *still* in love with him?"

His question amazed her. "Why would I tell you if I weren't?"

"When we first met, your sister insinuated you had thought of wishing for things to change, or something like that. Am I right?"

Sophya began to feel uneasy. She stood up and walked over to the tallow tree near the water. She touched a twig of the tree and began twirling it with her fingers.

"I think we need to change the subject, William. In fact, I think we probably need to *leave.*" She turned toward the blanket to start packing up.

He had already gotten up quickly behind her without her realizing it. When she turned, he grabbed her left hand with his right. Then he pinned her right shoulder with his left against the tree.

"Stop it!" she yelled.

He smashed his mouth on hers. His tongue tried to pry her mouth open more, and with his knee he raised her skirt up between her legs. When he felt her squirming away, he smashed his body harder against hers.

She turned her head sideways, away from his mouth and cried out with a gasp.

"You want something *better*? I can give it to you, besides, I want something *different* to tide me over until I marry." he snidely remarked. It won't matter, since you are already married, you might need *someone* right now, too! Besides, if I don't really *exist,* what's the harm? And, no one will hear you out here, by the way."

He tried to reach his right hand under her blouse that had come un-tucked.

Sophya screamed in anguish that she had gotten herself into this.

About that time, a noise, or something, whizzed right past William's head. Then, Sophya heard a rustle in the bushes from across the stream.

William loosened his grip to look in the direction it came from, just long enough for her to get loose.

Sophya ran to Rusty, jumped on, and steered the horse in the direction she wanted to go.

"You bastard! And, that's in the Bible too, if you ever bothered to really read it! Clean up your *own* mess!" She kicked Rusty in the flanks and rode off after seeing William looking dazed and torn. She imagined he couldn't decide whether to run after her or find who saw him.

The horse showed his speed. Ducking her head she cleared the trees and distanced herself from the valley quickly. Sophya steered him in another direction that she hoped would be a clearing that she knew of.

It was. Tears burned her cheeks. She kept a pace, patting Rusty's mane and soothing and encouraging him. "What a fool. What a fool I've been."

Sophya couldn't soothe herself, though.

"God, please forgive me." Now tears of repentance, not fear, flowed.

She reined the horse down a path that would be a country road one day and breathed easy, glad it existed. It led to Panola County. That word had been derived from the Indian word "ponolo" meaning cotton, and she saw plenty of it planted in front of her. Cotton on one side and acres and acres of Indian corn on the other side.

Sophya finally reached the main road that went to the front of the plantation. She wanted to be in clear view, so nothing else could happen.

When she arrived all disheveled at the mansion, it seemed so settled and quiet, displaying a normal Sunday peace about it. "This place doesn't even show evidences of knowing there's a war going on, elsewhere in the country, or down by the creek," she muttered to herself.

She felt dirty. She felt sad. She felt betrayed.

Sophya quickly dismounted Rusty in front of the house. She turned him in the direction of the barn and walked around the house. She peeked on the west side of the plantation to make sure William hadn't made it to the barn yet. Then she walked quietly and briskly to it.

She opened the same creaky door her sister and she had come through just a few days ago. It seemed a million years ago, they fell "back in time"-- a hundred and something years!

Quietness prevailed here also. Sophya led Rusty to the stalls, ungirthed his saddle and took it off. It was heavy, but she hauled it to the stump. Then, she took off his blanket and brushed his back to cool the sweat and murmured to him with a calming voice. She would throw it at William and run out if he came in.

Sophya looked around the tack room….the desk where William had been *rehearsing* his sermon…the saddles…the blacksmithing corner. She smelled the hay and leather, just as before. Then, she fell on her knees and cried unto the Lord…

"Oh, *please,* forgive me for wishing for this! *Please,* help me not to throw that pitchfork if he comes in right now! Get me and Anya back, please, please. I know what you wanted me to see. I know now: Things could be worse. I'll be more grateful, just *please*, get us *back!"*

She wept hard, but no answer came. Rusty neighed and ended the silence. She got back to the barn door and opened it slowly, peeking out. "Thank God, he's not here. But, God, you could zap me *now* and Anya too somehow!"

But nothing happened.

Sophya slipped back to the west side of the house avoiding the cookhouse. She carefully opened the side door that entered the small hall. She waited and listened. She didn't hear any voices in the dining room or in William's study. She tiptoed to where she could see into the dining area. It was clear. She walked into the great hall. Clear also. The door to the study had been shut. She dashed up the stairs into her room and closed the door behind her.

She sat on the edge of the bed, still not believing all that had happened. She hugged herself and tightly rocked herself, in a comforting manner, to heal all her emotional wounds, because there was no one else to do it. Then, Sophya turned over and cried into her pillow for all her troubles, which seemed unsolvable in *both* centuries. That made her sob even more deeply.

"Oh, God, help me. Help this stupid child get back to *her* children! Oh, Mama, be praying for me, for Anya," tears streamed quietly as she tried to figure a way to get back home.

The door slipped open.

Sophya sat up, wiping her eyes.

Katy stood there looking at her, questioningly, almost compassionately.

"I will bring you a bowl of water to freshen up for church services," she said.

"Church!" Sophya looked away, then realized her mistake. She looked down at the floor and said, "I don't want to go."

"Did he have his way with you?" Katy asked in a lowered voice.

Sophya looked at Katy quickly, not knowing if she could trust her. "Did he with you?"

"No. I'm not *pretty* enough," she replied with what sounded like bitterness.

Is she jealous of this?

Caught off guard, Sophya waited, then asked, "Has he with Lillie?"

Katy nodded her head, showing no emotion at that moment.

Sophya's thoughts raced. Her anger flared. "Does Mama Sara know? Does Flo know? How can he *do* this and still call himself a *minister*?"

"Sara knows, but she's the one that spoiled him, so she accepts it. Miss Flo knows, but plans to change it soon, I guess. And as far as for being a minister, no one's perfect. He's unmarried and has needs just like everyone else."

Sophya gasped when she said that.

She looked away, not really knowing what to say. Then, decided to clarify. "He didn't get to *totally* do what he wanted to do." She looked at Katy warily.

Katy looked down, almost breathing relief, it seemed. As she turned to leave, she looked back and flatly stated, "Everyone goes to church around here."

When the door closed, Sophya prayed, "Lord, help her, help me, to accept our fate in life. Thank you for balancing judgment with mercy. But one day, would You *please* let me really be loved by a man, like You intended and let me love him back? For now, I will *live* with my consequences."

She walked over to the window and looked out, wishing to be free in *this* century.

Lillie knocked lightly and came in. She had the water bowl and towel and some clothes draped across her arm. The empathy in her eyes showed. She walked over and placed the bowl on the bedside table beside Sophya. Then, she laid the clothes and towel on the bed and turned to Sophya with outstretched arms.

Sophya fell into her motherly arms and wept. She wept with her, until no more tears came.

She scooped up the clothes placing them on top of the pillow, sat and patted the spot next to her on the bed and then Sophya sat where she had patted.

"That snake! I don't want to hear that bas…" Sophya looked up apologetically. "*Reverend* Hawkins preach!"

"Deys no one else heah to do it."

"Well, we're in trouble then," Sophya said resentfully and looked down at her hands. She wrung them nervously. "I may not have felt like I was worth much in my other life, but no one deserves this."

Lillie began to speak, patting her hands with hers. "You know dat pretty vase you at-mired in da dinin' room, missy?"

Sophya looked at her, surprised, and wondered what that had to do with anything.

"You da vase," she said and smiled. "Or da vessel. Gawd can make sumpin be-u-ti-ful outta ever-thin' dat happen."

Sophya let out a deep sigh, knowing the scripture she referred to and said it, "In a great house there are not only vessels of gold and silver, but wood and clay, some to honor and some to dishonor."

They looked at each other and smiled.

"Till you go thu da fi-yah, you won't be made perfec'. You won't be made gold. Dat great Gawd of glory will fi-yah all dat beauty and per-fek-shun He can, into you, dat you will *let* Him. But, He's goin' thu da fi-yah wid you." Her face looked aglow.

The biggest peace fell on Sophya. She closed her eyes for that to sink in.

After the silence, she said, "I'm going to be alright now. Thank you, Lillie." They hugged.

Lillie pointed upward.

"Thank You, Lord!" Sophya said and smiled again.

"Now, you fix up, 'cause we gonna make it thu dis."

"Where's Beth and Anya?" Sophya asked.

"Dey baked dem cookies and ate some dinnah, and dey lef' early fo' chuch.'

"Why?"

"You know dat fella, Steve? Beth hopes to see him. He get dere early to hep out. She giv' him one mo' chance to notice huh, or you sistah. She see which one."

They smiled.

"Ah be back. We kin walk togettah." She patted Sophya's hand again and got up to leave.

Sophya remembered another scripture. "If two or three agree, as touching, anything that they ask, it shall be done for them…"

Chapter Seven
Trying to Find Her Way

("Come let us cross over the river." Stonewall Jackson)

The mood stood somewhere between somber and anxious. Sophya couldn't figure it out. The church was small. The pews were hard, but, oh, the windows had beautiful colors of stained glass. It reminded her of when her grandfather helped rebuild this little church later into brick. Sophya got to see some other country churches, also, when she spent summers with Granddad and Grandmother Braden. She got to travel with him to interim or circuit-preach, in small towns. She loved it.

Some of the congregation were becoming recognizable here, some of the blacks that worked for William, also, people she had seen at the ball. The bright, elaborate clothing of the Negroes surprised her. Lillie's dress was not so loud of a color. She dressed humbly. Her dress looked crisp and clean, though. She sat on the back row and shooed Sophya up front.

Sophya smiled, thinking of their walk and talk there together. Lillie led the conversation, keeping the topics light, probably to steer Sophya's mind off the disappointing day. *Lillie will make someone a wonderful wife one day with her good sense of humor and inward and outward beauty and wisdom.*

Beth and Anya were sitting about halfway up toward the front of the church. She recognized them in their finery. *Wonder how Anya talked Beth out of that outfit and hat!*

Sophya stopped, forcing a smile and stepped across them. They smiled mischievously and scooted down to let her sit on the end instead.

The pianist started to play, "What a Friend We Have in Jesus." It surprised Sophya. A male song leader went up to the pulpit and motioned for the congregation to stand, which they did, with a lot of spirit!

Reverend William Hawkins walked up to one of the chairs on the podium. He picked up one of the song books and found the page and began to sing with them. He didn't even look at Sophya.

She fumed.

The song leader asked them to sing another song. It was from scripture, but Sophya couldn't tell where, maybe Psalms. When they got through, he motioned for them to sit down.

He started to read the announcements. Some things never change. Prayer was given for the sick and those away fighting. It jolted Sophya when she heard the name Seth Morris. She looked at Anya, but she didn't catch the name. William just glanced at his notes.

The song leader nodded to a young woman that had a pained look on her face. *She must be nervous.* She came up to the podium to sing and the man sat down. Sophya never heard her song before. She stated she would sing, "My Lord is Near in Time of Trouble." While she sang, hot tears came to Sophya's eyes. The young lady sang words from Psalms 91. A hush fell over the congregation. They must have known this would be like stepping into the gates of heaven. More tears came.

Being caught off guard, Sophya blinked hard to clear her eyelids and her tears. She looked over at Anya, who sat amazed also, and she turned to Sophya with tears in her eyes. They were being reminded: God was near…even *here.*

Then, *Reverend* Hawkins called on a man in the group to pray a thanksgiving over the offering. After great lengths, the prayer finally ended. Some men passed the basket. Sophya was embarrassed because she had nothing to give.

The commotion settled down when William stood up to the podium again. He still didn't look at Sophya.

"These are troubled times."

Some of the congregation answered, "Amen."

He went on, "There's wars and rumors of wars."

More "Amen's!"

"*What* doth the Lord require of us?" William asked.

Sophya looked up from her hands, in shock, at his face.

He stared coolly at her, then faced the next person across the aisle from her, with a more compassionate look.

She closed her eyes then opened them to focus on the hymnal in her lap.

"God wants you to repent."

She looked up in anger as he gazed straight at her and smiled.

Jackass! Lord, help me get through this! Help me never to be sitting here again under these circumstances!

"What does the Lord require of thee but to do justly and walk uprighteously?"

"Have you taken inventory? Are you *doing* what He has required of you?"

Oh, please, Sophya thought.

"God wants us to love Him and our neighbor as much as ourselves," he continued.

Sophya stared at him with a chilly stare. *You perform that a bit too much, Brother.*

He went on. "*If* we were doing that, would we be having war right now? If you, children, loved your parents, would you be disobeying them? If you, adults, loved God like you are supposed to, would you cheat and lie to your neighbor? How about church attendance and tithes, couldn't that be considered an act of obedience or *dis*-obedience? And Negroes, in the Book of Philemon, in the New Testament, didn't the slave, Onesimus, still serve the apostle Paul well, even after he became a Christian? Are you disobedient to your masters?"

Another hush fell over the church.

"We are *all* going to be judged. And, *none* of us have the promise of tomorrow, with this war going on. I urge you to do some soul-searching between now and next week's service. Ask God, in prayer, what you need to *do* or *stop* doing in order to enter His Kingdom."

He stopped and looked at Sophya.

"Ohhh!" She muttered under her breath and looked at him with hate.

Beth, sitting next to Anya, glanced over quickly, questioningly.

Sophya closed her eyes and uttered a short prayer again. Then, she faced William. She had a peaceful, confident façade that he could easily read... *And I know where you're going.*

Their eyes didn't make contact again for a long, long time.

"Open your Bibles to Revelation Chapter three, verse eleven."

Beth shared hers with Anya and Sophya.

He waited then he read: "Behold, I come quickly; hold that fast which thou hast, let no man take thy crown. Him that overcomes will I make a pillar in the temple. I will write upon him the name of my God, and the name of the city of God, which is, NEW JERUSALEM, which cometh down out of heaven from my God; and I will write upon him my new name. He that hath an ear, let him hear what the Spirit saith unto the churches. And unto the angel of the church of the Laodoceans, write: These things saith the Amen, the Faithful and true Witness, the beginning of the creation of God, I know thy works, that thou are neither *cold* nor *hot;* I would that thou wert *cold* or *hot.* So, then because thou art *lukewarm,* neither cold or hot, I will spue thee out of my mouth."

Then *Reverend* Hawkins closed his Bible and looked straight at Sophya and said, "Is there any among you that would like to come to the altar of repentance today?"

She blinked her eyes hard in disbelief!

Then, he looked out over the rest of congregation. "The waters of baptism await you! The Sabine River is a good temperature today, to wash away your sins! Come! You don't *know* if you have tomorrow!"

He motioned for everyone to rise and the people stood. Then, he stretched out his arms for them to come to the altar. He stepped down from the podium to greet the souls that actually came.

Sophya chose that time for her hurried exit back out of the front door. She knew it would appear like a bathroom break, or whatever.

She dashed by Lillie but kept going.

The sun shone hot outside, but the little church stood under a shade tree. The raised church windows and the paper fans of the saints had helped chase away the heat for a little while on the inside.

Reluctantly, she headed in the direction of the plantation home.

Without her knowing it Lillie slipped out of her pew to follow her. Sophya heard her whisper, "*Wait!*"

Lillie caught up with her.

"Ohhhh, that hell-bound bastard!"

Lillie looked at her, shocked.

She knew Sophya's face showed pain. "Thank God he didn't get to finish what he started with me! I could've gone back to my husband in 1980 with an *immaculate conception*! *That* would be hard to explain since I haven't slept with him because of his infidelities!"

Lillie's eyes widened.

Then she put her arm through Sophya's to comfort her as they walked.

"Naw, missy, he fix it ta where d'on happen."

Sophya stopped, took a deep breath, looked out into space, and then down at Lillie's hard-working hand looped around her arm. She patted it, and they began walking again.

"How can he *do* these things and think he's going to heaven?" Sophya asked.

"Mens deez days das normal ting 'cept if one marry or sumpin.' Das looked down on a bit mo'." Lillie's eyes were full of acceptance.

"Ohhh," Sophya replied angrily, then she smiled at Lillie.

What she said next, really affected her.

"You may not huhd 'bout dis in you time, but Negro women ah in *sub-jec-shun* mo' ways dan Negro mens."

Sophya glanced at her with sympathy.

"But, uthawise, we be taken good cah of in dis household."

Sophya tightened her lips, sighed and smiled at Lillie.

"Dem Yanks say dey bettah ta us, but sum d'one want ta leave sum plantashuns. We may be wus off." She hesitated. "Do tangs gets bettah?"

Sophya thought for a moment, then answered, "In some ways, Lillie. The Negro does win freedom. Women and blacks get to vote." She looked at her and smiled. "And women get to take men to court that violate them."

Lillie thought deep on these revelations.

"But, the Negroes don't really get more respect as a whole until about the 1960's.

Lillie nodded at that.

"In fact, in my time, 1980, the blacks have been grouped together as bad, again, and some are falsely accused for committing crimes just for being black. The pendulum has swung the other way. I hate to tell you this, but a large part of the blacks hate all the whites for that and for the Civil War. Sometimes I feel like saying, 'I wasn't there, that wasn't me that did that to you.' I've never been prejudiced against anyone, though, that I can remember, except old, fresh drunks." Sophya laughed. "But I've tried not to be."

"As compaih ta young fresh drunks?" Lillie snickered.

Sophya spit out a snicker, too. "Well, I guess, yes!" She nudged her to hush.

"Hmmm," she said, thinking about the rest.

Sophya felt like she needed to add one more thing.

"Lillie, no matter what has happened to you, don't think you are ruined or damaged. I am sure whoever God has for you will love you for who you are, like that nice man Mr. Brooks!"

She jerked her head hard to look at Sophya. "Oh, no, he not in'trests in *me*, just *kind,* das all. He know, prob'ly, ah at-miyah him. But he da spihtial leadah of his tribe. He hafta choose from deyah. Das dey rules."

"Ohhh." Sophya digested that. She hugged her. "I wish I could take you back with me."

Lillie smiled a big smile. "Commone, les go sneak sumpin' outta Sare's kitchen! She be gone a good while. Das her grandson, Samuel, dat went down fo' da bap'tizm."

Sophya looked shocked. "Mama Sara is *married*?"

"Yes." Lillie chuckled. "Das ta Big Bob. He sat by huh in church. She da boss, doh," she whispered.

Sophya raised her eyebrows.

Lillie passed her hand over Sophya's eyes to shut them.

They snickered again.

"OK," Sophya said. "Then I need some *alone* time out of this mansion, either at the barn or going on a walk!"

"Das good. Me too. Ah likes dat. I be off now till tomorrah. You go."

***

Sophya dashed up the stairs to change, wishing for something other than that fateful riding skirt. This time she wore her tennis shoes for speed and hurried out the back door.

Lillie went to her servant's quarters. Those were little houses out to the side of the cook's house. She had her own separate one.

Sophya glanced at the barn. Then, she took off in a run, across the pasture, through the woods, and down to the creek. She knew it would probably never bring good memories again, though. The last one would surely over-shadow the rest. It felt like she had to go look for footprints across the creek or *something*! She wanted to find what whizzed by William and shocked him.

She passed the clay embankment, down the hill to where her other memories had been. "At least my husband never tried to rape me!"

He would just go elsewhere. She shook her head sadly.

Through the narrow path, she kicked up some doves. She

115

stopped in awe. "Oh, God, You *are* here! You are beautiful, and You can make something *beautiful* even out of this."

Sophya finally relaxed. She knew the *Reverend* would be tied up for the rest of the day, or that Lillie would hint she was resting.

It felt cooler now, down by the creek...cooler, shadier, with gorgeous patches of wild flowers, and dewberries. She reached to pick some to eat, checking them for redbugs first. Her spirit already began to feel lighter.

Sophya walked over to the sandy bottom curve in the creek and stopped. "God, help me figure this out." She breathed a quiet prayer while pacing in a circle.

She saw where their horses' hooves had been. She noticed the grass smashed where the picnic blanket had been. She turned toward the tree and walked over to it where she saw the twig she had twisted. She leaned her head against the tree and let out a sob. "Oh, God..." she cried.

She looked at the creek. She walked over to it and slipped off her tennis shoes. her bare feet felt the cool, damp sand.

She held up her skirt and walked across the shallow part of the creek to the other side. Looking for tracks she found some indentations in the soil. *Could have been.* She stared around long and hard in the thicket. Then she saw it: the broken twig she had heard snap while William and she were skirmishing. She touched it with her hand and glanced around again.

Who has been here? Nothing but quietness answered her thoughts. She heard a bird chirp. It felt so peaceful at that moment.

Sophya tiptoed back to the creek so as not to disturb the other tracks. She held up her skirt and crossed back through the water.

The stream seemed so inviting. She knew right past the sand bar to the left used to be a cove about four feet deep where the water was cool and clear.

She stepped out of her skirt, laid it on top of her shoes and took off her blouse, leaving only her undies and bra on. She gazed at the

116

water longingly. *No one will know but me.*

She waded knee deep into the water, until she found the spot. She stopped and then dove into the cove. "Ahhh." She dipped her hair into the water. She swam, first forward, then flipped over, back-stroking. "Oh, God," Sophya cried as the creek water rinsed her tears. "Baptize me again. Wash away my sins, again, if this is my fault." She laid back and immersed herself completely, releasing the stress of the morning and all her guilt of being in this situation and involving Anya.

She stood up with her eyes closed and wiped her face and began to walk to the shallow end. She shook her hair out and started to shiver. When she opened her eyes, a blanket was being held up in front of her face and handed to her.

A familiar voice said, "Is it not too dangerous for a lady to swim here alone?"

"Ayyye!" she started to scream but he snatched her out of the water, swooping her up with a strong hand and throwing the blanket over her head.

"Hush! I won't *hurt* you! It's me, Brooks! But screaming may bring someone who *will!*"

She stopped screaming.

He slowly pulled the blanket off of her head and face, and tucked it warmly around her body. She had never been this close to him before. His eyes were the most beautiful green she had ever seen. His medium brown hair, not in a pony-tail now, looked *good*, even though she didn't usually like long hair on men. But it made him look so handsome. He was wearing a tan, suede, Indian-looking vest over his bare chest and britches.

She could never speak immediately when suddenly shocked or hurt. At times she wished she could throw a quick barb. *But I've already had to repent enough today.*

"Hello," was all he said, smiling, strong, comforting.

She swallowed and finally regained her composure. "Do you always spy on ladies while they are swimming in their underwear?"

"Only if I happen upon them." He smiled again…a tempting smile.

She couldn't help but smile back.

"Besides, this is my creek you are in."

Her face showed her surprise. "I thought this belonged to William Hawkins!"

"It does, to here." His foot drew a line to the water's edge on William's side.

"Oh," she said looking down at the stream then back up to him.

"Would you like to accompany me to the other side? I will build a fire and warm you."

She blinked hard at the double meaning that passed through her mind. Then she began feeling self-conscious about being in just her underwear under the blanket.

Brooks sensed her distrust.

"You don't know me," he added. "But if you ask, anyone can vouch for my character. I would never force myself on a woman." He looked down to her lips, then back up to her eyes, though. "But a lovely woman shouldn't swim alone to tempt us."

She blinked and caught her breath. "It was *you*! *You* were here when William…"

"Yes."

She thought a moment more. "At the ball, outside the window when that devil DeVille grabbed me?"

"Yes," he answered quietly.

"Why? Why make yourself my *protector*?" she asked, amazed.

Brooks laughed lightly. It sounded euphoric to her senses.

"You seem to *need* protecting!" he continued smiling.

"No…I'm…" she stopped. "Well, I *used* to be…" She glanced up at his face after briefly looking down at the blanket, feeling her face blush. "I guess I do seem to bring out the *worst* in men. Oh, *never mind*!" she shook her head.

He laughed again, "Come let us make a fire."

She stopped short, still, at his choice of words, not feeling up to anymore confrontations today. She stared over at the path they would take across the creek. Her forehead furrowed in deep thought.

Brooks spoke softly, "I will never harm you."

Something in his voice was so soothing. She could not look him in the eye at that moment. She felt his eyes piercing right through the cognitive part of her brain that received all information and hitherto would make a clear decision.

She sighed and said, "Well, Lillie seems trusts you."

"Miss Lillie is a wise woman," he replied.

Before Sophya could say another word, Brooks grabbed her clothes and shoes from the bank with his right hand. He quickly propped that hand, items and all, behind her back. Then, he swooped her up with his left hand, blanket and all.

"Ayyye!" she squealed again.

"Shhh! I'm only carrying you across to the other side!" He was so agile and with one step he crossed the creek!

Once on the other bank, his left arm slowly let her lower body down, but he still held her close to him.

Such strong muscles! Sophya felt his chest breathing in and out with hers and his warm breath on her ear. *What am I feeling? Oh God, help me!*

Her legs were weak. She waited a moment. Then, she tried to look in control. She made the mistake of staring into his deep, green eyes. They looked back, deeper into hers. She had never seen anyone's eyes do that before. They almost seem transfixed or something, like they were looking into her soul.

She sighed again and said, "Thank you," trying to hide her trembling emotions.

Brooks smiled disarmingly, but never stepped away. "Shall we go?"

His question almost appeared to have an eternal meaning.

She closed her eyes once more. Her analytical mind formed no opinion right then. She tried to make her foggy brain think. Her stomach turned to mush.

"Yes," she answered and smiled with a fake confidence. That combined with weak limbs didn't mesh well at all to propel a body to motion.

Brooks never removed his right arm from around the blanket at her waist, guiding her. It almost felt as if he thought he might lose her. Maybe he just wanted to keep her from falling.

"It's just a little ways," he said, coaxing in a comforting manner and nodding easterly.

They went through the woods, then over a little ridge, or levee.

Once on the other side, her eyes experienced the most beautiful valley she had ever seen! There were fruit trees and flowers and a precious log cabin with a front porch!

"These weren't here...*before!*"

She looked inquisitively at Brooks.

"Come," was all he said, while he stared into her eyes, waiting for her to make the choice. Then he handed her her clothes, which she stuffed under the blanket embarrassingly.

She managed to smile and say, "The lilies in this valley are so gorgeous!" Then, *she* led the way.

He laughed and soon appeared close by her side again.

She admired the pretty flowers and trees. Rabbits, gophers, then a road runner ran across their path! Everything was so and lush and green!

This must be what heaven is like!

"Ohhh," she exclaimed as she looked at Brooks and found him watching her. It embarrassed her, so she blushed again, but managed to speak, "This is so heavenly!"

She glanced at the valley to escape his intense gaze.

"Yes."

Sophya turned twice toward his face, but saw no mockery there. She want to run down the hill but I didn't want to appear *too* childish. She tightened her grip on the blanket to get ready to run.

"Bet I can *beat* you!" Brooks said and started to run. He let her catch up and reach the porch first. She panted for a breath. He was not panting! They looked at each other and started laughing.

He stepped up to the first step, then stepped back down by the post. "After you."

His eyes pierced hers, then he turned his head and nodded in the direction of the door. Sophya walked up the steps to the door. Brooks quickly came to open it for her. She stepped into its peace. It had such cozy, comforting surroundings.

"Ohhh," was all she could say.

Brooks laughed as he came into the doorway.

The cabin had been made into one open room. The floors were fairly smooth wood. The walls were the rough interior of the logs.

A kitchen with open cabinets was on her right side. They formed an L-shape, meeting in the corner of two walls. Each wall contained a window with curtains. She had seen the opened shutters on the outside. What appeared to be a free-standing table with cabinets and two stools stood in the middle of the kitchen near the cabinets, like an island cabinet.

A large closet with doors graced the whole other right corner and back wall, next to a back door. A lamp, a night table and a ¾ wooden bed and wooden chair had been placed in the left corner.

A beautiful stone fireplace and hearth with a wooden mantle sat on the left wall. In front of it stood a wooden coffee table and two stuffed chairs. The bright fabrics that covered it were patchwork. The pattern matched the quilt on the bed.

To her immediate left were what seemed to be a hundred books on shelves. She gasped in surprise and walked over to them and touched them as if they were sacred.

"I love books and reading too!" *They get me through many lonely times.* Sophya glanced back at Brooks, who had been patient, and saw him smiling at her delight. He started to walk towards her as she read some of the titles. "*Law, Tribal Matters, Strong's Concordance, How to Grow Fruit Trees...?*" she looked at his face with surprise.

"I learned," he said with a smile. "Come, sit. I'll get some logs to burning." He nodded towards the stuffed chairs.

Sophya sat down. The chair was large enough and comfortable. "You *built* all this?"

Brooks turned from squatting at the fireplace and faced her. "Yes." He showed amazement at her question.

"I thought Indians…"

"Live in teepees?" he finished her sentence, chuckling.

"Well…yes!" She slumped, intimidated and hugged the blanket tighter after she laid her clothes beside her.

"My people commune together, and with the Tejas Indians, over the next hill. Some live in tents or teepees. Some build stronger dwellings. We have trading stores within the camp that are wooden structures."

He turned back to stoke the fire. "I am in my tent most nights." Then he turned back, looking straight into her eyes. He showed no apology for his race.

"Why do you have a separate cabin?" Her curiosity got the better of her. She thought of William and how he probably used a separate dwelling to abuse Lillie.

"I read. I also study. I am, like William Hawkins is to his people, a spiritual guide," Brooks said modestly.

"Huh!" Sophya exclaimed and looked away.

"I do try to spend more time with God than politics," Brooks continued, "or taking advantage of people." His eyes showed disapproval.

Sophya looked down and asked, "Why did you invite me here and why do you protect me?"

"You were wet!" he laughed. Then he got serious. "I don't know. You do seem to *need* protecting, though." His answer seemed honest. His eyes meet hers, speaking so many unspoken things, making her gut turn to mush again.

"Are you hungry?" He got up and went to the cabinets. He opened a container and brought her something that looked like beef jerky and a pear.

She pulled one hand out of her blanket to take it and asked him, "What's this?"

"Try it!" he urged. "I'll be right back." He went out the back door with two cups in his hand.

She tasted the beef jerky. "Hmmm, better, moister than moist," she decided.

Brooks came back in and gave her a cool drink of water.

"Where did you get that?" she questioned excitedly.

He smiled jokingly. "From a well."

"You know what I mean!"

"Come," he insisted, reaching for her hand.

His hand looked so strong and tan. She put her snacks on the coffee table, smiled at him, and took his hand. Brooks helped her up and guided her to the back door and opened it.

Sophya looked outside. "An *outhouse*! You have an *outdoor toilet*!"

Brooks sighed. "Not *that*! But I did copy that from the *white* man, though." he said it almost like his present company was *not* white! Then, he turned her to the left and pointed to something on the porch. "Look."

"A well! A well on the porch!" She sounded so gleeful. "My great-grandmother's porch has a well!"

"I didn't know anyone else had that."

He waited for her to reveal more, she guessed. She clammed up, not thinking she could explain it. She bit her lip, then said, "You have a beautiful, convenient, place!"

Brooks grinned and then stopped and looked into her eyes with that wonderful compassion of his. Something intimate passed between them. He looked like he did not want to her to leave, but again said, "Come."

He motioned for them to walk back into the cabin. He did not put his hand around her waist this time. She was grateful.

Once inside, she sat in the chair in front of the fireplace and watched it crackle, even though her body had finished drying.

Brooks sat in the chair nearby, watching the fire, also, like he, too, knew their time together would be short.

"How do you know Hawkins?"

"I don't, really," Sophya answered reluctantly.

That surprised him.

"He hasn't told you anything about me?"

"Only that you are his guest," he responded.

"Huh!" she retorted.

"If you don't know him, why are you there?"

Sophya sighed. "Actually, my sister and I were traveling and got lost. He found us on his property and, let us stay," she spoke softly.

"I saw you dance with him. I thought you knew him."

She shot Brooks a quick glance. She had forgotten he stood outside the window during the ball, waiting to speak to William.

"I thought he was related to me."

Brooks drew that information in.

"How did you know where the deep cove was in the stream?"

She couldn't think of an answer and bit her lip. "I have been there before."

"When?"

"Uhhh!" she sounded exasperated by his probing. "I have another relative that *does* live near here."

"Who?" he smiled tempting her.

"Ohhh, you'd make a good reporter!" she blurted out.

"Why are you so secretive?" His eyes became more intense.

Sophya stood up quickly, almost losing the blanket. She grabbed it back onto her shoulders and began to pace by the fireplace.

"Louanna Morris, for one," she looked back at him.

Brooks' eyes widened. "Oh?"

It seemed several things went through his mind.

"I haven't gotten to meet, er…see her yet. She wasn't in church this morning." *I am speaking too nervously!*

"She doesn't have a well on her porch. She has a dogtrot. And, she's not old enough to be a *great-grandmother*," he stated calmly.

Sophya smiled. Her eyes must've shown that her mind wandered in time…back…forwards…or *wherever*!

Brooks' chin tilted as if trying to figure her out.

She came back to the present-- past. "I know. It's *another* relative, not her."

He stared a moment, questioningly.

"She's on my mom's side. Mom's dad was Spanish and Cherokee," she hoped to change the subject.

"Cherokee? You are Cherokee?" Brooks didn't hide his delight. "I am Cherokee, also." He reached up and touched her drying hair. "Your hair is curly."

"Yes, it is. I know how to do that," she smiled, still a bit skittishly.

He leaned back in his chair, not camouflaging his attraction now.

"It makes you uneasy to talk about yourself?" he contemplated out loud.

She glanced at him, twice. She let out a deep sigh and stared at the fire.

"There are things you might not understand or believe…I'm not going to say yet."

"Yet?" he smiled a comforting smile to alleviate her fears and showed gratitude for another chance to talk later.

"Yes, yet," she smiled, comforted, and reached for her clothes.

"Where can I get dressed?" she asked.

Brooks waved his hand around the room they were in.

"Tuh," she said exasperatedly.

"I will leave you a moment," his face was reassuring.

Before he left, she prodded, "Brooks is an unusual name for an

Indian, isn't it?"

"My name is Running Brook. Chief Running Brook. The white men call me 'Brooks'." He looked into her eyes for her reaction.

"It's a comforting name, not that of a warrior though," she commented.

"Then, I have fulfilled my mother's wishes." He had a twinkle in his eyes.

She sighed again, noticing he didn't reveal much of *himself* either.

Brooks tilted his head again in that irresistible way he had of looking at her, then walked out of the door.

Her knees nearly buckled. She sat on the chair and finished dressing, then threw her pear core into the fire and listened to it sizzle.

"You will, with the temptation, provide the *will* to escape, right, Lord?" she asked before she walked out the door.

Then she wondered why Brooks never spoke of the Civil War going on.

Oh well.

***

Brooks led her back to the stream and lifted her across. Sophya went to shake his hand and he lifted hers almost to his lips like he might kiss it. He breathed on it a moment, then put his other strong hand to cover her hand also.

That stunned her. Her heart leaped, her stomach fluttered. She couldn't tell if it was out of affection or for a prayer of protection.

She glanced down at their clasped hands. He did too. Then their eyes met one more time. He closed his, so she closed hers.

"May the God we both serve, bring these hands," and he took her other hand to hold with both of his, "back safely."

Then he opened her hands, palms up. "May He open them up to a deep, abiding friendship." Brooks then placed one of her opened

126

hands onto her heart.

"May her heart," his eyes settled back on hers once again opened, embracing, though not touching, "be open to love again one day."

She closed her eyes. She felt a tear fall and a heat go straight through her hand to her heart when he said the prayer. It burned throughout her. As soon as she came to her senses and open her eyes, Brooks was gone.

Chapter Eight
Sister Talk

("There is a friend that sticketh closer than a brother. It's a sister.)

Sophya look around at what now appeared to be a wonderland. *Something good out of something bad.* "Thank You, Lord."

She realized it must be about five in the afternoon. The sun was beginning to set. She made a dash through the woods, across the pasture and back to the house.

No activity in the kitchen. She hurried through the cook's house, across the plank and through the dining room. Everything seemed quiet. Up the stairs she dashed.

She opened her bedroom door and saw Anya's door was open and went in.

"*Where* have you been?" Anya sat on the bed playing solitaire with the deck of cards.

"Well, *hello*! How are you doing?" Sophya acted insulted.

Anya didn't hide her exasperation. "How are *you* and *what* have you been doing?" She washed her face and hands in the bowl. Then, she sat in the chair in the corner by the bed and began taking off her tennis shoes. She let them fall to the floor with a clunk and sighed, "Ugh!" in relief. She propped her feet on the bed and started pushing Anya with them.

"Hey!" Her card playing messed up so she stopped and said irritably, "I repeat--"

She got serious. "You don't have to repeat it. I will tell you."

Anya recognized the somberness in her tone. She gathered the cards and turned to put them on the end table and faced her, finally showing concern. "What happened?"

Sophya sighed deeply. "You know that *picnic* William took me on this morning?"

"Yes," she answered slowly.

"Well, he had ulterior motives."

"*Reverend* William Hawkins?"

"The Reverend," she stated bluntly. "He took me to that bend in the creek by the sandbar. The *food* was good!"

"Hmmm," Anya's mind wandered.

"We had a great conversation. I almost started to trust him. He asked me questions about the war. I told him some things I remembered, but not all. Then, he started asking me about my marriage. I decided not to be too detailed."

Anya raised her brows.

"He started leading up to the fact that my marriage must not be that great. Said he remembered me and you talking about how I wanted to *change* it since I wished for *this.*"

Sophya waved her hand, insinuating the mansion and surroundings and the time period, showing her aggravation.

"Mercy." Anya sympathized. "Did he…"

"No," Sophya said solemnly. "Thank God, but not because he didn't *try* hard enough!"

Anya's eyes widened then she said, "You wished for a preacher. Guess most men are-- men-- huh."

"I don't know, Anya. I'm a Pollyanna, victim of high hope, usually. You know me; I also always think I'm being punished if something goes wrong. Maybe this time it's for not being grateful for what I have."

"Tuh! I *doubt* it," she stated bluntly. "Abuse victims get used to abuse, they say. They begin to think it's normal and that they deserve it. You've heard that."

"Yeh," Sophya said pensively. "If I'm not being punished, then I haven't figured out why we're here."

"Hmph," Anya grumbled as she scooted back to prop against the headboard and pillow. "Call me when you do."

Sophya rolled her eyes. "Yeh, on my telephone, right?"

Anya folded her arms on her chest huffily.

129

"Something good *did* happen today," Sophya added.

"*Now* you tell me. I thought you looked different, but then you tell me this bad stuff."

"I mean other than that fine sermon we heard this morning."

She coughed. "Pa-leeze!" Anya closed her eyes tightly remembering.

Sophya laughed and shook her head. "Well, while I scrambled to get away from the *1864 William*, that thinks women are for *one* thing only..." she thought back a moment. "1980 William thinks it's two things, *to go work and give sex*!" She looked stoically proud that she had figured that out.

Anya closed her eyes and shook her head, "And?"

"I hate how you cut me off like that!" She looked at her sister's disdain *with* disdain.

"Alright, I'm sorry. You've had a rough enough day."

"Thank you," Sophya blinked with injured pride.

Her eyes widened as she began to tell her good tale. "While Reverend Hawkins had me pinned to a tree we heard something *swish* right by his head! Then, something rustled in the bushes. He stopped what he was *trying* to do, to look at who caught him. I thought someone had shot at him but I wasn't sure with what."

Anya's eyes opened wide. "Who? What?"

"When he loosened his grip on me, I ran and hopped back on Rusty."

Anya blinked hard.

"Yeh, *Rusty*!" Sophya reiterated and laughed. "Then, I rode off into the sunset--or woods, rather--fast! And, if you get on to me about this next thing, I swear I'll..."

"Just *tell* me!" Anya exclaimed.

Sophya took a deep breath. "Lillie said William would be gone for this afternoon. So, I told her I'd take a walk. I went back to look for evidence of who had been there. I saw where the picnic blanket had been, the broken twig on the tree..."

"Ms. Indian Scout."

Sophya looked aggravated at her sister.

"Alright!" she said.

"I took my shoes off to cross the creek. I saw what might be some covered prints. Then I saw it."

"*What?*" Anya asked impatiently.

"The freshly broken twig on that branch of the tree on the other side!"

"Do you honestly think…" she started to say.

Sophya got excited. "It's confirmed!"

"How?" she looked at Sophya in disbelief.

"Someone told me!"

Anya tilted her head questioningly.

"Anyway, I went back across."

"Anya, do you know of that cove where the creek is deeper?"

"Yes."

"It beckoned me."

"Oh, no."

"I know, I know."

"I stripped down to my bra and panties. I felt like *I* had sinned, like *I* was dirty. So, I re-baptized myself."

"Huh!" Anya sucked in her breath. She would never be so bold or sacreligious.

Sophya bit her lip.

"I felt clean again, or at least *better*. Then, I felt cold!"

"Good!" Anya exclaimed. "Serves you right for stripping!"

She just rolled her eyes at her sister's judgmental attitude and continued. "When I opened my eyes, a blanket was in front of me."

Anya's eyes got real big.

"An Indian blanket."

She sucked in her breath.

"So I screamed."

"Oh my gosh," Anya said slowly, taking it all in.

Sophya bit her lip again and nodded.

"Someone threw it over my head and a male voice told me to hush before someone that really wants to harm me hears me! Then he said he was Brooks.

She studied Anya's face before going on. She had leaned away from the bed in anticipation, listening to her sister's every word. Then, she leaned back real hard against the bed.

"My, my, my," was all she could say.

"Amen," Sophya added.

"What happened next?"

She had aroused Anya's curiosity. She was eating this up. "He let the blanket down off my head slowly. I've never seen him up that close before. *Oh,* Anya, his eyes are so *green*! His muscles so *strong*! His breathing…" Sophya blushed, "so enticing and rhythmic.." She mumbled her last words, just remembering.

"Oh my gosh! Mush!"

Anya didn't seem up to any love story with them being in the wrong time zone, Sophya supposed. She threw her legs off the bed to get up and leave.

"Sit back down until I'm through, young lady, or I'll give you a thrashin'!"

Anya looked at Sophya, blankly, showing doubt, then sat back down. "Have you even *tried* to go back to the barn and get us out of here before you fall in love with it?"

"Yes," she answered, afraid she'd ask more.

"So did I."

"Without me? You little brat!"

"Look who's talking, big Sis!"

Sophya couldn't hold back laughing. She hopped over the bed to squeeze Anya into subjection and laughter. And, it worked.

"Oh, God, help us both," she said whimsically, and sat up.

"Anya, Brooks swept me and my clothes up and crossed the creek and then a ridge. He has a cabin! With a fireplace! Separate from his tribe. He warmed me and my things up."

"I bet," Anya said sarcastically.

Sophya ignored her comment. "Oh, Anya, it was so quaint, so exquisite! I don't know why I've met him, but it's for a reason. I found out *he* was the one that protected me at the brook….hey Brooks at the brook! And at the ball when that devil DeVille squeezed my arm. He looked outside, and then he stopped. He saw Brooks!"

That got Anya's approval. "Good," she said, "you *need* it."

She smirked. "That's what *he* said."

"We agree!"

"Tell me about y'all," Sophya insisted.

"Welll…" Anya stretched it out. "Not near as exciting as your day-- but unusual." She scooted back to the headboard. "The cookie making was fun, and delicious. I'm glad Mama Sara likes *me!* Did you know her grandson got baptized today?"

"Yes. Lillie told me."

"Well, Beth and I ate breakfast in the kitchen, then came up and got dressed for church. Thank goodness they keep finding clothes to fit us!"

"Amen," Sophya said. "And those weird button-up shoes I'd like to take them home!"

Anya continued, "We got there early to help *Stevie* make sure the church was ready."

"Stevie?" Sophie joked.

Anya shut her eyes to dismiss the insinuation. "We did! We helped him sweep and put out tithing cards and straighten the song books."

"I see," Sophya said and raised her eyebrows.

"It wasn't anything as hair-raisin' as *your* escapades, like I said, but I'm trying to build some friendships here with Beth and Steve, not just have a *fling!*"

Sophie supposed she looked like she had been slapped, because she couldn't speak.

"I'm sorry, I'm sorry," Anya quickly said and hugged her.

Sophya tightened her lip, but smiled forgivingly.

"Anyway, it was nice, helping them out and all. It reminded me of my secretarial job at my church." Anya looked out into space sadly, then back at Sophya. "Steve reminds me of someone I know, but I can't figure out whom."

"He looks like Steve Lawrence, the singer, to me, except with darker hair. He's so cute. And he wants to get *your* attention, not Beth's. I adore her, but all's fair in love and war, Sis!"

"Tuh! Speak for yourself!" Anya stated sharply.

"There you go again, doing *without.* You've got to *grab* adventure and love, whenever it comes, Anya!"

"That's *your* theory. Which got you into trouble real good this time," she retorted. "Just because *you've* been in a prison and are glad to get out—doesn't mean I have."

"You just watch. When this is all over, you'll thank me for it," Sophya said.

"I'll thank you right now for not messing up my life anymore!" she pouted.

Sophya reached over and hugged her again. "Anything else *good* happen?"

"We went to the baptism and they had dinner on the ground. It was great. It looked just like that picture in the hall at the top of the stairs. Beth introduced me to some more folks, but Stevie didn't come around much after church."

"Louanna Morris wasn't there, Lillie told me."

"I know," Anya replied.

"Anya, let's sneak out of here and go see her early in the morning. OK?" Sophya said excitedly.

"Yes!" she exclaimed. "Oh, there you go again."

"Anya, we have to leave before William, or he won't *let* us leave!"

"Alright."

"Deal?'

"Deal."

134

Sophya snatched the pillow beside Anya and started hitting her with it. She squealed and grabbed the pillow from behind her to fight back.

Beth entered through the door. "Hey, no fair having fun without me!"

Sophya laughed and threw a pillow at Beth, who caught it after stumbling.

"Did anyone ever have fun in this house before?" Sophya asked.

Anya hit her with her pillow from one direction and Beth threw hers at her from the other. Sophya fell down on the bed.

"Yes," Beth laughed.

Anya dove in to tickle Sophya. They all laughed.

"Come on you two, I have something just as fun to do!" Beth said.

They looked up and she beckoned them to follow her to her room.

Sophya grabbed Anya one more time and tickled her back.

"Hey, truce!" she yelled.

Sophie hopped off the bed on the left side, walking around a safe distance from her sister. Anya scooted off on the right side, ahead of her, blocking her and going first.

When they entered Beth's beautiful pastel pink bedroom, she said, "Come see!"

Sophya finally noticed the surroundings in this room. Her bed, on her right, had a deeper pink satin spread on it than the wall color. She hadn't noticed it before, when she and Anya were sitting on it.

Beth walked past the bed and the antique white, French armoire and fireplace in the corner of the room. A gold, oval-shaped pipe, Sophya hadn't seen before, hung from the ceiling near the south wall in front of Sophya. It had a pink and white eyelet curtain draped from it. She thought a room divider had been in front of it. Beth pulled the curtain back. Hiding behind it sat an ornate, white, claw-foot bath tub!

"Ohhh," Sophya exclaimed.

"Ahh," Anya let out her breath.

Beth laughed gleefully.

"You kept this from us all this time?" Sophie feigned hurt feelings.

Anya laughed.

Beth laughed too. "I only share it with my *real* good friends! And y'all are the first I've had."

Anya and Sophya looked at each other, not knowing whether to laugh or cry, so they hugged her.

"How do you get water in here?" Anya asked.

"And out?" Sophya added.

Beth laughed again. "That's the problem! It takes *ten* buckets! I have to get the maids to help me pull it up on a rope and pulley across a special spot on the banister. Then we drain it with a pipe that goes out alongside the house outside.

Anya and Sophya looked at each other. Then they remembered the surly-faced maid named Katy, the maid on duty.

Together they said, "Never mind!"

Beth crumbled giggling. When she straightened up again, she said, "*Katy* suggested it and offered to help! She's been boiling water in the cook's house for us."

They looked at each other in surprise.

"Where's your brother?" Sophya asked.

"Uh, I'm not sure," Beth answered.

"Where's the room he sleeps in?"

Beth showed surprise. "My brother?"

Sophya nodded.

"It's the one across the hall from mine."

"I wouldn't want to disturb him," Sophya replied. *Or him disturb me.*

"Oh," Beth said. "He'll be gone until late, I think."

Sophya glanced at Anya. She tried to hide any concern from Beth. "Who's first?" she asked to distract Beth.

"You go first and we can play cards! We'll get something to eat from the kitchen first.

Thus began the toting and pulleying.

***

Ohhh these bubbles and this *fragrance!*"

Beth and Anya laughed from their card game.

Chapter Nine
A Virtuous Woman

("Who can find a virtuous woman? Her price is far above rubies."
Prov.31:10)

"Anya, get up!" Sophya whispered urgently.

"What?" she opened her eyes.

"Come *on* and get *up*!" Sophya stressed. "It's almost daylight!"

"Ohhh," moaned Anya, "we're not back home yet?"

"No, Dorothy, we're not in Kansas yet! Let's go enjoy anyway!" She swatted her sister's rear.

"Ohhh," she moaned again.

Sophya stripped the covers off of her.

"Hey!"

"Get *up*, sleepyhead! Are you hung over from that card game last night?"

"Well, Beth did win all but two of my buttons."

"That's what you get for gambling."

She moaned some more and rolled out of bed.

"Here." She handed her a wet cloth for her face.

"Ugh! It's cold!"

"What did you expect, more of last night's luxuries?" Sophya asked.

She blotted her face and frowned at her sister.

Sophya handed her the clothes that lay beside the bed on the chair. Then, Sophya scooted the "chamber pot" close by.

"Thanks," Anya said sarcastically.

"Put your tennis shoes on. We have a lot of walking to do."

If looks could kill....

***

Sophya led the way out of the bedroom, down the stairs, and through the front doors. She had saved some of Lillie's lotion to apply to the hinges to make sure they didn't squeak.

Anya, sleepily, followed behind, out the door and down the front stairs of the plantation home's front porch.

Sophya tiptoed around the azalea bushes to the corner of the porch and stopped quickly. She held her hand back, motioning for Anya to stop.

She peeked around the building and snapped back, sucking in her breath.

"What's the matter?" Anya whispered insistently.

Sophya put her finger to her mouth to shush her to wait then whispered, *"William."*

"Where?" she whispered back in surprise.

"Sneaking out of Lillie's cabin," she answered disgustedly.

"Are you sure?"

"Um hm."

"Oh, my, gosh," came her reply.

Sophya waved for Anya to proceed again behind her. Then they made a dash to the road.

Walking down the road, heading east from the mansion, Sophya felt safe to speak in a normal tone. "Way I figure, it's about a mile before the farm road takes us to the right."

"OK...." Anya stated, not eagerly or trustingly.

"Remember where Grandmother Morris' house was, on that farm-to-market road?"

"Yes, but that was now and this is *then*!" Anya's face, which Sophya could see better then, looked like it had a frown.

"Aren't you even a *little* excited that we are fixin' to get to meet our ancestor?" Sophya sounded exasperated.

"Well, yes," Anya finally answered.

"Good," she sighed. "Here, let's turn."

They trudged in silence for a while, down the curvy, dirt road.

"About how far, ya think?" Anya asked.

"Probably about two more miles."

Silence on the other end.

Then, "Mercy," came her reply.

"No...exercise!"

She closed her eyes then opened them and looked toward heaven, hoping Sophya would disappear, she guessed.

So Sophya decided to sing. "Glory, glory, halleluiah. Glory, glory, halleluiah. Glory, glory hal--le--luiah! His Truth is marching oooonnn!" She sang softly to cheer herself, and, if at all possible, Anya, too, who probably knew it. So, she let Sophya sing. Over and over.

"Mine eyes have seen the glory of the coming of the Lord. He is trampling out the vintage where the 'grapes of wrath' are stored."

Anya trodded, Sophya plodded.

"He hath loosed the fateful lightning of His terrible swift sword! His Truth is marching on! Glory, glory, halleluiah. Glory, glory, halleluiah. Glory, glory, hall-el-uiah..."

A cow stopped chewing grass and looked up at them.

"You know, that song was first written by an abolitionist, Julia Ward Howe, during the Civil War?"

"Yeh, I know," Anya answered.

When they were almost there, Anya sighed, "Oh no, I just realized we are going to have to walk all the way back, too!"

A mischievous smile came over Sophya's face. "His Truth is marching on!"

She trudged on. Then, just over the last hill, the sun rose boldly and they saw their great-great grandmother's house.

"Huh!" Anya's breath caught.

"Oh, God, thank you, God." Sophya's eyes watered with tears.

They held hands and walked down the hill together.

***

The white-washed, wooden house needed painting, even back then. The picket fence that surrounded it looked in better shape. The house and fence stood near the country road.

There appeared to be a pecan orchard on one side and a fruit orchard on the other side. An old barn separated the two orchards in the back of the farm house.

Some cows and a few horses grazed in a pasture further behind that. Chickens were in the fence directly in back of the house. Cows mooed, a rooster crowed.

By the front fence, to the left, lay nice rows of new growth vegetables. Flowers grew near the house's front and around the shade tree on the right side of the front yard. A gate and stone sidewalk in the middle separated the left and right front yard.

"Oh, look, Anya, there's the dogtrot porch!" Sophya stood in awe as they walked to the front gate.

They heard what sounded like the back porch screen door creak open and slam shut. A middle-aged woman wearing an apron came out. Apparently, she was headed to the barn in the back.

Sophya and Anya sucked their breath in and looked at each other. Anya walked up to the gate of the picket fence. Sophya followed. Then they just stood and stared while the chickens in the barn raised a ruckus. Soon, the woman came out of the barn with eggs tucked in her apron. When she saw the girls staring at her, *she* gasped and stepped backwards.

"Hello," Sophya said, shakily.

"Hello," their grandmother answered warily.

"My name is Sophya. This is my sister, Anya."

She looked from Sophya to Anya, doubtfully, because of the difference in their height.

"Really," Sophya said.

"Tuh," Anya tried to suppress a painful laugh.

The woman stepped up to the stairs and walked through the dogtrot porch with the eggs still in her apron. "My name is Louanna

Morris. What can I do for you?"

"Well," Sophya said, unusually shy. "We came to meet you. We've been staying at Reverend Hawkins' place."

"Oh," Ms. Louanna said with a dawning recognition.

"We came to thank you for the dress."

She looked around. "Oh. How'd you get here?"

"We *walked*," Anya answered disdainfully.

The woman looked from one to the other and smiled. "So early?"

"You *are* Louanna Morris?" Sophya wanted to make sure.

"Yes," she said bluntly, then walked closer to the edge of the porch. "Come in, come on in the gate."

Sophya opened it and went in. Anya followed. Then they stopped.

"We think we are related to you," Sophya laid it out.

She raised her eyebrows. "I don't recognize your names. What's your last name?"

Sophya laughed lightly. Anya and she looked at each other and smiled.

"Well, may we sit on your porch and try to explain?" Sophya asked.

"Sure, sure, come on up." She motioned to some chairs leaning against the house and a swing hanging from the ceiling with rope cords.

They sat on the swing, on the right side of the front porch.

"Thanks for loaning your beautiful, black velvet dress to me."

Ms. Louanna relaxed. She had sat in one of the chairs. Then she leaned forward with a gleam in her luminous, bright blue eyes. Her eyes looked like our immediate grandmother's clear blue, Scotch-Irish eyes. Her whitening, strawberry-blonde hair was pulled back in a bun. "Oh, yes, yes. Did you have a *ball*?" She leaned back and chuckled.

Sophya and Anya laughed.

"Yes!" Sophya exclaimed. She nudged Anya with her foot to

shut her up about the *real* time they had at the party.

"Oh, I used to be the 'belle of the ball', too, when I was young!" She had a far off look in her eyes. Then, she focused back on Sophya and Anya.

"I can imagine!" Sophya said. "Where ever did you get that gorgeous dress, with no hoop and such a *scoop* neckline?"

She leaned over again, excitedly laughing, and told them her 'deep, dark' secret.

Anya and Sophya leaned closer.

"Once, I was engaged to a fella *straight* from Paris!" She sat back straight in her chair and showed her pride.

"Engaged!" they said together.

"You mean we could have had some *French* blood in us?" they asked excitedly.

A questioning look crossed Ms. Louanna's face.

Anya caught it and got the conversation back on track. "He gave you the dress?"

"And the gloves," she beamed.

"Ohhh," Sophya said and leaned back, thinking of the high honor to wear such an outfit.

Ms. Louanna still had a twinkle in her eyes. "But then, I met Seth Morris. I knew my Frenchman wanted me to go back to France with him. I decided right then and there, I couldn't leave Seth Morris or my home."

"Can we meet your husband? Is he asleep?" Anya asked.

"Oh no, honey, he's not here." Her blue eyes turned tender. She had a lovely, wide-boned face and a long, graceful neck. She only had a few wrinkles, even though she should have been weathered from farming.

"He's off fighting this horrible war. He had been in Vicksburg, till it fell." Tears well up in her bright eyes. "He hasn't been on any list saying he's been killed."

They sat silent, not knowing what to say next.

She cheered up. "Sometimes, those young Confederate soldiers

143

come right down my road!"

They smiled at their great-great-grandmother, who verified stories they had heard.

"That's why I always keep enough food cooked for them. In my small way, I pray someone will be feeding my Seth a good meal in return." She sat back with her warm thoughts of her husband.

Anya's stomach growled thinking of food.

Then, Louanna remembered the eggs in her apron and looked down at them. "Oh, dear, I need to be cooking right now! Come on, you girls could probably use some breakfast, too."

"Oh, yes," Sophya murmured.

Anya tried to suppress a giggle.

Ms. Louanna got up carefully with her eggs and motioned for them to follow. She headed for the screen door to the front room on the left section of the house.

Sophya opened the door for her.

They had come to this house years before. It had been a broken down shack by then. Amazingly, they had been in this very same living room. The fireplace still sat in a corner--the north wall corner. The room looked homey instead of desolate, though.

They followed their grandmother into the kitchen.

"What a bright kitchen!" Anya spoke up.

"Thank you, child," she said. Then Ms. Louanna walked to the table by the back wall and door that faced the other porch. She placed the eggs in a container on the table. The table and chairs were painted red. A fresh bouquet of yellow daffodils and red poppies added to the attraction of the table. Red and white checkered curtains and tablecloth graced the quaint kitchen.

Their great-great-grandmother offered them some strong coffee with sweet cream when they sat down. She winked.

"I boot-legged that!" she said with pride, touching the coffee cup. Then, she went to cracking and scrambling eggs in the bowl. The sisters smiled at each other.

Ms. Louanna asked if one of them would peel some peaches and cut them up in the other bowl. Anya volunteered.

Sophya asked where the plates and silverware were so she could set the cute little table. Their grandmother pointed and said, "Over there, honey."

They watched in wonder, like she might disappear at any moment. She reminded them so much of their very own grandmother, her granddaughter, now gone. She took the biscuits out of the oven connected to a pot-bellied stove and buttered them. The girls' mouths watered. She picked the bacon up from the skillet and drained the grease into a bowl. Then, she quickly soft-scrambled the eggs, just like Grandmother Braden did. Just the way Sophya loved them. Anya didn't even ask for hers to stay in a little longer to be firmer that time. They sat mesmerized.

Then Louanna Morris dipped the food onto their plates. She pulled some bottled milk from a sort of cooling bin and put it on top of the table. She pulled out the end chair and sat down with them.

They didn't want this moment to end, really.

Louanna bowed her head, so did they.

"Lord, bless this food. Thank You for it. Bless my Seth with food for his body, wherever he is. Protect him and his troops. Remind others to be praying for them. Help me to be a blessing to these girls today."

Anya and Sophya slowly looked up at each other across the table, with tears glimmering in their eyes and smiled. Then they looked at their grandmother, who wasn't but ten or fifteen years older than Sophya. They saw tears in her eyes too, and she smiled at them.

"Now, tell me how you girls happen to know Reverend Hawkins and how you might be related to me."

Sophya choked on the coffee she had started.

Anya let out an attempt to suppress a laugh again.

"Mercy!" Ms. Louanna exclaimed.

They laughed hard together, since, "mercy" had been their own dear grandmother's favorite expression.

Louanna Morris sat back in her chair and studied them.

Anya's face filled with compassion.

Sophya turned towards her great-great-grandmother to touch her hand, but her foot hit the table leg.

Ms. Louanna looked down at Sophya's foot to make sure it was alright.

"Goodness, what kind of shoes are those? They sure look serviceable."

Anya and Sophya glanced at each other. She waited for Sophya to speak first.

"These are *tennis* shoes, gran...uh!" she realized what she almost said and straightened back up in her chair, looking shocked.

Louanna tilted her head to look at her more intently.

Sophya bit her lip.

Anya watched.

"Tennis shoes, Ms. Louanna. People invented them to play tennis in, or run, or to walk distances in them." She sighed deeply with relief that she came up with such an answer.

"Oh," Louanna seemed to revert back to her distrust with their unwillingness to reveal very much. She took another sip of her coffee.

"When we tell you how we know, or *met* Reverend Hawkins, you might not believe us."

Ms. Louanna looked down at her coffee cup. "Does it *matter* if I believe you? You really don't have to tell me if you don't want to." She looked up at Sophya.

Anya spoke up. "We'd like to tell you. We'd like for you to *believe* us. In fact, it's very important to us that you do."

Her facial expression softened. "Well, looks like there are no soldiers coming by for breakfast this morning. They are usually here by now. So, I've got time to listen."

Sophya decided to begin by using her shoes as an example. "The reason you haven't seen shoes like my shoes before is because..."

"Speak up, girl, I don't bite!"

Anya jumped when she used that tone and chose to answer, "We don't *know* how we came to meet William."

Ms. Louanna appeared to be shocked at the familiar use of her Pastor's name.

"Er, Reverend Hawkins," Anya added.

"It's my fault," Sophya spoke up.

Louanna turned to look at her.

Anya forked her food and ate a little.

"We, my sister and I, live near here and were out walking one day," Sophya glanced from Anya to Louanna. "In these shoes. We decided to look inside an old barn of my aunt's. We had never been inside it before. And, Lord, I promise *never* to go into it again!" She looked heavenward.

Anya whimpered a laugh.

Sophya sighed deeply. "When we went inside, something hit us both in the head. We were knocked down, maybe out for a while. When we came to, we were facing Reverend Hawkins in *his* barn. And it wasn't old anymore."

Louanna Morris blinked hard but tried to hide her surprise.

Sophya rubbed her forehead.

"Do you believe in-- time travel?" Sophya asked.

Louanna blinked again and showed she was trying patiently think through her answer.

Anya then bit her lip.

"Have you ever *read*, or *heard* of people going forward or backward in time?" Sophya tried to ask as politely as she knew how.

"No, well, maybe. But to say I *believe* in it, can't say as I do," replied Mrs. Morris. "I know strange things can happen though."

"Well, it happened to us," Sophya stated bitterly, which surprised Anya.

Their great-great-grandmother looked from one back to the other.

"Go on, child," she said.

Child.

"We live in 1980," Sophya bit her lip again.

Ms. Louanna sat back in her chair. "How can that be?"

Sophya sat back hard in hers. "*God alone* knows!"

Anya managed a painful laugh, which surprised Sophya.

"How did…" she looked from one back to the other again "You get here today?" she asks politely, trying to believe them, Sophya guessed.

"My little sister," she nodded towards Anya. "lives in this area with my mother and brother."

Louanna smiled at Anya.

"I live in southern Louisiana and came for a visit."

Ms. Louanna gave her full attention to figuring this out, or acting like it, and took a bite of her breakfast.

"In my time, I have had a very bad marriage." Sophya smiled so as to relieve her troubled expression. "And I have wished, many, many times, to go *back* in time, to start over."

"Oh, child," Louanna slapped her hand on the table. "It's appointed a man once to die…"

"And then the judgment." Sophya completed the scripture from Hebrews chapter nine.

Louanna smiled.

"I know I don't *deserve* to get to start over and try and do it right."

"No honey, that's not what I meant. Everything happens for a reason. *God* has a purpose, a plan for *all* our lives. He can't let everyone start over, once they learn from their mistakes. That would be utter chaos!"

Anya smiled sympathetically.

"Then *what* are we doing here?" Sophya waved her hand around and her voice cracked.

Ms. Louanna looked very serious. "I don't know how, or why you ended up at Reverend Hawkins's place!"

Anya and Sophya glanced quickly at each other.

"What? What's the matter now?" she asked.

"That's who I am married to in my time," Sophya stated solemnly.

Ms. Louanna's mouth fell open. "Oh, dear--"

"Yes ma'am. His name is William *Blackwell*, and he's *not* a minister."

Louanna leaned back in her chair and stayed silent a moment, exhaling.

Anya and Sophya were silent also, not knowing what to say anymore.

"Does Reverend Hawkins *know* this?" she inquired.

"Yes ma'am. When we came to, or *whatever,* he asked who we were and how we got there. I thought he was joking, so I sarcastically asked him the same thing, and why he dressed the weird way he did." She turned to Anya to see if she wanted to add anything, but she didn't. As usual! Sophya frowned at her.

Ms. Louanna laughed, maybe about the clothes, lightening the mood.

Sophya continued, "Then *he* sarcastically asked me why I dress the way *I* did. I wore short pants, Ms. Louanna." She touched her leg to where the shorts went to.

Louanna Morris smiled.

"Then he asked why I acted like I knew him," Sophya sighed. "I went up to him *real* close and told him he knew why, that I was *married* to him! And, you can imagine how it went from there."

"Hmmm," she said, slumping back in her chair again.

"He told us to leave," Sophya went on. "So we said 'gladly' and went back outside, but everything had changed and we freaked out. He came out of the barn door to see what had upset us. And, he decided to house us until we could find out the crux of the matter."

"And," Sophya looked at Anya. "We do appreciate it. However, he thinks we're spies, so we're sort of under house arrest. He's holding us until he can get to the bottom of this. We had to sneak out to meet you while it was still dark this morning and walk here."

"Oh dear. Nonsense, you're not spies, anyone can see that!"

"Thank you," Anya said, truly grateful for the camaraderie.

"He did sorta, kinda start to believe me at the ball when I called your husband Isaiah Morris instead of Seth."

"Hmmm, my, my, my. We must figure this out," Ms. Louanna said.

Maybe she finally has started to believe us.

"Well, I'm pretty sure I have. I think it's God's way of making me appreciate what I *did* have," Sophya exhaled.

"Ha!" Anya snipped.

Louanna looked at her questioningly. Then she looked at Sophya. "I don't recall God ever going to that extreme before." She thought for a moment. "Do you have any children?"

"Yes, three," she beamed.

"Seems like God is blessing the relationship, anyway, then," she added.

"Then I haven't figured out *why* this is happening!" Sophya cried out.

"I just wouldn't have believed Reverend Hawkins to be low enough to keep anybody as a prisoner," Louanna said pensively.

"He's very…" Sophya chose her words carefully. "Political."

"Oh, don't I know it! Sometimes he brings his views to the pulpit!" She looked down while thinking. "But, he's been very good to me and my husband. He's been very attentive to me while Seth's been away fighting."

She looked from Sophya to Anya.

"Well, I was glad when he finally began to believe me when I called Seth *Isaiah*. He said only someone looking at baptismal records would know your husband's proper name."

"My, my. Yes, everyone calls him 'Seth'. Well, I will pray for God to soften Reverend Hawkins' heart through all of this. We have enough pain in this troubled time without him creating more. I will

150

also pray God helps you girls find His will and your way home."

Anya's head jerked back, surprised at being included in needing to *find God's will and her way home.*

Ms. Louanna caught the twinkle in Sophya's eyes when she saw Anya's surprised face. Louanna winked at her.

"Now, how do you girls think you are related to me, because I'm not related to Reverend Hawkins?" She patted their hands and reached to pour them more coffee.

"We *are* related to you. We just didn't know how to tell you in the beginning," Sophya said slowly.

Louanna sat back in her chair once more, and drank her coffee, girding herself for more surprises.

Anya sighed.

"How?" Louanna repeated.

"You are our great-great-grandmother." Now Sophya leaned back, her eyes sparkling.

"Huh!" Ms. Louanna drew in her breath.

"And, we are *pleased* to *meet* you!" Anya said and patted Ms. Louanna's hand.

Louanna Morris smiled and began shaking her head, unable to take it all in.

"You have a daughter named Loula, right?" Anya asked.

Louanna looked surprised. She seemed to be a woman not afraid to speak, usually, but she had trouble at the moment. Then, she slowly nodded her head taking in the information.

"Well, *she* has a daughter named Priscilla."

"Later," Sophya added.

Ms. Louanna appeared amazed, then answered, "Wonderful! She has two boys now."

Anya smiled and continued. "Then *her* daughter has a daughter," she smiled bigger. "Whom she names *Christian*, which is *our* mother."

She laughed when Louanna Morris jerked her head trying to figure it all out.

Louanna bent forward and then back again, letting all her breath deflate.

"Mercy!" was all she said.

"And *our* grandmother, *Priscilla's,* favorite word was, "*Mercy*!"

They all three giggled.

"But, she passed." Sophya tightened her lips.

"My, my," Louanna shook her head. "This is amazing. Yes, I have a daughter named Loula. She lives in Shreveport. She has two sons. But you say she'll have a daughter?"

"Yes, ma'am," Sophya said and Anya agreed.

"And, she apparently moves back here with her family later," Anya added.

Louanna Morris grinned, with a distant look in her eyes. "Good," she finally said.

"Our menfolk…Do you know if our husbands make it?" she looked afraid to ask.

"Mr. Isaiah Seth Morris comes home," Sophya gladly told her.

Louanna clasped her hands together and brought them to her lips. Tears of joy came to her eyes. None of them had dry eyes.

When she regained her composure she asked, "What can you tell me about the war?"

Sophya spoke up excitedly. "The South is going to win a great battle at Mansfield, April 8th, and one that's considered a draw the next day at Pleasant Hill! But, it makes Banks back out of Louisiana!"

"Ohhh," Louanna clasped her hands together again.

"But," Sophya said, "I hate to tell you, the South does not win the war."

Ms. Louanna sat back in her chair sadly, staring at the flowers on the table. "Recon, why?" She almost asked the air.

Anya and Sophya looked at each other.

Sophya spoke up. "General Richard Taylor's excellent strategy helps win the victory at Mansfield and hold 'em off at Pleasant Hill, *and* the creek!" Sophya said proudly. "However, he and General Kirby Smith don't decide to mend their differences for the good of the South, like General Banks and General A. J. Smith did for the North's remaining victories. But really, only ole Stonewall Jackson believed in Richard Taylor enough to listen to his advice. He said they could have won the whole war if they'd have listened to General Taylor!"

"I knew it!" Louanna slapped her knee.

Sophya guessed she and Anya look surprised.

Louanna set their minds at ease. "My Seth served with Richard and his father, Zachary Taylor in Mexico."

Sophya gasped, "Oh, my Lord!"

Anya said, "Oh, Lord, help us. Richard Taylor's her hero."

"He's camped near here right now," Louanna added. "Reverend Hawkins knows him."

"Oh, my, gosh," Anya mumbled.

"Oh my, Lord!" Sophya exclaimed excitedly. "If I could just get to *meet* him, maybe all this would be *worth* it! Where?"

"Oh, child, you can't go by yourself. It's too dangerous," Louanna said.

"Are you going back to Reverend Hawkins's?" she hesitantly asked. "You are welcome to stay here."

Anya and Sophya glanced at each other.

"What a tempting offer. Unfortunately, I feel we are *supposed* to be there for now. I don't think I've apparently learned everything I'm supposed to learn yet," she looked at Anya apologetically.

Anya looked down a moment, then up. "You met Brooks."

"Oh, you met Chief Running Brook?" Ms. Louanna asked excitedly.

Anya blinked hard.

Sophya caught it and smiled. "Yes, but I haven't figured how I can bring him back home and explain him to my husband, yet!"

They all laughed.

"Well, let me take you back to Reverend Hawkins's in my buggy. I will encourage him to take you to meet General Taylor,"

Louanna said, matter-of-factly.

"Oh my gosh!" Sophya squealed.

"Ohhh, *thank you* for the ride!" Anya leaped for joy and hugged her.

"And for Richard Taylor!" Sophya exclaimed and hugged her too.

"Mercy." She glanced at both of them, overwhelmed.

They laughed again.

All got still.

"We wish we could take you back, Grandmother Morris," Anya spoke softly.

Ms. Louanna touched their hands and looked from one to the other. Settling her eyes on Sophya, she replied, "We must live the lives God intended for us to live."

They all had tears glistening on their cheeks.

"But what if you make a mistake and marry the wrong person? Or what if you put a curse on your marriage by having an affair first with him?" Tears flooded Sophya's eyes.

Anya reached over and held her hand.

"I wasn't involved in church for a few years in my teens. I fell in love with him. The others, because I didn't give in, I lost them. Maybe they were the wrong kind. I don't know. But I didn't want to lose William so I threw myself at him." Her eyes pleaded for forgiveness.

Louanna stood up and hugged her.

Sophya buried her head in her shoulder and let out all her tears for her past and present troubles. "Oh God, what have I done?"

Anya whimpered a deep cry of sympathy for their situation.

Their grandmother sighed and sat down, holding Sophya's hands in hers.

"Sophya," she said.

Sophya opened her drenched blue-grey eyes to look into her great-great grandmother's crystal blue ones.

"Yes ma'am?"

"Only *God* can put it in a person's heart to love, and only *God* can take it out."

Sophya's eyes blinked that in.

"Nothing happens by accident," she added. "God is a forgiving God. Have you repented and turned back to Him?"

"Yes."

"Yes, but what?" she asked.

"How do you *know* when you are forgiven?"

"I believe you know the scriptures as well as me," she says. "He forgives as soon as we ask and stop sinning."

She sighed deeply.

"But have you forgiven yourself?" Louanna tilted her head slightly, softly saying it, encouragingly.

Anya and Sophya both looked down, knowing she had not.

Louanna Morris took hold of Anya's hand too. "I'm going to pray. But I also want you girls to think about going with me to one of Brooks' meetings sometimes. He will lead you to higher and deeper things of God. OK?"

They glanced at each other knowingly, and looked back at Louanna. They agreed and followed their grandmother's lead and closed their eyes to pray.

"Dear Lord, what a day You have blessed us with. We thank You for that. We praise Your most holy name for the victories in our lives and soon, at Mansfield and Pleasant Hill. Help us to *draw* from these victories, in our moments in the valley. Lead and guide and bless Sophya and Anya. Thank You for bringing them to my door. Help them to be a blessing to each other and to Reverend Hawkins and he to them. Change his heart. Bring Sophya safely to see General Taylor. Bless that time. Help Anya and Sophya see Your purpose for their lives and for this situation. Bring them back safely to their own time. And, now, Lord, *thank You* for blessing my Seth and bringing him back home safely to me. We pray these things in Jesus name, Amen."

155

When Anya and Sophya raised their heads, big tears rolled down Grandmother Louanna's face. She opened her eyes and smiled.

"We still wish we could bring you back with us," Anya said.

They laughed, relieving the somber mood.

"Oh, child, I need to be *here* when my Seth comes home!" She had a faraway look in her eyes again. Then, she came back to the present. "Oh, I want each of you to take one of my embroidered handkerchiefs back with you. Wouldn't that be *something* for you to show your great-great-grandmother's initials on them?"

"Oh, my, gosh!" Anya emulated slowly.

"It will be heavenly." Sophya smiled at her grandmother. "And thank you for that *heavenly* breakfast!" she added.

Laughter ensued.

***

Ms. Louanna's buggy pulled up in front of Rev. Hawkins's plantation home at about ten thirty that morning. Lillie opened the front door and saw them and clasped her hands together. "Glory be!" she shouted back into the house. "Rev-end Hawkins! Dey heah!"

She hurried out onto the porch. He followed soon afterward.

"*Where* have y'all been!" he sounded exasperated. "I have been looking all over for you! I've even been down to the Indian settlement!"

Anya and Sophya looked at each other. Then Sophya asked, "Why'd you go there?"

"No matter," he said. "You're safe now."

"There, there, hold your horses," Ms. Louanna Morris demanded.

Lillie snickered. William glanced over at her in surprise. She put her hand on her mouth acting like she was coughing instead.

"These girls have been with *me*!" Ms. Louanna proclaimed. "And, they have an open invitation to *stay* with me for their duration!" She reprimanded him.

Rev. William Hawkins calmed down.

"These *are* my great-great-granddaughters," she explained, knowing he knew. "Even though it may not appear so today." She looked from one of them to the other with affection.

William appeared shocked that she knew their secret and believed them.

"I am *demanding*, Reverend Hawkins, that you let these girls have *freedom*, to come and go as they please! They need to be able to find out why they are here. And, they need your *support*, not hindrance."

William shuffled his feet as though off-balance from being slapped.

Sophya raised her eyebrows in amazement at Lillie when Louanna used the word *freedom*.

Louanna then pointed toward Lillie. "We all need to be free, as God's *equal* creatures."

Lillie's eyes widened. "Yes'm," she said and looked at Rev. Hawkins.

William gazed from Lillie to Louanna. "Ms. Louanna, you are not suggesting…"

"I'm suggesting just what I said." She backed up what she said next. "My Seth agrees." She turned quickly to all of them and added. "Oh, he's off fighting for the *South*, alright, but he went so we wouldn't be dominated by them *Yanks*! Anyone works for *me,*" she squinted her eyes at Rev. Hawkins, "Gets *paid,* and they come and go as they *please*! Dark, white or German immigrants. And, they get treated with *respect*."

William Hawkins blinked hard but held his tongue. Sophya guessed this must have been out of respect for Louanna's age.

Anya and Sophya were silently shocked.

Lillie smiled at Ms. Louanna, relaxed and folded her arms.

"Another thing, Reverend, this young woman knows a lot about General Richard Taylor. She admires him tremendously. I suggest you take her to meet him."

"I've already arranged that, Ms. Louanna."

Lillie looked surprised at him.

Sophya grabbed Anya's and Louanna's hands and let out a squeal of satisfaction!

"Good!" Louanna said.

They all laughed as the tension was relieved.

Louanna Morris held onto Sophya and Anya a little longer. She stared intently from Sophie's eyes to Anya's. William and Lillie remained silent. "You girls have blessed me beyond measure this day. I would like to bless you whenever I can." She smiled. "Please come back and visit me, anytime," she said and glared at William.

"You have blessed us," Sophya answered, to lighten their parting.

"Yes," Anya agreed.

They hugged each other good-bye.

"If you don't get to come back and see me," she glanced at William. "I'll come back looking for you."

William kept silent.

Ms. Louanna hugged them again, her great-great-granddaughters. "Give this to your mother for me." She kissed each of them on the cheek. Her twinkling blue eyes glistened with love. So did theirs. "Till we meet again," she said and they dismounted the buggy.

As she clucked her horses, Rev. Hawkins said, "We missed you in church last Sunday."

Louanna Morris looked back and replied, "Thank you." Then she faced forward retorting., "My ox was in the ditch." She shook her reins and turned the horses back toward the road.

The girls laughed, wishing they would have missed that sermon, too.

William turned to Sophya. "I would appreciate it if you will let me know your whereabouts next time."

She let out a sigh, but made no promises. *My husband would have demanded it even after he had been with another woman like this*

William has.

William glared at her a moment, then abruptly turned to go into the manse.

The women let him, and then they noticed he was waiting at the door with it opened, for them to walk in.

"Commone," Lillie said with a sigh of acceptance and took them arm in arm.

Chapter Ten
Wandering and Wondering

("Entreat me not to leave thee, or to return from following after thee..." Ruth 1:16)

Rev. William Hawkins turned to walk into his study. He stopped, then faced Sophya and Anya. He glanced almost apologetically at Lillie--for whatever reason, maybe for excluding her--and spoke, "I'll bring you two ladies to see General Taylor when I return from Shreveport after completing some business. I've sent a messenger to tell Richard."

Sophya looked at him with surprise. Then she looked from Anya to Lillie and back to him. "Thanks," she said. Then, her mouth, needing hot coals, too quickly added, "If you see Kirby Smith, tell him to quit trading with the enemy, we have a war to fight!"

"Huh!" she realized too late what she said.

Lillie tilted her head and looked hard at her.

Anya raised her eyebrows and let out a sigh.

William blinked hard, let out a sigh and said, "Sophie..."

Her eyes widened at this familiar address, so did Lillie's.

"Never mind," Sophya clipped, biting her lip and turned and walked up the stairs.

Anya and Lillie seemed glad to follow. As Sophya turned the corner at the top of the stairs, she caught him still watching her. He shook his head and walked into his study.

Once inside the room, she flopped on the bed. "Where's Flo when you need her!"

"Couldn't you think of anytang bettah ta say dan dat, Missy?" Lillie got straight to the point.

Sophya let out a deep, deep sigh.

"Maybe if you took a bar of *soap* to her mouth, Lillie," Anya

160

surmised, but with a smile on her face instead of her former anger.

Anya tapped on Beth's door and entered after she heard a soft invitation to come in, then closed it behind her. *We have made some dear friends here that we must leave behind someday.*

Lillie sat on the edge of the bed. Sophya sat up and leaned against the headboard.

"You wanna talk, Miz Sophie?"

Sophya outlined her lips with her finger while she thought for a moment, then she said, "Do *you,* Lillie?"

Lillie blinked her eyes and jerked her head back, but no words came.

Sophya proceed. "We had the best time at Ms-- our great-grandmother's house!" She hugged herself tight and had a dreamy look in her eyes.

Lillie relaxed and smiled.

"But, while we were sneaking away before dawn, we peeked around the corner of the front of the house and thought we saw 'the Rev' coming out of your cabin."

Lillie looked down at her hands.

"Did he…"

"Yes'm."

"Oh God," Sophya leaned forwards and touched her hand. Then she got angry. "I wish to God he'd get caught and have to pay!"

"Yes'm, he will," she said still looking at her hands. "Ah makes shur o' dat today. Ah makes like I enjoy, and hold onto him dis time."

Sophya got dizzy with the thoughts of repercussions. Her head went back against the wall by the headboard where she sat. "Uh ohhh," she moaned.

"Is time he pay up, Missy, is time." She looked up at Sophya so sadly. "Ah mostly say we gotta forgive, but is time he need to stop making us *have* to." She touched Sophya's hand, too.

Sophya took her other hand and patted Lillie's. Saving all judgment, uncharacteristically, and not wanting to ruin the mood of the day, she only replied, "I'm tired," and yawned.

"Come eat a little dinnah fo' you rest."

Lillie got up and knocked on Beth's door lightly, and opened it. "You guls, commone eat sumpin' with Miz Sophie."

"Alright," Anya and Beth answered.

***

"Visions of sugar plums" danced in Sophya's head as she fell back on the pillow to take a nap. "Hmmm, I could learn to really enjoy retirement!" But for now, she dozed off thinking of Ms. Louanna and meeting *General Richard Taylor*!

***

"No," Beth whispered to Anya. "Let's go through my hall door instead of disturbing Sophya."

"OK," Anya agreed.

They went into Beth's bedroom.

"Do you want to play cards or do you want to rest?" Beth asked as she sat on the edge of her bed and began to reach in the drawer of the table beside the bed.

"I feel like-- I need to take a walk and get some more fresh air, exercise and sunshine, believe it or not, after all that this morning!"

Something stirred within Anya that she couldn't explain.

"Oh, OK," Beth said half-heartedly. "I'm not much of an outside person," she apologized.

"I need to go alone anyway," Anya said politely.

"Oh!" Beth responded light-heartedly.

"You don't mind?" Anya asked.

"No! Actually, I'm relieved!" Beth smiled.

"Good."

"Where will you go?"

"I don't know. I guess I'll know when I get there!" Anya

hugged Beth.

***

"Oh, that barn! I'm not trying that again, not without Sophya." Anya looked across the pasture to the woods instead. She thought of the stream she loved to take her nieces and nephews wading in. *Sophya certainly had some memories there yesterday.* She picked a piece of field grass to chew on and headed in that direction.

The pasture was awesome with eucalyptus and field flowers. She loved eucalyptus. The cows and horses out grazing had a contentment Anya envied.

She stopped where her mother's house was supposed to be. "Oh Mom, I miss you and Urich so much." Then, she put her chin up with a new found strength. She decided right then and there to make the best of this situation, like Sophie had asked. "I *will* find my way out of here with Your help, God. I *will* glean *nuggets* from this experience to take back with me. Please, take care of Mom and Urich until then."

She felt a weight lift off her shoulders. A peace came over her.

"Wow!" she exclaimed, enjoying the lightness.

Off she trudged, across the pasture and into the woods, pushing aside jutting small limbs and trampling the pine straw on the ground.

What a fresh smell the pine straw makes! Those yellow, blacked-eyed susans are sent just for me!

Past the clay ridge, Anya went down into the valley where the wild, lavender irises were growing. The new grass there hit her at the knees. She followed the trail around the bend hoping her allergies didn't act up and then…

"Oops!" she was surprised. There sat Steve on a log beside the stream, fishing with a cane pole.

He quickly turned around, startled, before she could slip away.

"Oh, I'm sorry. I didn't mean, I mean I didn't *know*…"

Steve put his pole down and stood up. "Oh, it's OK."

"I didn't think anyone would *be* here!" Anya felt shy.

"Some people might *still* think no one's here," he laughed humbly.

"Oh," was all she could manage to say. Then it came to her. "Why?"

He smiled. "Well, I'm not the most important person in this community."

Anya thought about that a minute and struggled to come up with a reply.

"But, I don't *bite,* if you've been told otherwise."

"No," she still struggled to speak. "I haven't been told anything. I mean…" Why couldn't she *speak?* She usually had *no* trouble. She just usually chose not to!

"We haven't been *properly* introduced. My name is Steve Garrett." He walked toward her slowly and tried to gain her trust.

"My name is Anya Stolsky." She blushed. "You *know* me!" She sounded exasperated and wanted to hide her blushing.

"I know," he answered, smiling, "but you mainly stuck by Miss Hawkins at church."

"Do you like to fish?" he asked.

"Never tried it," Anya responded truthfully. "I've only been a bystander,…so far."

"Would you like to?" He tilted his head, smiling. "There's plenty of room on this log if you care to sit," he added.

Anya looked at the log, and the inviting stream, then his face. Sophie was right, *for a change,* he did look like a younger version of Steve Lawrence, except for darker hair. *And his name is Steve!* His face was trusting as an angel's. But Steve Lawrence was in Sophie's time.

"Alright," she said, slowly walking towards him.

"Good!" he replied, and turned around to sit on the log and check his pole.

Anya sat down. She longed to take her shoes off and wade in the water, but she wanted to clear something up first.

"Were you raised around here?" she probed.

"Yes," he glanced over at her then back at his bobbing cork.

Anya waited. She watched him and the excitement on his face about the fish.

He stood up. "Whoa," he blurted out and let the fish swim with the bait a bit. Then he jerked it out. It was a good size perch.

"Whoa ho, babe!" He grabbed the flapping fish to unhook it.

"Want me to do something?" Anya asked.

"Thought you said you never fished!" he said amazed.

"I have been *present*, many-a-time when my nieces and nephews did!" she exclaimed.

Steve laughed.

What light-hearted laughter! I could become accustomed to hearing that often. What a winning smile, too.

Catching her watching him so intently, caught him off guard. He dropped the fish back into the water.

"Oops!" He snatched it back up. "Will you grab that string out of the water next to you? It's on that spike. Watch it, it's got some other fish on the stringer."

Anya stood up and walked over to the cord and pulled it up slowly. "Wow, you've been busy!" There were seven good-sized brim and perch on the line.

"Yuk." She shook the dirt off her hand she got from the stake end.

"Yep," Steve said and she notice that he blushed at being that close to her.

Anya held the string while Steve unhooked the fish with ease. Putting his pole down first, he laced the new fish onto the string through the gill with the others. Then he handed it to her and rinsed his hands in the stream. He pointed for her to put the fish back in the water. "That's why I couldn't shake your hand."

"Oh, I didn't realize men shook hands with women, here..." she trailed off realizing what she has said.

Steve laughed again. "Why sure, ma'am!"

165

Anya laughed. "Well shake my dirty hand!" She held out her hand.

A twinkle came into Steve's eyes. He reached out to shake her hand. "And you can call me *Stevie*, when you forgive me."

"Forgive you for *what?*" Anya asked innocently.

Then he pulled her hand and made her fall into the creek!

"Ohhh!" she exclaimed and stood up.

He reached to help her out. She acted as though she was slipping and pulled *him* in!

"Ahhh!" Steve yelled as he fell in.

Anya was knocked down again by his body. "Ohhh," she mumbled, standing back up and gurgling and spitting out water.

"Hey! You're scaring the fish!" Steve blurted out.

"Who started this?" She reached and gave him a hand to help him up.

"Oh no. I'll get up by myself!" Then he feigned helplessness and pushed her over again with his shoulder.

"Huh!" she muttered as she went under.

He snatched her back up, "Hey, no fair drowning, my conscience would bother me!"

Anya, befuddled, got her bearings. She realized she looked a sight. She shook her short hair out and tried to peel the adhering skirt and blouse away from her body.

"I doubt it," she replied.

They burst out laughing.

He helped her to the shore. "Oh well, that's enough of a mess of fish to fry. Want to stay for lunch?"

"I've *had* lunch," she retorted.

"Aw, come on, the least you can do is let me start a fire so you can get dry."

Anya looked down at her clothes. She thought of *all* the explaining she'd have to do. She also thought of the fact that she hadn't had this much fun in a long, long, time. She smiled at Steve and said, "Alright."

He smiled back and motioned for her to sit back on the log.

"I'll gather some sticks." He pulled a blanket out of his pack that sat on the ground and handed it to her. "You can wrap this around yourself."

"Thanks. Do all men keep blankets with them out in the woods for damsels in distress?"

He tilted his head again questioningly.

"Never mind. But what about you? You're wet too."

"Aw, I'm tough," he added with a twinkle in his eyes.

Anya smiled and slowly shook her head then wrapped the blanket around her shoulders and wiped her face dry. "OK, but I'll dry quicker if I can help gather sticks, Ste-*vie!*"

He looked up. "Suit yourself."

"What made you think I wouldn't get mad if you threw me in?"

"Just a hunch, and the way you looked longingly at the water."

Smiling, she stacked sticks in a pile a safe enough distance from the log. "Here?"

"That's good," Steve added his to the stack. He then got some matches and a pan, oil and a potato out of his pack. He crossed some strong sticks about the fire and hooked the pan and oil over the fire. He pulled out a plate and knife. "Here, you want to peel this potato and cut it up?"

Anya leaned her head back as if foregoing it, but took it anyway.

Steve scaled the fish on a stump and threw the heads back into the stream. He took a bottle of water out of his pack and rinsed the fish, sprinkled some seasoned corn meal on the fish and put them to fry in the heated pan.

He sat on the stump beside Anya and watched her peel the big potato. "If you cut it in half, it may be easier for your hands."

She looked over at him. *How considerate.* "Who's doing this?"

His eyes got wide and his head snapped back.

She sighed. "I'm sorry. I'm used to being in charge, tending to my mom and my brother, when he's home."

He tightened his lips in a brief smile of acceptance for her apology.

"And, I'm not good at manipulating men, and acting like I'm helpless."

"Good!" Steve said quickly.

"But I sure could get used to one waiting on me hand and foot and cooking!" She said in deep thought and with a twinkle in *her* eye.

He laughed hard and slapped his knee.

Anya looked down, coyly, surprised at her own bold statement.

Steve got up to turn the fish with a big fork then sat back down again.

"Do you and your mom and brother live near here?" Steve asked.

Anya choked at the question and coughed, finally saying, "Not too far."

He looked over at her with a questioning smile.

She changed the subject. "How about you? Did you say you were raised in this area?"

"Yes, most of my life, but I was born in west Texas. I think the prairie dust chased my mom over to east Texas. We also have relatives near Shreveport".

"Oh," Anya said. "So you've known Beth Hawkins a long time."

He took the plate from her, scraped the potatoes into the hot grease to cook and put the fish on the plate and set it on the stump to cool.

At that moment, a raccoon came wandering out of the woods. Anya had the potato peelings in her skirt lap. "Awww," she embellished the moment.

"He wants some of those peelings," Steve pointed to her skirt. "He bugs me when I come here. Hold the peeling out in your hand to him."

Anya, for once, did as she is told.

The coon wobbled over to her slowly.

"Come on, guy," Steve said in a soft voice.

The coon came closer to Anya and took the peelings, licked them, then ate them.

"He's so cute," she said. "I love animals."

"Me too," Steve agreed. He took a peeling and fed the coon, also.

"I went to school with Beth Hawkins, to answer your question," he said. "But I mostly know her because Reverend Hawkins gets me to tend to his animals when I'm not working at the saddle shop."

"Oh." That surprised Anya.

"What do you think of Beth?" she delved.

Steve sat back and looked at her. "I think she's a rich kid, that hardly ever goes outside and she has very red hair! Why?" he asked with a teasing smile.

"You don't *like* her?"

"I don't *dislike* her. You mean like boyfriend, girlfriend?"

Anya sat back now.

Steve took that to mean yes.

"No, I don't like her for a *girlfriend!*"

Anya let out a deep sigh.

Steve laughed again. "She's nice and all, but she's not…"

"Not what?" Anya thought she may have to get defensive here for her friend.

"She's not *active!*" he smiled a mischievous smile again.

"Active." Anya looked straight ahead to think about that one.

The coon scampered off.

"Yes, active. For example, she wouldn't walk down here and sit by the creek, nor look longingly at it like she wanted to be *in* it! Much less *laugh* if someone threw her in!" He smiled bigger.

Anya closed her eyes and laughed with understanding, but said, "She might!"

Steve got up and picked up the fried potatoes and put them onto the plate on top of the fish to re-warm them and set it down. He looked back and said, "I doubt it."

She took off the blanket from her shoulders and handed it to him. "I'm almost dry."

He hung the blanket on a tree limb.

"Got any ketchup to go with this fish?" she asked.

"Ketchup? What's that? Besides, we're roughin' it. In fact, I didn't *know* I'd be having company, so I only have water to drink."

"I guess I'll just have to suffer," Anya feigned royal blood.

Then he came with the plate and sat on the log. "Taste it."

She did, and with surprise she added, "Wow."

He laughed, then joined in sitting to eat, but bowed his head to pray silently. She did too.

Then he decided to pry some. "Where, exactly, does your mom live?"

"You mean, where do I live?" Anya joked with him.

"Well, yes," Steve said, looking like he got caught in the cookie jar.

"I'm not going to tell you," she answered, assuming an out-of-character, demure look.

Steve practically choked on his fish to keep from laughing.

"Why?" he demanded jokingly.

She, again, unusually shy, stated, "It's a secret."

Now *he* turned, looked ahead, out into space and the woods, trying to figure her out.

"My name is Anya Marie Stolsky. I am twenty-one years of age. I am four foot, seven inches tall and wish I were more, and weigh blank pounds. Oh, and I am an American citizen, and *not* a spy."

"Not a spy?" he smiled quizzically.

Oh, that smile, she was mesmerized.

"No, not a spy," she added confidently.

"Did someone *say* you were a spy?"

Anya laughed mischievously. "Yep, the *Rev*!"

170

Steve looked surprised at her lack of respect for Rev. Hawkins but brushed it off. "*Reverend Hawkins* thinks you are a spy?"

"Well, not anymore, I guess," Anya began to wish she hadn't said anything.

Steve sighed.

"Can we change the subject?" she pleaded.

"No!" Steve said tenaciously. "Why did he think you were a spy?"

Anya's nervous stress of the whole situation manifested. She could not stop giggling enough to appear to be telling the truth. "I...we.." she laughed. "My sister and me..." *Gosh I can't stop!* "Got hit in the head and lost our memory!" *Oh my gosh, I'm acting drunk and can't stop!*

Anya laughed so hard, she leaned backwards almost falling off the log.

Steve dropped the plate off his lap and grabbed her in his arms.

The next thing Anya knew, she was starring into Steve's beautiful, hazel eyes, probably more seriously than she would like. *Oh my gosh, I can't think, I can't speak!*

He looked so serious! Then, he kissed her! It was quick, but so tender and sweet.

His lips! Anya's thoughts raced. She had never been kissed before, she was virtually inexperienced because she devoted her life to her mother and brother.

Then no sooner than he had kissed her, he held her away and smiled charismatically.

Anya, unable to handle these new emotions with all her other problems, decided to do what any other red-blooded, American girl would do, she got up and ran, dropping her plate.

"Hey!" Steve got up and ran after her, tackling her gently.

Spitting grass out of her mouth, Anya quipped, "Phooey, gees! Are you always this hard to get along with?" She tried to push up, but he held on.

"I won't let go of you till you *promise* to come back here this same time tomorrow!"

Anya looked back at Stevie. She dropped back down to the ground on her arm like she would be sleeping on it. Then she mumbled, "I don't know if I'll have any *energy* left!"

Steve sat up and let her get up. "I'm betting you do!"

He got up and offered her his hand to her.

Anya rolled over, looking at his hand, then his face, with an agitated look in her eyes. "*No* thank you!" She acted like she would get up, and then knocked Steve over. He pulled her down with him.

"Hey!" she retorted.

He rolled over, looking down at her, like he might kiss her again.

"Oh, Lord, help!" Anya hollered and closed her eyes.

That took Steve totally by surprise. He rolled away quickly, fearing he might have scared her.

At that opening, Anya scampered off in the other direction, and ran towards the plantation home.

She'd gone a safe enough distance through the little field up to the woods and heard no footsteps following her. Then she glanced back and saw him still sitting on the ground, watching her.

Anya laughed, waved her hands, like horns by her ears and shouted, "Na na na!" and turned to run again.

***

She sneaked in the side door of the small hallway. She peeked into the dining room, then into the great hall, not knowing this had become a familiar pathway. Then she darted up the stairs. *Oh, I wish I didn't have to go through Sophie's room!*

She gently opened the door and peeked in.

***

Sophya was lying on the bed. She appeared to still be asleep, facing the wall.

Anya tiptoed toward her room.

"*Where* have you been, young *lady!*"

Anya turned towards her and Sophya sat up on the bed.

She glanced back at Beth's door to make sure it was closed. Then she whispered, "*Oh, his eyes were so green! His muscles so strong!*" She started to giggle. "*He was so*...how'd you say it? *Enticing!*"

"Brooks?" Sophya asked indignantly, while her throat constricted.

Anya was crumbling, trying not to laugh, then she went into her room.

"Brooks?" Sophya repeated, getting up and following her into her room, showing a little more agitation. "You've been with *Brooks, you little hussy?*"

Anya motioned for her to shut the door behind her and said, "Noooo."

"Who?"

"No one! I was just joking," but she couldn't stop giggling.

Being the big sister, Sophya said, "Wait a minute. You look like you just had a roll in the hay!" She picked some grass out of Anya's hair.

Anya couldn't stop laughing. She sat on her bed. Then, she laid on the pillow and rolled over onto it to drown her laughter in it.

"*What* have *you* been drinking? Or smoking? Have you smoked that Indian knick-knick plant in the peace pipe or something?"

Anya looked at her like Sophya was unreal.

Sophya sat on the edge of the bed and said, "I'm going to tell Mom!"

Anya looked at her with pained laughter. "Yeh, right." She shook her head.

"I'm going to count to three..."

"You ought to know by now, you can't make me mind you

anymore!" She sat up and wiped her nose and mouth together.

Sophya let out a sigh, folded her arms and start tapping her foot. "I'm *waiting!*"

Anya tried to be serious. There was a pleading look in her eyes. She snickered and wiped her mouth and nose again, without a Kleenex, if they were even invented yet. Then she gained composure. "I'm not going to tell you." She whimpered a concealed laugh.

Sophya knew she was great at not telling her deepest thoughts, but she *had* to get to the bottom of this!

"*An-ya!*" Sophya looked deep into her eyes. Then she got tickled and hugged her. "What's up?"

"I..." she began, "don't want you to be held responsible for what you don't know," she added with a compassionate smile on her face and a painfully shaking belly.

"Oh," Sophya said, clamping her jaw.

About that time, Beth knocked lightly on Anya's door and said, "Can I come in?"

Anya appeared so surprised and guilty, she jumped!

Then Sophya realized she must've been with Steve. She turn her head to the side in a knowing way and whispered, *"You little hussy, you've been with Steve!"*

"At least I'm not married!" she snapped back in a whisper.

Sophya's eyes closed tightly at being rebuked.

"I'm sorry," Anya said quickly and touched her sister's hand.

"Yes," she answered Beth and just raised her eyebrows in warning.

Beth entered in shyly, because she had interrupted their sister talk. Anya did not get up to reach for her hand this time in greeting, Sophya noticed.

"Lillie *and* Katy said they'd help us pulley the water up for a *grand* bath again!" Beth was excited.

Anya and Sophya looked at each other with a pleased expression and back to Beth.

"Mama Sara said we better come get a snack first," she added.

Sophya heard Anya whimper and saw her hold her stomach.

"Great!" Sophya said. "Let's go!" She got up to follow Beth out, then turned to raise her *motherly* eyebrows back to Anya.

"Then we can play cards *all* night since my brother's gone!" she looked back with a sweet, sneaky smile.

Anya and Sophya smiled.

More food! Anya tightened her lip and followed them.

Chapter Eleven
Updates

("Take no thought for the morrow; for the morrow shall take thought for itself." Matt. 6:33)

What a wonderful time Anya and I had with Beth last night! Anya kept her secret about Steve with the best poker-face at the card game. She had been extra giggly though. Sophya was sure Beth noticed. Maybe she was just glad Anya finally lightened up a bit. But, for whatever reason, Anya didn't seem one bit guilty about her feelings for Steve. That surprised Sophya, since she had been so concerned before, because Beth liked him.

Oh, well.

The daylight crept into her window. Sophya wanted to sleep late but couldn't. Rolling over, she sat up and opened the drapes. It appeared cloudy outside. She touched the window pane. "Ugh, still warm," she said to herself.

She took the Bible out of the drawer, glad to have found it. She finally had been given paper, by Lillie, to write on with this quill pen and ink. She tried and gave it up. *Thank goodness I have Mom's ink pen*! These supernatural days needed to be documented for later, for her and everyone else to believe, *whether they would believe it or not.*

"Have not I commanded thee? Be strong and of good courage;
Be not afraid, neither be thou dismayed: For the Lord *thy* God
Is with thee *withersoever thou goest.*" Joshua 1:9

Fear not. Surely, that could be for her that day. She was looking so forward to meeting Gen. Taylor! Sophya longed to be poised and smart and beautiful and win his approval. More than anything, she hoped to give him support and encouragement and conduct a good interview. *Speaking of believing, I can hardly believe I'll meet him!*

I wonder why I haven't heard Lillie up yet? She got up, looked in the mirror and shook her hair out, picking it and fluffing it with her fingers. Donning the robe and slippers that had been loaned to her. She picked up the pitcher to go get some warm water and a cloth and towel.

She peeked out of the door into the hall, quietly and slowly. *Things are so much better and quieter without William here.* "Now *there's* a similarity between the two men!"

She exited her room into the hall and went to the kitchen.

She walked past the beautiful picture of the baptism on the wall, wondering what kind of mood Mama Sara would be in. Down the gorgeous stairs to the great dining room she went, stopping and touching the intricately designed vase on the buffet, with its hues of royal blue, gold, red and purple—and gold. Sophya remembered Lillie's words, "You da vase, Missy." Her eyes moistened. She stopped and wiped a tear away before crossing into the kitchen.

The dash across the ramp into the kitchen met her with very warm, damp air. She entered and saw Mama Sara moving slowly.

"Good morning," Sophya said.

Sara turned around to look and managed to say, "Good mawnin.'"

"I haven't seen Lillie so I came to get some hot water for my basin."

"Lih-lee got da day off," Mama Sara said. "Ah tole huh no need be heah since Mastah gone."

Sophya took in a deep breath at the thought of a day without her friend.

Sara was good at detecting body language. "You be alright. Katy jes take both flohs."

Sophya didn't know if she had been reprimanded or what. "I can get my own water. I just wondered where the towels and cloths are." She didn't take a step closer.

"Sit down, chile. Have sum brek'fas."

She dipped the best looking *real* oatmeal Sophya had ever seen, into a bowl. It was thick and creamy, not like the instant kind. Sara handed Sophya a spoon and nodded her head towards the opposite counter where the *real* cream and sugar were.

Sophya melted and muttered. "Yes ma'am," Then she handed her a cup of deliciously, strong-smelling coffee, like the south Louisiana kind she liked.

Sara glanced at the pleased look on Sophya's face and said, "Coffee hahd ta cum by dees days. You bes enjoy." Then, she turned and started humming before she saw Sophya nod with approval.

Sophya sat and began to devour it, identifying with the early bird that caught the worm.

Bacon, oh my gosh, real bacon, not fat free! She handed her a saucer of bacon and a saucer of sliced peaches put up in their own juices. "Wow," she mumbled. She thought she heard Mama Sara laugh a little.

Sophya finished and offered to wash her dishes. Sara poured hot water from the kettle into Sophya's pitcher and replied, "Naw'sum, chile. Go git da towels from Katy. She upstaihz."

"Thank you," Sophya said humbly. Sara just kept stirring and humming. She didn't even turn around.

***

Upstairs Sophya tiptoed to look for Katy. She found her in her bedroom opposite from Sophya's. It looked neat and clean. It was large, about the size of Beth's. The walls were off-white with wood wainscot. The colors were muted earth tones of beige, tans, and light green-- nothing bold. The bed was made up with a pretty off-white lace spread over a solid-colored spread of tan. The bed was four-poster, mahogany wood. The furniture mostly matched. There were a couple of armoires and several dressers in the room.

Sophya nodded to Katy. She had already put her pitcher of hot water that Sara had given her in the room before walking into Katy's room.

"Will you show me where the towels and cloths are?" she asked as pleasantly as possible.

Katy was dusting. She stopped and walked over to one of the dressers and got some towels and cloths. "Bring some for the other two girls," she requested.

Sophya agreed

Katy actually smiled a bit then continued cleaning her room.

***

The morning was going cheerfully, like a day off away from your boss and your work load. Beth had some sewing she needed to catch up on. She irresistibly solicited Anya's reluctant help. "That leaves me time to catch up writing our 'adventures'," Sophya happily realized.

Anya and Sophya discussed visiting Grandmother Morris; they invited Beth to come along with them. She politely showed reserve. Mama Sara overheard and disagreed strongly, saying, "Naw'sum, is fixin' ta rain *hahd*!" So, they give in to a leisurely afternoon.

***

A horrendous rain and hail storm blew in right after supper. Sara and Katy hustled to build a fire in the fireplace on the south wall in the ballroom. The girls helped.

One-half of the ballroom was closed off now, with doors that had been hidden in the half-wall. Candles in this section of the room had been lit. A sofa and chairs replaced the ballroom chairs and tables. It was cozy with the oil lamp light.

The small, grand piano was kept in here. This room faced south and the large porch which afforded it with more warmth. They wrapped small blankets around them like shawls.

Sitting on the loveseat-type sofa, with her feet propped on it,

179

Sophya watched the fire flicker in the fireplace. She always wished for a fireplace and to be sitting near it with the man she loved. Her dream included a man that would be passionately in love with her, too. Sophya thought of the two Williams. *It won't be either of them!* She thought of Brooks. *Hmm.* Then she thought of her *children* and how they would love to pop corn or play music, or games around a fireplace like this. Her heart ached for them.

"Beth, play us something on the piano!" Sophya sweetly pleaded.

She had been all cozy in a chair with her feet propped on a little stool. She was intently watching Anya playing a game of solitaire with cards. Anya sat on the floor, by a low table, wrapped up and dealing cards.

"I don't know…" Beth answered, hesitantly.

Anya stopped playing and looked at her and said, "Please?" She smiled and batted her eye lashes.

Beth didn't budge.

"There's no one here but *us*," Sophya coaxed. "Katy's upstairs."

Beth blushed. She couldn't avoid their pleading eyes though. "Alright," she whispered. Getting up, she took her blanket with her and sat on the piano stool. A lamp on top of it gave a warm flame to encourage her and light the keys.

Beth began playing the "Blue Danube Waltz." She must have remembered how fond Anya and Sophya were of all the waltzes.

Sophya thought of the ball and how much had happened in just a few days.

Beth looked up like that must be her thoughts too.

Sophya smiled at her and she smiled back.

Anya stopped playing cards and listened in awe.

When Beth finished, they just sat absorbing the peace that had settled into the den. Sophya dared the raging storm outside to change their spirits.

Anya and Beth smiled at each other. Then, Anya gathered her

blanket and went to sit on the piano stool with Beth. Sophya gathered hers, too, and went to lean on the piano.

"Do you know how to play some church songs?" Sophya asked. "That's our favorite thing to do at Mother's. She'd play and we would sing along.

Beth nodded, "Yes."

Anya requested "Amazing Grace". Beth played it beautifully. Then Sophya asked for "It is Well". Beth didn't know that one, so Anya and Sophya harmonized it for her. She loved it. Next she played "What a Friend We Have in Jesus", and lastly, "He Leadeth Me".

Sophya thought of the song that said "Peace be still," as the storm still raged outside.

***

The next day, March 23, had *such* a chill to it. Cold, slushy mud and a sharp wind to greet them if they ventured out. So in their boredom, they helped Katy and Lillie clean and, when she let them, they even assisted Mama Sara in the kitchen.

***

March 24th offered a cool, crisp, sunny breeze. The temperature had climbed back up from the thirties to about sixty degrees, that morning, with a promise of rising a bit higher even. The wind was not as sharp or threatening to make one sick if going outside.

Anya and Sophya and Beth were in the kitchen with Mama Sara eating lunch or, as she called it, "dinner." The back door that faced north was opened to cool the hot kitchen.

About that time a buggy pulled up by the back door. Sara's grandson, Sammy Harrison, held the reins and Johnny Sims, the young man that had danced so wonderfully at the ball, was riding shotgun.

Johnny smiled a big smile at Sophya. She sat on the stool

closest to the back door. Sammy reined in the horses to stop. Johnny hopped off the buggy and up the steps.

"Well, howdy, Miss So-*phe*-ya!" he exclaimed. Then he took her hand and kissed it.

Sophya laughed and said, "Well, howdy, *back,* Mister Johnny Sims!"

He smiled wider. "You remembered *my* name!" he said excitedly.

"Ah nevah forget a *gentleman,* Suh!" she stretched out her southern drawl.

Sara rolled her eyes and looked back at the stove.

Johnny showed humorous appreciation.

He nodded to Sara, then Anya. Then, he looked at Beth like he was seeing her for the very first time! His head jerked back.

Beth noticed and blushed. She looked precious today in a rose-colored gingham dress that contrasted gorgeously with her auburn hair.

"Johnny, this is my sister, Anya, and this is…" *oh-my-gosh I almost introduced Beth as my sister-in-law!* Sophya cleared her throat. Anya smiled a painful, sympathetic smile.

Beth blushed again.

"This is Reverend Hawkins' sister, *Beth*!" she finally managed to say.

Johnny laughed and nodded his head. Approval boldly showed in his eyes.

Sophya sighed with relief. She caught Sara glancing over at her with a deep, thoughtful look on her face as she hugged her grandson.

Another stool had been placed in the kitchen since last time. Sophya motioned for Johnny to sit down, but he waited. "Sammy, you want me to get you another chair?"

Sara looked at her in surprise.

"I'm sorry I missed your baptism. Congratulations!"

"Thankee Miz Sophie. Naw'sum, we can't stayz long. Mastah

William sent us back from Shreveport ta fetch Missy Beth. We s'posed ta bring huh ta Nac-kee-doh-chez ta be wid huh auntie. Dem Yanks get-in closah."

Beth sucked in her breath but didn't speak..

Anya and Sophya glanced at each other.

Mama Sara went to stirring her pot faster. "Lawsey," she said. "Have muhsey, Lawd." She regained her composure and added, "You boyz needa eat sumpin' fust."

She didn't wait for an answer and started dipping food onto plates.

Sammy went to the opposite counter and stood by the other door to eat. Johnny sat down in the vacant chair by Sophya. Sara handed their plates to them.

Sophya wanted some answers even though Johnny had started eating, She decided to press on.

"Reverend Hawkins hasn't finished his business in Shreveport, yet, Johnny?"

Sara cleared her throat like Sophya may be out of line or that might be none of her business. She may have wanted to shelter Beth from any bad news.

But Sophya was determined.

"No ma'am," he smiled and nodded at Beth, Sophya guessed, since they were talking about her brother. "He's been meeting with General *Kirby Smith*!" he said with pride. "He's completing some business."

He made it sound real important, so Sophya smiled.

"He has to make plans to get his crops and his livestock out to market somehow."

Sophya tightened her lips thinking of the wheeling and dealing going on.

"Did you get to hear much other news about the war?" she continued to question.

Johnny smiled. "General Smith says them Yanks may be overconfident because of Gettysburg and Vicksburg and Chattanooga, but they can't have Texas and Louisiana without a fight!" He slapped his knee. Sammy laughed, not even knowing what that would mean.

Sophya knew Kirby Smith must be borrowing Gen. Richard Taylor's brave words, since historically speaking, Smith, himself, traded with the enemy more than planning the war.

"Where are the Yanks now?" Sophya asked.

Johnny laughed again. "General Richard Taylor out-smarted them Yanks! By the time they got to Alexandria, he done had it deserted! He got the people and most their stuff out already! Said Banks arrived with a *pomp ceremony* though!"

Sophya laughed. She even thought she heard Mama Sara laugh a little.

"What of Fort DeRussy?" Sophya persisted.

Mama Sara looked at Sophya again with almost a warning look, like women and politics don't mix.

"Sophie!" Anya added her warning.

Sophya glanced at them both but nodded to Johnny to continue.

"General Kirby Smith said that General A. J. Smith took it--and our men, too--but blowed a few of his *own men* up in the process, along with his ego!"

"My, my," Sophie shook her head.

"General Banks had Admiral Porter's fleet coming by way of the Red River, but Kirby Smith said they'll never make it over the falls 'less the river rises. And General Kirby Smith told General Taylor he couldn't believe General Halleck was so infatuated with Shreveport that he'd take his troops from east of the Mississippi. That made Halleck so mad!"

"Is he in command of the Union forces down here still?" Sophya wanted to know what point they were at.

"Halleck's being replaced by General Grant now," Johnny said.

"Well, at least he's got more sense then Halleck!" Sophya commented. To her surprise, Sara and her grandson, Sammy, both laughed. Maybe Sara now enjoyed being around this conversation *and* gaining some information, too.

About that time Lillie came in and listened.

"Yes'm. He even had General Sherman send *10,000* troops to go up river with Banks," Johnny added.

His audience mulled that over for awhile.

"Has General Taylor been able to round up enough men?" Sophya acted ignorant.

"Well, ma'am," Johnny said. "It's been hard. That's why I aim to join them and fight them despots!"

She smiled at his big word.

"But," he continued, "General Taylor is *real* mad because he lost his mounted Calvary, and Colonel Vincent and his men. They climbed Henderson Hill near Co-tile in that ice storm only to be bush-whacked and captured by A. J. Smith. *Two hundred and fifty men* taken by him and Mower, without even a fight!"

Sophya shook her head feigning disbelief and let him take another bite of his food. She noticed that this all had gotten Mama Sara's undivided attention.

"Was Kirby Smith surprised Banks chose the Red River instead of Mobile or somewhere else? What made them head for Shreveport?"

"Well, General Kirby Smith said he and General Richard Taylor had an inkling about that last summer. Come January, it was looking for sure. Then them Yanks drug their feet about that very same decision…Shreveport or Mobile," he laughed. "Said ole Banks must've partied too much in New Or-leens at that Governor Michael Hahn's inauguration to be able to make a decision!"

Anya even smiled when Sophya shook her head and looked at her, acting with disbelief.

Johnny continued. "He said General Banks probably felt too victorious after sticking that Yank flag at the Rio Gran-day at Brazos. Shucks, that didn't mean nothing to us Texas Rebs! 'Member when he tried to fight real-life Reb at the Sabine Pass? He got *whooped* by them Texan and Lousisanan Rebs!" He slapped his knee again.

Sophya laughed a little but noticed Sara turned around to the stove.

Then silence ensued as their thoughts settled in.

"But, them Yanks are moving closer, ma'am. So, we need to pack Miss Beth off to her Aunt Paula's, Reverend Hawkins said. Real soon. He said you two ladies," he nodded at her and Anya, "Have other business to stay for."

Mama Sara turned to Lillie. "Take Missy Beth ta pack huh things." She almost said it sadly.

Lillie didn't move at first.

Beth looked around at all of them, tears welled in her eyes. "I want to *stay!*" She pleaded with Sara.

"Missy…" Mama Sara said in a tone that made Beth reluctantly obey.

She slowly got up and hugged Anya so tight and looked at her face with her watery eyes. "I have never had a friend like you both except Jesus." She smiled through her tears. Then she hugged Sophya, too. "I have come to love you *both* as my own sisters."

Sophya almost couldn't speak for choking back her tears. None of them knew what laid ahead for them, really. "Well," Sophya whispered, "as one song says, '*MEMORY* is *one* thing even *death* can't take away'."

She hugged Sara and the girls again. The kitchen filled with somberness and not one dry eye.

"Commone," Lillie sniffed and touched Beth's arm to lead her.

"We'll help," Anya tried to sound cheerful.

Sophya took in a deep breath and put her hand on Johnny's shoulder. "Thank you for the news." She nodded to him and Sammy. "Take good care of our little Missy Beth."

***

The next morning, March 25th, Sophya walked into Anya's

186

room after they ate breakfast downstairs.

"You were mighty quiet at breakfast, young lady," she said to her sister.

Anya looked up from playing her game of solitaire while she sat on top of the bed. She smiled a little and replied, "Things aren't the same without Beth around. I mean, she's quiet, I know, but she's so sweet and fun."

"I know, I know," Sophie said. "Hey, you want to go visit Grandmother Morris today?"

Anya looked surprised, like she hadn't even thought about that. "Yes," she answered then reached for her shoes.

"This time, we'll ride horses!" Sophya suggested.

"Amen!" Anya responded.

***

"I notice our visit put you in a *little* better mood. I'm glad we stayed for lunch! Umm, that woman can flat cook!" Sophya stated happily.

Anya got a smirk on her face. "Yeh, but the way to your heart has always been through your stomach!"

"Sooo," Sophya touch her forehead to her sister's. "What can cheer *you* up?"

"I think..."Anya hesitated. "I think I need to go to the creek bank for that!"

"Huh!" Sophya sucked in her breath. "*That's* where you met with Steve?"

"Yesss," she dragged it out defensively. "Why?"

"*That's* where I met with Brooks!" Sophie laughed.

Anya smiled and shook her head.

Sophya didn't mention her bad experience with William being at that place also.

"Go *to* it, Chickadee!" she swatted Anya's fanny when she picked up her shoes.

187

"Hey!" she snapped.

***

Anya came back more joyful. Sophya was truly grateful she found a friend she could confide in. Now it's Sophya's turn.

She decided to go out of the front door even though it squeaked. She brought a piece of the lye bar soap to scrape on it. *Phew, it worked.* Silently she sneaked out the door, even if they *were* supposed to have freedom to come and go.

The coast was clear as she peeked around the house, slid past Lillie and Sara's quarters, to go across the field. "Oh Lord, I'd still rather be going back to Mom's house even though I've met Brooks."

She avoided the stream in case Steve might still be there and went way around, almost to the road, She saw the embankment and headed that way.

***

Sophya felt she'd burst if she didn't get to finally tell Brooks the truth about their being there. She came to his cabin from the east and walked toward the west side to what she considered to be the front door. Then she saw him. She accidentally sucked in her breath and uttered, "Huh!" at seeing his muscles flex. He still could take her breath away. He was planting a tree. Caught off guard, he turned quickly, suspiciously. He let out a sigh and smiled.

"Hello," she managed to say.

"Hello," he replied, still smiling. "You surprised me. I didn't know if you would ever want to return here." He pointed for them to walk into his cabin and collected his tools.

That statement surprised Sophya. "Why wouldn't I?" Their eyes penetrated each other.

"I may have been too bold."

188

She glanced at the ground to draw some words, then they came. "You are a perfect *gentleman* and host."

He thought on that a moment. "I also presumed your *other* host may have won you over by now, in his more civilized environment."

"Tuh," she sarcastically snorted, then stopped herself when she noticed his eyebrows raise. "That's why I came. I need to talk to you about that…him…why I'm here."

They stopped walking and only stared into each other's faces again. Brooks pointed for them to continue into the cabin. Once there, he propped his tools against the outside log wall of the cabin and opened the door for her. She went in, he followed.

"Please, sit down. I will pour us something to drink," he motioned towards the chair, so she obeyed.

She contemplated how to begin. Then he handed her a cup of something that looked like grape juice. She tasted it. "Hmm, this is good." It was blackberry juice. Brooks sat near-by and waited for her to speak.

"I don't even know how to begin and I don't have long to stay," she almost whimpered.

Brooks leaned forwards looking compassionately at her. "Begin with the truth, that is always a good place to start."

"The truth," she sighed. "OK." She looked imploringly at him. "Do you know how the truth is the *truth*, whether anybody believes it or not?"

He seemed amazed at what she said, and leaned back in his chair. "Yes."

Sophya put her cup down. "Oh, Brooks, you are such a good person. *Why* did I have to meet you?"

He almost painfully laughed. "Maybe because I *am* a good person? Is that bad?"

She couldn't bear to see him look like that so she quickly continued, overlooking what he had said. "The *truth* is, I hated my life and asked God to change it. I always longed to go back in time, to *this* time, the Civil War."

His eyes widened.

"I, in no way blame you for not believing what I'm about to say. One day, *a week and a half ago,* my younger sister and I were walking down Mom's driveway to her mailbox," she waited to see if he understood that.

"Driveway? Mailbox?" he asked.

Sophya continued, "And it was April 8, 1980." She stopped.

He let out a deep sigh.

"We decided to go into my aunt's old barn that we hadn't been in before." She kept watching his facial expression. "Whenever we went in, something hit us on the head rendering us unconscious. I heard the words, 'Frankincense, and myrrh to pure gold', and my sister mumbling, 'What's that smell?' When we came to, everything was different. And there stood William. A relative in real life whom I didn't get along with. Naturally, he didn't recognize us or believe our story and took us for spies. I asked him what the date was--because he looked so different-- and he said March 18, 1864. He took us to his house, sort of under house arrest."

She rested her case.

Brooks weighed his words very carefully. "It's because of your beauty he made you stay in his house. I was sorely tempted also."

She laughed weakly thinking this was his attempt at comic relief.

"This is an amazing story. Perhaps you will tell me more when you have time." He smiled, put his cup down and held her hands so gently and began to pray. "Lord, thank you for the Truth…"

Sophya cringed, knowing it was not the total truth.

"Help us unravel this and determine Your will," he opened his eyes and they appeared to have that x-ray vision again.

"I need to go. Oh, William is taking me to meet General Richard Taylor soon," she bashfully smiled. "He's one of my heroes. I will tell you more later."

Brooks' hands felt like a shock ran through it to hers. Then, he abruptly let go.

Sophya glanced down at her hands. They looked the same. Oh, how dearly she wished he could keep her there forever, also.

***

"Hey, did you find Brooks?" Anya asked as she looked up from reading her book.

"Yes. Oh, Anya, he is so kind and gentle and wise and compassionate. And good-looking!"

She laughed as Sophya closed her bedroom door and sat on her bed. "Especially the good-looking part, huh?"

'Well, it's all of him, really. I've never met a man like that, who loves God and respects women."

"Hmm," Anya had to agree with her on that one.

"Today turned out so good though. I just decided to enjoy the time we had."

A quiet stillness settled.

"You know, we don't know when we'll be going back," Anya said in a motherly tone.

Sophya sighed. Tears came to her eyes. "I'm not a prisoner of hate for right now, Anya. I am not tied to someone that hates me and God. Do you not see how special this time has been for me?"

Compassion showed on Anya's face. She hugged Sophya tightly and they both cried about everything. Then she added, "We know things will end one day. There are parts of *this* time period we will both miss." Anya hugged her again. "But I don't want to go until after tomorrow, though."

***

Reverend William Hawkins arrived back from Shreveport the afternoon of March 25th. He and Big Bob, Mama Sara's husband, came just in time for Sara's supper.

191

The next morning, Sophya put on the pretty baby-blue cotton dress William had bought for her in Shreveport. It had a full skirt with layers of cotton eyelet slips that showed a little, but no hoops! She thought of the nice, grey cotton church dress he had gotten for Lillie. *I guess he takes care of her too, for apology.* She looked in the mirror and fixed her hair. Lillie had long since stopped asking her if she needed help with that, after she found out Sophya was a hairdresser. "Exterior, interior, fix me, Lord, and mirror, mirror, with confidence and wisdom for today's interview with General Richard Taylor!"

"Come on, woman!" *Reverend* Hawkins called from downstairs.

She grabbed her paper and pen, and the quill and ink, just in case she needed it and could learn to use it. She put them in the cloth handbag William purchased. Then she went out to the banister and said, "I had hoped your vacation away would give you some patience!"

After you had some more women, she mused.

He shook his head, but it looked like she saw admiration in his eyes. He didn't look too bad in that brown suit and long jacket, either.

"If I don't, are you going to give me tribulation to learn patience—like the Bible says?"

I could hook you to the ceiling with cables, like I just saw in a movie. She smiled.

He smiled back at her, never imagining her thoughts, while she came down the stairs. Then, he took her hand, kissed it and held on to it.

She lifted her hand with his up to look at it and reminded him of Grandmother Morris's orders. "I'm free, remember?"

He shook his head again, but let go of her hand.

Off they went to the horses and buggy that waited at the front door of the manse.

***

"The air and the weather are perfect!" she smiled her sweetest smile, wishing she was with somebody else, and gathered her shawl around her shoulders.

William picked up a lovely white eyelet, folded umbrella from the buckboard and handed it to her. He glanced over at her intently. "This is in case it's not."

Surprised, Sophya said, "Thank you."

Then he added, "I sent word to General Taylor that I have some urgent business with him. I heard he's held up at Beasley's, south of Natchitoches. I said I would bring a female writer-friend of mine that wanted to interview him." He watched for her reply.

"Oh, I'm a writer-friend?"

"Well, yes. You do plan to write about him later, don't you?" he smiled teasingly.

"Well, yes. I just didn't know you knew!" Sophya smiled smugly, looking ahead, trying to analyze that.

"Lillie asked me for that writing paper for you," he replied.

Then he looked at her more intently. "Sophie--"

She glanced at his face, not approving of his familiar use of her nickname.

"Sophya," he said emphasizing her proper name instead. "I'm an artist as well as a preacher, you know. I have heard you at least approve of my *art* ability." He raised his eyebrows, while looking at her. "I would like to sketch General Taylor while you interview him, OK?"

She sighed at the reprimand and looked straight ahead again, squelching a hundred words.

"As an artist, I usually notice everything," he still looked at her for a response.

She didn't want to ruin her good mood or this trip or seem ungrateful to him today. She smiled sweetly and answered, "I see."

His head reared back and he laughed so hard it made the horses jump.

Then Sophya laughed and said, "Can we just enjoy the ride and

193

scenery and perfect weather today and not argue?"

"As you wish, madam!"

***

Sophya loved this country. This time of year, Spring-- her favorite. The pines and red dirt, awesome. *Oh, God, help me to know and do Your will today.*

William interrupted her thoughts. "It will take us two days to get there. We'll spend the night in Mansfield."

"What!" she exclaimed.

"Calm down. We have separate rooms."

"I didn't pack anything!" she said exasperated.

"I had Lillie pack you some extra things."

Sophya sighed in amazement at his trickery. She hadn't even *thought* about how long this trip would take at this time period or, spending overnight with *William*! She sighed.

He glanced over at her. "I promise we have separate rooms."

She looked at him and bit her lip, feeling guilty even for her thoughts of distrust. With great restraint, however, she said nothing, then took in a breath of fresh air and looked away. "What about Sunday? You have to preach!"

He looked at her, his face relaying he knew she disliked his sermon. "I'm taking this Sunday off."

He shook the reins of the horses again, but miraculously said nothing else.

They rode practically in silence the rest of the twenty-mile trip.

***

"Mansfield looks so different! It is smaller, for sure, but *busier*, somehow, I guess with the war, huh."

Rev. William Hawkins got down to tie the horses to the hotel

194

post. They had eaten a snack lunch along the way.

It must be about 4 p.m., she thought.

"I would imagine," he said, reining in his words as he reined in the horses.

Is he pouting about the separate rooms?

"Let's go get cleaned up before supper."

He got their bags and helped her out of the buggy. He stared into her eyes a moment. *So different.* She stared back. *Except they both live a double standard.* Sophya turned and took the lead.

"This looks just like in the cowboy movies I've seen on television!" she whispered as he checked them in at the desk.

He laughed. His mood seemed to perk up at her childish excitement. "What's movies and television?" he asked.

Sophya laughed, but not sarcastically. "It's a glass-front box that shows...*shows!*" was all she could think to say. "Pre-recorded, *moving* pictures!"

He mulled that over. "That sounds nice," he said as he ushered her up the stairs. Once in front of her room, he handed her the key.

"I'm down at the *end* of the hall." He nodded in that direction.

She didn't know if that had been to appease her or give her general information, or an invitation.

She just gave a tight-lipped smile.

"I'll be back for you in about an hour for us to go to supper."

"Thank you," Sophya said and just kept smiling until she made sure he walked away. Then she let herself in and sighed with relief.

***

"My dress still looks OK today. Thanks for having it pressed for me. But, had I known, I would have worn something different yesterday."

William glanced at her dress, then at her face. "What's the matter, I'm not worth wearing it for? You will still be able to swagger ole Richard when he sees how blue it makes your eyes look."

She raised her eyebrows and gave a curt smile.

They had been gone from Mansfield about a half hour, heading into woodsier country, narrower roads. *Beautiful*, Sophya mused.

"Swagger?" she later said and acted offended. "He's married," she added.

"So are you," he reminded her. "Oh come now, we men know you women like to use your *wiles* to attract us!"

"Wiles?" Sophya questioned. "That sounds like something connected with the *devil*!"

He laughed heartily. His mood had been lighter today. He seemed pleased at the big fuss she had made over the good food they were served last night. He let her know he had it brought in from Shreveport and had left it with the innkeeper on his way back to Morristown the day before yesterday. She still couldn't believe this William made such a big fuss over her. She certainly was not used to it.

"I guess the devil did make me eat too much last night!" she commented.

"Is that why I saw you walking it off downtown early this morning?" he asked.

"You saw me?"

He smiled.

"Maybe," she said coyly. "But I really wanted to take it all in so I could *write* about it! It's so different...all the hubbub. They say General Taylor has well set-up hospital stations here for later," she added.

He stared an extra long time at her face, until it made her feel uncomfortable and she looked away.

"It was too dangerous with a *war* going on around here," he said sternly. "And, here I thought I was letting you have extra rest."

She raised her eyebrows, non-committing, not knowing if he had a real concern or a really controlling nature, like his twin.

She just sighed, so as to end the conversation. He had been

good at picking up on that, too. That was totally opposite from the real Will.

***

After they left the woods country and Pleasant Hill, they came to farming country, with corn and cotton.

"Let's stop here by the creek and take a break," William remarked.

He helped her down then spread a blanket near the stream. Sophya watched him but didn't move. Then he took some sandwiches and cool tea in a jar and water out. She still didn't get closer. She couldn't even bring herself to offer to help.

William stopped right in front of her, with his hands full. "I'm sorry for pushing myself on you before. Please, forgive me."

Sophya was sure he saw her eyes water. She felt her throat constrict and swallowed hard. *We always think these things are our own fault.*

"I will not do it again. That's not what this trip is for. Please, won't you sit with me and take a break?"

Forgiveness has to come on the part of a *real* Christian whether the offender asks for it, changes, or not. Trust, however, is whole 'nother story.

Her mouth was so dry she almost couldn't speak. She looked at his familiar, but un-familiar face. She thought of how the disciples didn't recognize Jesus' face when He came back after the cross. But that was a *totally* different situation.

Sophya let out a very, deep sigh, and turned and walked to the blanket and sat down.

This time, William stayed silent, mostly, only making small talk, serving her occasionally. *So different.* They passed through the busy city of Natchitoches, only to stop and be refreshed.

Chapter Twelve

A Mighty Man of Valor: General Richard Taylor

("And the Angel of the Lord appeared unto him and said unto him, 'The Lord is with thee, thou mighty man of valor." Judges 6:12)

Late that afternoon, William and Sophya arrived at Beasley's Landing. Once there, they saw a barn made into a store. It stood near a wide stretch of the Red River. The river looked so inviting. Sophya had begun to perspire as the heat of the day had worn on. Then it began letting up into a gentle breeze.

"There's your hero."

Sophya looked up and saw a man sitting on a log under the cool shade of a tree near the store. He was whittling on a stick.

"Wow," she said, in awe.

William drove closer and stopped the buggy.

"Hawkins!" the man called out.

"Hello, General Taylor," William spoke to his friend.

"How'd you get such a pretty woman to be seen riding with you?" Taylor asked.

Sophya smiled. She liked him immediately.

William hopped down, laced the reins to the tree and helped Sophya down.

"I promised her a kingdom and an interview with the king!" William answered smugly humorous.

He and Richard Taylor laughed.

Sophya smiled but she was so scared! She couldn't even walk to meet him!

"General Richard Taylor, meet Miss Sophya Blackwell," the Reverend said.

"How do you do, Miss Sophya Blackwell?" Gen. Taylor asked.

I will settle this 'Miss' part later. She smiled a toothy grin at William and looked back at Gen. Taylor.

"I am too hot and sweaty to meet a General!" she exclaimed nervously. He had gotten up to greet her. He stood about her same height, though stories she had read would make him out to be six foot five! He looked like Henry Fonda. He had brown hair and a beard. He was a nice-looking man.

"I don't bite, like your partner, here," he nodded to William, who stood stark still, not knowing how Sophya might respond to that.

She wondered how Gen. Taylor knew!

"I hope not!" she said and they all laughed as Sophya shook his hand excitedly.

"I understand you want to interview me," her hero said.

"Yes," she said shyly.

"Why?"

She glanced at William, not knowing how to answer. Rev. Hawkins smiled like she was on her own but with an assured wink like he thought she could handle it.

So different, she thought, and looked away from him and back to Gen. Taylor. She didn't know if Gen. Taylor was being humble or inquisitive. So she waited to speak.

"Let's sit down," he said. He sat back down on the log, making room for her. He seemed at ease enough. "I apologize there are no other accommodations."

She reached for her quill and ink and paper in her little handbag and started to sit on the ground in front of him, to his surprise. "It's OK," Sophya said.

"Wait!" William rushed get the blanket out of the buggy and spread it on the ground. She stared in amazement at his concern.

"Whoa-ho!" Taylor exclaimed.

"Always willing to oblige a lady." William smiled as he bowed to her and Gen. Taylor. Then, he brought out a small stool. "Do you want this Sophya?"

She didn't really want to take her eyes off of the general. Afraid he'd disappear, she just glanced back at William and shook her head and sat on the blanket.

"Well, I'll take it," he said. "Mind if I sketch you, General?" He pulled out his tablet and a charcoal pencil.

General Taylor's head snapped back as he laughed. "I'm famous!" he joked.

Sophya and William spoke up, "Yes!"

He laughed again and smiled a comforting smile.

"No ma'am, not that famous."

"You will be one day," she said sincerely. "That's why I want to be the *first* one to interview you!"

"Thank you. Thank you, young lady, but I doubt it."

"Plus, we have the same birthday!"

"January 27th?" he asked.

She nodded vigorously.

"I'll be. How'd you find *that* out?"

She raised her eyebrows and took a deep breath, placing her finger over her lips, like it was a big secret.

He and William laughed.

"Where are your tents?" she looked around.

"My tents! Oh, no ma'am. My men sleep out under the sky. So do I. Besides, that's too much to carry around and make a quick exit with good timing."

"Oh," she said, still hating to lose his gaze, but she needed to start making notes. She dipped the quill slowly in the ink and tried to write with it. "Ugh!"

William laughed.

Gen. Taylor's eyebrows raised.

"Uh, I think I'll use this one," she took out her mom's pen.

Taylor blinked. "Is that something new?"

"Another *type* of ink pen," she assured him. Then she began to interview him.

200

"How are you feeling?" she knew of his bouts with rheumatoid arthritis.

"Is this part of the interview?" he asked laughing.

"Nooo," she blushed.

William laughed too.

"Stiff," came the general's answer. "But pretty good-- all things considered."

"You look relaxed," she noticed.

He smiled as if wondering if this was part of the interview too. "Looks are deceiving, dear. My reconnaissance are out right now. My men and I are ready to leave quickly, if need be."

"Oh," she looked around for the enemy.

"You're safe, for now," he added.

Sophya sighed. "I was afraid you might not let me interview you unless I was someone important like Belle Boyd or something."

He laughed and slapped his knee. "You know about that?"

"Why, I heard she gave the best soldier report ever received over there in the Shenandoah Valley, for a female civilian!" Sophya answered smartly.

"How'd you hear about *that*?"

"From a friend, who has a friend, who has a cousin!"

They laughed together.

Gen. Taylor thought a minute. "Yes, that was the great days with Stonewall Jackson. Great man. He thought I was wicked though!" They laughed. "But, I am thankful to be interviewed by someone who will tell the truth," he sighed, eyes piercing.

"Yes," she answered. "I will. I think if that doesn't work, though, I'll pose incognito as a female Confederate soldier and write the rest!"

"Oh, there's none of those around here!" He winked at William.

"Are you sure?" Sophya had a mischievous look on her face, knowing about the girl that stowed away and fought with him at Mansfield, but wasn't discovered until later.

He didn't miss a beat. "Why, do you want to come along?"

"I hadn't thought about that!" she quickly turned to William for permission.

"No!" he said emphatically

They laughed--teaming together against her.

"What do you think of this *Reverend*?" she asked aggravatedly.

"Oh, I've known William Hawkins a long time," the General said. "He's a good businessman." Then he leaned close to her. His hazel eyes had a sparkle in them; even after all he'd been through. "But I don't like his preaching!"

He and Sophya laughed heartily.

William cleared his throat loudly and blurted, "This is about Taylor, not me."

She smiled mischievously at Gen. Taylor and said, "I'll behave."

He smiled back in camaraderie.

She cleared her throat and began the real interview.

"First, General Taylor, let me say what an honor and privilege this is that you have given me."

He nodded humbly. "The honor is mine."

"I have followed your career since learning we had such a distinguished son of President Zachary Taylor, residing in Louisiana with us."

He smiled and closed his eyes in a moment of memories, it appeared, of the former Louisiana in better times.

"Word has come back to me, from my relatives fighting in this cruel war, of your bravery and your loyalty. The uniqueness of how you were chosen, one of merely three, to be Brigadier General without even prior military experience other than graduating from Yale for your military training and serving as secretary of war to your father in Mexico. It is amazing."

Taylor had a poker face, whether in humbleness or his experience being called in question, she knew not. But he did know, her motives and admiration were sincere and genuine.

"My experience makes others wonder about it, too."

Sophya smiled a disbelieving smile, turning her head slightly, but chose to ignore his remark. "I may not beat you at a game of chess, but your reported brilliance in strategy and bravery amidst all odds has won mine and other's admiration. Surely it needs to be recorded in history. Is that reason enough for you?"

He smiled. "Genius is God-given, but men are responsible for their acts, as I've said before."

She took that in for a moment and wrote it down.

"I believe you saw the whole, big picture of this ugly war in advance. Since you were educated up North...you had friends on both sides and were against secession, right?"

He nodded and glanced up, from his thoughts, at her. "Think we'll win?"

She was silent, and then offered a non-committal smile.

He raised his brows to William, who stopped doing his sketch to look up.

She continued, "Talk about your opinion of both sides and of the conventions."

He sighed and said, "Let me say, first, thank you, Miss Sophya, for your comments and for coming. I will also say: I am just a man. I love this country and my state of Louisiana and freedom, like you apparently do, too. I have made many mistakes and will probably make more. So, keep that pedestal at ground level, please, ma'am."

She smiled.

He went on. "It's true I had friends on both sides. I went into the convention with the opinion the North and South should stay together. Yancey...Have you heard of him?"

She shook her head affirmative.

"Yancey and his Alabama crew wanted to secede, which brought Florida, Mississippi, Arkansas, and Texas to follow. After I spoke with him in private, he changed his mind. But, unfortunately, he couldn't change his friends' minds.

"After Alabama withdrew, the convention split moving to

Baltimore and Richmond, and Lincoln got elected to serve the North, as you know. But, in the beginning, even General Butler supported Jefferson Davis as president, along with others from New England. New York and some westerners wanted Douglas. Then, Jefferson Davis was chosen as president of the southern seceding states."

Sophya wrote quickly, "Hold on a moment."

He smiled at William. "Make me look young and good-looking, Rev."

William laughed. "I would, but you want this to be truthful!"

Laughter.

"What's your opinion of the differences of North and South's abilities?"

"Well, as you stated, I had been schooled up North. My dad had been the President. But, I fell in love, down South and *with* the South. I have a sugar plantation around the French settlements of Louisiana and also my wife's relatives."

"In 1861, my French friend, former governor Mouton of Louisiana, appointed me to be Chairman of the Military Defense. So, I scavenged around," he shook his head, "And found us lacking in ammunition and military training for the officers. It amazed me how the southern representatives were so complacent about these issues. I set out to rectify the situation."

"The southerners are truly braver and better horsemen and gun handlers, being farm boys and hunters. However, the Texans refused to walk anywhere. They said they *ride!* I had to train them how to march in infantry and keep up."

She smiled and glanced back at William, who had said that very same thing, but he was engrossed in sketching.

"Others saw the good effects of this and later asked for help in these areas of marching, which I willingly gave them."

"The North, being manufacturers, are superior to the South in numbers and wealth and mechanical resources, also in commanding the sea." He raised his brows and sighed.

Sophya looked up and sadly shook her head and said, "Wait," and wrote some more.

Gen. Taylor smiled. "Fear not, au contraire, we're not down for the count, yet, m'lady!"

She took in a deep breath. "In your opinion, why are we fighting this war?"

He shook his head again, sadly, then answered. "Cotton, greed, politics, and the lust for land, on the North's part. Oh, it may go down in history as being solely because of slaves in the South, but that's something started by some of the northern Abolitionists. Most of the southerners would send their sons off to fight instead of their darkie counterparts. They refer to them as servants instead of slaves. I have tried to start movements to send the Negroes back to Africa to their homes, but the North has not even been compassionate on that issue. No, my dear, on the whole, I've witnessed the Yanks treat Negroes as badly as some southern plantation owners. The enemy uses them for their infantry, and then leaves them behind, unaided, unattended; left to fend for themselves, and starve and die after skirmishes."

He sighed. "They just don't have as much need for them up north, not farming as much as having factories. Some can't afford them, but some do have them and are reconciling the chance of losing them too."

"Do you think some want to stay on their plantations?"

"It's true the Negroes didn't ask to be brought over to serve the southern plantations and *certainly* not to be abused." He looked over at William. Sophya slowly looked up from her writing. William stopped sketching a minute, and remained silent.

Taylor began again. "Some don't want to be uprooted from their protection and provender. Not all are mistreated, Miss Sophya. Mine aren't. But they are free to come and go. What's sad is; it was their own race that sold them into slavery to the traders to begin with. It just makes me sick that people treat people like that. That's why I believe I'm fighting for freedom and States' rights to choose what we want."

"Do you believe the Confederates have too much southern pride?" she asked.

William cleared his throat.

Taylor glanced over at him. "To be sure, Miss Blackwell."

She smiled unexpectedly at his admitting this.

"Pride in oneself or what one does may not always be a bad thing." The sparkle came back to his eyes. "But, this is about cotton and control, even probably to the extent of covetousness. Or, the North wanting to stamp out something they don't understand."

"Amen," William finally felt he could agree.

Sophya looked back at him, then Gen. Taylor and added, "That's probably true about a lot of things, but we all probably long to be free in America. That's what we're founded for."

"Yes ma'am," he said.

"You have been involved in three of the most important theatres of the war: Virginia, Tennessee, and now, the Trans-Mississippi Dept. What has been the most memorable so far?" she inquired.

Gen. Taylor looked at William. "This girl does her homework. Who did you say you were with?" he faced her again.

Sophya explained. "Not anybody, really, but I hope to get a copy of this interview to the Mansfield newspaper. With your permission of course."

He nodded. "Granted," he said.

She looked back at William.

He agreed.

Pen in position she glanced up for Gen. Taylor to continue.

"To answer your question, I will say the most memorable times were spent with Stonewall Jackson. He was unusual. He had his quirks, but brave in battle. He was a strong leader and full of faith."

"Did he really keep a stock of lemons to eat at all times?" she excitedly ask.

Richard Taylor glanced at William and back to Sophya. "How did you know about that?"

206

She smiled demurely.

"Yes!" he stated and leaned towards her and laughed.

Some of Gen. Richard Taylor's men were starting to notice their conversation and Sophya began to get anxious to complete the interview.

"General Taylor, tell me something of this campaign you're involved in now, and some of the leaders on both sides, and perhaps, what you hope to accomplish."

He raised his eyebrows. "How long did you say you plan to stay? We may have to take arms up before then!"

"Pleeeze," she pleaded.

William laughed.

Gen. Taylor sighed, fatigue showing, with a distant look in his eyes.

"I'll try." He stretched his hands out on his knees. "Louisiana is in a unique position, being located west of the Mississippi River and next to Texas. We are not like Mississippi, having a strategically located city of Vicksburg on the river. We lost New Orleans almost without a fight, then Vicksburg, too, by dragging our feet. Most of our men have been off fighting in other states' battles."

"The coveted state of Texas, this 'Red River Campaign' to save it, is what this is all about. The Union wants Texas because it has even more cotton than Louisiana. They also want it before France or Mexico claims it."

Sophya's eyes got big and she sighed, acting like she didn't know that.

"As early as last summer, Kirby Smith and I agreed that General Halleck might push to go into Louisiana. We were told General Grant wanted to take Mobile first. But," he hesitated, "he was overruled. General Banks was sent to New Orleans. The South thought they could take it back from him at that point."

"It's a shame how easily we lost New Orleans in '62 to Farragut's Fleet." Gen. Taylor looked down. "We got stopped the second time we tried, at Baton Rouge. General Mouton tried hard to

207

regain it, but couldn't. Louisiana had no soldiers, no arms, no ammunition and a lot of rivers and streams for easy access." He stopped, and then added, "I was determined Louisiana wasn't going to be *'lost without even a shot being fired'!"*

Sophya looked then at her notes and smiled. She heard William say, "Amen."

Richard Taylor continued. "I set out to round up men and horses and supplies. Major Brent was excellent help at getting supplies from out of nowhere. The French people of Louisiana were very brave. They helped us a lot."

"We set up protection of the salt wells with Judge Avery's help around Lafayette. I knew the topography of the land, which was an advantage over the Feds. When we had gained momentum, General Kirby Smith pulled my men and the ones under General John Walker from Texas to come help. We had to stand guard across the river from Vicksburg. He placed us near Monroe. We could have had victory at Vicksburg almost a year ago if General Smith would have struck while the iron was hot! But instead, he ordered us to at least, 'make a good show' and *'do something'* at that late date!"

William and Sophya commiserated with his frustration and sighed. Sophya, being inexperienced, excitedly, interrupted and said, "I met General Green and General DeBray at William's party last week!"

Gen. Taylor replied, "Oh whoa," and looked at William, his eyes penetrating. "Entertaining Green are you? You better let him attend to the plan at hand."

William's lips were tight, not knowing what Sophya would say next. He probably worried that she'd mention Andrew Hamilton, too, but she didn't.

"Two good men, Green's supposed to be on his way here now."

"You believe in that *Napoleonic Code* of striking while the enemy is confused?"

"Mercy!" he showed surprise. "Yes, I do." Gen. Taylor calmly spoke. Then his blood pressure seemed to rise. "Too bad I can't get Kirby Smith to agree."

William coughed.

"Oh yes, Kirby's a friend of yours, huh, William."

The Rev looked stoic.

Sophya continued, "What happened next on the Red River?"

"General A. J. Smith and his men reeked havoc along the river...burning property, stealing cotton."

Sophya wrote as Taylor spoke.

"I knew Ft. DeRussy and any other earthwork like that would be a sitting duck target for the Feds. but, General *Kirby* Smith insisted on our attempting to finish it. A. J. Smith was well trained by General Sherman in the area of devastation by the North. He conquered DeRussy. Several were killed." Richard Taylor became silent a moment, but didn't mention that A. J. Smith killed some of his own men in the process.

"And," Taylor added, "two hundred and fifty of our men were taken prisoners. When that ice storm blew in the other day, Colonel Vincent and his men were surrounded and taken--in that mud and ice--by General Mower and his men. That was most of my Calvary--gone."

Sophya looked numb, even though she had already been told that.

"What do you think of the North's plan of accompanying their men on land with Admiral Porter's fleet by water?" she asked.

"Not much," Taylor answered.

William laughed.

She glanced back as if to look at him but didn't. She did not want to lose the seriousness of this moment. "Why?" she persisted.

"Except for that last ice storm, you may know, we've been in a drought. As we speak, General Porter and his men will try to go over some very low falls at Alexandria. General Banks is there to win another *fixed* election, so to speak."

"You don't think much of General Banks, do you?"

"Tuh," Gen. Taylor muttered. "He's a *grandiose* one! But, I observed his tactics before. He's about as good a strategist as McClellan on the Peninsula Campaign. All talk, not much action."

"Hmm," Sophya mumbled.

So did William.

"What's next, General?"

"Well, we have awaited Green's troops from Texas, but don't write that."

She nodded.

"I have been made aware that General Walker's men have been detained in Shreveport by Kirby Smith. There's one you ought to interview, and if you figure *him* out, tell me!" he said emphatically.

"What do you mean?"

"He thinks the main theatre of this war in this state needs to be fought in Shreveport since Steele's army is descending from Arkansas. But I've insisted that the only possible way to defeat Steele's movement is to whip the enemy *now* in the heart of the Red River."

Sophya determined Gen. Taylor was getting antsy with these last statements. She hastened her reply and her end to the interview.

"We saw how you've prepared Mansfield and heard of supply stations you've set up along the way. Some say troops are to meet you from Keatchie, also, am I right?"

He smiled and slowly nodded. "But that's not to be common knowledge either."

Sophya nodded and looked back at William, who had stopped sketching long ago, and then she turned back to Taylor. "We have *no* doubt *victory* is within your hands and in the near future."

William added, "Amen."

Gen. Taylor expressed his gratitude for their vote of confidence.

Sophya got up and went to shake his hand, but decided to hug him instead. "God bless."

His voice cracked, "God bless you."

William shook Taylor's hand and said, "Thanks," and showed him the sketch.

Sophya peeked around his shoulder. The picture showed her sitting on the blanket interviewing Gen. Taylor!

She sucked in her breath and Gen. Taylor said, "Wow." His appreciation appeared real.

William's gratitude seemed to be truly genuine.

***

Sophya sat in awe in the buggy on the way back to Natchitoches. She kept looking through her notes and correcting some, and stating, "My, my."

William laughed at her inability to say more, for once.

"You did a very good interview," he stated.

She looked over, her eyes wide at that compliment.

***

They arrived at the bustling city of Natchitoches and checked into a hotel there. Sophya didn't even think to distrust William at this point. They dined at a Spanish restaurant first. She had a good time. *Am I beginning to trust him?*

He walked her to her door. She put her key into the lock, saying, "Thank you, so much and hope you have a good-night's rest." William turned her around and kissed her. "Stop!"she said, pushing him away and looked at him indignantly.

"Can't you do anything just to be nice, without expecting payment back for it?"

She opened the door, walked in and slammed it in his face!

Note: This interview is purely fictitious, and from the imagination of the author of this book. However, the answers, opinions and quotes of Gen. Richard were attained from: *Destruction*

& Reconstruction, by Richard Taylor; *Red River Campaign,* by Ludwell H. Johnson; and *Richard Taylor: Soldier Prince of Dixie,* by T. Michael Parrish.

Chapter Thirteen
A Sawmill Town

("What God hath cleansed, let no man call common." Acts 10:15)

Dawn rose a rosy red, Tuesday, March 29th.

"Red sky at morning, sailor take warning," Sophya mumbled to herself, looking out of the east window.

Today she planned to ride around the countryside alone. The longing to see how unfamiliar this old familiar county was so many years ago burned within her. So did her desire to be alone and think.

Anya, not being a morning person, was not awake yet. "She may need my company, with Beth gone," Sophya expressed out loud, "but today *I* need my company more."

She wanted to try and gain a clear perspective of why all this was happening.

Katy knocked lightly at the door and came in. "I heard you stirring, so I brought some warm water for you to wash with."

It's amazing how people bond and can change their attitudes and actions. "Thanks, Katy."

She smiled. "Master William left early on horseback. He still has to fix the buggy wheel. He wants you to go in the wagon today for your travels. He asked Brooks to take you."

"Brooks!" Sophya immediately tried to hide her emotions after her outburst. "I mean—great!" She smiled a fake smile.

A surprising, mischievous grin slowly came on Katy's face.

Blushing and looking down, Sophya shook her head masking her own smile and sighed, giving in.

"Okayyy."

"He'll be here in half an hour," she said, and walked out of the room.

After Katy left, Sophya moaned, "Oh, gosh. So much for my *clear* perspective on things today!"

Within thirty minutes she brushed past Lillie while she dusted the hutch in the dining room. Bumping her, Sophya said, "Oops!"

Lillie stopped, so as to gain Sophya's full attention and pointed to the Mosaic vase and snickered.

Sophya shook her head and whispered, "*I'm really married in another life, you know!*"

With her voice lowered Lillie stated, "*Dat was den, dis is now. What you tank he's doin' while you away?*"

Sophya rolled her eyes and noticed Lillie looked a little peeked. "You OK?"

Lillie smiled and nodded and quickly turned back to her dusting.

Sophya opened the door to go out to the kitchen. Mama Sara was humming. She stopped when Sophya came in. "Mistah Brooks not up wid da wagon yet. Have some brekfas'." She had her back to Sophya.

"I can't, yet." Her nerves were too active.

Sara slowly turned to peer into Sophya's face, and then turned back around.

"I'd love some coffee, though."

She took a cup from the shelf and poured the hot coffee from the stove top into it.

She reached to where the spoons were kept.

Sara, slowly, distrustfully, looked back at her hand to watch it. She turned back before she saw Sophya shake her head. *If I was going to steal a knife, I'd have done it by now,* Sophya thought disgustedly.

She heard the wagon drive up, so she stood up and started for the door.

"Wait, chile," she heard Mama Sara say. It surprised her so much her mouth fell open. Was that a sly smile she caught on Sara's face from this side?

Those words brought back a flood of warm memories. Sophya was eleven. She had a crush on Richard Crow in the fifth grade. There was to be a party at his house for his birthday. He had invited her. He and his mom were coming to get Sophya and drive her there. She heard their car drive up and started to run out of the door. "Wait, child," she heard her mother say. "He needs to come to the door and knock for you to come."

Her eyes misted over. *Oh, Mom, I miss you so much.*

Brooks knocked on the back door. "Come in," Sara and Sophya said together. Sophya laughed. Sara just shook her head and smiled.

"Well…" Brooks commented, glancing from Sophya to Sara, wondering about the joke. Then he saw her misted eyes. With one thumb, he wiped a tear. "What have I missed?"

The look in his eyes was so intense something shivered within her.

Mama Sara glanced back at what transpired between them then turned back to her stirring. "No telling," she murmured.

Brooks and Sophya laughed. Sophya looked away and wiped the other tear, shyly, and asked, "Ready?"

His eyes showed surprise then compassion. He stepped down the two outside steps and held out his hand to guide her. What a lovely, strong, tan hand her eyes beheld. *I will take this hand offered.*

He was dressed in buckskin britches and a regular, western shirt that almost disguised his Indian heritage, but not his good looks or muscular chest. *What a lovely, strong person,* she also mused.

He helped her step up to the wagon's padded seat. Her skirt was not as cumbersome as she thought it would be. He sat beside her and looked at her eyes and then her lips. His penetrating green eyes were so desirable, along with his tan skin and brown hair.

"Where to?" he asked.

She looked ahead and thought, *that could have a world of answers.* All she could finally say was, "Hmm," as she looked straight ahead again.

He laughed, realizing he affected something within her.

"I know a place," he declared, rescuing the moment.

"Alright," she replied, regaining her composure enough to smile then look back at his handsome face. "Let's go."

Brooks steered the wagon to the road in front of the plantation home and headed east. They rode past where her great-grandmother's house would be later, then cousin's and her other aunt's. Nothing but trees and pasture now. Sophya failed to notice these things on her tense trip with *Master* William.

Brooks turned down the road by the church. Sophya thought of Reverend William Hawkins' two-faced, controlling sermon. She had walked with Lillie that day and they came to know one another deeper, right here on this spot. Sammy had been baptized in the river nearby that Sunday. Sophya chose to "think on these things," as instructed in Philippians 4:8 instead of William.

She sighed and glanced at Brooks, realizing he was allowing her revere, and said, "We are quiet."

"You were thinking," he replied with a smile. "Things must look very different."

"You *believe* me!"

He looked and saw her face light up with excitement. "Truth is truth whether anyone chooses to believe it or not. Isn't that what you said? It's the truth to you, yes?"

"Yes."

"Then it must *be* the truth."

She sighed with relief on that note. "Yes, thanks, and yes, things do look very different."

"Tell me what it looks like in your time." His request *seemed* sincere.

"Well, we just passed where my great-grandmother's house will be. She's the one with the well on her porch. Next to her are my cousin's and his parent's homes, which is her son, Bob, and grandson, Cleve, and their wives," Sophya stated happily.

"Later my grandfather, her son-in-law, enlarges and adds bricks to the outside of this church that William preaches in. He is the one with the Cherokee grandmother," she smiled.

216

"You have a good heritage, then?" he asked.

"Yes."

Brooks turned the wagon north to where the county line would soon be. Acres of cotton lay planted to the west. Corn spread out on the acres to the east. "Wow," she glanced at him, "I'd heard, but I never imagined how much cotton and corn were here!"

"Panolo--cotton," he stated. "That caused this war," he said sadly.

"Yes," Sophya remarked. Surprised, she turned to him and asked, "You knew?"

"Oh, yes, many *know*," he answered.

The mood changed. "Let's talk of something lighter."

"OK," he replied.

Brooks steered the wagon northward up the dirt road. When they were about to be adjacent to where his cabin would be--past the woods to the left--she looked to the right.

"Wow!" she exclaimed again. There were probably forty Indian residences lying out across the plains area. It looked like they extended to the Sabine River. Some were tent-shaped, made of leather hides. Some were dome shaped, made with tied timbers. Sophya sat mesmerized over the sight. There were a few wooden buildings. She looked at Brooks and shook her head disbelieving it.

"Is this your people?"

"This is a mixture of Indian nations. Some Caddo, some Cherokee, a few Choctaw left, and the ones called Tejas, the Texas Indians."

"That word means friendly!" she excitedly bragged on her knowledge.

"I know," he smiled and added, "the Caddo have been here the longest, for hundreds of years, though."

"Are you the Spiritual Leader of them all?"

"Yes, they have chosen me to be," he said modestly.

Sophya eyes scanned the area as the wagon stopped. There were almost a hundred people: men, women and children. Some were at

217

campfires cooking; some were grinding what looked like corn. Some were tanning hides, some cutting and smoothing timbers. Children laughed and played. In one area, some were being taught to basket weave.

"Wow," she kept saying.

He smiled. "Want to meet them?"

Sophya nodded slowly, with a mixture of anticipation and fear.

Brooks dismounted and came to help her down from the wagon.

"Will they want to scalp me?"

"Not today. Today is Friday."

She crumbled laughing, relieving her stress.

"This is amazing that they live and work together even though they have so many different backgrounds," she said.

"The different tribes are tired. Tired of running, and fighting, and tired of traveling--and giving up so much. They have found something to unify *against* but cohabitate *with.*" Brooks had a distant look in his eyes.

She stared at him. "The white man?"

"Yes. Come. I'll show you."

"Will they accept me?"

He led her by her arm. "They will accept you because you are with me."

She glanced cautiously at him, analyzing his reply. *Should I trust him? Should I trust that he would ever want someone like me to truly be with him?*

They came first to a young brave drying hides. He looked up in surprise.

"*Wind,* meet my friend, Sophya."

He smiled so searchingly. He stood and held her hand a moment. Brooks cleared his throat and Wind let her hand go and nodded.

"Nice to meet you," she replied.

"Same," he answered. He went back to his work, but he

watched as they walked away.

Brooks smiled. "His name is 'Goes with the Wind,' but we shorten things now, too, like the white man."

"He seems so sad," Sophya commented.

"He lost his wife a few months ago."

She became stricken with pity. Brooks saw it cross her face.

"Grief is a process. All must go through it. No *one* or *thing* can shorten it for us." He held out his hand and pointed for them to continue walking.

They came to an old woman studying her Bible. She looked at Sophya with such wisdom in her eyes. "*Shake*, meet Sophya."

Sophya looked from Brooks to the woman, trying to conceal a smile.

"Her name is *Shaking Rock*," they smiled at each other. "Her counsel is highly regarded by the others and me." He touched her cheek. Sophya saw mutual admiration.

Sophya clasped her hand. "I could use some of that sometime."

"Anytime." Her eyes were penetrating, her hand, welcoming.

An older warrior walked up. "Who do you bring?"

This caught her off guard. Sophya thought of many things when she looked at his weather-worn face: wisdom, compassion, knowledge, caution.

"Chief *Hawk*, meet Sophya, my friend. She is a visitor of William Hawkins'."

"That he *shares* her is a surprise," Chief Hawk replied, patting her shoulder.

She didn't contain her laugh that time.

Brooks shook his head and smiled. "Man can't be everywhere at one time, like God." *He meant William!*

Hawk patted Brooks' shoulder, laughed and said, "Miss Sophya."

He nodded and continued walking in the same direction he had been walking in and stopped to talk briefly to another, older squaw.

"Hello, Shy But Bold!" Brooks acknowledged her also as they

walked past.

Sophya presumed she was Chief Hawk's wife.

"There are many situations we may find ourselves in in this life. Not all may be unpleasant." He stopped at the group where a lovely dark-haired Indian woman was teaching the children to make baskets. "*Shining Star,* meet Sophya." Sophya wondered why Brooks said that prior to this introduction.

Star hopped up and took both of Sophya's hands into her hard-working hands. Sophya almost felt ashamed that her own hands must feel so pampered. She vainly, constantly covered her hands with lotion since they were in chemicals often as a beautician.

"So glad to make your acquaintance." Star's eyes sparkled like deep midnight blue crystals that Sophya had never seen before. She appeared so friendly and at ease, and so pretty!

"Is this the visiting woman you have told me about, Running Brook?" Her high esteem for Brooks showed in her eyes. It may even have bordered on love.

"Yes." He met her gaze with compassion.

Uh oh, Sophya thought.

"You may call me 'Star.' Would you like to sit for a session?" She spoke good English with pride.

Sophya glanced at Brooks.

"This is *your* day." He made it sound like a gift.

She looked back at Star and decided to quickly take a place by one of the young girls who had patted the ground where she wanted Sophya to sit by her. "What's your name?"

"Heather," she excitedly stated. "Lavender Heather."

Sophya's surprise must have shown at the lovely name and the lovely girl. They bonded immediately. *This must be what's called a spirit friend*, Sophya thought. She also thought so of Lillie as being a "Spirit friend" at that moment. "What a beautiful name."

Brooks nodded. "Excuse me," he said and walked a distance to talk to Chief Hawk.

Heather handed Sophya some of her pine straw to weave with.

Star began explaining to Sophya and the children how to gather the straw, tie it in bundles, and weave the smaller groups together. They practiced.

"Fascinating!" Sophya said excitedly. The children laugh at her. Star gently silenced them and continued teaching.

About that time a young, white, male child wandered by. "Sophya, would you take *Wandering Dependence* by the hand and lead him over here to study with us? His parents left him with us while they are traveling and looking for work. We are trying to help him," Star said.

"Sure!" She went and spoke kindly to him and asked him to join them. He seemed glad to have direction for the time being.

Then, a Caucasian infant child ran from out of nowhere and leaped into her arms! She looked into Sophya's eyes with her crystal blue eyes and hugged her and held on tight.

"Oh, my goodness!" Star said, and reached over to take the child from her. "Her parents need our help right now, but don't want to join our group yet. She looked at the child smiling up to her. "We call her *Bright Follower.*"

About that time, Brooks came back to their group. Sophya excused herself and stood up.

"Come back anytime!" Heather's sky blue eyes were imploring.

"Yes," Sophya smiled and touched her cheek. Touching Dependence and Bright Follower on the cheek, also, she said goodbye to the rest of them.

"Thank you so much," Sophya said to Star.

"Here," she happily offered. "Take this!" She gave her a finished basket.

Her graciousness caught Sophya off guard. "I... thank you, again."

Then, Star reached to touch Brooks' hand.

What passed through her? Jealousy? Oh, no! *She's so kind and beautiful, and he is not mine, nor am I free to be his.*

Another older, graceful Squaw stopped and extended her hand. "I am Generous Spirit. If ever you get the chance, come visit me one day."

Sophya smiled and said, "OK!" and looked at Brooks.

He nodded at the woman then told Star goodbye, and almost, possessively, put his arm against Sophya's waist, guiding her on.

"Come," was the only word that accompanied his intense look into her eyes.

She sighed and began walking, not wanting to separate from his touch, but wondering. She didn't understand the silence that ensued between them. She just knew she couldn't speak at that moment.

Sophya looked up over the prairie and wished this moment—this safe, comforting, loving, strong-attraction moment—would last forever.

"How is your day?" It seemed like such a childlike, pure question.

She looked at the ground and at the grass. She compared it with the time she first walked with William and Anya to his plantation home a few weeks ago. She sighed again. "Promising," was all she could said.

Brooks laughed out loud. Their spirits lifted for the moment.

"Here is a woman you really need to meet. She can do everything with food, and does! *Heavy Spirit,* meet Sophya."

Sophya's eyes opened wide at this introduction. The woman was grinding corn. Her hands were not free to shake Sophya's. There before her stood a short, squaw woman.

"Pleased…" Sophya started to say.

"If everyone else would just do their part, I wouldn't *have* to do *everything*!"

Sophya smarted at that retort. Some delicious smelling corn bread in a pan lured her. Then she smelled vegetable soup in another pot.

"Sit! Sit!" Heavy Spirit pointed to stumps of pine trees cut in the shape of stools.

Brooks looked at Sophya. "Shall we?"

"I usually never turn down..." She hated to reveal this part of her..."Food."

Brooks laughed and tilted his head appearing to *know* that this was hard for her to admit.

The smell of the food made her stomach growl after no breakfast that morning.

Heavy Spirit ignored the communication that passed between them. "You take Chief Hawk, for example. He can be helping *you* more, too. You have to be our spiritual guide, consort with the white man, and do a dance to keep from being drawn into this war!"

Brooks and Sophya glanced at each other acknowledging she totally disregarded that Sophya was white also. He shook his head. "You let me be concerned about that. You have enough to do getting our supplies and making it last."

"And so *deliciously!*" Sophya added.

She briefly smiled at Sophya. "Still, the same, you ought to fire up your people more."

Brooks tilted his head another way, a reprimanding way.

"Well, I speak my mind," she added.

"Is not one's tongue to be controlled, also?" Brooks asked lovingly.

Heavy Spirit waved her hand around at Brooks, ending the conversation. She must have known he already ended it anyway.

Then, from out of no where came a lovely Indian woman walking fast. She stopped.

"Spirit Friend, this is Sophya."

She laughed. "How nice to meet you!"

Before Sophya could say anything, another stoic woman came up behind the first one. "There you are. Come let's make some *real* soup!" she said as she disdainfully looked at Heavy Spirit and her soup.

"Hmph!" Heavy Spirit murmured and continued stirring her pot.

223

"Hard Taskmaster, this is Sophya." *"These women always compete with each other,"* Brooks whispered.

She smiled and turned and walked away.

Sophya blinked her eyes at what just took place.

***

An hour later, Brooks and Sophya were seated in the wagon, riding north again.

"What do you think of this time and this mixed Indian nation now?" he asked.

Neither of the Williams would have asked my opinion…what a difference.

"In my time," she tried to think how to phrase this. "Society is trying to give restitution."

"Restitution?" Brooks questioned.

"Yes." She looked out across the vast farm land, thinking of how great freedom actually felt for one moment. She glanced into his beautiful eyes and smiled gently.

"They are attempting to pay back to the Indian, and the Negro later, after a time, probably and other religious people-- all that have been oppressed."

"Pay back," he said slowly as he gazed across the land in deep thought, also.

"Well, *give* back," she stammered, still not sure her words were correct.

He looked at her with amusement. "Do you believe that is possible?"

Sophya swallowed hard. It came to mind how the Indians were stolen from and killed. The rest, put on reservations. Fenced in. Lillie crossed her mind and how she'd been forced to give up her virtue. Other Negroes had been enslaved, beaten or killed. The Jews endured a horrendous Holocaust. Her father's grandmother, a Russian Jew, had been killed in a concentration camp. A picture even flashed through her mind of abused women and children, prisoners and martyred Christians. Even Christ on the cross. She swallowed again answering, "No."

Brooks squinted his eyes. He seemed to try and read for a moment of all things that may have passed through her mind. Things he didn't know yet, nor would he. But, he knew enough. He was an Indian, himself. No telling what *he'd* been through already. He was now living through the Civil War.

Sophya touched his arm to help get through this moment to the next one. "The river is over there to the right. There used to be a ferry there."

"There still is," he replied grinning.

There were more woods than she remembered. They came to the flat embankment where the ferry landed. Sophya saw it docked on the other side of the river, near the little town there. She looked at Brooks in surprise. She didn't wait for protocol. She hopped down and ran to the water while Brooks halted the horses and wagon. The day had warmed up. "Wee," she squealed.

He sat amazed and shook his head at her child-likeness. Then he got down from the buggy and walked over to her.

She sat on a log and began unlacing her borrowed boots that were a size too small for her *not so Cinderella* feet!

Brooks kneeled to help her.

"You love the water?" he asked.

"Yes," she said and inhaled the cool air that surrounded the water and trees.

"Most women in *my time*," he emphasized. "Wear shoes. Are you going to re-baptize yourself again?"

Sophya sat back and started laughing. "No, I don't think I've sinned, at least not so far today anyway. But Spring is here and it's too beautiful not to feel it beneath my toes!"

He laughed and continued, "You are not afraid of…"

She smirked. "Snakes? No! A person can't live their life in

fear!"

Sophya hopped up and ran to the riverbank to dip her toes in the cool water. About at that time, a five foot long water moccasin, slithered out of the water towards her.

"Yikes!" she screamed and ran back to hop on the log.

Brooks was quick. Before she could figure out what happened, she saw his knife in the snake's head.

"Phew," she wilted. She looked around all over before she stepped off the log. "I keep needing to say, 'thank you', for rescuing me. I apologize."

He smiled and with another quick swipe, he retrieved his knife, threw the snake into the river, rinsed and wiped his knife and re-sheathed it. "One must learn to add *caution* to their *exuberance* for life wouldn't you say?"

She blushed at his reproof.

He came and touched her shoulder and added, "These are really *unfamiliar* territories during this time period and need greater regard."

"Oh, they're not unfamiliar."

His eyes opened wide with surprise.

"Well, I mean, it's more *wooded.*"

Brooks waited for her explanation.

"I mean…well…"

He looked at her like he realized she was hiding something.

She blurted it out, "This is one of the places my husband and I used to take our children fishing!"

Brooks recoiled. "*Husband!* You have a husband and you have been staying with William Hawkins and have been alone with me?"

"Look, I didn't ask to be with either *one* of you!"

Brooks looked stunned, hurt.

That hurt her heart so much. "I mean, I'm *glad* to have met *you*!"

Brooks relaxed a little and awaited her explanation. She thought she almost saw anger rising in him, though.

Her confidence and her good mood began to slip away, as well as her brief interlude with happiness. She looked into his eyes imploringly.

"Well?"

"I am married."

Brooks closed his eyes and looked like she had slapped him.

"My marriage is bad. I have three children that I love dearly, though."

Brooks eyes opened wider.

"My husband has not been faithful to me."

Now she thought she saw a hint of sympathy coming from his eyes.

"I have been in the process of deciding whether I want a divorce or not. We have not been in the same bed together for a year now."

He thought for a minute. "What have you decided?"

"I don't know."

Brooks lifted his eyebrows and sighed. "This trip to stay with Hawkins is to decide if you wanted *him* instead?"

"No! I told you the *truth* about that! My younger sister and I were just walking down my mother's driveway and decided to go into this old barn and check it out. *What* a deal! It was *1980*! We ended up in *William's* barn and back in *1864*! He acted real offended we bothered him while he practiced his sermon!"

Brooks sighed.

"We tried to explain to him what happened, and said we must be lost, but he didn't believe us and held us as traitors."

"Lost when you know this area so well? When you say your relatives live all around here? Please, forgive me; I must look like the fool!" He turned to face the wagon.

"William Hawkins is my husband in real life." There, she said that, too.

Brooks slowly turned around. He looked her up and down, but not with desire this time. This time it was with disgust. "Let's go," he said.

"Brooks, forgive me! I didn't *do* this! I'll tell you like I told my sister; *I don't have the power to transport myself from 1980 to 1864!*" Sophya began to sob.

"All I know is, I was hated for apparently taking away my *husband's* freedom and strapping him down with *responsibility* and children he didn't want! I *loved* him. *I'm* the fool. He never..." she cried out. "He *never* loved me. He never really *wanted* marriage, just to satisfy his flesh. I didn't realize I was temporary. I thought I could prove marriage could be *forever*. Unlike my parents."

She looked at him like she couldn't even *think* of any more words to justify herself. But then more came. "I have *never* met anyone like you before. I've never felt so *loved* by someone that can actually be *trusted.*"

She spoke softer, "I didn't mean for this to happen. I never wanted to hurt anyone. I've just asked God if it could have been *different* if *I* did something different, or *married* someone different. I didn't know He'd give me the chance to see!"

She rested her case.

He picked up a rock and skipped it across the water. "Are you ready to go?"

Her heart hurt with such heaviness. "No."

He sighed and thought a minute. "There is a sawmill or logging village down the river from here. I think that's where Sara's grandson, Sammy, works. Would you like to go see it in operation before we go back?"

"Yes."

They rode in silence. She longed to ask him about Star and if he had feelings for her but changed her mind, when they passed by the Indian camp.

Coming back to the main road, Brooks headed the wagon east back towards the other end of the Sabine River south. The closer they got, the more she heard the noise of the timbers being sawed and falling to the ground. She didn't remember hearing that when she was with William.

She looked excitedly at Brooks, knowing the sawmill would not be active in her time. He glanced back at her with an unreadable expression. She decided right then and there, that love, like money, was hard to come by and hard to keep, no matter what *time* she was in.

Brooks turned right, to drive the wagon alongside the road which was probably made by the loggers. It followed the river southward. "Giddy up!" he urged the horses to go down a steep hill on the road.

A buzz of activity surrounded them when they arrived at the camp shortly thereafter. Sophya took it all in with awe.

Brooks pointed to a section of the camp. Sophya saw Sammy standing next to a man who appeared to be giving him instructions. Sammy waved at them. He must've gotten permission to come speak to them, because he started walking towards them.

"Hey, Miss Sophie and Mistah Brooks! What brings you fokes heah?"

Brooks didn't answer. Sophya guessed that was her cue. She glanced back at him, then to Sammy. "Ya'll had a good trip, taking Miss Beth, Sammy?"

"Yes'm, mighty good. Miss Beth and Johnny talked da whole way to each utta. Looks like dey been knowin' each utta dey whole life, but not knowin' it."

She smiled. "Well, Brooks brought me here for you to show me how all this operates. You don't have a mill here?"

"No ma'am, but dey do southa heah. Dey jis call it a sawmill." He pointed to the rafts on the river. "We chops 'em and sends 'em on dem or we floats 'em down da rivah," he said proudly.

Sophya looked back at the rafts. So did Brooks.

Sammy pointed in the direction of the tall Texas pines being sawed down. "Dey dangerous, doh. You might'n oughta stay heah long." He looked at Brooks.

"Well, do you mind just telling me briefly how it works?"

Sophya prodded.

Sammy dusted his hands on his britches as if it helped him think where to start. "Welll, you see dat tall tick pine ovah deh?" he pointed.

She followed his hand and nodded.

"Dat's about da tickness an' tallness dey need ta be." He pointed to two men using a band saw on another tree. "Dat's how we cuts 'em."

"Phew!" Sophya gasped. "Looks like a lot of work."

Sammy beamed. "Ah's strong. Ain't dat right, Mistah Brooks?"

"You are very strong, Sammy," Brooks agreed.

She glanced back at Brooks then to Sammy. He continued.

"When dey ready to drop da tree, dey call dat 'fellin' da tree." He pointed in another direction of the camp. "Dat man's is 'scalin' da trees." He looked back at Sophya and saw her interest was sincere.

He pointed to two men with metal looking clamps in their hands. "Dem fellas is 'hookers.' "

She didn't let on that word had another meaning in her time. She swallowed hard and smiled.

"Dem men hook da timbahs and dey load dem on da wagon and pull dem to da rivah neah da rafs."

Then Sammy pointed to men stationed there with more band saws. "Dey cuts da timbahs inta trans-po-table size. Dats dat. Dey ready." He ended proudly.

"*Thank* you, Sammy!"

He smiled. "Welcum, ma'am."

The man he spoke with in the beginning called him back to work.

"I bes' be goin'," he nodded.

They thanked Sammy and told him good-bye.

Sophya sat back in the wagon pleased with his explanation that she would *write about*!

Brooks clicked his tongue to rouse the horses.

Sophya rehearsed over and over, in her mind, this next thing that happened. Was it her fault? Was it Sammy's? Or just fate?

She heard men screaming. She heard a tree fall. It must have been going the wrong direction. Brooks jerked the wagon to a stop. They both turned in time to see the timber fall. At least it was the top half of the tree that hit Sammy. It was still very thick. They rushed to get out of the wagon at the same time and ran towards Sammy. His foreman ran towards him too--along with the other men. They lifted the treetop off of Sammy. His foreman quickly got on his knees and listened to Sammy's chest. He looked up panicking. "He's not breathing!"

Sophya looked to see if Brooks would do anything. He knelt down to touch the artery on Sammy's neck for a pulse, then shook his head and slowly looked up at her. Then he began to pray. They all prayed with him. He listened to his chest again and just bowed his head once more, not wanting to look in Sophya's eyes. This seemed to take forever.

"Don't ya'll know CPR?" she screamed. They all looked at her like she was crazy. She just started crying.

"C..P..R!" She thought of how proud Mama Sara was of her grandson. She thought of his baptism and their good time talking in the kitchen.

"Ohhhh!" she screamed and dropped to her knees and propped his head back and begin puffing breaths into his mouth, then listening. She didn't know if the chest could take it, but felt they didn't have anything to lose at this point. She gently pumped his chest a few times. Blew in his mouth; pushed on his chest, blew, and pushed. Over and over. She was getting so tired. It seemed like an hour, but it must have been just a few minutes. She felt she would explode with the stress of it all. She touched his neck. "He has a pulse!"

She looked around. No one acknowledged her comment. "He has a pulse!"

She blew into his mouth once more and his chest finally began to rise and fall on its own.

Brooks said, "He's breathing!"

She sat back on her knees and put her hands to her face and sobbed.

Everyone clapped!

Brooks touched her shoulder.

Then the men backed away, embarrassed. She never thought about what time period she was in or what she had just done. She looked around and shook her head. She looked down at the sweet young man.

"He's breathing," she repeated what Brooks said and added, "thank God, he's breathing."

Sophya was out of breath, worn out. Brooks lifted her up and put his arm around her shoulder a moment while she wearily stood beside him. *Why do I always fall apart after I'm brave?*

Then, he started yelling orders as he headed for their wagon. "Help get this man in the wagon so we can bring him to the doctor!"

The men obeyed even though he was an Indian. They knew he was the leader. He hauled their wagon over. Before Sophya knew it, Sammy was carefully loaded in.

She remembered hearing the foreman tell Brooks the camp doctor was in his office that day back up on the main road and thanked him. She was in a daze. Things moved in slow-motion and appeared to be on a movie screen instead of right around her.

Someone said, "She's in shock. Throw a blanket around her." She saw the foreman's hand help her up into the wagon as he wrapped the blanket around her. He was a white man, but his eyes seemed full of gratitude that Sammy was alive.

She vaguely remembered Brooks getting into the wagon and driving them off.

***

Sammy would have to stay with the doctor. He was still

sedated, but with a promise of tomorrow in his future. He had a concussion and a broken left arm and a few broken ribs. Doc said they would know more about his spine later. By all appearances, his motor skills were still good. The doctor finally asked Sophya, "How did you learn to do that, young lady?"

Brooks looked up quickly. He must've planned to ask her that same thing.

A tear rolled down her cheek as she answered him, whimpering, "My mother's a nurse, she taught me, and, I miss her very much right now."

The two men laughed gently. Doc patted her shoulder. "Well, she will be very proud of you."

She smiled a half-smile, knowing she could never tell her. Brooks took her hand as she stood up woozily, and said, "Come, let's go."

Brooks and Sophya headed for home in the wagon. The doctor gave her a sedative and she became sleepy. Daylight wanted to depart, almost apologetically, but stayed to help them see their way home. While she rested her head on Brooks' shoulder, the most beautiful, red sunset spread across the sky. "Red sky at night, sailors delight," she mumbled.

Brooks looked over and smiled.

They arrived at the back door of the kitchen to the plantation. She did not want to face this bunch again. Every muscle in her body ached. Maybe the sedative would help soon.

Sophya looked at Brooks, knowing she had disappointed him today, before all this with Sammy happened. She knew, also, he may never want to see her again. His face was still not readable, a good Indian trait she wished she'd inherited. He held her hand so she could stand. She did not know *how* she was going to hop down to the ground on her own strength. All of the sudden, Brooks' two hands circle her waist and lifted her like a feather to the ground. She didn't look up but leaned her head forward saying, "Thanks."

A sigh was his only reply. Maybe he wanted to say more—bad

233

or good, she didn't know. Right now, fatigue almost kept her from feeling or saying anything.

He opened the back door to the kitchen and there stood Mama Sara, Lillie, Katy and Anya, and Big Bob! But, thank God, no William. "Surprise!" they shouted.

Sophya almost fainted. Brooks held her up.

Tears welled up--big-time now. She cried and cried. Even Brooks' compassion couldn't stop her crying. All the women and Big Bob swarmed her and took her from him and helped her onto the stool. She sat, embarrassed, and just kept shaking her head in relief and disbelief.

Mama Sara said, "Tank you! Tank you, tank you, Miss Sophie, for saving my granson, t'day! His fo'man cum and d'one tole us what you did!"

That must've been the first time she ever called Sophya by her name. Her eyes had tears, they *all* had tears.

"You're welcome," she mumbled and smiled.

"Lookie, chile. Fried chicken, and your fav'rite, peach cobblah!" Sara exclaimed.

She felt almost too tired to eat now, even though it had been about five of six hours since the soup. They had packed only water and cookies. The latter went unnoticed…rare.

"Oh wow," Sophya stated, trying to get enough energy to show her gratitude.

"And guess what?" Anya asked.

Sophya shook her head numbly.

"We hauled you a tub of hot water filled with bubbles!"

She opened her eyes wide with thankfulness, nothing else seemed to be able to move.

Brooks chuckled. "I'd better be going."

"Oh no!" the women said, and a plate was fixed for both of them. So, they tried to eat.

After their raves over the food, Brooks got up to leave and

thanked them. She looked into his eyes and tried to hide her love for him. What a more blessed surprise to see: his eyes weren't hiding it anymore! That would be a look she would take with her to her grave, whether she ever saw him again, or not. She could make it now.

***

"This tub, this water, these bubbles…Oh, *thank You, God*!"

Anya walked into her room to say good night.

"Good night," Sophya said. "Oh, Anya…"

She stuck her head back in. "Where's Sammy's parents?"

"Uh, I don't think he even knows who his dad is. They say his mom was real wild, and died."

"Oh," she said sadly.

"Want to talk more about today?" Anya asked.

"No, thanks, maybe tomorrow."

She came and hugged her.

"Proud of you, Sis," she said and left.

I don't remember her ever saying that before.

Sophya thought about the day, all of it, the Indian camp, the scene at the old ferry sight, and the episode at the logging camp. "Oh, God, would it have happened if I *hadn't* been there? Did the accident happen because I *was* there? Would Sammy have *died* had I *not* been there? Only You know. You were there."

She thought of the last look in Brooks' eyes. "What am I doing? What am I doing? *Why* am I here if I have to *leave? Please* let me know. You know, I always *want to know, want to know!* You *made* me that way. Please, please, let me know."

Then she remember Philippians 4:13. "I can do all things through Christ, which strengthens me."

235

Chapter Fourteen
Beth and Johnny

("Many waters cannot quench love, neither can the floods drown it."
Song/Sol. 8:7)

Sara had just washed the last supper dish and put it away when she heard a horse and rider hastily approach the barn. She looked out of the open back door. "Miss Beth! What you doin' heah? Miss Beth?"

Beth slid off the horse and hurriedly opened the barn door. "I need the wagon! I need the wagon!" She was crying so hard until it came out in sobs.

"Oh, Lawsey," Mama Sara moaned. She carried her full weight as fast as she could to William's study. "Massah, Massah, it's Miss Beth!" Sara pointed in the direction of the barn.

"Beth?" William started toward the kitchen, in the direction Sara pointed.

"No suh, the *bahn*--she in the *bahn*--grabbin' yo *wagon*!" She panted.

William skipped past the dining room and ran out of the side door of the little hall. He approached the opened barn door. "Beth! Beth!"

When he ran into the barn door he saw Beth hitching the wagon and crying uncontrollably. Attempting to calm his younger sister, he assumed a gentle tone, "Beth, hey, hon, where ya goin'?"

Beth looked at her older brother with contempt in her eyes he'd never seen before. "I'm going to Mansfield!" she kept sobbing.

"Mansfield!" William shouted.

"Yes, and don't you try and stop me! This is *our* wagon, not just *your* wagon! This is *our* house, everything's *ours*, not just *yours*!"

William stepped back, unable to believe his ears.

Beth swallowed hard to think that she had finally verbalized it.

She couldn't stop crying. She began hitching the wagon again.

William snapped back from his daze. "Beth, why do you want to go where the hottest battle has been fought right now?" He put his hand on hers to stop her frantic movements.

Beth sobbed more. "Johnny.." Her voice tapered off as she rested her head on her hand grasping the horse's bridle. "I need to go bury Johnny."

"Johnny?" William asked. "Johnny *who*?"

Beth gasped and almost crumbled. William reached to hold her up. She shook her brother off and looked hatefully at him. "Johnny Sims. Johnny Sims, who you know *nothing* about and are *nothing* like. Johnny who asked me to marry him! Johnny who's not *afraid* to love. Johnny who was not afraid, period. Not afraid to *fight*, not a hypocrite *preacher* who forces himself on women!"

"Huh?" William felt as though the breath was knocked out of him. He had no idea she knew. He had no idea she felt like that about him either. He gained control of his emotions. He knew he could not let her go. He grabbed the featherweight wisp of a girl up and carried her into the house despite her screams.

"Lawsey, Lawsey," Sara exclaimed. She had been listening at the back door. Then she saw her master come toward the plantation house carrying his kicking, and screaming, little sister. His face showed no emotion. Sara backed up and let him come in. William carried his fighting package straight into his study and slammed the door shut.

Sara followed him but stopped short when he slammed the door.

Anya and Sophya came out of the bedroom to see what caused the commotion, only to see Katy come out from her bedroom. Lillie was off now that it was evening. They looked at Mama Sara. She looked back up at them and just shook her head.

Anya and Sophya slowly descended the stairs and sat on the bottom step.

Katy approached the stairs, but stayed at the top.

Mama Sara came to lean on the banister beside Anya. From there, they could hear William and Beth shouting.

In the other room, William set his charge down hard in a chair. "You are *not* going to that battlefield and endanger your life looking for Johnny, whatever his name is, and be around all that and stragglers who might harm you," he yelled.

"Sims!" Beth screamed until she almost screeched. "Johnny *Sims.* Mona Sims' son! Johnny who *finally* was somebody that loved me!"

William blinked hard at the accusation.

"I can't believe you are saying that, Beth. I have tended to you, and taken *care* of you…"

"But you can't say *loved*, can you?"

William looked as though she slapped him.

"*Can* you? *Who* do you love? No one but *yourself!* What do you even *know* about me to love? Johnny found out everything about me," she whimpered. "And I found out everything about him. Just in that short amount of time," she sniffed. "We bothered to find *out* about each other! You just *use* people, and you're never home long enough to learn anything about me or to care."

William's mouth fell open.

"You just use *Lillie* and *Flo,* and you even tried to use *Sophya*!"

Mama Sara glanced over at Sophya, who looked up and tightened her lip.

They heard William continuing the conversation, "Now just a minute, young lady, you don't know what you're talking about." He began to state his case.

Beth's tear-stained eyes glared into her brother's. "I know that's not *love.* I know that's for the sanctity of *marriage, Reverend* Hawkins!'

Sophya couldn't contain her emotions any longer. She ran and opened the study door and shouted at William, "Let her *go*! Let her go find Johnny. She's right about you and you know it!"

About that time William turned and grabbed Sophya to shove her out the study door, mumbling, "Mind your own business!"

Beth lurched forward past him and out the front door, slamming it behind her.

Sophya grabbed William's arm and struggled with him. He grumbled an expletive, to her surprise. They fought a while longer, and then Sophya ended up with his jacket in her hands as he flew out the same door Beth had left through.

William got out in time to see Beth leaving in the wagon. She probably hoped the horses remembered the way since her eyes were too full of tears to see.

William hadn't ridden bareback in several years. He found his cream-colored horse, Sally, and tried to soothe her out of her stall. She reared up, sensing his stress. "Come on, girl. Come on." He put her bridle on then slipped on and led her out of the barn.

Sophya, Anya, Sara and Katy all ran outside just in time to glimpse him riding away.

***

William could see the dust of the wagon on its trail. He ate it and coughed all the way, blinking hard. Then he saw Beth almost at the river. She must've planned to get a ride on the ferry.

About that time, Beth took her eyes off the dirt road and looked back to see her brother following her. Still looking back, she stood up and clicked the horses to go faster.

Before William could blink an eye, the wagon wheel hit a rut in the road as she was turning north opposite the ferry. It toppled over, spilling Beth and landing on top of her.

William reached the scene within a few minutes. He slid down and pushed the wagon off of his sister. Dropping to his knees, he embraced her limp body.

"*Sorry, sorry...*" she whispered with her last breath.

Her brother crumbled, kissing his sister's pretty face and

239

rocking her in his arms. "No! No! No! Give me another *chance*, God. No!" He wept and wept. Then he remembered how Sophya had saved Sammy, not too far from that very spot.

"We'll make it, Beth. We'll make it. I'll change. You'll see. Sophya can help. Ugh!" He struggled to stand upright with her body, supporting her neck, as tears streamed down his face. He gently laid his sister in the back of the up-righted wagon.

***

About fifteen minutes after Beth and William left, he appeared back at the front door of the plantation. "Sara, Sara, get Sophya!"

Sara hustled her body to the front hall and glanced out the door at the wagon and the lifeless body of Beth.

"Miz Sophie!" she hollered. Her tears began to pour, seeing Beth lying in the back of the wagon was so overwhelming.

Sophya and Anya had been sitting in the kitchen with Sara, hoping to hear some news. She and Anya followed right behind Sara. Sophya heard her name called and ran to the porch. William was dashing up the steps.

"Sophya, come help me with Beth! Like you did with Sammy!"

Sophya's heart almost fainted. She ran to the wagon and climbed in and supported Beth's limp head. Sophya looked imploringly at William after touching her. "There's no pulse!" She began crying.

He looked pleadingly at her.

Sophya straightened Beth's sweet, gentle neck and tried to listen for a heartbeat or look for respiration. She realized her neck was broken. Nothing happened. She breathed into Beth's mouth. She pressed her chest gently. She blew. She pressed. Blew and pressed, knowing there probably wasn't any hope. She knew she may be doing more damage. For their sakes, those alive and watching, Sophya kept trying.

"I think her neck is broken," she sobbed. *God, she looks like an angel already.* God had already taken His angel. She could not bring her back. Sophya put her head on Beth's chest and wept.

William let out the loudest yell she'd ever heard and sobbed, followed by Sara's and Anya's and Katy's sobs.

Lillie came out of her cabin rounding the front of the house after hearing the loud voices. She ran to the wagon and looked in at Beth's still body. She glanced around at all of them for an answer. William was inconsolable. He didn't look up. None of them could speak. Mama Sara only shook her head. Lillie slithered to the ground moaning, "No, no… oh no…"

No one could compose themselves. Finally, Anya came to the foot of the wagon and just held on to Beth's feet and leaned on them, sobbing.

William put his face in his hands. "It's my fault. It's all my fault."

Sophya cleared her mind. "No, it's *mine!* Had I…" she choked back tears. "If I had *not* interfered, you could have kept her here."

He just kept shaking his head and mumbled, "She would have found a way. I should have just taken her, but, I did it my way…"

All of the sudden, he seemed to come to his senses. Tears flowed hard as he got up resignedly from the doorstep, like two hundred pounds were added to his weight, and he went to the wagon. Anya stepped back slowly, wiping her nose on her sleeve.

"Beth, oh Beth," William wept. He got in the wagon and picked her limp body up and walked to the edge of the wagon, gently holding her head to keep it from falling back. He caressed her close to his own body, sat down on the end of the wagon, then stood up on the ground and turned to walk up the stairs with her.

The rest of them watched him walk by as if they were in a daze. Then he went across the porch and down the hall, into the dining room. He let the bottom half of his sister's body slip onto the corner of the dining table and he slung the china place settings down to the other end of dining the table. Some fell off onto the floor. With his free arm, he lovingly placed her on the table, straightening her head and neck and smoothing out her dirty dress and her hair.

Katy immediately began cleaning it all up. At least it gave her something to do to feel like she was helping. Lillie knew it was her job but she couldn't seem to move.

William crumbled over Beth's body, sobbing and slid into a dining chair.

Tear-filled, Sara touched his arm. "Mastah William…"

He shook her arm off, as if not deserving any comfort.

"Sara," Sophya took over. "Can someone be sent for the doctor to verify this?"

She nodded, tears streaming and slowly, turned to Lillie and nodded for her to go out the back door and to the cabins to find someone.

Anya slid into a chair across from William. She just kept stroking Beth's arm while she heaved tears.

Sophya had not sat that close to death before. Now, she did, numbly, at the end of the table.

***

Beth's small, frail body had lain in the same spot on the huge dining table for two days. The signed death certificate lay right beside her. William had not come out of his study the whole two days. Well-wishers were turned away at the beautiful front doors. Mama Sara tried from time to time to coax the white man she had raised from a boy to eat or drink. His only reply, through the door, was "No."

His grief over the loss of the younger sister *he* had raised would not be consoled. None of the women left the house in case he needed them. Brooks stopped by in an attempt to minister to William only to be turned away, also. Lillie even looked unconsolable these days. Anya was in the same category. Katy knew how to keep a stoic face. She had done it all her life. This, Sophya found out, had been due to the death of her parents right after her birth and being shuffled about to so many of the wrong people. Sophya finally supposed that even this William must have some good in him, along with the bad, for taking her in.

Sophya stayed to herself, writing a great deal, even helping Sara fix the meals they made that nobody really wanted to eat. This they did, even knowing Beth's lifeless body lay in the dining room across the walkway from them where they used to share big meals.

Finally, on the morning of the third day, April 13th, Sophya was in her bedroom reading and heard William's study door open. She got up and peeked out her door. What she witnessed coming out was a hollow, desolate man.

Katy came out of her bedroom, that she was allowed to have separately since she was not Negro. She looked questioningly at Sophya, who shrugged her shoulders and looked at William. Sophya eased over to the top of the stairs and stopped. Her face couldn't hide the shock when she saw William's aged face. He never noticed or looked. He just walked towards the dining room.

She hurried down the stairs. Katy came slowly, halfway down. They heard Sara hustling her stocky body as quickly as she could across the plank and into the dining room. Sophya stopped quickly at the doorway into the dining room, in time to see William's posture crumble when he saw Beth's cold body again. Sara stopped her broad self suddenly.

He slowly ran his fingers, lovingly, along Beth's chilled little arm. "Mama Sara, do you know, or can you find out, where Johnny Sims lived?"

That startled Sophya. She slipped deep into thought a moment as she saw Sara's face sadly showing no knowledge of what he'd just asked.

"I know-- about where…" Sophya said.

William slowly turned towards her. He managed to smile slightly despite the weight of grief evident on his face.

"Will you take me there?" he asked humbly.

243

Sophya saw no threat left in this shell of a man. She smiled back. "Yes, let me get my shoes."

He looked down at her bare feet, in a foggy, deep thought, appearing to try and clear his head. He looked back up into her face. "Thank you," he managed to say.

***

About an hour later, after William got cleaned up and the buggy got hitched, they were on a dusty road with directions from the sawmill camp heading south along the river. A few minutes later, they arrived at the pretty white house with a picket fence. William and Sophya sighed in relief at the same time. They looked at each other and smiled. No breeze stirred.

William helped her out of the buggy. A blonde-haired woman with an apron on came out of the door. She appeared to be about Sophya and William's age age.

Wiping her hands on the apron she asked, "May I help you?"

William almost couldn't move forward. Sophya took his arm to encourage him. He began walking toward the woman. Upon approaching the woman, Sophya was sure even William noticed how attractive she was, in a pure, country sense.

She repeated, "May I help you?"

Sophya noticed William shook his head as if to clear his thoughts again, a trait he'd adopted now. He reached to touch her hand and shake it. She reluctantly began to raise her hand.

"I'm William Hawkins, Reverend William Hawkins." This time he said it to comfort her instead of in a prideful way. Sophya raised her brows, seeing him in a new light.

"I'm Mona Sims," she looked into his face with compassion at his information. "I heard about your sister's passing."

"This is my friend, Sophya Blackwell," William added.

Sophya put both of her hands around Mrs. Sims' hand. "I'm

244

sorry to hear about Johnny's death. Mona looked at Sophya's hands. Huge tears welled up in Mona's eyes. Sophya could tell William wanted to hug her, but for once, he kept a respectful distance. Sophya closed the gap between them and hugged her. They just wept for a while. Then, Sophya bashfully stepped back and noticed William's face filled with tears. He was standing stoic, unable to move.

Mona touched his hand. "I am so sorry about Beth," she said.

William looked down at her hand, tears dripping. He sighed deeply.

"Won't you come in?" Mona waved her hand to the house and blotted her face with her apron.

"Thank you," Sophya answered and pushed William's arm to move him forwards again.

He suddenly replied, "No, no thank you. Can we just sit on the porch?"

Surprised, Mona replied, "Why yes, whatever you want."

There was a swing at each one of her porch and some wicker or straw seated chairs nearby. She chose a chair so they chose the swing. A breeze finally began to blow.

William finally spoke, "I am very sorry to hear your son didn't make it..." his voice faltered. "Through the battles at Mansfield and Pleasant Hill." Embarrassed, he wasn't sure which.

Mona controlled her emotion. "Me too." She blinked hard, probably thinking back "It was Pleasant Hill, he lasted until Pleasant Hill. He was very brave and loyal. He was a good son, Reverend Hawkins. He died like he would have wanted to die—fighting for freedom."

She smiled slightly, and then turned the subject to him. "Johnny thought very highly of your sister."

William had been looking down at his folded hands. At that remark he glanced up quickly and nodded his head in gratitude. He hesitated a minute. "Do you have a picture of your son? I'd like to see him."

She looked intently at William then smiled and answered, "Yes,

245

let me get it for you."

William stared at who would have been his brother-in-law, smiled, looked up and asked, "Have you had services for you son yet?"

Mona fiddled with her hands. "Well," she looked at him intently, "sort of."

William waited.

"Our preacher across the river left. They, he and his wife, moved." She didn't offer any further explanation.

Not a gossip-- good trait, Sophya surmised.

"I…" his voice almost failed him again. "I haven't had Beth's service yet."

The gallant, grieving mother sighed with empathy.

"Would I be asking too much...did you know my sister and your son were more than just friends?"

William struggling for words. Amazing.

Mona's mouth quivered as she looked into his eyes. "Yes," she smiled and a tear dropped. "He told me."

William seemed relieved.

She continued, "My son told me he came to know Beth very well." Mona almost whispered these last words. She knotted her hands into fists and held them tightly together. "Johnny told me he and Beth fell in love and he asked her to marry him and she agreed."

William swallowed hard at the confirmation of the information. "Would you consider….please forgive me if I'm being bold, but would you and your husband consider letting me bury Beth beside Johnny? I could hold a service for both."

His voice cracked. "I'll gladly pay you anything you want for the plot. I think Beth would have liked that."

William held his breath awaiting her answer.

"Reverend Hawkins, you don't have to pay anything."

William started to object.

Mrs. Sims raised her hand to silence him. "If it will make you feel more comfortable, we can swap the price of your services for the plot. I'd be *honored* for a real preacher to hold a real service over my son. *Johnny* would be grateful," her voice quaked. "I'd imagine, too, *so* grateful, to know Beth..." she wiped her eyes. "will be beside him for eternity."

William stood up and shook her hand. "*Thank* you, Mrs. Sims."

He's so different now, so humble, so grateful. Sophya watched in awe.

"Mrs. Sims, what about your husband, is he here?"

She gently raised her hand again, this time almost with no strength left in it. "He's not. We received," she sucked in her breath to have to say it out loud, "we received word he's not coming back." She put her head in her hands. "He was killed at Shen..." she sobbed "Shenandoah. We got word after Johnny left for Mansfield." She began sobbing uncontrollably.

At this point, William dropped to his knees and wept, not being able to handle anything more. Mona dropped down on hers and hugged him, even though it was she who had suffered more loss. They wept together. So did Sophya as she stepped forward to put a hand on each one's shoulder...

Oh God, how much sorrow can one heart hold? I am so fortunate. Please forgive me. Get me back and I'll be grateful. Please, deliver me.

***

The afternoon of April 14th arrived with a gentle breeze. The small group that was gathered--on about an acre family plot--behind the Sims's home, were dressed in their Sunday best.

Up on the hill under the shade of a tree lay the fresh grave of Johnny Sims. Right next to him was the fresh dug grave of Elizabeth Angela Hawkins, their Beth.

"We are gathered together..." William struggled. "To put to rest, the souls of Johnny Sims and Beth Hawkins. From all accounts given…" he sighed. "He was much like her: Sweet, innocent, friendly, loyal and…" his voice cracked. "brave and loving."

Mona cried out, so did Johnny's sister, Jenny. They held on to each other.

Mama Sara hadn't stopped sobbing the whole time. Sammy supported her weight mostly, as tears streamed down his face. Her husband, Big Bob held her up on the other side.

"It is common to read Psalms 23, where God *promises that even though* 'I walk through the valley of the shadow of death…He is with me.' Or, John 14, where He speaks through Jesus and encourages us, *'Let not your heart be troubled…In my Father's house are many mansions. I go to prepare a place for you…and the Comforter, whom the Father will send, in my name, He shall teach you all things…His peace I leave with you.'*"

"These are comforts and truths indeed. But the words I would like to say today, that I consider more fitting, come from the Book of Ruth…"

Anya and Sophya clutched one another and cried out loud. Lillie grabbed Katy, even though Katy probably did not know what William was about to say.

A huge peace came over Mona and Jenny. They breathed in and stood tall, as if strengthened.

"Entreat me not to leave thee, or return from following after thee: for whither thou goest, I will go; and whither thou lodgest, I will lodge; thy people shall be my people and thy God, my God…"

"We know this was Naomi's daughter-in-law, Ruth, speaking to her. Today, this verse is used in many weddings. I believe, without a shadow of a doubt, that…" He breathed a faltering breath. "Had Johnny and Beth lived, they would have been married. And in my opinion, and with my blessing, would have been in God's perfect will."

Chapter Fifteen
Florence

("Blessed is the man that walks not in the counsel of the ungodly, nor stands in the way of sinners, nor sits in the seat of the scornful."
Psalms 1:1)

Friday, April 15th, arrived whether those in William Hawkins' household had the strength left to face it or not. Had it been up to their strength alone to bring it on, it would have failed to have shown up on the calendar. The comfort that Spring brings—new beginnings, new flowers, new hopes— God alone must have spring-boarded it to come.

Sitting out on the front porch in the rocker, Sophya was trying to write down her feelings about Beth. She inhaled, again, the lovely scent of wisteria and honeysuckle. Thoughts of the night of the ball came back to mind. Thank God, William had left early that morning for Shreveport to update his will, now that Beth was gone. Although he hadn't much fight left in him, Sophya could think better this way.

She wrote, *Friday, April 15th, the day after Beth Hawkin's and Johnny Sims' funeral. United in the ground and throughout eternity. Had they lived, there's no doubt, like her brother said, they would have been united in marriage forever...*

Why had God cut off the bud before the blossom? Maybe to save something worse from happening? Sophya didn't know. Can something good come from something bad? Maybe-- to save SOMEONE-- from himself. For that, Beth would have willingly died.

"...Beth was gentle. Beth was kind. She loved being a friend. She lived life to the fullest, even in her own shy way. She liked to look for small things in life to enjoy each day as a gift given to her personally."

About that time Sophya's revere was disturbed. She heard a buggy approaching. She looked up to see Flo coming down the road.

"Uh oh." *She's seen me.* "Oh well, I refuse to run and hide. Gees." She shot up a prayer. They were coming more easily these days. She sighed and waited.

"Well, look at my welcoming committee." Flo smiled a fake smile. Her driver, an older man, nodded to Sophya and helped *Florence* down.

"We would have a bigger committee, had we had more warning" Sophya smiled sweetly.

Flo glanced at her slowly, up and down with disdain. Flo was gorgeous, her lilac outfit accentuated her raven hair. Sophya had on a borrowed beige house robe. Her worst color.

"I told William I'd probably arrive today," she huffed.

"He must not have remembered." Sophya smiled, degrading her of her importance.

"He remembered." Her gaze leveled Sophya.

"Hmm, he's had a lot on his mind lately," Sophya reminded her.

"I know. He telegraphed me all about Beth." A little contriteness showed through. "He told me he had to go to Shreveport today."

"I'm surprised you came anyway."

"Dahling, we need to get to *know* one another better, don't you think?"

Sophya's eyes must have relayed her doubts.

"Oh pooh," Flo tapped her nails on the porch column. "Let's go inside. I'm famished and dusty. Randal, park the buggy in the barn and meet me in the house," she instructed and brushed past Sophya.

Sophya followed her inside noticing the sway in her walk, rivaling a porch swing, probably over-emphasized for Sophya's benefit. About the time Flo turned towards the dining room, Sophya heard Lillie coming out of Sophie's room, dust cloth in hand. Sophya looked up, put her hands on her hips to walk like Flo, almost getting a catch in her back. She smiled up at Lillie, who rolled her eyes while she came down the stairs.

"Come on!" Sophya whispered and motioned for Lillie to come protect her.

When she passed Sophya she held up her nails and said, "Sisss," like a cat and shook her head no. Then, she went in to clean William's study.

Sophya sighed again. *Oh, I've got to quit sighing!* She shook *her* head and trailed Flo into the dining room.

Flo prissed across the boardwalk acting disgusted to have to walk the plank.

Sophya, however, envisioned waters and a crocodile below.

"Well, Sara, we made it. I hope William told you I'd be coming today."

For once, Mama Sara was *sitting,* peeling potatoes. She looked up slowly and said with no emotion, "Yes'm, he tole me. You be served a late brk'fas. Dinnah ain't ready yet. Waih you wants to eat at?"

Flo looked shocked. "In the *dining* room, of course!" She gazed around the kitchen in a condescending way. She had no idea none of the others had ventured to use the dining table that week, painfully thinking of Beth's body lying there.

"Yes'm. Have a seat. Ah serves you." When Sara lifted her face it showed how her age had finally caught up with her.

"I'll bring it, Sara, just tell me what you want me to dish up."

Flo's head popped up in surprise. Randal came in the back door. Sophya nodded and told him, "If you'll sit in the dining room, I'll bring your breakfast."

He appeared to be a kindly man. He smiled and followed Flo, who walked off with an indignant air.

Mama Sara stood and uncovered the oatmeal, eggs, bacon, biscuits and preserves. Sophya got some china down from the shelf. "It's OK, Sara; you can finish what you were doing."

She nodded in appreciation.

Sophya carried the plates across the plank and into the dining room. Placing one down by Flo and another by Randal, she asked,

"What would you like to drink?"

"Coffee," they both answered at the same time. Flo glanced at Randal like he was out of place not letting her speak first. Randal, tired--Sophya figured--ignored her and closed his eyes in a silent prayer. Flo waited, aggravated, until he started to eat.

Sophya stood amazed. *And she's going to be a preacher's wife?*

After delivering their coffee, she excused herself. "I'm going to get dressed."

Flo didn't even acknowledge her.

Randal nodded.

Sophya peeked into the study. Lillie looked up and Sophya and stuck her tongue out at her.

"You water's getting' cole up in you room," she stated, then smiled and finished dusting. *Katy must be off today--with Lillie doing both floors.*

***

In this room (Sophie's room as it was called for now), there had been comfort, fun, melancholy moments, time recorded, and decisions made. It had served a good purpose. As she look around, she got the distinct feeling her time here would be ending soon.

"My, my," she washed her face, looked in the mirror, "Ohhh, my *hair*!" and put the brush and comb to good use. "Decision: I will wear my blue and eyelet dress William bought me!" *What's up with that?*

"Hey Anya," Sophie said as she peeked into her sister's room. She turned over to face Sophya. "How are you today?" She smiled patronizingly, and turned back over. "*Flo* is here visiting us," Sophya said in her cheeriest voice.

"Oh, God. Oh, no." Anya hesitated, and then turned her covers back. She sat on the edge of the bed, head in hands, wiping her eyes. "What's up with that?"

252

Sophya laughed at the repeat of her thoughts and reached and hugged her. "She *says* she wants to get *know* me better."

Anya looked up grumpily. "Count me out. Got any warm water?"

"Anya! I at least expect *you* to back me!"

"In a *cat* fight?" She smirked. "You can handle it, Sis. *Do you have any water?*"

"I'll get my bowl out of my room and bring it. It's lukewarm," Sophya smiled.

"Huh!" Anya sighed indignantly and slipped off the bed onto the chamber pot. Then, she slowly followed Sophya into her room. Blotting her face, she muttered, "Ugh," then used the towel Sophya had handed her.

"Anya, I feel we need to be tying up loose ends around here."

She glanced up in surprise. "You mean, you really think there's a way *out* of here, finally? Oh, I miss Mother and Urich so much."

"Yes, I miss them and my children and Mikki and her family, too."

"Think about all that's happened. The Battles are over. The War in this area is coming to an end, and for whatever reason, we were in it this time."

Anya quickly camouflaged her disdain and covered her face again.

Sophya continued, "Beth is dead. Johnny is dead." She sighed.

"But you saved Sammy!" she finally found something to be grateful for.

"God saved Sammy," Sophie smiled. "I thanked Him for letting me be present to help."

Anya put the towel down. "Yes, a lot *has* happened, and in a short time. Have you figured out why we're here yet?"

"No," she sighed again. "I've got to quit *sighing*!" They smiled at each other. Sophya took Anya's hands. "It could be a kaleidoscope of reasons."

Anya raised her eyebrows at her sister's big word.

"I don't think it was just to win Mama Sara and William over."

"Huh!" Anya laughed.

One more, deep sigh. "Nor just to meet Beth and Johnny, even though these have been heart-warming experiences."

Anya smiled.

"Being there with Sammy may have been one thing that changed history, who knows, but I can't think of anything else earthshaking. I mean, we met Brooks and Steve…" Sophya looked down at her hand with no wedding ring on it. "We will probably never forget them."

A tear appeared from out of nowhere in both of their eyes. Sophya blotted Anya's and she in turn, blotted Sophya's. They hugged.

Anya remembered another blessing. "You had an interview published in that paper they get in Mansfield!"

"*The Charleston Daily Courier!* Yes, and that paper in Natchitoches, *The Red River Herald.* At least the truth will get out this time," she perked up.

"But we can't take Steve and Brooks back with us, can we," Anya analyzed. She patted Sophya's hand while tossing her towel across her shoulder.

"No, but for some reason, we *were* supposed to meet them," Sophya deduced. "Maybe they will be in our *futures*!" She looked at her sister questioningly.

"Maybe," Anya said, looking into Sophya's eyes then down at her hands.

"I do believe this has granted me my wish to live back in this time," Sophya replied.

Anya looked despairingly.

"And to see what William would be like as a preacher!" she added. They both closed their eyes and shook their heads doubtingly.

"And we got to meet our great-great-grandmother!" Anya exclaimed.

"Yes, I loved that part too," Sophie mused. "And we need to say goodbye to her."

"Yes," Anya smiled exuberantly. "Have you made any decisions, yet?"

Sighing, "I don't like either of the Williams." Sophya frowned.

They laughed lightly. Then, Sophie patted her sister's hand. "Well, child…"

Anya rolled her eyes.

"I must get dressed and *visit the Queen*!"

"Tuh," Anya muttered again. "I'm going out walking or something."

Sophya smiled at her sister, knowing where she was going. They hugged again.

***

Sophya went into the dining room. No Flo there. She crossed the plank. "Sara, got any coffee left?"

"You sistah 'bout took it all," she chuckled.

"Some things never change." She shook her head while she poured the remainder.

"Miz Flo out front ah believes."

Sophya forced a smile and managed to say, "Thanks," and walked the plank.

She thought she heard Sara chuckling some more.

She hurried past the study and glanced in. Lillie had William's framed picture in her hand. She had stopped cleaning and was staring at it.

How odd, she didn't even notice me going by.

Sophya squeaked open the front door. There sat the "Queen" in a rocker.

"Oh, your blue dress is very flattering. Wherever did you get it?"

Sophie's time to shine. Then go straight to hell. Do not get to go

255

to heaven if she dies in her sin! "Oh, *William* got it for me in Shreveport."

"*William*!" Flo spit it out, and then calmed herself down.

"Yes, William. I didn't have very many clothes when I arrived here for my visit, so he bought me some."

She practically stared a hole through Sophya.

"You didn't have very many clothes? Why is that? And why are you visiting here? How do you know William anyway?"

Sophya sat back in shock. Apparently William hadn't told her anything. She said a quick prayer not to be too haughty back to her. "William is related to me."

Flo absorbed that for a moment, sitting up like she didn't hear Sophya correctly.

"How?" She *was* trying to be nice.

"By marriage," she sighed. *Gees!*

Drawing that info in, Flo stretched her mouth in an agitated way.

"Something happened to me and I needed to get away for a while, so he let me come here. And, my sister came with me."

Flo sat back hard in the rocker. "*What* happened to you?"

"I'd rather not say," she looked embarrassed to share it.

Flo shook her head. "Are you married?" she asked almost angrily at that point, trying to get to the bottom of it.

"Well, if you must know, I'm separated and considering divorce." There, she said it.

"Hmph!" She sounded disgusted then caught herself, probably not knowing what William would say about her inquisition. "How long do you intend to be here?"

Gulp. *I didn't intend to be here at all.* Sophya looked at the flowers, now tainted by Flo's presence. She looked out at the dirt road that used to be a paved highway. She looked down at her ring-less finger, then she looked into Flo's eyes and said, "I honestly don't know."

Flo stood up, almost in a rage. "Look, you little snip, if you have any designs on William, you can *forget it*!"

"Designs?" she laughed at the word.

"Yes! He and I have been engaged for a long time and plan to marry as soon as the war is over!"

The noise of a horse riding up made Sophya turn around. It was Brooks. The sun sure looked good outlining his handsome self. She'd never seen him on a horse either.

Flo saw the attraction in Sophya's eyes, evidently, and turned to see if it was William. It must've surprised her to see Brooks. She took full advantage of it by hopping up to meet him. "Oh, Brooks, how good to see you! What brings you here?"

She glanced over at Sophya, who felt her x-ray eyes.

He was perceptive enough to look at Sophya also, for her reaction. "I have been trying to get to talk with Reverend Hawkins since Beth's passing, just to give my condolences." He smiled at both of them.

Sophya jumped up and said at the very same time Flo did, "That's very nice of you."

Flo smiled when Sophya saw her turn red, but curbed her temper.

"William is in Shreveport until tomorrow," Flo gladly took the stage.

Brooks looked down, maybe disappointed that he's missed him again,.

"Please tell him I came by," he said.

Sophya butted in, "We will."

He looked up at her quickly.

Flo wasn't to be out-done. "Won't you come in for a while?"

"No," he answered politely, "I'll be going." He nodded to Flo, then looked at Sophya with an intensity that made her blush! He turned the horse around and rode off.

Flo turned to Sophya with a *double* accusatory look.

"Flo, you are a very beautiful woman, why would you have to

257

worry about me and William, or me and *anybody*!"

Flo sighed.

"I have no *designs* or plans or *anything* except to get through today and heal from some things that happened in my past!"

She looked at Sophya as though she were a fly bugging her. "Well, I'm going to *demand* that William send you back to your home, or husband, or *whatever*!"

Sophya got up quickly from the rocker and put her face *real* close to Flo's. "You do whatever you feel is necessary, but stay away from me or I'll pour cold water on that pretty hairdo, face and *temper*!"

Flo jumped back, surprised by her actions.

Going into the manse, Sophya slammed the front door. Lillie stepped out of the library-- study-- and looked surprised. She must've overheard them. Sophya raised her eyebrows and pressed her lips tightly and went up to her room.

***

Later, she heard voices below, "No ma'am, Mastah William say for you to stay in Katy's room, not Miz Beth's. Katy stay with some of her kinfolk tonight."

"I may be here more than one night!" Flo exclaimed.

"All I know is all I know," Lillie answered.

"Get Randal to bring my things up!" Flo retorted.

Sophya heard the shuffling of feet and hurried to prop the chair under her door knob.

***

The next morning, Saturday, April 16th, Sophya realized she must've dozed off while writing. She had heard Flo coming and going all afternoon. Anya's door was closed. She never heard her come in

258

after she took the chair away from her door. Just then, she heard William's voice downstairs and Flo rushing out of Katy's room.

"Oh, *William*, I'm so glad to *see* you!"

Sophya could only visualize the rest in her mind. She sat up and the journal booklet she had been writing in fell off her chest. "Huh!"

She walked over to look at herself in the mirror. Straightening her hair, she wondered, *Am I even nearly as pretty as she is?* She thought of Brooks and Star, the Indian Squaw. Brooks seemed to think she was pretty, and Star was much prettier than Flo. Sophya walked off, not giving it another thought.

She went into Beth's room and walked around and touched her bed. *And that tub!* She pushed back the pink curtain. Tears came to her eyes. "So many memories in such a short time. Will William make this into a shrine? Or someday, will *life* appear in here again?"

***

Downstairs in the kitchen, Sara stood stirring a pot on the stove, as usual. "Hey Sara, how ya doin'?"

She looked back at Sophya and smiled. Ignoring her question, she instead said, "Sit down, Missy, have some beans and conebread."

My favorite. She sat down.

Sara handed her some tea to drink. *Oh, for ice cubes.*

"Missy, do you lak Mastah William?"

She 'bout choked on her tea! That was completely out of character for Sara and the Negroes of her generation. They were taught not to pry.

She smiled. "I *like* him, but not they way you are asking about." Sophya tried to show her in her eyes the love that she had come to feel for her, though. Sophya was glad Sara had finally come to *trust* her.

She turned back around to stir her pot.

"Mama Sara, I have been through some rough stuff before I came here. I am related to William by marriage…"

She glanced back at Sophya.

"…And he took me in, even though he didn't really know or trust me. I am grateful that he has let me and my sister stay here awhile. But I am not in love with him."

Sara raised her eyebrows and sighed. Sophya really believed that disappointed her. She dished up a plate and handed it to her.

"Ummm," Sophya smelled it and smiled again, back at Sara's smiling face.

"Where's William and Flo?" Sophya asked.

"No tellin', Missy, no tellin'."

Chapter Sixteen
Steve and Anya

("To everything there is a season, and a time to every purpose under the heaven…a time to love and a time to hate, a time of war and a time of peace." Ecc. 3:1&8)

"This barn…"

Anya looked around. "Time travel. Who'd a thought?"

She walked to where the stalls were and took the bridle off of the hook. She had not seen Steve come to work and tend William's stock for a few days. So, she decided to go look for him at the tack and saddle shop where he also helped out. Rusty neighed and reared his head back when she went to pet him.

"Hey fella," she petted his nose. "I like animals, too. So what if I prefer cats and Sophya likes horses?"

Rusty whimpered as if in thought.

"I have ridden before. It's just not much, but you'll help me do it again, huh?" The horse shook his head affirmatively.

Anya was so petite compared to the critter. She opened the stall after lacing the bridle in his mouth. Rusty resisted at first.

"Come on, fella." She got it in and laced it around his ears, then pulled the leather reins to guide the horse out.

She held onto the reins and looked around again. "Let's see…blanket…"

She draped it across his back. "Yeh, that's warm, huh, buddy."

She glanced at the heavy saddle. "Where's my tall sister when I need her?"

Rusty turned his head to look at her as if he couldn't answer that. She pulled him closer to the saddle and stool. Looping the reins over the rail, Anya stepped on the stool and bent over to get the heavy saddle. "Ugh, Steve, I sure hope this is worth it."

When she had flung the saddle onto Rusty he jumped a bit.

"Hey, hey."

Anya stepped off the stool and patted the horse. "It's OK, boy, I don't weigh as much as this saddle. You'll see, it'll be O.K."

He sniffed her back pocket. "Ah ha! I forgot about the cookies. Now we'll be best friends, huh."

She pulled the cookies wrapped in a cloth out of her pocket. Rusty was impatient and nudged her hand. "Wait, fella."

Holding her hand *real* flat, she gave him a cookie. He gulped it down and nodded his head so quickly it made Anya jump. "Huh!"

That made *him* jump. "Uh oh."

She patted him again and hugged his neck. Then, she stepped off the stool and reached down around to get the girth under his belly and looped it in the round ring. She examined the stirrup to see how to shorten it and led him to the barn door, muttering, "Oh, help, Lord."

Anya brought the stool, stepped up and took the reins from the rail. She put her foot in the stirrup and hiked herself up onto the saddle. Rusty shuffled his feet a bit. "Whoa, guy," she mumbled to settle him. "Phew. Don't forget, you're the *famous* 'Trusty Rusty'!"

He snorted.

"Now, *slowly* Rusty," she clucked her tongue, ducked and rode the horse out of the opened, double-barn door. He walked out of the door and kept that gait. *Today, Rusty, while it is still called today, though!*

Anya headed the horse in the direction of the stream. She clucked again, shook the reins and pressed the stirrups into his flanks. Rusty increased his pace to a gallop.

"Ahhh," she hollered as she and the horse raced across the pasture towards the woods.

Almost an hour later, Anya rode Rusty up to Hank Wood's Tack and Saddle Shop. "Whoa, boy," she patted Rusty's neck again.

Hank slowly came out of the store to greet the new customer he hadn't met before.

Praise God I don't have to dismount and remount, Anya

262

thought.

"Hep you, ma'am?"

"Uh, hello." She smiled at the store owner. "I am looking for Steve Garrett."

"Oh," Mr. Hank stated. "Well, he ain't here."

Anya waited for more of an explanation, but none came.

"Well, how do you do? I'm Anya Stolsky, a friend of his." She reached to shake his hand.

He approached her, shook her hand, spit tobacco and said, "Pleased."

Anya sighed, "Hmm."

She decided to reveal more. "I'm a relative of Reverend William Hawkins."

Mr. Woods nodded, but said nothing.

"Uh, my sister and I have been visiting him."

Silence.

"I became friends with Steve and really need to tell him I may be leaving."

Still silence.

"Is he at work today?"

"Nawsum. He sent a message his ma got sicker."

Anya thought about that news a moment. "I know he lives up the road to the north of here, but I don't remember how far. Will you tell me how to get there?"

"Oh," he scratches his jaw. "He lives 'bout halfway up to Pulaski Settlement, ma'am."

"Pulaski?"

"Yep."

"How far is that?"

He mulled the dip in his mouth and spit again. "Oh, 'bout twenty miles."

"Jesus!" Anya said, thinking of how sore her rear would be tomorrow.

Mr. Hank raised his eyebrows at the slang use of the word

coming from a girl.

"I'm sorry," she said.

"Do you know what the place looks like, or what color the house is, or if there's a mailbox with their name on it?"

He sighed a minute. "Ain't no mailbox, ma'am. People get their mail here or Center or Pulaski, dependin' on where they live."

"Oh," Anya considered this.

"But, it's a wat, two-story house, needin' paintin'. It's on the rat side of the road. Got a big oak in the front yard with a swing hangin' from it."

"*Thank* you!" she said very grateful to finally get some information out of him, and started backing the horse up.

"Don't mention it, ma'am," he said and smiled with a twinkle in his eye.

Anya couldn't help but smile back and blushed at the same time.

"Come on, Rusty," she clicked her tongue.

***

The house truly did need painting. Her rear truly was sore. But, Steve's house looked so homey, right down to the old swing in the yard. Grass didn't grow much under all the shade of the big oak tree. The bushes and flowers against the porch helped the looks, though.

Anya halted the horse to take in the scene.

"Come on, fella," she said then shook the reins.

By the time she approached the porch, Steve had opened the front door.

"Phewee!" he whistled. "Will you look at what ole Rusty brought up today!"

Anya smiled. "My rear's numb and tomorrow it'll sing a *different* tune!"

Steve laughed deep at the raw statement.

'What are *you* doin' here?"

"I just want to talk to you for a while."

The look in his eyes was *too* inviting. "You came all this way just to talk?"

Anya smiled again, shaking her head at the rough trip. "Well you've been absent."

"How'd you find me?"

"Oh, your boss, Mr. Woods, gave me directions...*finally.*"

Steve tightened his lips, admiring her tenacity. "Come on in."

"Uh, could you *possibly* help me off this animal and get him some water?"

Steve rushed to her, regretting that he hadn't thought to offer. "Sure!"

He then acted like he'd fling her over his shoulder.

"Hey, no funny stuff!" Anya exclaimed. "I'm *tired*!"

Steve let her slide down close to his body.

What's *that?* She's never felt like *mush* before.

"None of that either please," she mumbled, looking at the button on his shirt.

He tipped her chin up to look into his green eyes, while he looked into her blue ones. "Alll--right, ma'am." He waited a moment, and then backed a step away from her.

Anya sighed with relief.

Steve laughed.

He put his hand on her back to guide her to the steps. Anya's legs almost gave way. Steve caught her quickly. She laughed, and then decided to make the best of the situation. Turning to face him, she took his right hand with her left. Exaggerating her gait, she walked bow-legged and talked like a cowgirl. "Welll suh, if you'll jus' hole mah hand and hep me make it, we can take these steps, ah believe."

Steve laughed so hard he almost *couldn't* take another step. Then, he did something that totally took her by surprise. He grabbed her and kissed her. And she let him. *How did this country boy learn how to do that-- like that?* Now she *really wa*sn't in control of body *or* mind. She opened her eyes and looked at him mischievously. Biding her time to gain control again she asked him, "How'd you learn how to do that-- like that?"

Steve looked mischievously back at her and answered, "You don't expect a genta-men to kiss and *tell*, do ya?"

Anya rolled her eyes. Steve cupped her face with his hands. Gazing into her eyes with love, he bent down and kissed her again, tenderly this time, and held her close.

Anya pushed him away. "Steve…stop-- *please*!"

He didn't move. "Why?"

His voice was low and husky. She hit his chest and replied, "Ugh!" Then she ran up the steps shouting, "Ow, ow, ow!"

Steve chuckled and followed close behind her, scooped his arms around her, and pulled her up the rest of the steps with him.

'Hey!" she retorted. "I didn't come to wrestle with you again, you ruffian!"

He put his hands on her shoulders and held her at arm's length. "You need *somebody* to wrestle with."

"Huh!" Anya spit out her disagreement and started to turn towards the screen door.

"I would *like* to wrestle with you for the rest of our lives," came his soft reply, as he continued to hold onto her shoulders.

Heart hurt. She emotionally froze so as to stop the tears before they started. It didn't work. She slowly looked up into his eyes with her beautiful blue ones, and she couldn't speak.

He hated the heaviness that just settled on their mood. He hadn't made her happy by expressing his feelings for her. She *sure* didn't take the bait and confirm her feelings for him. He touched her teary cheek.

"Come. I want you to meet my mom." He decided not to confront what made her cry at that moment. He had the feeling he didn't want to know.

266

Anya looked back at him and smiled as she walked into the house. She was grateful he gave her time to collect herself, and she did want to meet Mrs. Garrett. Steve directed her to a bedroom door on the left at the end of a long, wide hall. They passed a living room on the right, a bedroom, and then bathroom on the left. There must've been a dining room between the kitchen and living room on the right, with no door to it from the hall.

"Where's the stairs and the dining room?" she asked Steve.

He smiled at her curiosity. "Next to the living room."

Approaching the last bedroom, she heard a child's voice. She glanced up questioningly at Steve. He just smiled again and directed her into the room. Anya saw a lady lying on the bed with her eyes closed-- probably Steve's mom. A boy, about five years old, sat on a rug coloring in a book. His eyes shot up to her.

"Anya, this is Bengy, my brother."

Anya smiled and said, "Hi."

Bengy finally smiled back at her. He had cotton-top hair.

Mrs. Garrett opened her eyes and turned her head towards them and smiled.

"Mom, this is Anya, the friend I told you about."

Her beauty showed through her paleness. Her hair was darker than Steve's.

"It is good to finally meet you. Anya. Sorry I'm having a bad day."

Anya looked over at Steve then approached the woman and took her hand. "I'm sorry you are not feeling well, too. It's very nice to meet *you.*" She stumbled for something further to say. "May I help you with anything?"

The bed-ridden woman closed her eyes. "No, Steve is very good to help. Wish I didn't have to keep him home from work today, though."

Steve sighed. "It's OK, Mama."

"Bengy keeps me company and gives me pretty pictures," she added, smiling at him.

"I stay in the lines!" he said excitedly to Anya.

"That's good! You do better than my sister, Sophie, and she's *old*!"

Bengy seemed proud knowing that.

"Umm, I'm telling'" Steve said.

Anya just shook her head.

"Mom, Anya and I will be out on the front porch talking if you need me, OK?"

"That's fine, son."

"Can I come?" his brother asked.

"No, you *could* be gathering eggs. That hasn't been done today yet."

Bengy stared down at his book. "I don't…"

Mrs. Garrett laughed a little.

"Or, you could stay here and watch Mom and if y'all need me, come and get me."

That suited his younger brother better. He nodded his head in acceptance.

"Come on," Steve pointed Anya back into the hall.

"Nice meeting you," she said glancing back at Steve's mother and brother.

"You, too," Mrs. Garrett mumbled.

"Wait," Steve stopped. "Let me get you something to drink. Tea? Water?"

Coke! With a McDonald's cheeseburger! Anya thought but smiled and said, "Tea, thank you."

*****

They were sitting on the front porch with their feet dangling off the side. Anya drank her tea thankfully. Rusty had made a trip around back to the watering trough.

Steve watched her then said, "Well…"

She looked at the liquid in the glass, turned it around in her hands, and then glanced into his green eyes. "I've never met anyone like you before."

He sighed, glad that might be all she might came to say. "Am I weird?"

She chuckled. "Unusual."

"Unusual?" he feigned offense.

"Yes."

"How?"

The thoughts of the words she wanted to say didn't stop the flow of tears that came.

"Hey!" Steve turned her chin to him and touched her tears with his thumb again.

She whimpered a laugh and wiped the other cheek and stared at her glass.

"What's the matter?" Steve asked gently.

Anya sighed. "We're probably going to be leaving soon."

"What?" His raised voice and didn't camouflage his hurt. He turned her shoulders toward him this time, spilling her tea. They both looked at the liquid drenching her riding skirt. Anya set the glass down on the other side of her, not answering him.

"Why?'

"*Why?*" she cried bitterly. "Why *everything?* Why this, why did I have to meet you?" she said angrily.

Steve got quiet and took his hands off her, his face relaying his pain at her words.

"I'm sorry," Anya sobbed more then gazed, into his eyes. "I'm sorry; I didn't mean it like *that*."

"What *did* you mean?"

"There is so much I haven't told you about myself…"

"I don't *need* to know anything else!" he grabbed her and hugged her.

She squirmed out of his grip and looked pleadingly into his eyes.

"What do I need to know but how I feel…how *we* feel?"

Anya just shook her head. "There are some *obligations* I have back home that keep me from committing to what you are talking about."

"What could possibly be so *obliging* to keep two people in love away from each other?" he demanded.

She stared at the face she had come to love. She stroked his hand then put his palm up to her face, but said nothing, knowing he would only analyze everything anyway.

"Anya!" He jerked his hand away and grabbed her two in his. "*What* would keep us from marrying?"

She let out a sigh and looked at their hands. Steve slowly let their hands drift down to her lap.

"What?" he repeated in a lower tone.

"Life," came her reply.

He raised his eyebrows. "Are you engaged?"

"Tuh!" she muttered.

"What, then?" he said pleadingly.

"*If* it is God's will for us to be together, then we will." She raised her hand to his lips to hush him as he started to speak. "Please, if you *really* care about me, you'll let me go back and wait and see."

Steve sighed deeply and backed away to look at her intensely.

"How long?" he asked.

"I don't know," she answered. "But we will both know when and if."

"You're wanting to *test* my love for you?"

She sucked in a painful sigh. "No!"

"Anya," he said softly and turned her chin towards his face gently with his finger. "This kind of love doesn't come around everyday. I really *love* you. I have since I first saw you. I think of you in my arms all the time."

Her eyes opened wide.

"I think of you in my kitchen."

They laughed.

"I think of you in my bed…"

She smashed her palm on his mouth. "Stop! I get the picture!"

He held her and whispered her name over and over, "Anya, Anya..."

Anya heaved a deep breath and began to cry. She cried until she had no breath left.

"You're really going to leave, aren't you."

Without pulling away, she nodded her head into his chest.

Steve kissed the top of her head, dropped his arms from around her, and let her go.

***

Sophya awoke to harsh voices downstairs. She had fallen asleep while writing again after lunch. She looked into Anya's room and she still wasn't there. She went to open the hall door to see if she could help if someone dropped something or fell. She saw William and Flo, but no one else.

"I told you, things are different now!" William loudly stated his case.

"Oh, you and that…*twit*…that's what's different, not just Beth's death!" Flo's voice was louder.

William looked up and saw Sophya watching. Then so did Flo. He pulled her by the arm into his study and slammed the door.

Sophya continued to hear their voices raised in argument.

Lillie came from the dining room, through the small hall and into the main hall. She looked up at Sophya in surprise. It stopped her a moment. Sophya smiled. She nodded and went to the study door and knocked.

"Mistah Randal ready fo' Miz Flo," she said and glanced back up at Sophya.

Maybe I'm not supposed to be hearing this, Sophya thought as she stepped back into the door. *Lillie's still looking pale, too.*

A moment later, Sophya peaked through the crack in her door when she heard William and Flo's angry voices again.

"You're going to *regret* this, William. My daddy has a *lot* of influence and you know it!"

Sophya heard William come out of his study sounding whipped in spirit. "Come on, *Florence,* I'll escort you out." He had his hand on her arm.

"My *things* are in the bedroom!"

"No they're not. Are they, Lillie?"

Sophya heard Lillie affirm, "No suh."

Sophya listened as the voices got distant and Lillie apparently followed them out. Sophya looked away for a moment to analyze this and got knocked to the floor by the door. "Agh!" She glanced up to see Anya entering.

"Gads!" She stopped to look down at her sister.

Sophya just shook her head. Before she could reprimand her, she noticed her face was red and her eyes swollen. "Help me up, please."

Anya pulled.

Sophya got her balance and hugged her. Her shoulders shook.

"Why, oh why, did I have to meet Steve?" she cried.

She pulled back and looked at her and then hugged her again.

"Mercy, mercy," was all Sophya could say. They laughed lightly, thinking of their grandmother.

"And what in God's name is happening between William and Flo?"

"The end of a dysfunctional relationship, I think."

"Hmm," Anya stated.

***

Anya went down with Sophya for supper, even though she didn't want to eat--rare indeed that she'd go anyway. Mama Sara looked glad for their friendly company in her kitchen.

After she'd fixed their plates, they heard Flo's buggy drive off and looked at each other and raised their eyebrows. William came in the back door looking flushed, then embarrassed, that they heard it all. He nodded briefly.

Sara broke the silence. "Suppah, Mastah William?"

"No…yes, yes, Sara, thanks."

She quickly got a plate and dipped what she knew he liked.

"Tea, suh?"

"Yes." He smiled at her, then at Sophya and Anya, and took his plate and sat on a stool. How weird.

Anya and Sophya slowly began eating again.

"I'm sorry y'all had to hear everything," he said.

They looked up.

"I'm sorry for everything," he looked at Sophya.

Oh my gosh. She didn't know if she could handle this contrite William.

He bowed and said a silent prayer then took a sip of the tea.

"Things have been rough around here, with Beth gone and all…" He almost couldn't speak for a moment. "I promise you girls, things are going to be better. I'll *see* to it that things are more joyful for you." He gazed at them intently.

Anya and Sophya couldn't speak, as his words sank in. They glanced at each other and back to him. "Thanks," Sophya mustered to say.

They ate silently a moment.

Mama Sara started humming. It was a church hymn.

William ate quietly, and then got up. "Things will be different from now on. Beth or no Beth, South's victory or no victory, for richer or poorer…"

They laughed.

He hugged Sara and said, "I believe I just got my sermon for tomorrow."

He patted Sophya and Anya on their backs and left.

273

They glanced at Mama Sara with their brows raised. She raised hers too sighing, "Um, um."

Anya and Sophya shook their heads.

Chapter Seventeen
The Good Sermon

("And when thou art converted, strengthen thy brethren." Luke 22:32)

"Sophya wake up!" Anya hollered. "There's some excitement outside I don't think you'll want to miss!" She had come into Sophya's room, leaving the door open as usual.

Sophya had stayed awake writing and slept like a *log* after such a peaceful evening in Sara's kitchen with William and Anya last night...Flo being gone out of their lives helped.

"What's going on? Gees! It's usually *me* having to wake *you*! And, as I recall, with a little more *compassion!*"

"Huh!" Anya smirked, looked at her sister doubtfully, grabbed her skirt off the chair and tossed it to her. "Here!"

Sophya looked at her in dismay. "*What* is so important?"

She shivered as she uncovered.

"Since this cold front came through, Mama Sara says Big Bob and Sammy and some others went hog-killing last night. They are going to dress them and hang 'em in the smokehouse to *cure*! Then, they'll make sausage out of the rest!"

Sophya looked around dazed then back at Anya. "This doesn't *sound* like something that would interest you." She blinked trying to gain understanding.

"I *know*, that's why it's so cool! We may *never* get to see this done in *our* time! Come on...*please*?"

Sophya glanced up at her after slipping into the skirt. She sat back down to put her *tennis* shoes on, not those *button up* leathers! *It is so seldom she gets excited about anything anymore.* "Oh, alright."

Anya clasped her hands together, squeezed the rag out and handed it, and her toothbrush, to her.

Sophya opened her eyes wide. "Do you *mind* if I do these two things separately, like *you* probably got to do this morning?" *Must be my hormone time.*

She sighed. "Oh, alright," she mumbled and sat on the edge of the bed.

Sophya was impressed with her brief display of humbleness. After the quickest swipe of the face and teeth and hair tie-up, she said, "I'm done."

Anya looked over at her in disbelief. "Miss Vanity?"

"If any in my fan club shows up today, I'll just hide."

She liked that.

Sophya pushed her. "Let's go get a hog."

She smiled and hopped up.

***

They scampered past the Negro quarters. Behind them there was a little wooden, fenced-in area. Next to it, the smokehouse. Then stood a connected area that had a roof over it extending from the smokehouse roof. There was a long table at the edge of that area. A big cook stove at had been placed the end of the table. Mama Sara was at the stove, naturally. A few other women were in the covered area. One was standing at the table and one sitting near it, working on some of the by-products of the hogs, Sophya supposed.

About the time the girls passed the corner of the Negro cabins they saw the women working, they also saw some hogs that were still alive in the pen. They arrived just in time to see Big Bob, the gentle giant, whack a hog right between the eyes with a sledge hammer.

Anya almost fainted! Sophya's knees got weak but she caught her sister. Anya gained composure and started to turn and leave. "Oh no, little sister. *We*," she pointed to both of them. "Are stayin'. *You* woke me up early and we're *both* staying!"

Anya looked up at her and seemed to be a pale shade of green.

"Oh, God," she mumbled.

"Come on. We'll watch, and *you* can write about it!"

She shook her head no.

Big Bob stabbed the hog in the heart after it fell. Sammy looked over and saw the girls. As Sophya closed her eyes tight, she heard him walking over.

"Miz Sophie, Miz Anya."

She heard the smile in his voice and opened her eyes. Her sister mustered some strength and reached over the fence to shake his hand. He shook hers and then Sophya offered her hand.

"We're trying to watch," Sophya replied. "How ya feeling, Sammy?"

He smiled bashfully and glanced over at the hog that had just been slain. "Betta'n that hog, thanks to you, Miz Sophie." He waved his left arm which still had the sling on it.

Sophya sighed at the remembrance.

Anya thought highly of Sammy, so Sophya assumed her silence was due to a queasy stomach. Sophya could barely speak with the way hers was rolling, also.

"Will you tell us what's going to happen next?" Sophya asked.

Anya whimpered.

Sammy glanced at her, smiling, and proceeded, "Well, deys boiling some water ovah deah." He nodded in the direction of Mama Sara. "Dey gone wash the carcass aftah dey bleeds it. One end, den da utta. Dat heps 'em take da bristles out."

They looked over towards the shed.

"Den, dey runs a gramblin' stick thew da two back legs ta hang him by. Dey dress it, makes a long cut, ta get da inerds out. Dem palmetta leaves heps hang it, too."

Anya looked down. "Ewe."

Sammy laughed.

Sophya raised her brows trying to take it all in.

"Den, dey wash and dries dat cavity and lays it on da table. Dey cuts a coupla hams roun da back legs and front shoulda and some spaih ribs and bacon off da sides."

Anya raised *her* brows at the mention of bacon and ham.

"Dey packs it in tubs o' salt all night. Den dey hangs da meat in the smokehouse and cures it. Dey boils da backbone and lime bone off da ribs. Da stomach and intestines is fo' tripe and chittlins and sausage." He smiled real big.

Sophya smiled back.

Anya looked up and appeared to still be interested in the conversation.

"Next, dey make da lard an' soap outta da fat and da liver." He winked at them.

Anya swooned and leaned against Sophya, apparently tired from it all.

Sammy and Sophya laughed.

"Well, how do you know where to find the hogs and when to…" Sophya waved her hand…"*do* all this?"

"Dat cold front, dat makes hog-killin' day. Mastah William and dem utta ranchers, dey marks dey hogs with slits or holes in dey ears and feeds 'em all winter. Dey roams and feeds on nuts and tangs an' fattens 'em. Dey know which is deys unless some ole greedy gut like Mr. Woods leaves 'em a trail o' corn to his land. He make 'em pay to get dey *own* hogs back!"

They all laughed.

Sophya realized about what time it was getting to be. "Well, Anya and I need to go be getting ready for church," she said.

"Amen," Anya mused.

Sammy snickered.

'It's so good to see you doing so well, really, Sammy." She patted his good arm. "And thanks for telling us about the hogs."

Anya fibbed and said, "Yeh," and nodded good-bye to him.

He grinned. "Bye, Miz Sophie, and Miz Anya."

***

Anya helped Sophya lace the corset tight. "Oh gosh, I'll be glad

278

when this is over."

"I wore it to the ball, but that's all!" Anya added.

They walked out of the bedroom door and saw William leaning against the banister, waiting for them. He looked up and smiled.

"Wow, thanks for waiting for us," Sophya said. "I figured everyone was gone."

"They are," he replied. "But they can't start without me." He looked almost bashful. *So humble.* Sophya stared at him still amazed by his transformation.

***

They hurried in to get a seat. Lillie sat in the back as usual. Sophya knew Mama Sara and Big Bob were tied up with the hog killing. Sammy was sitting near Lillie. He beamed when he saw them. Sophya didn't see Steve. Apparently, Anya refused to acknowledge his absence. She was still dealing with *not* seeing Beth. The girls saw Ms. Louanna on the right side. She motioned for them to sit in the two seats she had saved. Then Sophya noticed Jenny, Johnny's twin sister, leaning forward around her mother. She waved from across the aisle. Mona came out of her revere and glanced over, then smiled through her sadness.

***

William stood up after the singing and the announcements. This was his first time back in the pulpit since his sister's death. He looked whipped. Scanning the congregation and not seeing his sister must have been heart-breaking, and then he spotted Mona and his face lit up. He looked at Sophya and Anya and smiled then glanced down at his open Bible.

"In everything give thanks" he heaved a deep sigh, "I Thessalonians 5:18 tells us."

Sophya figured the congregation viewed his transformation as surprising as she did.

"I recently told someone that I plan to live a more joyful life."

Sophya's heart felt warmed by his courage. She caught Anya glancing over at her, but she didn't look at her.

He continued, "I said whether the South wins or not, victory or no victory, for richer or for poorer."

The crowd laughed lightly, also, at this comparison.

"Seriously, Saints, think about it. Think of all the heroes in the Bible. These were recorded as a witness to us. They, surely, had wars and rumors of wars, and famine, drought and pestilence, even earthquakes!"

Some amens sounded around the room.

"Abraham had to wait for what must've seemed like forever for his promised heir. Jacob, his grandson, the deceiver, had to escape for twenty years for lying. But, he later had a *name change*, to Israel, which meant '*power with God*'! Joseph, his son, was lied about and thrown into prison unfairly. He had to wait almost twenty years to see the fulfillment of his dreams. King David had to wait about the same, and almost got killed waiting for his promise of the kingdom. Then there's Job. He lost everything…" William's voice cracked.

Tears quickly came to Sophya's eyes and, she was sure, others'. She glanced over at Mona, who slowly looked from William to Sophya and had big tears in her eyes. Jenny took her mother's hand. She leaned her head to her daughter's and stared at the Bible in her lap.

"And Jesus," Rev. Hawkins added, "was beaten and bruised and rejected, then nailed to a cross to die for our sins. Folks, we don't really have problems."

Some more in the congregation said amen.

"Our God is Faithful."

Someone said, "Yeh."

"And, He is *well able* to work something good out of

something bad, even this old war."

Ms. Louanna surprised Sophya and shouted a loud, "Amen!"

Anya patted her hand.

"God expects us, pleads with us, to be thankful *in* everything: Icy rain, drought, abundance, *lack* of abundance, good health, bad health, loss..." William looked down. Tears dropped.

Oh my gosh. Sophya's eyes flooded.

"Folks," his voice cracked again. "Love one another while you still have the chance. Be thankful you have one another and, for sure, that you have Jesus Christ."

Chapter Eighteen
DeVille the Devil

("I beheld Satan, as lightning, fall from Heaven." Luke 10:18)

As the sun rose on the quiet, calm morning, most houses in Texas continued their daily activities. It seemed as though not much has happened. But it had. The Battle of Mansfield had been won. There had been a draw concerning the Battle of Pleasant Hill. Abraham Lincoln shakily held his position as President of the North. Jefferson Davis barely held onto his position as President of the failing South. Andrew Hamilton, traitor, was acting Governor of Texas. The Texas Rangers still enforced the law. Cotton and corn still flourished. The German settlers worked the crops for pay or to earn a parcel of land and the Negro slaves work it for blood, sweat and no pay--just housing and sometimes sad conditions. Texas soil was not that affected by the War Between the States. The men that came home from fighting for other states would be affected forever, however, if they made it back at all. Louisiana lost 3,059 lives. Texas lost 1,260, plus Beth Hawkins and Johnny Sims.

***

"Mama Sara, did William say when we would be leaving to visit Mona today?"

Sophya asked as she entered the kitchen from the main house.

"Naw'sum, he jes say he cum git you and Miss Anya when he ready," Sara said.

"Oh. OK. Where's Katy? I haven't seen her today?"

"She-- in-de-sposd."

That's strange. She doesn't have much family. She is loyal to William and seldom misses work or seems to be sick.

282

"Thank you. I'll go make sure Anya is ready."

Sophya turned towards the outside plank leading back to the manse and bumped right into Anya. "Aghh!"

"Hey, watch where you're going, Sophie!" Anya snapped.

"Hey, *you* quit tail-gating!"

"I'm *not* tail-gating. You're not watching where you're going!"

"Hmm," Mama Sara said then clucked her tongue at the sisters. "Tsh, tsh, you two beat all."

They realized how foolish they sounded. Sophya looked at Anya and raised her brows. Anya just shook her head and went to sit on a stool.

"Hav sum coffee, guls, we finely got sum now," Sara added to lighten the mood.

Sophya poured the cups and brought them to the counter for Anya then the cream and sugar. She now raised her brows at Sophya, who, in turn, shook *her* head back at her. *Doesn't she think I can be nice?*

Slowly stirring her coffee she said, "It's going to seem weird, going to Johnny's Mama's house again."

"I know," Sophya said contemplatively. "Somehow, I believe William can help her though."

"How?" Anya asked.

"Well, Beth was like a daughter to him, and Johnny *was* Mona's son."

Anya sighed and drank her coffee quietly.

"D'one go match-makin', Missy. Dey bofe need healin'. Time and God da only Healah," Sara commented.

"Hmm..." Sophie digested that one. "Man, it's not like William to be late," She thought out loud.

"It's not like you to wait patiently either," Anya muttered and glared at her sister.

"He has sum biz'nes to tend to," Sara mumbled.

It struck Sophya as unusual that he would detain their plans though. She looked at Anya to ease the qualm she felt. She saw Anya staring at her coffee cup. "You OK?"

"Yes," she replied.

"You don't *have* to visit Beth's grave, Anya."

"I don't *have* to follow your foolish whims, either," she stated bitterly.

Mama Sara looked back at them.

Sophya glanced at Anya. She must've realized she was back-sliding into her bitter blame-game.

"Sorry," she quietly said.

Sophya smiled a forgiving smile.

Sara caught it. "Das right. You guls need ta gets along. Life is shote."

They gazed at each other, knowing *time* might also be short. Sophya sighed and looked into her coffee cup. Before she could ponder much, William rode up.

Sara looked out the back door, almost more anxious than the girls. "Massah."

William dismounted his horse and hopped the steps in one leap, and pecked a kiss on her forehead calmly, but his face showed stress. "Sara."

"Coffee?" Sophya offered and scooted off the stool to get a cup.

William's expression changed to surprise. Sara even glanced back at her and mumbled, "My, my."

"Thanks," he answered, so she poured then touched the sugar bowl and looked back at him.

"No," he said and sat on the first stool by Anya. "Sorry I'm late. I had unexpected business. You girls ready?"

Simultaneously, Anya and Sophya answered, "Yes."

His face relaxed and they smiled. "Hold on a minute," he said, drinking his coffee. "I'll get the buggy."

***

Once in the buggy and on the road they turned west not east.

"Where…?" Sophya started to ask.

"I have some unfinished business still. I apologize for involving you ladies, but I didn't want to keep you waiting any longer." He didn't offer any other explanation or conversation so Anya and Sophya just looked at each other and then ahead.

***

In about thirty minutes they arrived at what later would be called shanty town. It was located southeast of the county seat. At that time, it was a shabby-looking plantation.

As they rode up, they saw Negro children working out in the field with the adults. They were picking cotton under the already hot sun. Anya and Sophya looked at each other in disgust.

There were shade trees shadowing a run-down house that very badly needed painting. The grounds were dirt, no flowers or beauty anywhere. They passed a shed, or lean-to barn, on the right. From inside the structure they heard screams. They glared closer inside the opening and saw a man beating a Negro with a strap. While Sophya was adjusting to the shock, Anya jumped up and yelled, "Stop that, you jackass!"

William grabbed her and pulled her back.

"But, they can't *do* that!"

Sophya was so glad her sister could react quickly. She still sat, dazed.

William helped her to be seated again. "But they do, Anya."

His dark eyes looked from Sophya back to her, sadly.

"Please, just stay sitting in the buggy. I'll take care of it when we're leaving soon." His tone was consoling in spite of their surroundings.

They rode up closer to the plantation house. A woman was sitting in a make-shift wheel chair on the front porch. A young girl, about ten years of age, sat playing in the dirt in the yard right in front of the woman. A teen-aged girl came out of the door and handed the woman a glass of something to drink.

As Hawkins and the sisters drew close, they heard a male voice cursing from inside the house. All three of the females stopped what they were doing and looked toward the front door.

Even from where William, Sophya and Anya sat, they could see the fear on their faces.

About that time old devil DeVille opened the screen door and slammed it behind himself. He walked toward the teenage girl and hit her, knocking her down. "I told you, girl, *wash the dishes*!"

The crippled woman tried to yell with her weak voice, "Sledge, stop!"

Anya and Sophya gasped.

DeVille started to swing at the lady in the wheelchair yelling, "I told you to keep your trap *shut,* woman!"

They jumped up at the same time William did. He held his hand out. "Stay here. I'll take care of this jackass," he said out loud.

DeVille looked up and saw them. "Oh, Hawkins, I suppose you're the one to tell *me* how to act? And at my own house!" He spit on the ground.

"I don't hit women and children," William answered. "Or Negroes."

"No, you just *use* them, eh, Rev?"

William hopped from the buggy and up the porch steps in what seemed like one fluid motion. Sledge backed up like he thought William might hit him. William looked at him with disgust and in a low voice said, "Not anymore. I got smart."

DeVille spit again. "Oh yeh, how's zat?"

"I lost someone I loved." Will looked at Sledge's family then back to him.

"Tuh!" DeVille mocked. "You never loved anyone but yourself!"

William Hawkins actually appeared embarrassed with this truth being confirmed. He turned his head back toward the buggy, briefly, then back to DeVille. "I'm not here to talk about me, Sledge. I'm here to address an issue about *you*."

"Oh?" DeVille smiled his toothy grin.

"Yes," William answered as Sledge swerved like he'd been drinking.

DeVille shook his head. "You've come quite a distance and gone to a lot of trouble, knowing I come to your place every *week*."

"That's what I'm here for," William stiffened into an unyielding stance. "I came to make *sure* you stay *off* my property and keep your *hands* off anyone connected with me."

DeVille now looked guiltily down at his wife in the wheelchair. She, in turn, looked at him with hatred. DeVille leaped at William. "Why you, hypocrite bastard. You musta really got religion."

Quick as a streak, William met him in the air and they both fell off the porch. William struggled to get up and tackled Sledge, who was trying to get up. His youngest daughter cried out and scampered away, while his oldest squealed in fear.

His wife's arms stretched out to comfort the oldest one, as the youngest girl jumped up on the porch to be near her mother. They watched the men scuffle on the ground and roll over and over, struggling in the dirt.

Anya moaned, "Oh no, can't we do *something*?"

"This has to be William's fight with that devil, I suppose, Anya," Sophya said sadly. "But don't worry, if he's losing badly…" She pushed open a little board in the bottom of the buggy with her foot and showed her William's pistol.

Anya sighed. She hated guns.

A person that's never suffered abuse or had children to protect might think that way, I guess, Sophya thought.

About that time DeVille shouted more obscenities. His rage boiled and he slugged William while he had an advantage. His teenage daughter gathered closer to her mom.

Anya and Sophya watched the men fighting. William pinned

Sledge to the ground. Then Sledge cursed and flipped him over. What they didn't see was DeVille slipping a knife out of his boot. Mrs. DeVille screamed. Sophya looked from her to the men fighting in time to see Sledge stab William in the right shoulder. *Left-handed bastard!*

Blood gushed out. William yelled in pain, then in anger and rustled his enemy back to the ground.

At the same time Sophya reached for the pistol, Sledge squealed a bludgeoning squeal. William barely missed Sledge's heart when he grabbed the knife and stabbed Sledge right above it near his shoulder. A gunshot kicked the dust up beside them at that instant. A man with a Texas Ranger badge hopped down off his horse and called, "Hawkins, you OK?"

"Yeh." William rolled off and pulled his bandanna out to tie a tourniquet around his arm.

The stranger hurried over to DeVille and tied his bandanna under DeVille's arm to the top of his shoulder near his wound. He stood up, pulling Sledge to his feet and said, "I'm arresting you for the assault and rape of Hawkins' white maid, Katy Willis."

Anya and Sophya sucked in their breath, looked at each other, and said, "Katy!"

Quicker than they thought possible, in his condition, DeVille tried to run. Will grabbed him and the Ranger pulled DeVille back to the ground. The stranger punched him out and cuffed him. "That'll take the care of him for a while."

His wife and daughters cried out again.

"I wanted to do that, Tad."

"Sorry, Hawkins."

William turned back to them. "Ladies, meet Tad Walker, a friend of mine.

They nodded.

Walker stepped up on the porch, touched the teen-age girl's shoulder and said, "Honey, get me your dad's horse."

She answered, "Yes sir," and left to get it.

The smaller girl hugged her Mama tighter.

Walker stooped down at eye level with Mrs. DeVille and the girl. "You will be taken care of."

She wept and nodded, not saying a word.

He patted the little girl.

The older girl brought the horse. "Help me get him up here, Hawkins. Then you need to meet us at Doc's."

William reached to help pick up DeVille. "I'll be alright. Sara knows how to treat this. Thanks."

Tad Walker tipped his hat to Anya and Sophya and left with his cargo. He led DeVille and his horse past the buggy, nodding again as he went by.

Rev. William Hawkins went to speak to Mrs. DeVille. "Janette, this had to happen. Sledge had to be stopped. I'm sorry it was in front of everybody."

She looked down. Her girls wept quietly.

"Like Ranger Walker said, we won't forget about you. You will be taken care of."

She stared into space, nodded her head, then gave a brief smile.

"Is there anything you need now?"

She shook her head.

William patted her hand and walked back to the buggy and climbed in. Riding back by the shed, William stopped. The foreman had come outside to watch the commotion and Walker take his boss, DeVille, off.

"Smith, if I hear of you whipping anymore Negroes, Walker *and* I will come back after you next, you hear?"

Smith looked hatefully at him.

"Do you hear?"

Smith glared.

"You mind Mrs. DeVille and her daughters. We'll be checking on you to make sure."

Smith's mouth twitched.

"You *hear*?"

"Yeh," Smith answered.

It wasn't until they rode off that William Hawkins finally sighed heavily.

Chapter Nineteen
Louanna and Isaiah

("In a moment, in the twinkling of an eye, at the last trump: for the trumpet shall sound and the dead shall be raised incorruptible..." I Cor. 15:52)

Sitting in her kitchen, soaking her feet in a pan, Louanna Morris had succumbed to letting big tears drop down her cheeks. "Lord, it's been so long. My faith is gone. Seth isn't coming home. He'd a been here by now. The Battle in Mansfield is over. Thank You, God, we won. But Lord, the Battle of Vicksburg has been over for a year. If my husband was alive, You'd a brought him back to me by now." She put one hand over her eyes and drew her apron up to dry them with the other hand.

***

"Click, click," Sophya made the horses obey and guided the buggy by clicking her tongue.

"You don't even know if Ms. Louanna will be home this late in the morning, Sophya," Anya despaired.

Sophya sighed. She didn't even feel up to way-laying Anya's doubts this morning. She looked at her sister with no expression and shook the reins again. She had told Anya she believed their time was running out. They needed to say goodbye to their great-great grandmother. That was the bottom line.

Anya saw Sophya's resolve, sighed and looked ahead.

Sophya surveyed the surrounding scene, taking it all into her memory. They got to the country road that turned right to go down to their grandmother's: Sophya finally commented, "I really like the buggy ride compared to walking."

"Amen," Anya seconded the statement.

291

That ended their conversation.

***

They pulled up to their grandmother's house. All looked well, but quiet. Sophya glanced at Anya, who remained non-committal. Then Sophya hopped down and tied the reins to the fence. "Come on. Let's go say goodbye."

Anya looked sadly at Sophya and slowly scooted off the buggy.

After walking onto the porch, Sophya looked through the screen door and knocked. "Ms. Louanna? Grandmother?"

In a moment she said, "In here, honey, come on in."

Sophya looked at Anya, surprised by Louanna's unhappy voice tone. Anya tightened her lip, appearing to try to be figuring it out, also.

Pushing the screen door open, they went in and found Louanna in the kitchen with her feet in a pan of water, wiping her eyes with her apron.

Sophya was shocked, but Anya immediately rushed to comfort her. She patted her on the shoulder and asked, "What's the matter?"

Sophya walked closer to hear the answer.

Louanna sobbed more and doubled over, putting her head in her lap.

Sophya knelt down in front of her. "Louanna?"

Louanna sat back up. "Oh, girls, I'm so sorry. I can't help it. I'm tired of being strong. I appreciate your efforts to convince me, but I don't believe my Seth is coming home."

They looked at one another again.

"Have you heard otherwise?" Sophya asked.

Louanna shook her head and whimpered.

Then it hit Sophya. "You *don't* believe that we are your great-granddaughters?"

She looked up and smiled, comfortingly, but replied, "I believe

292

you are two very sweet girls that just, maybe, stopped by to visit an old woman."

Sophya sat back on her knees. Then she recalled that discouragement was the devil's best tool and could blind the truth.

"Ms. Louanna," she became determined. "How did we just choose your road to walk down that morning, that early?"

Anya sarcastically sighed and said, "Tuh, yeh!"

Louanna Morris looked at them through her watery, crystal blue eyes, but didn't answer.

She proceeded. "How did we know about your children?"

She started to say, "Reverend…"

"No," Sophya stated emphatically. "Even *he* believed me because we knew Seth's full name to be Isaiah Seth."

She thought for a minute.

Anya interjected, "I assure you, neither Sophya, nor any other angel, could prod me to wake that early and without breakfast, walk that far, except to meet my great-grandmother."

This made Louanna laugh a little and she blotted her snotty nose with her apron saying, "Uh oh." She took off her messy apron and put it on the floor beside her. Then, she just looked at them a moment. She sighed and took the towel from the next chair and began wiping her feet.

"Here, let me," Sophya said.

Louanna stretched her lips tight to acquiesce.

"I'm sorry you found me like this."

"Everyone has their down days," Anya mumbled looking at Sophya, knowing she would agree because of Anya's mood that morning.

Sophya dried Louanna's feet and took the pan out back to pour out the water. When she came back in, Anya had gotten their grandmother to laugh about something. At that point, Sophya didn't even care if she had been the butt of the joke.

"What?" she demanded.

Anya laughed again, so did Louanna as she said, "It's good to have sisters."

"Hmm," Sophya replied looking from one to the other.

Louanna slapped her hands on to her knees with determination--after sliding her feet into her slippers and stood up. "Well, you girls have missed breakfast, and there's no more soldiers coming anymore. Do you want to help with dinner and stay and eat?"

"What are we having?" Sophya asked.

"As if it matters to you," Anya snickered.

Louanna smiled and shook her head at them. "Fried chicken?" She raised her brows questioningly.

"Hmm," Sophie replied. "Will you also teach me how *you* make peach cobbler?"

"Yes," she smiled.

"I hate cutting up chickens!" Anya blurted.

"You hate doing anything unless it's your idea and *easy*!"

Anya stuck her tongue out at Sophya.

"Mercy," Louanna said.

They laughed.

Grandmother Morris began cutting up the chicken after it was rinsed. A bowl filled with batter made of egg and buttermilk along with a bowl of seasoned flour to dip it in awaited.

Sophya broke up green snap beans. Anya peeled peaches.

"Will you tell us about our grandfather Isaiah?" Sophya asked.

Louanna looked out the window, as if being reminded to look for him again. Then, she glanced back toward the girls and began. "When I met Seth, I least expected it."

She sighed. "I was engaged to Charles." She raised a haughty chin and continued. "I had gone to the market in Mansfield, near the feed store. My parents had come here to Texas from the Carolinas, but we were about as close to the other market, too. Anyway, I liked the one in Mansfield best. That day seemed especially perfect to go to the market. While I came out of the store, Seth came out of the feed store next door at the same time. I had parked my buggy in front of the feed store because he had parked his wagon in front of the grocery store. We criss-crossed to walk out and bumped right into each other! His wagon was loaded. He had been paying his bill. I dropped all my groceries on the sidewalk planks. Neither of us could blame the other. Neither of us was paying any attention. He immediately started apologizing and helping me pick up my groceries. His horses reared at me and he quickly calmed them so they wouldn't scare me."

She stopped and smiled another moment looking back at them, then she dropped the chicken pieces into the sizzling grease pot. "He was tall and good-looking, with piercing dark eyes and hair. I instantly liked him and felt attracted to him and...well, somehow protected."

Louanna turned and faced us as she leaned her back against the counter. She appeared to be in deep thought. "It dawned on me, I had never felt *protected* when I was with Charles. Oh, he was good-looking, almost carelessly good-looking. My mother liked him, but Dad always warned me to be very *sure* before I married him. He never said that about Seth."

She smiled at Anya and Sophya. "Anyway, I'm jumping ahead." She raised her brows and sighed. "I felt the *excitement* with Charles, but not the trust, I guess you could say. He was even wealthy." She winked at us both. "But deep down, I felt he was a lady's man. I saw how women looked at him. It took me a while to see how he was looking back at them."

She tightened her lips, turned around to check the chicken, and back to the girls. "Seth introduced himself that day. Said his parents had a spread over closer to Center, the county seat, but liked to shop here, away from everybody, sometimes. Later, I was glad he picked *that time* to do it. He seemed so confident and caring. He asked if I was married. I said no, but engaged. That didn't seem to faze him. He asked where I lived. I vaguely told him. But, he had already *seen* the attraction in my eyes. I had seen it in his, too, but I believed in being honorable. At least, I believed it until one day when I caught Charles and my cousin in a questionable predicament. They convinced me it was innocent, but a seed of doubt had been planted. Another time, at a country dance, Charles left me unattended for quite a while. When he reappeared, he didn't mind the other gentlemen's attentions to me, and he smelled like someone else's perfume, not mine. I broke up with him that night."

"I didn't know how to get in touch with Isaiah Seth Morris. I thought about leaving a note at the feed store, and then erased that thought for being too forward. I just handed it over to God. Seth, later, asked the grocer my whereabouts and he told him. One day, he just showed up at my doorstep. I was sitting out on that very porch shelling peas. My parents died soon after I married and left the place to me." Louanna looked out the back window this time, at the farmland. "Anyway, he surprised me when he drove up. Sophya smiled. He asked permission to come through the gate. I nodded. I was in an old dress. My hair was sweaty and wiry and *red*. I hated that!" They laughed.

"Isaiah Seth came up the steps and got down on his knees. He said, 'Ms. Louanna, I think it'd be a mistake if you marry your fiancée. I think it's the Lord's will for you to marry me!' I blushed. My dad had come to the screen door. He nodded his approval. I acted like I didn't see it and looked straight into Seth's eyes and asked, 'Why is that?' He smiled and said, 'God told me.' I told him, 'I'll *consider* it, but you and I need to get to *know* one another first!' Seth smiled again, and said, 'Thank you,' and stood up. I motioned for him to sit by me, and he did, every day after that." She sighed. "Until this old war. But, I always felt safe and protected, even while he was away. I knew by him fighting to protect our homeland, he was protecting me in his own way." Her eyes glistened.

Anya and Sophya sighed after being so enthralled with her story of their grandfather.

"Wow," Sophya replied as Louanna took the chicken pieces out and set them to drain on a plate. The potatoes she'd handed Anya were peeled, and were now boiling and the green beans were simmering with bacon fat.

Anya sat mesmerized still by her story.

"How about you?" Louanna asked. "Have you seen Brooks again? What have you decided about your marriage?"

Sophya took a deep breath as she helped place the chicken, beans, mashed potatoes and gravy on the table.

"After we eat I'll tell you."

They laughed again.

***

Sophya finished her peach cobbler first and wiped her mouth with her napkin. "Brooks has been marvelous."

Anya laughed.

Louanna looked up. "How?"

"He has restored my faith in men." Sophya tightened her lip as Louanna looked intently into her eyes. "Yes, men, not mankind. He is all of those things you mentioned that attracted you to Seth and Charles. He's exciting, and actually, comforting, good looking, protective, but not careless-- ever." Sophya jutted her jaw out while she analyzed. "I don't know why I met him, except, maybe, to restore my faith."

Louanna smiled at that answer. "And your marriage?"

She glanced over at Anya almost apologetically. "I have decided to wait on God."

Anya's eyes showed disbelief.

Louanna looked at her and back to Sophya.

"If God can throw two women back in time, He can surely change my husband or deliver me from him." She closed her eyes at the pain involving that decision.

The other two women stayed silent.

Her voice quaked, "God has changed William Hawkins. He may change William Blackwell."

"Look at the cost!" Anya sobbed.

297

Louanna glanced kindly at Anya and back to Sophya.

Sophya raised her eyebrows and sighed at the loss of the lovely Beth. "I know. This has been, otherwise, an exciting time for me. It's given me a chance to think things through and see them in a different perspective. Time is nothing to God, even though it's *everything* to someone as impatient as me."

Louanna laughed lightly.

"Meeting Beth and Brooks and Lillie and *you*, even William and Katy, has been an experience I'm glad to have had. Mama Sara and *Flo* and that *devil* DeVille were a real trial!"

They laughed.

"Sweet Johnny and his mom and sister have been a blessing, so was helping Sammy. And *oh,* General Richard Taylor…*wow*!"

Louanna and Anya smiled.

"God has been good to me, in spite of me."

They got quiet at this reminder to be thankful.

"What about you, Anya? Has anything good happened to you through this?" Our grandmother asked.

Anya sighed.

Sophya wasn't sure she'd open up so she, typically, jumped in. "She met *Stev--ie*!"

Anya blushed and Louanna looked at her and questioned, "Oh?"

"Yes, thank you very much, So--phe--ya!" Anya smiled at Louanna. "I met Steve Garrett through Beth. I don't know why, either. But maybe, someday, I'll meet someone in real life," she sighed, "who's just like him." She got a distant look in her eyes then realized they were staring and holding their breath. She smiled to comfort them. "He's perfect." She sighed and stopped talking.

"Oh, girls, Life is amazing. I pray the Lord forgives me for forgetting that a moment." Louanna got up to bring the dishes to the sink. "My life, with my Seth, has truly been a blessing." She flattened her lips, then smiled.

"Grandmother," Sophya said, needing to hear that word. "We

think our time here may be up soon." Her eyes moistened.

Ms. Louanna stiffened at that deduction. The she smiled, realizing what Sophya just called her. She went and hugged them.

There were no dry eyes.

***

"Click, click," Sophya clicked her tongue to the horses. "We love you, Grandmother Louanna."

She, sporting a clean apron, wiped her eyes and waved. "I have come to love you two girls, too. Pray for me and Seth. I'll pray for you."

They nodded.

"Thanks," a teary-eyed Anya mumbled and waved.

Sophya steered the horses to go to the top of the hill. Anya was still looking back waving at Louanna, who stood at the fence waving to them. Sophya saw a man approaching over the hill on the other side of the road. He was wearing ragged clothes and a hat, and walking with the aid of a big stick. His left arm was missing. That shirt sleeve was tied in a knot. He looked to be in his early fifties. All of the sudden Sophya's breath caught in her throat.

"*Huh! Anya!*" she whispered.

Anya turned. "What?"

"*Look!*"

She gazed at the man. He looked down while he walked. Then Anya stared at her sister in wonder.

"Sir," Sophya's voice almost failed. "May I offer you a ride?"

He stopped and looked up. *Such weary eyes.* He looked in the direction she was heading and back to her.

Sophya smiled.

"No ma'am. I'm almost home," he sighed and added, "just over this hill. Thanks, though." He took a deep breath and stuck his stick in the dirt and began walking again.

Ain't no way I'm moving this buggy.

Anya understood the unspoken words.

They stayed there and watched as he walked over the hill. He looked back at them and nodded, as if assuring them they could go now that they'd seen he'd made it over.

Sophya turned back to look at Louanna while Anya watched the man.

Louanna had just about turned to go in, when she saw the buggy stop at the top of the hill. She turned back to the fence to see if they had a problem.

As the man made it over the hill and headed down the road, the girls heard Louanna yell,

"Ohhhh!"

The man looked up and almost crumbled in delight. He picked up his pace as she ran to meet him halfway. She greeted him with hugs and kisses and more hugging and kissing! Then, she remembered to wave to Anya and Sophya, displaying her happiness. She must've told him something about them. He, weakly, turned and waved, also. Then, Louanna Morris ushered Isaiah Seth Morris home.

Chapter Twenty
The Proposal and the Fire!

("And now, behold, I go bound in the Spirit to Jerusalem, not knowing the things that shall befall me there." Acts 20:22)

"Tuesday, April the 19th, hmm. the day I met the real William," Sophya said, looking out of the window. "Wonder what today holds? Oh well, I'm going horseback riding to the creek--and to see Brooks!"

Not wanting to disturb Anya, she set out for the kitchen. Walking down the stairs, she thought, *Rev. William sure was quiet yesterday and stayed to himself after his good sermon on Sunday. The other William would have been hanging around constantly to be bragged on.*

She didn't see Lillie or Katy. Strange. She was glad Katy was doing better, though.

Crossing the plank she smelled Sara's good cooking. "Good morning, Sara."

"Good mawnin', Miz Sophie," she actually smiled.

"Where *is* everybody?"

Sara looked up in surprise. "Katy upstaihz. Lillie late. Mastah, he out in da bahn. He do his haws-shoe makin' taday."

"Oh. Wonder where he was yesterday," she said, thinking out loud.

Sara turned to look at her in surprise.

Sophya raised her eyebrows and plopped on the stool. "I don't handle boredom very well." She smiled briefly.

"Mastah go ta town." That's all she offered.

So Sophya changed the subject. "Those eggs and bacon sure smell good."

Sara flipped some onto a plate with a biscuit and some bacon for her.

"Ummm." She glanced down and said a blessing.

When Sophya's head came up, Sara said, "Git you cup o' coffee."

Sophya obeyed, saying, "Great-- we've got some!"

"Umhmm," came her comment.

After eating, Sophya told Sara she wanted to saddle a horse and ride to the creek.

Once in the barn Sophya saw William sweating over a hot iron. She presumed he was shaping it into a horseshoe. He glanced up and smiled a quick smile. "How are you doing?"

Analytical Sophya wondered, *What does he mean by that?* "I'm…fine?" she said questioningly.

William smirked a little that his question was so general. "I mean, I've been gone and wondered how your day was yesterday and so forth."

And so *forth...* She smiled. "Good. I stayed in my room a lot, writing. Today, I'm feeling bored. This routine of having *servants* to do all the work is weird."

He laughed out loud.

"May I saddle Rusty and go riding?"

Was that a flash of disappointment she saw cross William's face?

"Sure," he hesitated. "Where to?" He shook his thoughts away. "Never mind. Sure." He tightened his bottom lip and nodded. "Can we talk for a while first?"

She sighed unconsciously, and then felt badly for it. "OK." She sat on the stump and looked up at him. "I won't bother your work?"

"Nah," he said and hammered the horseshoe into shape. Then, he looked in deep thought and slacked off hammering. "May I ask you about your life? I don't want to offend you, though."

Another sigh. "Alright. Shoot."

He laid his half-formed horseshoe down on the brick stone ledge, then his sledge hammer.

"I never even bothered to asked, do you have any children?"

She smiled. *That's not too intimidating.* "Yes, three."

"Do you mind telling me about them?"

"I miss them terribly," she said.

He smiled. "I would imagine so. I bet you're a good mother."

She closed her eyes. "I try, but, the jury's still out on that one."

William chuckled. "I bet not."

She shook her head debating why they didn't even want to come with her. "Deidra is thirteen, Bobby is ten and Billy is five. Their hair is blonde, black and brown, respectively," Sophya laughed. "Diedra wishes she didn't have brothers. Bobby says the same about Billy!"

He smiled.

"Do you mind telling me what you fell in love with about your husband?"

She weighed that for a moment, whether to tell him and what to tell. "When I first met him, I was attracted because he was tall and handsome and neat, and had a clean cut hair cut and was well-shaven."

William blinked at that information. She supposed he may have remembered how she questioned him about his hair and mustache in the beginning. He stoked the fire in the clay-bottom of the 'smithing pit.

"Surely you loved something deeper than that."

She blinked hard at the reprimand but continued, "He seemed kind and considerate. Generous. But all that changed after we married."

"How so?"

She swallowed hard, debating how much to reveal. "A marriage license changes things...apparently," she tightened her lips.

William looked sad for her.

She supposed that prodded her to go on. "It seems that a piece of paper, called a *marriage license*, gives some men the *license* to stop doing some things but start doing others."

"Like what?"

"Sometimes, and I've conferred with my friends for confirmation, men are only into the *hunt*!"

William opened his eyes wide gaining understanding and trying not to be defensive. He opened his mouth to speak.

Sophya held up her hand to stop him. "You know, it's in y'all's *nature* so I guess we can't kill you for that! Once you marry us, the hunt is over and the trophy is put on the shelf."

William shook his head.

"Not all, I know, but at least *half* of you. Some *may* want you more once they have you, but many *stop* wanting you."

He continued to shake his head, but didn't speak, probably since he had no experience.

"What, or who *used* to be important, now is not. Someone, whose opinion *used* to be valued, is now stupid. Someone, who *used* to be exciting, is now boring and possibly pregnant. And, *you* may be the very spouse that thinks pregnant is ugly, and children are a nuisance and expense that *you* didn't necessarily bargain for!" She was getting mad just talking about it!

William looked shocked. "Not all."

Sophya held her hand up again. "Then, this exciting, attractive *trophy* is now an inanimate object placed on a shelf. The only time you spend with it is to curse it out because it got dusty and lost its *sheen,* because *you* didn't think it was important enough to take down and dust and polish it. It was just to show your friends or use to relieve your sexual desire." She closed her eyes to keep back her tears. "*You* are too busy going to a job you hate because you now have a family to support."

William tried to touch and comfort her.

Sophya continued and but didn't let him touch her. "So, *you* go out to *saloons,*" She used a word he understood. "And spend your time and money on women that *sparkle* and haven't lost their luster yet. They don't have children to tend to and are *temporary*! They won't *tie you down*! Plus, you are paying double or triple for those *drinks* you could have bought cheaper down at the store near your home, but complaining your *family* costs you too much!"

William was silent.

Sophya relaxed.

"I fell in love listening to all of his life experiences and past troubles. I thought my love could heal his hurts."

William looked down at the fire, probably thinking what she found out…that healing is God's job.

"All that listening and backing him in all he wanted to try, except for other women, didn't pay off. It just set the pattern. He was never willing to listen to me without arguing, or back me in anything I believed in."

William looked at her in sympathy.

"So, a bitter pattern began-- of spite. What he did to me, I got back at him for. And," she looked around, "and this is the most I've gotten to vent to a *male* in twenty years!"

Sophya realized she actually felt lighter, and laughed.

William dropped to his knees and surprised her. He dug something out of his pocket, after shedding his 'smithing gloves. It was wrapped in a black velvet cloth.

He opened his conversation with, "Sophie…Sophya, *I* wouldn't *do* those things to you. *You* are the most exciting, sincere, beautiful woman I've ever met! Please, do me the honor of being my wife." He looked away, then back, refusing to let her answer yet.

"I am financially well off enough to where supporting a family would not make me bitter. Please, Sophya, God is giving you a chance to do it over again…right." His eyes pleaded and he went to put the ring with the huge diamond on her finger.

Right outside, Brooks walked up to place his hand on the barn door after asking Sara about Sophya's whereabouts. Then, Chief Running Brook put his head against the barn door, closing the small slit he had just opened after hearing William's proposal. He lifted his head back up, placed a kiss on his fingertips and pressed them to the barn door, then quietly left.

Sophya was startled by William's proposal. When she came out of her daze, she took the ring off and handed it back to him. "Are you *out* of your mind? We couldn't make it the *first* time!"

"I'm not *him*."

Oh, God, help.

William looked like she had just slapped him and he fell back, leaning on his rear instead of his knees.

Sophya started pacing. When she saw him fall back she turned back to help him up.

He waved her away, even in his stunned condition, mumbling, "No, no!"

She looked at him with all the compassion she could muster. He had been through so much. He *had* changed…and for the better.

"Oh, William, I am so sorry if I led you on in any way."

He rolled over onto his knees to get up. "No, no. It's OK." He dusted himself off, then he started coming towards her. "Sophya, *this* is the chance you've always *wanted!* You've admitted that. This is the time in history, this is the *place*…" he waved his hand around. "And I *have* changed." He looked at her pleadingly.

She held her hand up to keep him at a distance, but his words softened her heart. She stepped towards him and held her hands over his hand that clutched the diamond ring. He was holding it out again for her to reconsider.

She closed her eyes and hoped for the right words. She opened them and saw his eyes staring at her in pain, waiting for her answer. "But, I don't love you."

He dropped his hand from hers in defeat and sat on the stump.

Sophya sighed and walked over to him while he stared into space. "I mean, I'm not *in* love with you."

William closed his eyes to block out those words.

"All those things you said are true. I love this place and time and you *have* changed for the better. And God *knows* I love living 'high on the hog'."

He looked up and laughed sarcastically at her analogy.

"There's something you are discounting though."

William raised his brows questioningly and said, "Oh?" almost uninterested.

"My children are my life."

He closed his eyes tight and sighed.

"Oh, they might not realize it, or appreciate it. But, I did without food and clothes *and* a father, while growing up. I do *not* want to put them through that."

William was listening now.

"And you know they didn't come *with* me, back in time, so I'm praying I'll get back to *them*, soon!"

After a moment, William replied, "I understand."

She believed he actually did, since he raised Beth like his own child.

Then her confidence rose to speak up, now that this man was finally listening to her. "William…"

He sighed and looked at her after standing up and putting the ring back into its cover and in his pocket.

Sophya held her hands around his hand again. "There's some*one* else that you are discounting, also."

"Who?"

"I believe God has brought *Mona* into your life for this purpose…not me."

"Mona?" he showed surprise and started to shake his head.

"*Think* about it. *Think* about all y'all have in common."

He sighed a non-committal sigh and looked away; maybe thinking the only thing they had in common was pain.

"William," she clasped his hands tighter. "I am a woman. I noticed something in her eyes toward you…love. *Promise* me you will pray about it. And," she smiled, "I saw a good heart in *her*."

He looked up knowing she meant Flo had lacked that.

Sighing, he patted her hand and smiled. "OK. Now let's get you saddled up."

Through the woods she went to the creek.

He was not there.

Sophya urged Rusty across the creek and over the ridge to his cabin. She looped the reins around the porch post. "Brooks, Brooks!" But, he was not there. She walked out to the back porch, remembering it had been there they both realized they didn't want to part from each other. He was not there. *If I go back to the brook and wish for him hard enough, he'll show up, I just know it.*

She slid off Rusty, not even bothering to tie him. He loved people. He'd stay here if she stayed nearby. She patted his face and nuzzled his muzzle. "Oh, Rusty, where is Brooks?"

He neighed and nodded his head.

She sat on the log near the bank, knowing it was time to say goodbye to Brooks. *Surely, God will give me the chance to say goodbye.*

She heard a horse approaching and looked up. It was that man, the Ranger that arrested Sledge DeVille the other day. Sophya blotted her eyes and stood up to hold onto Rusty to keep him from spooking. She didn't appreciate any company right now.

"Ma'am," the Ranger spoke and tipped his hat. His dark curly, *unruly* hair needed a haircut, she noticed. It probably represented his personality too, she also, deducted.

Oh, God, I just pre-judged him.

"Do you know Chief Running Brook?" Sophya asked holding her hand over her eyes to block off the approaching noon sun.

"Yes, ma'am."

Pure, Texas drawl.

"Have you seen him today?"

The Ranger took his hat off. His hand still rested on the saddle horn and his hat dangled from his fingertips. He sighed and wiped his brow with the other hand, like he'd rather not discuss it. "Yes, he's gone."

"*Gone?*" Sophya's hand fell to her side.

"Yes'm."

She started feeling sick. She felt queasy. He watched her. "Where to?" she managed to ask, shakily.

He sighed, "I told him earlier this morning his people were being escorted north to Oklahoma today, to where the Cherokees were taken. I gave them time to prepare and am just now coming back to check on them."

Sophya felt as though she would faint and slumped to the log, scaring Rusty.

The Ranger, she couldn't remember his name...Walker or something, started to dismount.

"Ma'am, are you going to be alright?"

She lifted her head from staring into space and glared at him, daring him to dismount and help her.

He stopped.

Sophya glanced over at the cool stream--with all its memories-- and back to the Ranger, with tears streaming now. "That doesn't really matter anymore."

She surprised herself at her bitterness. Then, it dawned on her, "Maybe I can catch up with him to say goodbye."

"Tuh," the pesky stranger mumbled. "I doubt it."

Sophya looked defiant at him. "Why not?"

"He disappeared when I told him the troops were coming to escort the Indians north."

"Disappeared?" she looked down trying to figure it out, then back up to the Ranger.

"Yeh, vanished, or whatever hoo-doo he does."

"Hoo-doo?" She looked angrily up at him. "He's a very religious man, how dare you say that!"

He sighed, "Are you going to be alright?"

She shook her head. "No, but you can *leave*. I *sure* don't need *your* compassion!"

"Look ma'am…"

Sophya looked down, shaking her head, still trying to figure it all out.

"I am only the messenger, ma'am. Running Brook won't be back. The Rangers will be the law over this area now."

She looked back at him doubtfully.

He shook his head and turned his horse to leave.

Then she crumbled and wept, finally glad to be alone and get to do it. She looked longingly at the stream. Through it flowed the water that washed away the guilt of William's forceful touch on her. This was where Brooks covered her shame. Water could be peaceful to the soul. Water could be a treacherous, a damaging flood. *Death by drowning must be a peaceful death*, she thought.

***

Later, back in Mama Sara's kitchen, Sophya sat numbly on a stool. She couldn't even think of going up the stairs to be alone in her room right now. She had just tied Rusty out by the kitchen.

Sara had started cooking dinner. While her back was to Sophya she asked, "Mistah Brooks find you? Ah tole him you went to da bahn."

She looked over at Sara in amazement, unable to speak. Big tears barreled down her cheeks. *He must've overheard me talking with William!*

Sara turned to look at Sophya. *Was that sympathy in her eyes?*

About the time Sophya tried to speak, Lillie entered the kitchen through the back door. Then she rushed through the kitchen only to throw up outside over the plank, and ran into the plantation home.

"That chile mus' hav' sum kind a *stomach* trouble or sumpin'. She been throwin' up evah mawning," Sara realized what she just said and gasped and dropped her soup ladle into the pot.

Sophya gasped at the same time and Sara turned slowly to look at her with fear in her eyes, realizing the implication.

About that time, Anya ran across the plank from the manse, screaming, "The barn's on fire! The barn's on fire! Sophie…help…help!" She yanked her off the stool.

Sara started pumping water into pots and met them outside. They saw William running out of the barn with an exasperated look and yelling, "I must've carelessly sparked a spark!" He hollered apologetically, knowing the girls probably felt it was their only way home.

"Oh, *God!*" Sophya stared at the flames of the barn reaching toward the sky, destroying their only hope. About that time Sophya came to her senses and started to help the others carry the water from the outside pump. Then she saw Anya, staring at the barn in shock. Then she started running into the barn screaming, "Mom! Urich!"

Sophya dropped her bucket and ran after her sister as she heard William yell, "Nooo…Sophie!"

As soon as Sophya entered the barn she felt that same sensation as before…a blow to the head. But, this time she felt propelled upward instead of falling. "Ayyy!"

***

Silence.

She looked around the dark, old barn. *Dark? Old?*

Anya was coming to her senses. She glanced around, looked over at Sophie and shook her head clear. Then, she stood up fast and ran for the door. "*Mom! Urich!*"

"Anya! No! Don't *tell* them!" Then Sophie whispered, "*They won't understand.*" She mumbled the last words, but her sister was gone.

She looked around in disbelief. *Well, this is what I decided I wanted, right?* She felt a sadness settle in on her. She got up from her rear onto her knees. Then she crumbled, face down in the dirt crying,

311

"Why, why, why, God? Why did you let me meet Brooks, then take him away?" She sobbed and sobbed, stretching flat out on the ground. Now, she was back to face, face to face, the life she had failed at, again. But a scripture came to her mind; *I can do all things through Christ, which strengthens me.*

Sophya sat back up and wiped her eyes. She looked around. She had on her Bermuda shorts. Same torn shoulder. *Same bra!* "Huh!" she exclaimed. Slowly, she put her right hand into her left bra cup. "It's there!" She pulled out the folded picture that William drew of her and Gen. Richard Taylor! She was so thankful! It traveled through time with her! She unwrapped Grandmother Louanna's kerchief from around it and opened it. She wept and wept, and thanked God over and over. She felt something in the pocket of her shorts. She stood up slowly and pulled it out. *It's my writing paper!* As she unfolded the paper, the pen fell out!

"Oh, God!" She walked around in a circle crying, "Thank You, God."

***

"Why didn't you call me yesterday?" William Blackwell demanded, on the other end of the phone.

"I'm calling you *now,* to tell you, I'm heading home this afternoon."

"Is that all you have to say for yourself?" he asked.

"Yep," Sophya suppressed a laugh.

"You're different," he said, trying to analyze the situation.

Sophya sighed and didn't say anything.

"Have you met someone else?" he pushed for an answer.

"Yes, Jesus Christ. I saw Him in church today and He said He *really* loves me."

"Tuh!" Will spat out. "Exactly *when* will you be leaving so I'll know *when* you'll be home in that car?"

312

"I'm not sure."

"You're not *sure*? Have you lost your *mind* while you were up there?"

Only my heart.

Nothing. She said nothing. She would *not* let him bully *her*, or the kids, anymore.

"You miss me, huh," he decided.

"I miss the kids. I'm getting ready to leave. *You* could have called *me* yesterday. Oh, wait, no, I forgot, it's long *distance*! You could have had *Mikki* call and check on me. Yeh! Mikki! Now, *if* you don't hang up and quit detaining me, I may change my mind and stay longer!"

"What's gotten into you?" Will asked confused.

"Courage," Sophya answered. "Bye." She began to hang up the receiver.

She didn't realize her mother had come into the living room and sat in her recliner. When Sophya turned around, her mom lowered the book she was reading and looked at her.

"This has been a wonderful trip, Mom." she said.

Christian smiled. "Sure you don't want to stay a little longer?"

"That's never been the question, it's *can Mikki handle all the kids*?"

They laughed as Anya came in and hugged Sophya, staring deeply into her eyes. Then Anya said, "I'm sorry, Sophie."

She realized her sister's double meaning. She hugged her back offering her forgiveness.

Sophya went and bent over and hugged Mom, motioning for her not to get up.

"Let's see, oh yeh, *If God be for me, who can be against me?* There!"

They laughed.

"Where's Urich?"

"Here I am." He walked in as if on cue.

Sophya hugged him, too. "Well, I'm heading out."

"You *sure*?" Mom said again.

"I'm sure-- for now, anyway."

She checked her pockets. "Oh, here's your pen."

Chapter Twenty-One
Hero Hall of Fame

("These all died in the faith not having received the promises but having seen them afar off and were persuaded of them and embraced them and confessed, they were strangers and pilgrims on earth…declaring plainly that they seek a country." Heb. 11:1 & 8)

Albert Blanchard:

Albert Blanchard arrived, in 1846, from Tennessee to settle in Sabinetown, Texas, the "entrance to the Sabine River" at that time. His older sister, Melvina, also came with him and his parents, Franklin and Emma. Franklin was twenty-eight and Emma was twenty-four. Their destination had been the home of John and Elizabeth Clark and their daughter, Ava and their adopted son, Joaquin. Elizabeth and Franklin were brother and sister. Their children became close friends as well as cousins. Joaquin's real mother, Many Shining Stars was Hias or Caddo Indian. She had been raped by a Mexican bandit and conceived Joaquin Salazar. She was killed five years later by another Mexican bandit, since Sabinetown was near "No Man's Land"--an unmarked territory between Louisiana and Texas where murderers and thieves hid out.

April 1846, Franklin and John left to fight with Brig. Gen. Robert K. Goodlow. He had come seeking volunteers to help fight and keep Mexico from taking over Texas at Ft. Brown (Brownsville). Franklin was injured by a lead ball and died May 26th, before going home. His wife, Emma fought grief and depression for a year until Elizabeth came and read to her out of the Bible. Emma felt encouraged and decided to live. One night, a neighbor's house caught on fire. She told her children to stay in bed while she went to help. Albert had a bad feeling about it and pleaded for his mom not to go.

She felt obligated and went anyway. (*Sabinetown,* by Robert Beddoe, pp. 28-29).

Emma's wagon was swept away off the icy ferry into swift flood waters. She died instantly. The news was brought to her children that they were orphaned. That week, Albert and Melvina were visited by Lila Coffee and her daughter, Mollie, and they took them home with them.

Albert grew to love Mollie and happily married her later. Melvina fell in love with a tall, dark stranger, named Joseph Sturrock. Joseph was smitten with Melvina, also. He came to town as the new surveyor from Tennessee, following in Earl Beddoe's job, in Nacogdoches, TX. (*Sabinetown,* p. 121 #3).

One Saturday morning, March 1864, Brig. Gen. Hampton Bee's Calvary from south Texas arrived in Sabinetown to camp. Union forces had captured Ft. DeRussy, LA. Gen. Bee posted a "call to arms" for a hundred volunteers to fight for the Confederacy. Judson Smith was appointed captain without popular vote. Albert Blanchard was elected first lieutenant and Earl Beddoe was elected second lieutenant. This was due to their popularity, academic background and hunting skills. For these reasons, also, Joseph Sturrock was commanded to be second lieutenant to quartermaster under Gen. Bee's staff. Joaquin Salazar signed up also. (*Sabinetown,* p. 123 #6).

Capt. Smith proved to be an evil, cowardly leader. He degraded Joaquin as a "half-breed" often and rode his men unnecessarily hard. But, after many drills, the area's 23rd Texas Calvary mounted up and marched out of Sabinetown. (p. 126 #1). Church bells tolled all over, as the Confederate flags were displayed and the men marched off valiantly to fight. The women gathered to see them off and the men took courage to defend and protect them.

April 3, 1864, Union Gen. Banks and his troops arrived in Natchitoches, LA. His plan was to move north and take Shreveport. (p. 131 #10). The size of Banks' army, the length of the train, and also his 1,000 wagons and their direction was reported to Gen. Bee. Word needed to be sent to Confederate Gen. Richard Taylor. Lt. Earl Beddoe was chosen for his knowledge of the area to deliver the message secretly and swiftly. He rode across the land and the Sabine River at night by changing horses in people's barns without their awaking. He crossed the Sabine by Myricks Ferry at Logansport. He reached Taylor's troops at Keatchie by 2 a.m. This act of bravery initiated the victory into motion for Mansfield, LA and the Battle of Mansfield.

The 23rd Texas Infantry Regiment were first to open fire at Major Davidson's command. Then, they were followed by a storm of other hidden Confederates. There, Capt. Sibley saw the advance from the north from Sabinetown and swung his entire company around and filled them with lead for three hours. (p. 135 #7). It was here that Judson Smith was shot for cowardice by Sergeant Raymond Waglerski, Sr. as Smith ran. Waglerski immediately received a promotion to lieutenant and led a terrific attack. The Yankees retreated and Confederate Gen. Mouton's men met them head-on. After Mouton and many others were mortally wounded, the rebels came out the victors.

Banks retreated to Pleasant Hill, about ten miles south of Mansfield. The next day's battle there was called a draw. The Union retreated out of Louisiana from that point, being chased by Gen. Taylor, who then took time to grieve his losses.

Joseph Sturrock located Earl Beddoe, who informed him Albert Blanchard had been wounded and taken to a hospital. Joaquin couldn't be found yet, but had survived. As Earl walked off, Joseph turned to help a soldier he recognized, who then died. Joseph was captured by a band of Yanks who in turn were wiped out by another group of Rebels. Joseph was wounded in the hip and taken to a near-by plantation to heal. (p.139 #1).

As the first casualties of the battle arrived at a home made into a hospital, at Keatchie, Mollie Blanchard set out with another woman named Phoebe to help. They traveled by wagon that night through Pulaski (Carthage) and crossed with the Sabine River Ferry. They helped Dr. McGuire, of Sabinetown, also, to tend Union and Confederate soldiers alike. (p. 144 #1; p. 146 #12).

At 3:30 a.m. more wounded arrived in wagons. "this one's hurt bad, Doc." Doc McGurie turned and said, "My God, it's Albert!" Mollie ran to him and screamed when she saw her husband. As blood trickled out of Albert's mouth, he opened his eyes and turned to his wife. His hand went to touch her face and she grabbed it with both of hers. She kissed his dying lips and said, "Albert, I love you." Then, brave Albert died.

Mollie left Keatchie with her dead husband in a wagon and headed home. After his funeral she put Texas and her past behind her with a move to her sister's in Arkansas.

Joseph healed and later found his way back home to Melvina. Then, Earl and Joaquin came home alive.

Sabinetown no longer exists except at the bottom of Toledo Bend Reservoir.

***

Leopold L. Armant:

Armant became major in May of 1862. By July, he was made a colonel. In July and August of 1863, he was Commander in Mouton's brigade, the 18th LA and the Yellow Jacket Battery of LA Infantry.

He was a native of St. James parish in Louisiana, advanced in education, culture and wealth. He was the most efficient lieutenant in the 18th regt. He was accomplished, agreeable and sociable, reportedly, as he fought in the Battle of Shiloh. Alfred Mouton requested information on the Union movement in that area. It was a dangerous assignment, but Col. Armant accepted this duty. He stole by night and climbed a tree to witness the Yankee activity and gave report to Col. Mouton. Mouton, in turn, gave specific recognition of Armant as gallant, daring, bold and reliable.

Col. Mouton, became Brig. Gen. while at home healing in the

Attakapas Indian region of Louisiana. Col. Armant was sent to the Trans-Mississippi Dept. and promoted to major.

After ill winds and ill health, Col. Roman resigned his post at Tupelo and left for home. Lt. Col. Bush left for Trans-Miss. Dept. for the same reasons. At the time Armant was to be promoted, Capt. Collins got promoted to lieutenant colonel and Mouton to major. The 18th LA was then sent to Pollard, Alabama. There, politics tried to oust Armant's promotion. Some stood up for him and an election was held. He won by majority. In Oct. 1862, they were ordered to New Iberia, LA in the Trans-Miss. Dept. The Union bore down hard. Col. Mouton became afflicted with rheumatism. Armant's group kept the Union in check for six hours, through swamps and bayous. Capt. Ralston was wounded and Col. McPheeters was killed on the Federal side and one hundred were taken as prisoners. Union leader Gen. Weitzel commended the Rebels for such a small group.

Col. Armant was a brave leader through all these engagements. Also, later, he proved strong at Berwick Bayou on the Teche River and Bisland. All this was with a small amount of troops, supplies, clothing and shoes. He then gallantly marched the 18th LA to north Louisiana.

April 8, 1864, he fought in the collision at Mansfield, south of Shreveport. He was ordered to stay and hold back half of his men in reserve. Instead, he went with his men and led them in the first half of the battle. He was killed, along with Alfred Mouton, Beard, Clack, Walker (not John), Canfield, Beatty, Lavery, "and many other heroes".

In the thickest part of the fight in that battle, Col. Armant's horse was shot. His color-bearer (flag person) also went down. Armant grabbed the flag from him and carried it, marching bravely as he was shot down. He still held the flag upright as he died on the battlefield.

"He formed one of the brightest parts in the War of Secession" it was said. He was buried with the other heroes at Mansfield cemetery until his remains were re-buried in St. James parish. His name is engraved on the monument at Mansfield Museum.

***

James Hamilton Beard:

James Beard moved to Red Bluff, LA on the Caddo-DeSoto parish line early in the 1850s. He became the manager of a dry goods store. He married Catherine Tomkies of Kingston, LA in 1857. They had a very happy marriage. He left the store to be a steamboat captain in 1858 but returned to the dry goods store in Shreveport. By 1860, he had become a wealthy man. He and his wife then had a daughter.

New Year's Day 1861, Beard formed a company of volunteers, weeks before the state of Louisiana seceded. He was elected captain of the "Shreveport Greys". they were untrained and ill-equipped, but ready to fight. William Moore of Shreveport, who would become their last captain, wrote how they finally had uniforms and were trained in marching. They drilled in public the first time on the year anniversary of the Battle of New Orleans in January.

Beard left for Baton Rouge, LA to canvas for weapons. He came back with them twelve days later. Theirs was the first company to leave to fight for the Confederacy, in April of 1861. They boarded a steamer and left New Orleans for Pensacola, FL. A reporter from *The Shreveport Times* witnessed their departure. He called their appearance "beyond all praise" and exclaimed, "the best citizens, the very best men of Shreveport-- its gentlemen-- make up the file of the company". He claimed Capt. Beard, "worthy". Big fanfare went on, even including Gov. Mouton from Alexandria. When they departed from Florida to Virginia, William Moore stated they were "jolly glad to leave".

The men went through rough times but continued to improve their skills. Aug. 15th, Beard was promoted to major. His wife, Kate, kept him informed of his daughter, Corinne's, progress, about how she attempted to scribble her papa a letter, and that she called every man "papa". She enclosed a lock of her hair for Maj. Beard. When he was given leave to come home, Kate conceived a son.

Beard was assigned to Monroe in May 1862, then Baton Rouge, then back to Kingston in Feb. 1863. November 1863, he was promoted to Colonel and served under Gen. Richard Taylor and Alfred Mouton.

April, 3, 1864, Taylor continued to withdraw from Grand Ecore toward Shreveport. April 5th, Taylor gave his army a respite. Gen. Banks was approaching from south of Natchitoches. Banks didn't bother to send out a reconnaissance. He felt he did not have time. There, he made a grave mistake. He didn't realize the location of a road that followed the river. Instead, he led his men and a twenty-mile long caravan of wagons through the woods keeping the end dangerously separated from the lead wagon. This was "the turning point of the Campaign", according to author, Ludwell Johnson, in his book, *The Red River Campaign.*

Banks played into Taylor's hand, continuing into Louisiana. A group of his men met stiff resistance April 7th, north of Pleasant Hill at Wilson's Farm, but still pushed toward Shreveport. Confederate Gen. Tom Green gave one more empty punch and withdrew stating prophetically, "We'll give 'em hell tomorrow".

After Mouton, Walker, and Green rested and convened with Taylor, they began marching south from Keatchie at 2 a.m. Earl Beddoe had ridden all night to report Banks' whereabouts to Taylor. Taylor had readied Mansfield to be a hospital station. Then they met up with Col. Beard and the 18th LA Consolidated Crescent and Col. Gray's LA regiment at the chosen battlefield at 6:30 a.m. Taylor had chosen Wilson's Farm three miles south of Mansfield for its strategic location. He spent the morning forming a curved Rebel battle line, off of what is now Hwy. 175, at a crossroads that ran west to the Sabine River on a slope called Honeycutt Hill.

In Col. Beard's last letter to his wife, he signed, "Good-bye", which he never had done before. His command, along with Gray's 28th LA made the first charge against Banks's men that afternoon.

Col. Beard was struck with a minie ball and killed. His brother pulled him off the battlefield and took him home--twelve miles away--in a borrowed wagon. The lock of his daughter's hair and her baby shoe was found still in his pocket. One account stated his baby boy had died five days before he did at just a few days old. Another said his son was eleven days old when his body was returned.

After her husband's burial at Kingston, Kate Beard dedicated her life to serving the Confederacy by commemeration in the UDC Chapter, named after her, in DeSoto parish.

***

Alfred Mouton:

Jean Jacques Alfred Mouton was graduate of the United States Military Academy. He became a Confederate general in the American Civil War.

Alfred Mouton was born in Opelousas, LA to the former governor of the state of Louisiana, Alexander Mouton. Due to the elder Mouton wanting his children to receive the best education, he enrolled his son in St. Charles College in Grand Coteau, LA. He secured a position for his son at the military academy in West Point, N.Y. Alfred only spoke French, so he was hesitant. His dad was adamant, so he enrolled in 1846.

Young Alfred became an average student but graduated in 1850. He resigned from the Army in September and took up civil engineering, for the New Orleans, Opelousas, and Great Western Railroad, 1852-53. He then took up sugar cane farming. His bloodline made him a prominent member of the community of Lafayette parish.

He served as leader of the Lafayette Vigilante Committee. They had formed to ensure justice to those who paid off jurors or perjured witnesses. He also served as Brig. Gen. in LA state militia, 1850-1861. This consisted mostly of farmers from around the area. Mouton was elected captain then colonel when it organized into the 18th LA

Infantry. He made a reputation as a strict disciplinarian and efficient drillmaster, along with his soldiers. One said, "He had a few, if any, equals". He never allowed any to deviate from orders but "mingled freely" with them after drill.

Weeks before the Battle of Shiloh, the 18th LA was one of the regiments called to Corinth, MS for Confederate Gen. Albert Sidney Johnston's planned attack on Union forces near Pittsburg Landing, TN. During the Battle of Shiloh, the 28th LA organized into Col. Preston Pond's brigade. Here, they received their "baptism by fire". Pond's brigade attacked a Federal right division of Union Generals William Tecumseh Sherman and John McClernand. Mouton was wounded. After Confederate defeat, P.G.T. Beauregard ordered LA 18th back to Corinth, then to Louisiana. There, Mouton was made Interim Commander of W. Virginia. He did what he could with limited men and supplies to thwart the Federal attempts to movement into Louisiana. His army attempted to protect the sugar cane farms along Bayou Lafourche. They were "brushed aside" by Union Gen. Godfrey Weitzel at the Battle of Labadieville. Weitzel destroyed many crops in that area.

When Confederate Gen. Richard Taylor arrived, Mouton was made Brig. Gen. This duo, along with Calvary Commander Tom Green would prove to be the "most efficient" during the war. They harassed, confused, frustrated and delayed Union attempts to secure Bayou Teche in south Louisiana.

Mouton's leadership helped Louisiana brigades undermine Union attempts to access the rich Bayou Teche. He played key roles at the Battle of Irish Bend, Ft. Bisland, Franklin, Bayou Borbeau and numerous others.

Mouton's brigade was used as lead unit in the Confederate attack in the Battle of Manfield, LA, where he was mortally wounded. Gen. Taylor lamented him by saying, "above all, the death of the gallant Mouton affected me most…modest, unselfish, patriotic. He showed best action always leading his men".

John George Walker:

Confederate Gen. John G. Walker was born July 22, 1821. He died July 20, 1893. Born in Jefferson City, MO, he grew up in St. Louis. He graduated from what became Washington University in 1844.

Walker joined the U.S. Army as a first lieutenant, U.S. Mounted Rifles in 1846. He served with honor in the Mexican-American War. He became captain for San Juan de los Llanos but was wounded at Molina del Rey. He stayed in the Army until 1861, when he joined the Confederate States of America (CSA). He was a major in the Calvary.

He was promoted to lieutenant colonel in the 8th TX Calvary, Aug. 1861 and served in the Dept. of North Caribbean. Sept. 1861, he was promoted to colonel.

January 1862, Walker became brigadier general and served in the Peninsula Campaign under Brig. Gen. Holmes. He was wounded at Malvern Hill. His division over-looked Harper's Ferry, W. VA., at Loudon Heights, before they surrendered to Gen. Stonewall Jackson of the Confederacy, Sept. 15, 1862. Walker served Maj. Gen. James Longstreet at South Mountain and Antietam next.

Nov. 1862, Walker was promoted to major general and transferred to Trans-Miss. Dept. He commanded twelve Texas regiments numbering 12,000 men, at Camp Nelson, AR. He formed them into divisions that became known as "Walker's Greyhounds" with the ability to move quickly on foot over many miles. From Nov. 1862 until the end of the war, the Greyhounds were exclusively used from Texas and served the Trans-Miss. Dept.

March 1863, the new commander of Trans-Miss. Dept., Lt. Gen. Edmund Kirby Smith, assigned the Greyhounds to Maj. Gen. Richard Taylor's Western LA command. They were to attack Maj. Gen. Ulysses S. Grant's supply line on the bank of the Mississippi River and from Louisiana they were to besiege the Union hold at

Vicksburg.

Grant moved his supply lines, side-stepping this attack. Hawes' brigade engaged in combat against the Federals at the Battle of Young's Point. McCollough's brigade fought African-American Union troops at the Battle of Milliken's Bend, June 6, 1863. This was the first fight for the untrained African-American corps. They fought bravely and suffered heavy casualties from Walker's men. When gunboats arrived to support the Yankee troops, driving McCollough and his men back, this turned into a Yankee victory. Gen. Richard Taylor and Gen. Walker had argued against this campaign with Gen. E. Kirby Smith. Taylor insisted Walker and his men were much more needed to "strike while the iron was hot" (Napoleonic Code) and confusion still ruled in New Orleans to get it back. This would block Gen. Nathaniel Banks' (who took Butler's place) continued movement up the Mississippi River from Port Hudson.

After Milliken's Bend, Taylor requested and was denied again, for Walker's troops to help where they needed more-- New Orleans. Walker wasted time for weeks patrolling the bank of the Mississippi River across from Vicksburg, MS. unable to cross.

Walker went back to Arkansas in late 1863. March 1864, he joined Taylor again in Alexandria, LA. He helped fight Banks in the Red River Campaign. Walker's troops played a critical role in the Confederate victory at the Battle of Mansfield, LA, April 8, 1864. Walker was then sent with his unit, the Greyhounds, back to Arkansas to fight Union Gen. Frederick Steele, at the Battle of Jenkin's Ferry, April 30, 1864, south of Little Rock. This left Taylor short-handed to chase Banks out of Louisiana.

Steele fled northward and didn't join Banks. There was no attempt to capture Shreveport, as Kirby Smith had supposed. Walker was sent back to join Taylor against Banks. He arrived only in time to see the Union troops leaving on Federal transports across the river at Simmesport.

After Taylor's request to be transferred out of Kirby Smith's command, Walker replaced him in the district of W. LA. By the end of the war he transferred further west to the District of Texas, New Mexico and Arizona.

At the close of the Civil War, he fled to Mexico as did several other Confederate leaders.

Years later he returned and served as U.S. Consul in Bogota, Columbia and Special Commissioner to the Pan-American Convention.

When he died in July 1893, he was buried in Stonewall Jackson Cemetery in Winchester, VA.

***

Thomas Green:

Tom Green was a Texas landowner, politician and soldier. He served as brigadier general in the Confederate Army during the American Civil War. He was considered to be one of the finest Calvary leaders in the Trans-Mississippi Theatre.

Green was born in Amelia County, VA. His family moved to Tennessee in 1817 when he was an infant. Green attended Jackson College in Tennessee and Princeton College in Kentucky. He received a degree at the University of Tennessee in 1834. He studied law with his father who was a prominent judge on the Tennessee Supreme Court.

Green left Tennessee for Nagogdoches, TX in Dec. 1835, when the Texas Revolution began. He enlisted in Isaac Moreland's Company on Jan. 14, 1836. During the Battle of San Jacinto, for Texas independence, April 21st, Green helped operate the famed "Twin Sisters" cannons. This was the only artillery of Sam Houston's army. Houston awarded Green a commissioned lieutenant spot a few days after that great victory. By early May, he was promoted to major and was assigned as aid-de-camp to Gen. Thomas Rusk. When hostilities rested, he resigned May 30th, to return to Tennessee to resume the study of law.

In 1837, the legislature of the new Republic of Texas granted large tracts of land to leading veterans of the Revolution. This included Tom Green. He relocated to Fayette County and became a county surveyor at LaGrange. A San Jacinto vet, William Gant, nominated Green, at that time to be engrossing clerk for Texas House of Representatives in the Fourth Texas Congress until 1839. He served as Secretary to Senate during the Sixth and Eighth Congresses. From 1841 until 1861, he served as clerk of the Texas Supreme Court, in the Republic and as U.S. state.

Between sessions, Green served in military campaigns against the Indians and Mexico. Fall of 1840, he joined John H. Moore to go up the Colorado River against the Comanches. After that, his men were identified by their loud Indian yells while attacking in battle, baffling their Yankee cohorts, and later their leader, Richard Taylor. After Rafael Vasquez's invasion of San Antonio, March 1842, Green recruited volunteers and had served as captain of the Travis County Volunteers. They did not see battle, however. That fall he served as Inspector General for the Somervell Expedition, after Adrian Wall's foray in San Antonio.

When the U. S. went to war with Mexico, Green recruited and commanded a company of Texas Rangers in LaGrange. These were part of the First Texas Regiment of Mounted Riflemen led by John Coffee Hayes. They helped Zachary Taylor capture Monterrey, Nuevo Leon, Sept. 1846.

After returning home from the Mexican-American War, Green married Mary Wallace Chalmers, Jan. 31, 1847. They had five daughters and one son.

Later, Texas seceded from the Union in 1861 and Green was elected colonel of the 5th Texas Calvary, part of the brigade led by Gen. Henry Sibley that had joined against the attempted invasion of Texas in 1862. Green led the Confederate victory there, boarding his men on the river steamer, "Bayou City", assisting in the recapture of Galveston, Jan. 1, 1863. He was also involved in the seizure of the Union steamer, the "Harriet Lane" the same day.

Spring 1863, Green commanded the First Calvary Brigade in Richard Taylor's division, fighting along Bayou Teche in Louisiana. May 20th, Green became the brigadier general. In June he captured a Union garrison at Brashear (Morgan) City, LA. They failed to seize Ft. Butler on the Mississipppi River, however.

Green's Calvary routed the advancing Union troops of Godfrey Weitzel and Cuvier Grover at Koch's (Cox's) Plantation, July 13. In Sept., First Calvary Brigade captured another Union detachment at Stirling's Plantation. Another success followed in Nov. at the Battle of Bayou Barbeaux. The four victories inflicted 3,000 casualties on their enemy but cost them only 600. Green was then assigned command of the Calvary division of the Trans-Miss. Dept.

During the Red River Campaign, Green commanded a brigade of Texas Calvary in the division of Brig. Gen. John S. Marmaduke. April 8, 1864, Green led successful attacks against Union Maj. Gen. Nathaniel Banks at the Battle of Mansfield and against Maj. Gen. William Emory at the Battle of Pleasant Hill, the next day.

A few day later, on April 12, 1864, Green was mortally wounded by a shell from a Federal gunboat patrolling the Red River at Blair's Landing, LA. Union Admiral David Dixon Porter paid tribute to the fallen Confederate Calvary leader by saying, "Green was one in whom the Rebels place more confidence than anyone else…losing Green was worth 5,000 other men". His men felt the same and backed off from battle that day, along with Gen. Richard Taylor, to grieve the loss of this "intelligent, brave, friend of men, but wild as a Comanche in battle". Green's "victory yell" lay silent.

***

General Richard Taylor:
Richard Taylor held a command at different times in all three main theatres of the war-- Virginia, the Tennessee Valley and the Trans-Mississippi. He was the son of President Zachary Taylor and

the brother-in-law of Confederate President, Jefferson Davis. These situations gave him unexpected social status and opportunity to observe a number of the great battles and to know, personally, many of the most important players on both sides. As Taylor put it, he followed the Confederacy from "cradle to hearse".

Taylor states several times in his memoir, *Destruction and Reconstruction,* that Louisiana was his native state. That was not literally true. He was born January 27, 1826, at an old family plantation near Louisville, Kentucky, but his family had settled in Louisiana and he soon returned there.

He was named after his grandfather, an officer of the Virginia Continentals in the Revolution. His father, Col. Zachary Taylor, ranking officer of the small U.S. Army, was connected to many prominent VA and KY cousins. His mother was similarly connected in Maryland. When he was nine years old, his older sister married Jefferson Davis, but she died shortly thereafter.

By the time Taylor graduated from Yale in 1845, he was widely traveled and well known. Soon after, he spent time with his father at Army headquarters in Mexico--as his secretary during the war with Mexico. That was his nearest contact with military action before the Civil War. He was then sent home with an acute case of rheumatoid arthritis.

His father's year as President of America broadened young Taylor's acquaintances at the highest levels from the North and the South.

In the 1850's, Taylor owned a prosperous sugar plantation in St. Charles parish in Louisiana. He married Louise Marie Bringer from a prominent Creole family, served in the Legislature and attended national political conventions as a delegate. His greatest interest was his vast library of classical literature and military history. The latter he gleaned from and used later in his military victories. No one who met him doubted his cultivation, power and distinction. The sub-title of a biography by T. Michael Parrish (1992) sums it up: *Richard Taylor: Soldier Prince of Dixie.*

Taylor was a conservative Unionist. He lacked enthusiasm for states rights or radical action. He swayed to the side of moderation. He viewed the break-up of the Democratic party at Charleston in 1860 with regret, but, he never doubted the cause of the South as being right (as did France and England). By 1861 he agreed with the majority of his state (LA) in favor of secession. He came to regard himself, primarily, as a "soldier bound to duty and swept up in events that might be understood but not controlled". He referred to all involved as "scene-shifters in some awful tragedy".

Taylor's accomplishments as a soldier are all the more remarkable when we consider: he did not expect success for his cause; he suffered from severe arthritis during the war; his plantation was gratuitously plundered, leaving his slaves to starve, then it was confiscated; his wife was reduced to the status of refugee; and his two sons died of disease while Taylor was away fighting the war, thus leaving him three daughters.

By Autumn of 1861 Taylor was made Brigadier General. He commanded what became the notable, LA brigade of the Army of Northern VA. They played a dire part in Stonewall Jackson's Shenandoah Valley Campaign. Jackson admired Taylor's devotion and discipline even to being hauled in a wagon to direct his men in battle while suffering with arthritis. Once, Taylor chased his men on horseback cursing them on to victory in the Shenandoah Valley. Stonewall called him a "wicked fellow". That had been when Stonewall Jackson promoted him to Brig. Gen., even though Taylor had appealed to his brother-in-law, not to promote a relative. He was informed that Stonewall Jackson recommended him for promotion for his working with "steadiness under fire".

Taylor, in turn, commended the men he worked under and these events and their quirky personalities in his book, *Destruction and Reconstruction.* This included Jackson, Ewell, Ashby, Bedford Forrest and even the Union generals that didn't destroy everything in their path, like Gen. Sherman did.

July 1862, Richard Taylor was promoted to Major General to command LA west of the Mississippi River. His hopes were to restore morale and contain the Federal invasion of the state. He also planned to relieve Vicksburg and re-capture New Orleans. There, Taylor showed his real worth by restoring morale among the depressed civilian population; creating war production; arming and organizing troops and with an inferiority of forces; and inflicting checks and losses on the enemy. The most culminating achievement was his victory in the Red River Campaign, Spring of 1864, aided by such sterling soldiers as Alexander Mouton and Texas frontiersman, Gen. Thomas Green-- even though being out-numbered, seven-to-one.

Taylor always believed and argued that he was prevented from further gains for the state and for the South by the "obstinate caution and blindness" of his superior, Gen. Edmund Kirby Smith, Commander of the Trans-Mississippi Dept. History bears this out. After the victory of the Battle of Mansfield and the draw at Pleasant Hill, the Yankees exited LA. Taylor was promoted to Lt. Gen., Aug. 1864 and requested leave of being under Kirby Smith. He was assigned to command Alabama, Mississippi, and east LA.

Bedford Forrest said of Taylor, "He's the biggest man in the lot. If we had more like him, we would have licked the Yankees long ago".

Taylor surrendered the last of the Confederate forces east of MS to Gen. Canby. Taylor's own words: "On the 8th of May, 1865, at Citronelle (AL), forty miles north of Mobile, I delivered the epilogue of the great drama in which I had played a humble part".

Chapter Twenty-Two
The Civil War in Louisiana

("…And when these things begin to come to pass, then look up, and lift up your heads, for your redemption draws nigh." Luke 21:28)

The Civil War had come to the door of Louisiana. The South's Army and navy failed to make efforts to unite, so New Orleans fell to the North.

The campaign to take Louisiana by Union forces was referred to as the "Red River Campaign". Union or Federal leaders finally made up their minds to take Texas through Louisiana. Texas, rich in cotton, had been well fought over by Mexico and Spain, thus, altering the Atlanta Campaign and delaying the Mobile Campaign. *(Red River Campaign/XIII)*

History books lay out the sole reason for the Civil War to be slavery. Research bears out through references from "The Oracles of War" and many letters written between leaders and soldiers, that wasn't the whole truth. Those lives and properties and prides were lost because of cotton, politics, slavery and greed for the land.

Gen. E. Kirby Smith had been placed as head of the Trans-Miss. Department, and stationed at Shreveport. Early June 1863, Gen. Smith believed the Yanks would come up the Red River to overtake Shreveport and enter into Texas.

The Union's early attempts to take Texas had not gained much recognition. The pompous Gen. Nathaniel Banks had placed a Union flag at Brazos Santiago, Nov. 2, 1862 "over a few acres of barren dunes". (*RRC*, p.39 #2) On Sept. 7th, before that, Federal gunboats had unsuccessfully met with "a hornet's nest" of Confederate Cajuns and Texans at Sabine Pass near the Gulf of Mexico. (*RRC*, p.38 #2)

Maj. Gen. Richard Taylor had been newly appointed Commander of Louisiana, west of the Mississippi River. He concluded that the Union would push up the Red River one month after his commander, Kirby Smith had realized that they would. (*RRC*, p.86).

Taylor attempted to get supplies from the depressed Alexandria, LA. Then, he went to Monroe to meet with Lt. Gen. Pemberton to secure co-operation on the river.

(From the "Report on Conduct of the War"): While Gen. Taylor attempted to supply Vicksburg, it fell to the Union.

Taylor's chief of artillery, Maj. J. L. Brent, a lawyer, proved to be of extreme value in scavenging supplies. He had served under Gen. Magruder in the Richmond Campaign. He asked to follow Taylor to Louisiana, where he had family. He proved to be a worthy spirit, for his men and in filling Gov. Moore's workshop with supplies. During the last days of January, 1863, Gen. Ulysses S. Grant and his large army landed at Vicksburg. Porter and his fleet accompanied him. They attempted to dig a canal through the peninsula opposite Vicksburg while in flood stage-- then abandoned their plan.

Taylor set out to prove that tin-clad boats, like sitting ducks, could not withstand field gunfire. This he did, giving his men confidence.

Feb. 14th was cold, icy and rainy with sharp wind. Sudden shots from Ft. DeRussy were heard. He found the "Queen of the West" had been taken by his men. Confusion took place at Alexandria when the "Queen" was ushered there, until the Confederates realized they had control of the steamer.

Feb. 22, the expedition entered the Mississippi River. They met up with the steamer from Port Hudson sent to destroy the "Queen of the West". They didn't know she had already been captured by their own men!

Feb. 23, they reached Natchez, MS. The "Indianola" fired open on the "Queen". Flames of the cotton bales had to be extinguished on the "Queen". They wet the cotton down to prevent more fires from spreading.

Taylor eluded to that victory as a great historical feat, regaining control of that section of the Mississippi River. He was saddened that losing at Vicksburg and at Gettysburg overshadowed this later.

Brent returned to the Red River with his tattered boats. Union Adm. Farragut and his ships passed Port Hudson and gained control of the Mississippi R. for the Federals again.

(From *Destruction & Reconstruction,* p.125 #3) Taylor took time to inject: "Of the brave and distinguished, Adm. Farragut, as of Gen. Grant, it can be said that they always respected non-combatants and property, and made war only against armed men".

***

March 1863, Lt. Gen. E. Kirby Smith arrived from the east to take command of the Trans-Miss. Dept. This included Missouri, Arkansas, Louisiana, Texas and the Indian Territory of New Mexico. He had graduated from West Point and gained experience in several campaigns on the Eastern Theatre of the war. (*D&R,* p.126 #3).

Taylor believed Smith would have been "spared some embarrassment" had he attended to the Federals occupying the territory he commanded. (*D&R,* pp.126-7). Taylor felt Smith wasted his time on lost causes and unwise moves. Smith landed in Alexandria and was advised of the situation, but had to advance north due to the enemy's movement from the southeast.

Re-opening the Mississippi R. for navigation at that time was the primary concern of the Union forces. Gen. Grant operated at Vicksburg. Gen. Banks, who took Gen. Butler's place, was sent to Port Hudson. Vicksburg needed to be taken first, so as to have clear communication with New Orleans.

***

Mouton traveled safely back over the Yokely Bridge. Gen. Green entered the town of Franklin. Semmes backed them up, but stayed too long, and he was captured. The South had possession of Bisland. Even though Taylor gained support and sympathy from Louisiana, most of their number were away fighting for other states.

Green and Mouton followed the enemy and burned the bridges to stop them. Plans were to capture their small force on the Teche. Taylor expected the Union to turn east after Alexandria and overtake Port Hudson on the Mississippi River. This he did.

Semmes, Fuller and Fusilier were taken captive by the Feds, along with the "Queen". Semmes and Fuller managed to escape. Fuller was wounded and couldn't walk. He kept charge of the "Maple Leaf" until his buddies escaped then returned her to the Feds. Fuller was taken to Delaware and died in prison. Taylor stated, "A braver man never lived". (*D&R*, p.13)

The Union troops reached Opelousas on April 20th. They stayed until May 5th, held back by Gen. Mouton. However, having to leave to Sabine for supplies, one hundred miles away, put him out of commission a while.

Taylor discovered in the "Report on the Conduct of War", vol. ii, pp. 309-10, that Banks had well-exaggerated his feats in Louisiana. Had it been true, most of Taylor's men would have been captured, along with his boats, and he would have been receiving his orders from the governor. This was a surprise to Taylor!

The Union's delay to leave Opelousas gave Taylor's men time to remove supplies from Alexandria. E. Kirby Smith was advised to go to Shreveport to set up stores. There, he would be away from "danger and disturbance".

Ft. DeRussy began being dismantled. The Red River was open to the enemy. Adm. Porter arrived at Vicksburg on April 16th and at Alexandria May 9th, right before Banks.

Ft. Beauregard was bombarded from the 8th-11th by the Yanks. Then, the South's Col. Logan drove them off.

Taylor read in Banks' report that Weitzel and Dwight pursued and dispersed the enemy rendering them unable to regroup until July. This humored Taylor, but he set the record straight: A mounted

Federal horseman did chase him and an orderly for four miles from the Cane River and Monette's Ferry. They then turned back toward Alexandria. *BUT,* Taylor and the orderly were *not* dispersed, and did *not* have to re-group!

The Union left Alexandria on the 13th of May. They crossed the Mississippi R. toward Port Hudson on the 23rd. Taylor took a steamer back to Alexandria. He had his infantry at Natchitoches to begin a march to the Teche to reunite with Mouton.

Green had been promoted to Brig. Gen. for gallantry, in the meantime. He and Mouton had gathered supplies at Sabine. They reached Teche too late. The enemy had plundered the whole area.

Kirby Smith communicated with Taylor back at Alexandria to receive assistance from Maj. Gen. Walker, arriving from Arkansas. They were trying to follow Kirby Smith's command to "do *something*" to help out at Vicksburg. (*D&R,* p.139 #1). Taylor strongly disagreed with these orders. He had hoped to conquer Berwick's Bay and break Banks' communication with New Orleans. Seeing the Confederates across from New Orleans would have increased the citizens' morale. Kirby Smith was adamant, so Taylor hurried Walker's forces to Washita (Ouachita). Walker harassed some Yanks first.

Grant's men rested on the bend of the Mississippi River near Yazoo City.

Nothing came of Walker's efforts. He was directed to Monroe. Taylor wanted him to go to Alexandria. Kirby Smith arrived in time to stop it. Walker was sent back to the Tensas where he and his men *wasted* two weeks, according to Taylor.

Back at Alexandria, Taylor found three small regiments of Texans that arrived under Col. (later Brig. Gen.) Major. He was ordered to Morgan's Ferry on the Atchafalaya River. Taylor went to join Green and Mouton on the Teche.

The Federals had left their sick soldiers at Berwick's Bay. Taylor ordered Mouton and Green to collect all boats, skiffs and supplies they could. Extreme secrecy was ordered, guards doubled, only a few scouts were allowed.

Taylor went to Morgan's Ferry to meet Major and proceed to the Mississippi R. at Port Hudson. There they heard the enemy in battle. A few women saw them and told them the number to be about 1,000. Taylor left at night to go unnoticed to Plaquemines.

June 19th, Major was expected to reach the Boeuf by the 23rd. His promptness was urgent, Taylor stressed, for him to attack at Berwick's Bay. (*D&R*, p.141 #4).

Green's brigade had fifty-three small craft to transport three hundred men the twelve miles in a quiet manner, down the Teche. The water was calm. Maj. Hunter of Baylor's Texans was put in command. Maj. Blair, 2nd Louisiana, was the second command to go to Atchafalaya and Grand Lake. They needed to land on the island one mile from Berwick's railway. When they heard Gen. Green's guns on the west of the bay, they were to rush the rear of the Federals.

Green opened fire, surprising the Union troops. They attempted to fire back. Hunter and his men closed in. Engines and carriages were heard escaping. Taylor crossed in a pirogue with Green.

Taylor and his men found "much bounty" and were grateful. Mouton came across with his men. He fired on the train. Major took possession of the bridge and the train.

Green and Major, in the meantime, combed the land searching for the Union troops for the one hundred-mile span. They completed their mission as planned-- on time. This, Taylor accredited to "Fortune". (*D&R*, p.143 #4).

"The spoils of Berwick's Bay were of vast importance…for the first time since I reached western Louisiana, I had supplies, and in such abundance as to serve for the Red River Campaign of 1864". (*D&R*, p.144 #2)

Three-fourths of the prisoners Banks had left behind were sick. Taylor sent the ones that could travel with the surgeons to New Orleans. He kept the ones that couldn't.

Richard Taylor's goal was to place batteries to interrupt Bank's communication with New Orleans. Berwick took up much of his time. Taylor gave high praise to Major for scanning all the area from Fordoche to Berwick without artillery or wagons.

June 24th, Gen. Green, Major's men and Gen. Mouton, with two regiments of infantry traveled by rail to Thibodeaux to back up Bayou des Allemond, twenty-five miles from New Orleans.

Maj. Brent and his men stayed behind at Berwick's, mounting guns. Gunboats could stop any crossing since the entrance to the Gulf was open, but the enemy did not make any attempts there from June 23rd-July 22nd.

June 27th, Green reached an earthwork called Ft. Butler, near Donaldsonville, LA, where the Lafourche River met the Mississippi River. On the 28th, an attempt to attack was made at night. Many blunders were made due to misrepresentation. Green's Col. Phillips died and ninety-seven Confederates hid in a ditch and then surrendered. Taylor commended Green still: "Like an Irishman at Donnybrook…to strike an enemy whenever he saw him-- a most commendable rule in war, and covering a multitude of such small errors as the attack on Ft. Butler". (*D&R,* p.145 #1)

Taylor was preparing artillery at Berwick's Bay. The first week of July, he had placed twelve guns there. Green's men drove away many gunboats attempting to land. He had plans to regain New Orleans. For three days the river had been closed to boats. Taylor later lamented of E. Kirby Smith's command, "The unwise movement toward aiding Vicksburg retarded operations at Berwick's and on the river, and Port Hudson fell. During the night of the 10th of July, intelligence of its surrender on the previous day reached me, and some hours later, the fall of Vicksburg, on the 4th, was announced". (*D&R,* p.146 #2). Taylor added, "The outlook was not cheerful, but it was necessary to make the best of it, and at all hazards save our plunder." (#3) They "worked day and night crossing supplies to the west side of the bay". (Berwick's).

July 13th, Federal Gen. Weitzel, Grover and Dwight came down

338

from Port Hudson with 6,000 men to Donaldsonville. Taylor joined Green but didn't interfere with his "excellent" disposition of forces. Green led the charge "vigorously" and drove the Federals into Donaldsonville, LA, capturing 200 prisoners.

Taylor reported on Gen. Banks' report on the incident to recapture of Brashear City (Morgan City) on Berwick's Bay, in the "Report on Conduct of War", vol. ii, pp.313-314, as exaggerated and "remarkable" on the number of men the Confederates had and had captured.

Meanwhile, Grant's forces went from Natchez to Ft. Beauregard on the Ouachita, River. The Confederate garrison of fifty men had abandoned it on Sept. 23rd, leaving heavy artillery for the enemy to destroy or carry off. (*D&R,* p.148 #4)

***

Taylor regretted that large forces had been "shut up in fortifications without a relieving army near at hand". (*D&R,* p.149 #1). He adamantly reiterated that had less Confederate troops been used at Vicksburg and Port Hudson, more would have been available for other battles. Consequently, more could have been added to Gen. Joseph Johnston's forces on the other side. Now, control of the Mississippi River and the valley from Ouachita and Atchafalaya to the Pearl River was lost. Taylor began concentrating on the Red River Valley Campaign.

Three months had been wasted trying to divert the Mississippi River channel at Vicksburg. Then they crossed the river below it.

Confederate Gen. Pemberton sent Bowen with a weak force to fight at Vicksburg. Re-enforcements were vainly requested. Pemberton's many blunders not only lost Vicksburg, but the whole eastern side of the Mississippi River.

Taylor credited Grant with recouping his losses and speedily following the enemy. This gave him successes at Vicksburg and Donaldsonville. Taylor quoted, "Among the blind, the one-eyed are kings". (*D&R,* p.150 #3) He commended Grant by saying, "Genius is God-given, but men are responsible for their acts; and it should be said of Gen. Grant that, as far as I am aware, he made war in the true spirit of a soldier, never by deed or word inflicting wrong on non-combatants. It would be to the credit of the United States Army if similar statements could be made of Generals Sherman and Sheridan". (*D&R,* p.151 #2).

Taylor was then re-joined by Maj. Gen. J. G. Walker and his Texas Division. John Walker had served in Mexico and resigned the U.S. Army to serve the Confederacy. He had victory at Harper's Ferry in 1862 and Antietam. Then he transferred to Arkansas. He had a good brigade and disciplined them well, making them very efficient.

Sept. 1863, Green and some of Mouton's brigade crossed the Atchafalaya at Morgan's Ferry and rerouted the enemy on the Fordoche and captured 450 prisoners. By Oct., the Federals moved up the Teche R. In November, Green, with some of Walker's regiment, was ordered to attack. Six hundred prisoners were taken, then 125 on open prairie by New Iberia. Banks only mentioned the latter in his reports, but Taylor made sure Walker and his men were given credit.

Taylor had the prisoners from Barbeau taken and treated at Alexandria. He saw their leader walking and limping with them. He insisted on sending him home to his sick wife, with his report of safety and sending a replacement for himself. *LATER,* the soldier repaid that debt. After the war, Andrew Johnson insisted Taylor attend the convention in Philadelphia to heal the wounds of war. The newspaper slandered Taylor's presence there as a "rebel who, with hands dripping with loyal blood, had the audacity to show himself in a loyal community". (*D&R,* p.153 #2). The Wisconsin Commander that Taylor had helped, during the war, was present and condemned the statement. He pleaded with Taylor to let him right the wrong. Taylor refused, but said, "This was the difference between brave soldiers and non-fighting politicians, who grew fat by inflaming the passions of sectional hate". (*D&R,* p.153 #2).

The winter of 1863-1864 passed without much activity. Control of the Mississippi River flamed the fire of the enemy's gunboats interfering with Taylor's movement to the north and south of the Red River. From Alexandria, for twenty miles south, winded the Bouef to where the Red River meets the Sabine River and pine forests. Twenty miles from the Bouef, Opelousas intersects on the way to the abandoned Ft. Jessup. Further up the Red was Pleasant Hill, Mansfield and Shreveport. Taylor set up depots on the ninety miles from the Bouef to Pleasant Hill.

The Union drew its attention to the west coast of Texas. So, E. Kirby Smith detached Gen. Green to Galveston, leaving Taylor short-handed.

Taylor mocked Smith for fortifying his headquarters at Shreveport with too much staff. He was quoted as saying, "Hydrocephalus at Shreveport produced atrophy elsewhere". (*D&R*, p.154 #2). This agitated Smith more. Taylor had also condemned Kirby Smith's efforts of strengthening Ft. DeRussy, which proved ridiculous later only to increase the wedge between them.

Prince Charles de Polignac joined Taylor from Arkansas. The remaining Texans threatened mutiny for such a *one* commanding them. Taylor went to the leaders, pointed out consequence for disobedience but promised to remove the officer *after action* if he proved unworthy. (*D&R*, p.155 #2). Polignac and the men were sent to Ouachita in the beginning of 1864. He proved "coolness under fire" and won the men over. Taylor praised Polignac, and showed disdain that he wasn't used in a greater capacity when he returned to France.

Taylor had received info (Jan.-Feb. 1864) that Porter's fleet and Sherman's army were progressing toward him in the Spring. They were to join Banks. Gen. Steele was to meet them at Shreveport from Arkansas. Taylor requested re-enforcements from Shreveport from E. Kirby Smith but was put off. E. Kirby Smith seemed to be more concerned with the possibility of defending himself and Shreveport, than definitely stopping the Union at the Red River *before* they even arrived at Shreveport and going on to Texas.

Taylor noted the Union's increased activity at Berwick's Bay and Sherman's visit to New Orleans to see Banks, March 7th. Taylor directed Polignac to Alexandria, Mouton to guard the twenty-five miles south of the Bouef, and Harrison to the west of Ouachita to assist Liddel to the north of the Red River. Vincent was ordered to join Taylor at Burr's Ferry. Taylor ordered all supplies and cotton evacuated from Alexandria.

March 12, Federal Adm. Porter's 19 gunboats and 19,000 of Sherman's men entered the Red River. March 13, the troops embarked at Simmsport. March 14, A. J. Smith and his men left for Ft. DeRussy. There, the South lost ten--killed or wounded--and 185 were taken to be prisoners, eight heavy guns and two field pieces. "Thus much for our Red River Gibraltar", Taylor added. (*D&R,* p.157 #1)

Three of Walker's companies had to fall back on March 12, cut off by the enemy, thus, cutting communications. They were joined forty miles back by Mouton and Polignac March 15th.

March 15th, Porter's fleet reached the deserted Alexandria. One steamer went aground and had to be burned due to the low tide in the river.

"Report on Conduct of War" vol. ii p. 192, Banks' aide Col. Clack reported 28,000 men at this point. That included 18,000 under Franklin and 10,000 under A.J. Smith and expecting 7,000 of Steele's from Arkansas, plus, Porter's gunboats and fleet.

Had Taylor's men confronted Banks' at Alexandria, it would have been 18,000 on the North to about 5,400 on the South and Liddel had 500 men. If re-enforcements were to come, they would come from the Sabine road. So, Taylor decided to cover that route.

Taylor left the Bouef, March 16th, on Burr's Ferry to Carroll Jones' farm, arriving on the 18th. He camped at a depot he'd set up where Burr's Ferry and Natchitoches road meet.

Polignac's Louisiana Brigade under Col. Gray united in a division for Mouton. Vincent's Calvary joined on the 19th. On the

20th, they were sent to Bayou Rapides (12 mi.). There, they skirmished with some of the enemy from Alexandria, twenty miles south. Dawn, the 21st, Edgar's battery was sent to join Vincent's on a hill at James Store. A good "lookout" point, according to Taylor. Couriers were sent to Sabine with news of approaching re-enforcements of Taylor's position. He directed them to Ft. Jessup road.

March 21st was rainy, cold, icy and windy. Taylor commented that, "Vincent's pickets found their fires more agreeable than their posts". (D&R, p.158 #5). The enemy was prompt and vigilant. They captured them and the approaching Capt. Elgee, coming to warn them. Two hundred were captured without even a shot being fire--and all the horses.

March 22nd, Taylor and his men marched twelve miles to Beasley's depot near Natchitoches and remained there until the 29th, hoping for re-enforcements. Beasley's was located between roads to Ft. Jessup and Natchitoches. No re-enforcements came. Taylor ordered his troops to Pleasant Hill by Ft. Jessup, 40 miles, and to Natchitoches, 30 miles.

On the night of March 30th, Taylor met with Col. McNeill's regiment of Texas Calvary, 2,050 men. Fifty were without arms. March 31st, Col. Herbert came with 125 unarmed men. These were the first part of Green's men.

The enemy reached Natchitoches on the 31st.

McNeill and Herbert were commanded to fall back to Pleasant Hill, thirty-six miles. Taylor stayed until the enemy arrived. Then he rode four miles to Grand Ecore. He caught a steamer waiting for him on the Red River. He went up river forty miles and landed by a road that stretched sixteen miles to Pleasant Hill, and four to Bayou Pierre, where a ferry crossed a large arm of the river and viewed the area.

April 1st, Walker, Mouton and Green joined Taylor at Pleasant Hill. Green informed him that DeBray was marching in from Ft. Jessup and the enemy was leaving Natchitoches. DeBray was ordered to push his artillery and wagons forward to Pleasant Hill after dark.

The enemy attempted to stop him unsuccessfully. DeBray had five wounded. The next day, some of Taylor's Calvary had a skirmish toward Natchitoches.

Gen. Major could not arrive with the rest of Green's Calvary until the 6th. He was directed to cross the Sabine River at Logansport and march twenty miles to Mansfield. Taylor waited two days at Pleasant Hill and prepared for action. The enemy did not advance. April 4th and 5th, Taylor and the infantry moved to Mansfield. April 6th, Major arrived where his and Buchell's Calvary joined. Gen. Major was then sent to Pleasant Hill to take command of the advance.

DeBray and Buchell's regiments of Calvary had never left Texas before. They had been drilled and disciplined and armed with sabers. Buchell's had been organized from the German Settlement at New Braunfels.

"The men (German) had a distinct idea that they were fighting for their adopted country, and their conduct in battle was in marked contrast to that of the Germans whom I had encountered in the Federal Army of Virginia. Col. Buchell had served in the Prussian Army and was an instructed soldier. Three days after he joined me, he was mortally wounded in action and survived but a few hours. I sat beside him as his brave spirit passed away. The old "Fatherland" sent no bolder horseman to battle at Rossbach or Gravelott". (*D&R*, p.160 #3).

Taylor expressed frustration with his "long retreat of two hundred miles" from south Louisiana to the north. (*D&R*, p.160 #4). In correspondence with Gen. E. Kirby Smith, Taylor always expressed an intention to fight as soon as re-enforcements reached him. Smith thought his force would be too weak. He suggested: 1) "Hold the forces at Shreveport until he could concentrate a force to relieve him. 2) Or, retire to Texas, inducing the enemy to follow."

Taylor objected this would: 1) "Result in a surrender of troops and Shreveport couldn't raise more. 2) That would be disastrously abandoning Louisiana and Arkansas and Texas couldn't give more relief." (*D&R*, p.160).

Kirby Smith adopted neither suggestion. "But, when Mansfield was reached, a decision became necessary." (*D&R*, p.161 #2).

Three roads intersected at Mansfield, making it strategically the spot for confrontation with the Union. "This was pointed out to the 'Aulic Council' at Shreveport but failed to elicit any definite response", according to Taylor. (#3).

The 4,400 troops had reached Shreveport by March 21st. Taylor repeatedly asked for re-enforcements from there, but they were withheld until April 4th. They, then, marched to Keatchie on the 6th. Supplies were scarce in Mansfield. Taylor order them to stay there until supplies arrived.

Green had been promoted to Maj. Gen. He was placed in command over Generals Bee, Major and Bagby.

April 7th, Major was at Pleasant Hill and reported the enemy advancing. Green went to the front. Southerly winds carried sounds of firing to Mansfield. Taylor rode hard to get there and came upon about fifty men on the road. He stopped his horse to speak and received a rebuke: "General, if you won't curse us, we will go back with you." Taylor wrote, "I bowed to the implied homily, rode on, followed by the men, and found Green fighting a superior force of horse". (*D&R*, p.162 #2).

Taylor added his new found troops and joined Green and "enjoyed his method of managing his wild horsemen; he certainly accomplished more with them than anyone else could have done". (p.162) The enemy was stopped with "severe work". Green was able to camp by the mill stream that night, which was "a matter of importance".

The roads around Mansfield were on a high ridge. Water was scarce except for the mill stream, seven miles from Mansfield, and one closer to Mansfield. For the twenty miles between Pleasant Hill and Natchitoches, there was no water apart from the Red River. Wells had been exhausted.

Taylor left Green and returned to Mansfield and selected a field for the battle for the next day. It was an open, high area, three miles south of Mansfield, at Sabine Crossroad.

The Commander of the Missouri and Arkansas group at Keatchie, Gen. Churchill, was ordered to march to Mansfield April 8th for battle. A medical director was sent to Mansfield to set up houses for medical treatment. Quartermasters were to gather supplies. Officers were set up to guard the city and preserve order.

Walker and Mouton were ordered to prepare to move for battle in the morning. A staff officer was sent to Green to leave a small force in front of the enemy. A dispatch was sent to Kirby Smith at 9 p.m. on the 7th about the battle on the 8th.

Chapter Twenty-Three
Battles of Mansfield and Pleasant Hill

("And all this assembly shall know that the Lord saves not with sword and spear; for the battle is the Lord's and *He* will give you into our hands." I Sam. 17:47)

"My confidence of success in the impending engagement was inspired by accurate knowledge of the Federal movements, as well as the character of their commander, Gen. Banks, whose measure had been taken in the Virginia Campaign of 1862 and since". (*Destruction and Reconstruction,* by Richard Taylor, p.163 #3).

Taylor's staff closely watched Adm. Porter and his fleet of gunboats and troops leave Grand Ecore, Apr. 7th for Pleasant Hill.

Confederate Gen. Liddell watched Gen. Banks move toward Pleasant Hill on the 6th with 25,000 men. His wagon train was led by 5,000 mounted men. They were separated from the rear guard by twenty miles and their one thousand-wagon train.

Taylor's troops reached their position at Sabine Crossroads early Apr. 8th. Walker's infantry division of three brigades and two batteries were on the right of the Pleasant Hill road. Mouton's two brigades and two batteries were on the left. Green and his men dismounted and took position on Mouton's left. Regiments of Calvary were posted on each side of the parallel roads. DeBray's Calvary and McMahon's battery held in reserve on the main road. Dense forest held back much use of artillery except for McMahon's, though not used at this time.

Taylor stated, "I had on the field 5,300 infantry, 3,000 horse (Calvary) and 500 artillery--in all, 8,800 men, a very full estimate. But the vicious dispositions of the enemy made me confident of beating all the force he could concentrate during the day; and on the morrow, Churchill, with 4,400 muskets, would be up." (*D&R* p.164 #3)

In the afternoon on the 8th, Taylor's troops were getting into position. He rode through them and stopped by Mouton's brigade. He remarked to the men: "As they were fighting in defense of their own soil I wished the Louisiana troops to draw first blood". They were already outraged that their homes had been destroyed. Plus, by the rumor that Louisiana would be abandoned without a fight.

At that moment, Taylor's Calvary rushed in, followed by a shower of bullets on Mouton's line. One struck Taylor's horse. Then Union troops charged the 18th Louisiana, but were set back with heavy losses.

To his surprise, the infantry were reported to be on Taylor's left, in the woods. The day before there had only been Calvary. Randall strengthened Mouton from the right to meet this attack. DeBray's men were deployed on the field to cover this charge.

The enemy showed no advance. By 4 p.m., Taylor ordered forward movement of his whole line. Mouton's Louisiana troops advanced with ardor and could not be restrained. They crossed the field under heavy artillery fire. They reached the fence, paused to draw breath and rushed the enemy into the woods.

Taylor later wrote, "Here our loss was severe. Gen. Mouton was killed, as were Colonels Armant, Beard and Walker (not John), commanding the 18th Crescent, and the 28th Louisiana regiments of Gray's brigade. Major Canfield of the Crescent also fell, and Lt. Col. Clack of the same was mortally wounded." (D&R, p.165 #2). Polignac's brigade, left of Gray's, suffered heavily. Colonel Noble, 17th Texas, and many others were killed.

Adjutant Black seized the flag and led the men on. Polignac was left in command due to Mouton's death. He displayed his ability and pressed forward from the left to this shattered division. Randall and his "fine" brigade supported him on the right. Major's dismounted men were stressed by dense woods to Gen. Green's impatience. But, Green gradually turned the enemy's right and forced them back with loss of prisoners and guns.

General John Walker, stationed on the right of the main road with Scurry and Waul's brigades, encountered little resistance. They crossed the field and entered the woods. Walker found he outflanked the enemy's left. Keeping his right brigade, Scurry advanced "and swept everything before him". (*D&R*, p.166 #1).

The first Federal line of all mounted force, Calvary, and one division of the 13th Army Corps fled. They left behind prisoners, guns and wagons. From two miles back, the 2nd division of the 13th Corps was brought up but were "routed", leaving guns and prisoners as the Confederates advanced.

At sunset more Union troops of their 19th Army were found four miles further on a ridge over-looking a small stream. Taylor contended, "…my men made no impression for a time on this body of fresh troops; but possession of the water was all-important, for there was none other between this and Mansfield". (*D&R*, p.166 #2)

Walker, Green and Polignac, with Taylor, led the weary men down to the stream. After some "sharp work", the enemy fell back and Taylor gained control of the stream.

Twilight faded and thus ended the Battle of Mansfield.

***

"Defeat of the Federal Army was largely due to the ignorance and arrogance of its commander, Gen. Banks, who attributed my lone retreat to his own wonderful strategy".

That night Taylor sent a dispatch to Gen. Kirby Smith with results of the day's battle and intention to completely push the enemy the following day.

The next day, Taylor rode to Mansfield to look after the wounded and meet Churchill. The village seemed to be in order with the precautions taken beforehand. Churchill was directed to move toward Pleasant Hill at 3 a.m. with two days rations.

Reflecting that night by the campfire, Taylor's thoughts: "…the pleasure of victory was turned to grief as I counted the fearful cost at which it had been won. Of the Louisianans fallen, most were acquaintances, many had been neighbors and friends; and they were gone. Above all, the death of gallant Mouton affected me. He had joined me soon after I reached western Louisiana, and had ever proved faithful to duty. Modest, unselfish, and patriotic, he showed best in action, always leading his men. I thought of his wife and children, and his father, Gov. Mouton, whose noble character I have attempted to portray." (*D&R,* p.167 #2)

Taylor returned to the front to meet Generals John Walker and Green. He and Green led the infantry and Calvary and battery fourteen miles to Pleasant Hill. Walker and Polignac followed Churchill's men. They found stragglers, scattered arms and burning wagons left from the enemy's hasty retreat. No shots were fired.

A short mile before Pleasant Hill the enemy was found. Effort was made to gather Taylor's men.

The enemy appeared to be continuing his retreat. Taylor didn't want to miss a chance to harass them in case they decided to re-group at the junction at Blair's Landing, sixteen miles east on the Red River. He would take advantage of the morale gained.

Reconnaissance was sent out detecting the enemy lines stretched out across the plateau from Pleasant Hill to College Hill. Taylor immediately worked out his plan of attack and ordered canteens filled at the mill stream and trains parked there. Churchill and his men arrived exhausted from the forty-five mile march, so did Walker's and Polignac's. A two hour rest was ordered.

At 3 p.m. Churchill and his men were to move right and turn the enemy's left and attack from the south and west and keep right. Walker was to attack from the left. Maj. Brent had twelve guns in the woods and four on the road coming from Mansfield. There posted Buchell and DeBray's Calvary. General Bee's and Polignac's were in reserve. Major's two dismounted brigades were to drive back the enemy from the right and the woods from Blair's Landing direction. Taylor had 12,000 men to their 18,000, but, like he'd hoped, still had morale on their side.

At 4:30 p.m. Churchill was in position ready to attack. Maj. Brent advanced to call attention. First attack was successful with Churchill's men cheering. Walker led forward from the right. Brent advanced his guns. Major turned the enemy's right and gained the road to Blair's.

"Complete victory seemed assured when Churchill's troops gave way, and for a time, arrested the advance of Walker and Major". (*D&R*, p.169 #3).

Churchill formed two lines with the Missouri brigade, Parsons on the right and Tappan and two Arkansas brigades on the left, moving forward on the enemy through woods he was out-flanked. He later gave his judgment on misinformation he had received.

The Missouri brigade, assaulted on all sides, retreated in confusion into a gully. Colonel Hardiman checked the enemy. Parsons rallied his men. Arkansas troops were forced into the gully. Missouri retreated. Gause ran into Walker's right and Scurry stopped them. Gause thought his own man, Scurry, had fired on him. There appeared to be little grounds for that, with few killed and injured by such a big attack. Churchill followed Missouri and opened fire. Their three carriages broke and lost their guns.

Night ended the conflict with both sides occupying their original positions. The South gained 300 prisoners but lost 179 and three guns. Missouri lost 331 killed and injured. Arkansas lost 142.

General Walker was wounded in the groin. Gen. Taylor directed Polignac to take his place in charge. When Scurry had been disoriented by Gause, Waul and Randall were ordered to drive back the Union line. "Never was order more thoroughly executed". (*D&R*, p. 171 #2).

When Brent's guns over-powered the Federals, the confusion and fierce attack of Waul and Randall caused Green to believe the enemy retreated. He had ordered Bee to charge with Buchell and DeBray. They were met with heavy enemy fire on both sides from the woods. Buchell was then killed and Bee and DeBray were wounded, but great morale was gained.

Bee withdrew with "coolness and pluck", according to Taylor. Brent advanced his guns to close the opposite line. Polignac's "reduced but stubborn division" attacked on Randall's left. Green urged his dismounted men to clear the woods from Mansfield Rd. to Blair's Landing Rd. Even though nightfall came, Polignac, Randall, Waul and Scurry steadily drove the enemy back. Taylor urged them on to Pleasant Hill. They became separated by the ravine that concealed the Federals. They escaped through the woods with heavy loss. A letter was captured from their commander denouncing his superiors for deserting them there. Thickening gloom and confusion caused Taylor to order withdrawal.

The enemy made no attempt to regain the ground they had lost. Taylor sent his troops back to the only water at the millstream. Bee covered the field and foraged supplies. The wounded were cared for. Bee was ordered to pursue the enemy toward Grand Ecore in the morning. Taylor, exhausted, threw himself on the ground and slept.

The enemy retreated during the night, leaving four hundred wounded and unburied dead. Bee's pursuit in the morning of April 10th found stragglers burning wagons and supplies. Taylor proceeded to reprimand his strategy-- hind-sightedly. He should have led Churchill's attack and not entrusted it to one so inexperienced. Taylor evaluated himself, "Herein lies the vast difference between genius and commonplace: one anticipates errors, the other discovers them too late". (*D&R,* p.174 #2)

Recorded in "Report on the Conduct of War" pp.94-95, 2nd vol., Gen. Francis Fessenden of the Union Army, who took Col. Benedict's place when he was killed and Gen. A.L. Lee's account on p. 62, plus Adm. Porter's p. 239, backed Taylor's report. Neither the North nor the South claimed victory that day, except for Gen. Banks' deluded one on p.326. Pleasant Hill, therefore, was considered a draw, but the Union's withdrawal from Louisiana, rendered it a victory.

General Kirby Smith aroused Gen. Taylor from his revere of sleep on the ground after the battle. He refused to let Taylor follow Banks out of Louisiana. He feared Porter's fleet may bank nearby or go on to Shreveport. He also still concluded he needed backup if Steele came down to Shreveport from Arkansas.

Kirby Smith insisted the Trans-Mississippi Dept. headquarters needed Taylor nearby. Taylor uselessly pointed out the least likeliness of Steele or Porter landing. Taylor acquiesced that the "sacrifices" of his army would be wasted and he followed Smith's orders to go to Mansfield.

Taylor received a dispatch from Capt. McCloskey that the enemy's fleet had passed the Grand Bayou Landing off Bayou Pierre, eighteen miles from Mansfield, April 19th, in low tide. He expected the news of defeat would turn them back south to Grand Ecore. He sent Gen. Bagby to cut them off by April 11th. Bagby confirmed the Federals had turned back on the river by the 10th. He experienced delay in crossing Bayou Pierre without the pontoon arriving that Taylor had requested from Shreveport.

The Union came back, passed Grand Bayou Landing at 10 a.m. on the 11th, before Bagby. He pushed toward and arrived at Blair's Landing the night of the 12th, after Gen. Green that day.

"Green attacked at once and leading his men in his accustomed fearless way, (and) was killed by a discharge of grape from one of the gunboats. Deprived of their leader, the men soon fell back and the fleet reached Grand Ecore without further molestation from the west bank. The enemy's loss, supposed by our people to have been immense, was reported to be at seven on the gunboats and fifty on the transports. Per contra, the enemy believed that our loss was stupendous; whereas we had scarcely a casualty except the death of Green, and irreparable one". (*D&R,* p.181 #1)

Taylor eluded that little was accomplished and a lot was lost with Green's death. Taylor added that Green had come to him early in his western Louisiana duty and proved himself well for Taylor to recommend his promotion to Brig. Gen., then Maj. Gen.

"Upright, modest, and with the simplicity of a child, danger seemed to be his element, and he rejoiced in combat. His men adored him and would follow wherever he led; …and his death was a public calamity, and mourned as such by the people of Texas and Louisiana. To me, he was a tried and devoted friend. …The great Commonwealth, whose soil contains his remains will never send forth a bolder warrior, a better citizen, nor a more upright man than Thomas Green". (*D&R,* p.181 #3).

***

After Blair's Landing, April 12th, the Calvary returned to Pleasant Hill, then joined Bee near Grand Ecore. Banks and his Army concentrated with gunboats and transports on the river. Bee occupied Natchitoches.

Taylor and Smith continued to disagree on whether to go north in case Steele would fall further south to fight or whether to go south and continue to chase Banks and his men out of Louisiana. Steele never came south. Bee faced Banks at Monette's Ferry on his retreat, but gave way on the 23rd and fell back instead of attacking.

Disheartened, Taylor chased the enemy to Alexandria.

General Banks retreated so quickly that Adm. Porter wrote in "Report on Conduct of War" vol. ii pp. 234-5, that he feared he and his fleet would be left stuck at Alexandria with no communication and destroyed. His testimony later proved the "utter helplessness of gunboats in narrow streams, when deprived of protection of troops on the bank".

***

General Wharton was sent to replace Gen. Green. He helped

Gen. Taylor agitate the enemy and attempt to keep them from passing over the falls at Alexandria, along with (Conf.) Gen. Steele, Bagby and Major at different stations along the way, also Polignac Liddell and Covington.

Taylor conceded, "From first to last, Gen. Kirby Smith seemed determined to throw a protecting shield around the Federal Army and fleet". (*D&R,* p.193 #1) Taylor, again, lamented the fall of such good men as Green and Mouton and the gallant others. He commended the great efforts of Walker and Polignac, who "held every position entrusted to them..." He blessed the worthy valor of Gen. Robert E. Lee and his men.

"The affairs of mice and men oft gang alee," from sheer stupidity and pig-headed obstinacy. Gen. Kirby Smith had publicly announced that Bank's army was too strong to be fought and that proper policy was either to defend the works protecting Shreveport or retreat into Texas. People do not like to lose "their reputations as prophets or sons of prophets. Subsequently, it was given out that Gen. Kirby Smith had a wonderful plan for the destruction of the enemy, which I had disturbed by rashly beating his army at Mansfield and Pleasant Hill; but his plan, like Trochu's for the defense of Paris, was never disclosed-- undoubtedly, because c'etait le *secret* de Polichinelle." (*D&R,* p.195 #1).

***

A month after the Red River Campaign, Gen. Taylor requested to be relieved of Gen. Kirby Smith's command. He settled his family at Natchitoches, Louisiana and reported for duty east of the Mississippi River, commanding the Department of Alabama, East Louisiana and Mississippi. He remained there until the Rio Grande capitulated in May 1865. Richard Taylor was present at the signing of the Treaty at the end of the war, May 8th, at Citronelle, Alabama. He "followed the Civil War from cradle to hearse".

The End

About The Author

Ms. Blythe lives in the old homestead in east Texas.

She has three children and six grandchildren in southwest Louisiana, close enough to reach the same day. She has six grandchildren in Tennessee, also-- way too far off in her opinion.

She also has three tremendous siblings and a great brother-in-law! Annabelle spent her early years working in retail, cosmetology and nursing.

She has been free-lance writing and working on novels for the past ten years.

Fifty-percent of the profits from her books goes towards establishing Hope Rose Home for Unwed Mothers in her area. Her burden is to train the mothers, and the young men connected, in careers and community service. This will be coupled with the staff teaching them parenting skills and about the Lord Jesus Christ.

Also By Author:
(To come) *Another Time in Russia/Book I A;*
Beloved in Another Time, Another Place/Book II/Prophecy Fulfilled;
Beloved in Another Time, Another Place/Book III/Promises Fulfilled.